HUNTER

IN THE COMPANY OF SNIPERS
Book 14

IRISH WINTERS

WINDY DAYS
PRESS

COPYRIGHT

Hunter; In the Company of Snipers, 14

Cover design and author photo by Kelli Ann Morgan,
http://www.inspirecreativeservices.com

Interior book design by Bob Houston eBook Formatting

Editor: Lauren McKellar, McStellar editing,
http://mcstellarediting.blogspot.com

ISBN Paperback: 978-1-942895-43-5
ISBN eBook: 978-1-942895-44-2
Library of Congress Control Number: 2017901841

Irish Winter's websites: http://www.irishwinters.com
and irishwinters.blogspot.com

In the Company of Snipers

You can find Irish Winters on Facebook:
https://www.facebook.com/author.irishwinters

On Twitter: https://twitter.com/irishwinters1

For news on upcoming releases, sign up for Irish Winters' Newsletter at IrishWinters.com.

For more information about all my books, visit IrishWinters.com.

IN THE COMPANY OF SNIPERS

This series revolves around ex-Marine scout sniper, Alex Stewart, and his covert surveillance company, The TEAM, home-based out of Alexandria, Virginia. An obsessive patriot and workaholic, he created the company to give ex-military snipers like him a chance at returning to civilian life with a decent job.

This is not a serial with each book ending at a cliffhanger. I wouldn't do that to you. *In the Company of Snipers* is a collection of passionate love stories involving women and men who are tough enough to take on the world alone. Each is a stand-alone read, where in the course of an active TEAM operation, one agent comes face to face with his or her demons. The men and women I write about are all patriots and warriors, dealing with what they've lived through or the mistakes they've made

Spoiler alert: Every novel contains adult scenes including sexual situations (some explicit), language, and violence. I don't write sweet romance, so be forewarned.

At the end of each story, it's my hope that you, along with my heroes, will come to realize...

Love changes everything.

CHAPTER ONE

"I'm hit. Damn, I'm… I'm dead." With a pain-filled groan, Ky Winchester fell to his knees. His weapon hit the dirt seconds before his face did. Instead of grief, revenge flamed to life in the deepest recess of Hunter Christian's war-hardened heart. His buddy didn't deserve to die like that, and shooting a man's family jewels was as low as a person could get. Could a vengeful female shooter be in the enemy's ranks? A sicko with a vendetta against men?

Adrenaline spiked. Fight or flight? That'd be the day that Hunter ran from the enemy. Women maybe. Bastards never. Camouflaged, Hunter faded into the verdant mesh of the Amazon jungle around him. It was early autumn and nights were chilly at home on the East Coast, but it couldn't have been hotter here. Sweat beaded at his temples, stinging and his eyes. Buzzing insects annoyed at his nostrils, lips, and eyelashes. He brushed the distractions away. If only he could see the dirtbag who'd taken his buddy down.

Part of what was supposed to have been a joint exercise with McCormack Industries, Hunter and his three buddies had stumbled into an ambush. The enemy hadn't let up since. Where the hell was the friendly landing party that should have been at this rendezvous point?

Hunter stifled another curse, a burdensome feat for a guy with a combat-honed vocabulary, crafted with explicit care and plenty of practice to artfully condemn a man to Dante's Hell. Yes, he'd studied the epic poem back when he cared a fuck about literature. He'd even lived a few of the tortures within the concentric levels, from Limbo to the most rancid—Treachery.

He knew the warning at the gates of Hell: *"Lasciate ogne speranza, voi ch'intrate."* Translation: *"Abandon all hope, ye who enter here."*

The story of his life.

A twig cracked to his left, jolting him out of his waste-of-time reverie. Crap like that could get a man killed. No sooner thought than…

"Shit," his good buddy, Agent Eric Reynolds hissed—right before he dropped like a rock. Damn it. Eric was the agent-in-charge. He should've known better than to give his twenty away—even in death.

Two men down and within seconds of each other? Something's not right. Was a rat on Hunter's team? An informer? He hated betrayers with every last piece of his soul. God, how he hated them.

The need to kill something crept up his spine like a prickly spider with an attitude, compelling his number one rule of engagement. *Stay sharp. Stay angry. Let it build. Then let it loose to obliterate the son-of-a-bitchin' enemy.*

Oddly, the weakest link on his team, and the one with the worst PTSD, Seth McCray, had gone silent. Go figure. Maybe Seth and he could win this war. Hunter backed into the good-sized tree at his rear. Another rustle, this one starboard, caught his attention, but he didn't turn to look. Couldn't risk it. Whatever joker was out there would have to get close and personal before he'd fire the short stock rifle pressed under his chin.

When a barely discernable ripple fractured the leafy scenery directly in front of him, he nearly cursed out loud. No wonder Ky and Eric had fallen so quickly. The enemy had cloaked themselves in the latest ActiveCamouflage System. They were invisible. *Not anymore.*

Barely flexing his index finger, Hunter lined up his shot and fired. The unseen shooter hit the dirt with a grunt and a muffled, "They got me."

Finally. One down. Satisfaction added to the ferocious sense of competition that came with warfare. *If I can kill one, I can kill 'em all.* It didn't take long. In minutes, Hunter took out two more *invisible* men. There was nothing better in combat than a pissed off Marine, and Hunter was one angry SOB. He would've felt better if another shot hadn't boomed, and if Seth hadn't called out, "Don't... don't let 'em get you, Hunt."

Holy screaming shit! I've lost all my guys and the sun's was barely up. He steeled his jaw. Rolled one shoulder. Hunkered own. The game had changed to the ultimate standoff, one gunslinger against an unknown number of assassins. *Fine by me.*

Come to Brazil they said. It'll be fun they said. Yeah right.

This wasn't Meredith's idea of a good time. She could barely breathe in this bug-infested jungle, it was so hot. How could she be the last of her team alive? It didn't seem real or right or—*gulp*—possible. But there she was, a single working mother and an engineering assistant—a trainee—now her team's lone survivor. Yes, she knew how to shoot, even carried a concealed carry pistol, but to hunt another human being? To be faster on the draw? To kill a man before he killed her? Something else entirely.

But now was not the time to turn tail and run for cover like a sissy girl. Her pride wouldn't allow it. Another big gulp. The TEAM's last agent waited just ahead to her left in the giant kapok tree. That was the only place he could be.

She steeled her nerve. *It's all up to me now. I've got to beat this guy.*

Still, she played it safe. Her senses reached out through the jungle, feeling for any unnatural sound that didn't belong. A burp. A sniff. A scratch. A cocky guy snort. *Darn. Nothing.*

Seconds stretched into minutes. Still nothing. Not one whisper. Not one sigh. Until...

"Don't move," a deep voice ordered as the barrel of a gun jabbed her bicep. Hard.

This guy had to be black ops as stealthy as he'd been. As good. His body heat warmed her right shoulder; he was standing that close. The aromatic scent of single barrel whiskey rolled off of him. Cigarette smoke. Her nostrils flared at the heady scent of clean male sweat mixed with the barest hint of manly deodorant. Something else radiated off this guy, too. Pure male power. Dominance.

But she hadn't missed the telltale signs, darn it. Neither the crushed grass from the weight of heavy boots, nor the tiny bent tips of branches. They'd all proved he should've been ahead of her hiding in that tree, not sneaking up behind her. She'd been alert. How'd he get back there?

A large male hand lifted the invisible automatic rifle from her grip—like he knew precisely where it was and which way it pointed. She nearly shrieked at the rippling black tattoo on his arm. A snake. It moved! *Kind of.*

Okay, maybe not. But it could have. The artwork was just that good. Lifelike. The serpent's red eyes stared unblinking at her. Its forked-tongue stretched to the end of his middle finger in a continual obscene gesture. The handle of the knife blade piercing the serpent's head just below this guy's clenched knuckles, declared USMC. Even the detailed scales glistened as if this creature was part of the guy's rippling muscles, but… *man, he's got some power in that massive, sexy arm.*

A woman could be tempted, but didn't it figure? *An ex-Marine? She'd* been bested by one of America's best, the good guys. Thinking she could delay her inevitable surrender, she cocked an elbow, intent on going for his Adam's apple. *She could still win. It could happen.*

"Stop it," he hissed. A heavy hand caught her by the nape of her neck, his thumb digging into her skin just below her ear. "A shot this close will hurt like hell, but I'm game if you are, Bozo. Where do you want it, in the crotch like you bagged my first guy?"

Guess again, tough guy. I'm better than a man. I'm a woman.

She would've tossed that golden *up-yours* back at him, but Meredith was suddenly damp and hot for all the wrong reasons. She should've been scared, but, for some reason she—wasn't. It didn't make sense. Her starved-for-sex inner Mean Girl had sprung to life at some weird, elemental, possibly animalistic level. How—wonderful. Meredith could barely resist rubbing up against this stranger's chest like a feral cat in heat. *What's wrong with me?*

Strong, mean fingers twisted her head to the side as if to snap her neck. *Ouch.*

"Say it or die," he hissed, the barrel of his rifle stuck in her ribs hard enough to really hurt.

Fine. If he was playing for keeps, she would too. She belted out the requisite, "Yield!" for all still standing. *That would be you—Captain America.*

Meredith pressed one finger to the center pad of her gloved palm. Section by section, the densely woven, metallic fabric of her all-in-one invisibility suit blinked into view. This moron needed to know who he was dealing with, and it wasn't some guy he could bully. Shifting her weight, she lifted one booted foot to give this jock something to think about. Surprise sucker-punched her instead. "Hunter Christian? Is that really you? What are you doing here?"

But it wasn't surprise glowering on his handsome, chiseled face. Or delight. More like disgust. His top lip curled. He grunted, but offered no sign of recognition, just a curt, "ma'am," before he performed an abrupt military-style about-face.

"Wait," she called after the wide shoulders angling through the woody curtain of liana vines and away from her. "Don't you recognize me? It's me. Meredith Flynn. Your... friend?"

But he'd vanished—just like last time.

CHAPTER TWO

"Yeah, she's a wicked shot, but she hit me in the crotch. I'll be black and blue for a week." Ky readjusted his junk for the umpteenth time.

Hunter jerked his eyes off the conversation taking place front and center stage. It had to hurt, but damn, did Ky have to keep rubbing himself like he was?

"Sorry." Meredith ducked her head into her shoulders and grinned like the naughty little cheerleader she once was.

Sorry, my ass.

Hanging back from all the politically correct bullshit and good-old-boy congratulatory backslapping taking place in the *enemy's* camp, Hunter had nothing nice to say about the first day's *battle*. He stayed near the tent door to keep his second-hand cigarette smoke from the others, but it was past time to leave.

He and his teammates, Ky Winchester, Seth McCray, and Eric Reynolds, were on, what was supposed to have been, an easy op with the esteemed McCormack Industry's RDT&E, Research, Development, Test, and Evaluation, folks. The mission had been vetted as more vacation than work, their job to assist MI's beta test of their top-of-the-line ActiveCamouflage System One, the ACS_1. Each paintball war game had been designed to pit the MI team of techno geeks against Alex Stewart's very capable covert operators in various combat scenarios, including ambush.

It seemed an obvious outcome would've followed when civilians were matched against highly trained operators. That was what Jed McCormack wanted—the unskilled and possibly very scared soldiers, his people, to experience the adrenaline rush, the chaos, and confusion of warfare.

The games were supposed to have shown the system's unique reliability, expose any weaknesses, and hopefully, prove Jed's point—that invisibility was the confidence boost the American military and public needed.

Interestingly, the MI team had barely lost.

Rack one for The TEAM.

Barely.

That win should've given Hunter reason enough to gloat, but it didn't. His gut was talking to him. This was no beginner's luck scenario. *No fuckin' way.* There was a reason the MI folks had nearly won. Someone had betrayed The TEAM. Who the hell was it?

Lowering his chin to his chest, he let a calculating gaze cruise over the men who supposedly had his back. Hunter hadn't survived deployments to Libya, Ethiopia, and Iraq to die on *vacation.* He took another hit of nicotine and let the smoke settle in deep before he blew it away. One thing was sure. The MI folks had better prepare for a sound thrashing. They thought they could beat ex-military? They'd be lucky if they walked straight by the time these games ended.

"Oh, it's all right, ma'am. You got me good," Ky said, the front of his camouflaged pants still stained with bright red dye. No one had changed clothes yet. "I never saw you coming."

"Please. Call me Meredith." She extended her hand to Ky, flouncing her blonde hair over one shoulder, smiling brightly like she might burst into a ra-ra-cheer at any moment. Of course, Ky's face lit up. What guy's wouldn't? That was what Meredith did best. *Light 'em up and leave 'em.*

"That's precisely the point, Agent Winchester," Teague Horton, McCormack Industry's lead engineer and war games operator, explained. "Everything visible on a soldier's uniform in combat becomes invisible once he hits the palm pad to activate our system. All equipment and even his weapon, if he's using one of ours. You might as well try an ACS_1 suit on. See what you think. Tomorrow it'll be your turn in the barrel."

"Nah. I can wait," Ky replied. "We weren't expecting the game to commence the second we touched down. That was a long flight from D.C. I'm beat."

"You, my dear, are one helluva shot." Eric poured on the charm to the only woman on deck.

Sure enough, Meredith batted those extra-long, extra thick eyelashes and offered her best come-on-down-y'all smile. At least she still played by the same rules.

Hunter knew them too well. *Move in. Lean in close. Close your eyes. Think you're important to her. Be a fool. Believe she cares. Get burned. Never go back.*

When Eric moved an inch closer to Meredith, he sucked in another pull of nicotine. *Go for it, Reynolds. Make an ass of yourself. Just don't come crying to me when she hands you your balls.*

What Hunter hadn't figured out yet was where her hubby, Fast Eddy Welch, the high school jock who'd once upon a time rolled her socks down? Or up? Hunter didn't really care.

Still, why was she flirting with Eric if she had a husband back home to keep her cheating ass warm at night?

Hunter inhaled deeply, drawing the pleasant sting of smoke into his lungs before he let it out and blew it away. Still the same old Meredith—full of beauty, allure, and deception.

"How much does one suit cost?" Seth asked from his side of the table.

"You tell me," Lyle Salaz, another MI technician, spoke up. "How much should it cost to protect American military assets in the field?"

"You mean *men*," Hunter's big mouth declared before his brain had the chance to shut down the illusion he'd meant to share his opinion. He flicked the ash off the end of his cancer stick.

Lyle was the atypical scientist and the first one Hunter had 'killed' in the paintball battle, the one who'd yelled, 'Son-of-a-bitch! I'm hit! They got me!' like a little girl. A middle-aged man, complete with a paunch that hung over his belt, receding hairline, and black-rimmed glasses, he spoke with a touch of conceit whenever he addressed The TEAM. The man thought he was better than them. Smarter. It showed. Hunter didn't regret shooting him in the face.

Lyle shrugged indifferently. "Assets. Men. They're all the same."

Not in my book they're not. Hunter clenched the fist not holding his smoke, but kept his big mouth closed like he should have done in the first place. He hadn't meant to interact with anyone from the MI team. He left the charm and politics to Eric, The TEAM's lead agent on this operation. Schmoozing never was Hunter's strong suit. He preferred passive resistance or direct conflict, hit 'em hard or walk away. Anything in the gray area between was a waste of time.

He had to give Jed credit though. Billionaire or not, he was the common soldier's best friend. While other companies scrambled all over each other to create technology that would conceal military equipment, Jed had focused on protection for American boots on the ground. For the men and women who stood in the line of fire.

The grunt was often treated like a throwaway item by some generals and presidents, but not Jed. Word was that his son had been injured in Iraq. Jed had literally put his money where his mouth was. Hunter respected Jed and there weren't many men who'd earned that honor.

Fresh out of the MI test lab, ACS_1 had been designed primarily to camouflage American soldiers. But MI wasn't resting on its laurels with just one system. The ACS_2 was also in development to camouflage vehicles—Humvees, missile haulers, trucks, and tanks. But a full-up TUSK, as in a Tank Urban Survival Kit-equipped M1A1 Abrams tank? That pushed the realm of possibility into the realm of just plain ludicrous in Hunter's book. He'd have to see an ACS_2 at work to believe it could conceal heavy equipment.

Plain and simple—all that high-tech camouflage didn't mean squat until MI could also conceal the cloud of dust a tank raised when it fast-tracked to the frontline over desert and dirt. What about the noise and the thunderous reverberations that sixty-three short tons created on good old Mother Earth? How did MI expect to conceal that? Invisibility wasn't the whole answer.

Still, lighter tanks were being developed. Hunter had heard of plans for a smaller and more agile ground-combat vehicle. It could happen, but the paintball game they'd just played proved his point, not MI's. Yes, Ky, Seth, and Eric all got *'killed.'* The highly skilled snipers were nearly taken out of the game within short order. But Hunter had also proved that even the best line of high-tech defense could be breached by good old-fashioned know-how. By gut feeling.

He stretched the kinks out of his back, tired of listening to all the BS. Pinching his cigarette butt between two fingers, he killed his smoke and tucked the butt into his shirt pocket. It was past time to leave.

He had a pillow in the guise of a backpack and a bedroll calling his name. Thank goodness, he and his buddies had set up their camp a good distance from the MI folks. He didn't need to hear any more come-ons and flirting.

It never changed. All six guys now circled Meredith like tomcats on the prowl, trying to prove they were clever. She must be in her element, the center of the universe again.

Stepping out of the tent and into the jungle, he shrugged the tedium of human companionship off his shoulders and halted long enough to light another cigarette. The jungle air was fresh and sweet, full of night noises that might make a regular person's skin crawl. Not his. Even that gurgling growl and grunt that sounded a lot like a large carnivore protecting its prey seemed less menacing than the babble in the tent behind him.

Hunter blew out a satisfying puff, instantly at ease in the world he knew best. Something screamed with an eerie human-like tone of terror nearby. A shrill whistle lifted his gaze to the shadowy canopy overhead. Then silence. Whichever predator was out and about tonight, it must have hit its mark. *Well, good.*

That was the real world for you, a world he understood. A dog-eat-dog world where you either killed or were killed. Where you fought to live another day. Got up in the morning and did it all over again. Yeah. He'd rather spend a night alone in the jungle than another minute in the company of a bunch of fools vying for the attention of Meredith Flynn.

Walking into the vines and tangled brush, he left yesterday behind. Ky, Seth, and Eric could find their own way home.

CHAPTER THREE

The friendly get-together ran out of air when Hunter up and left without a word. Meredith tried not to notice, but how could she not? He'd stayed near the tent opening like a grumpy shadow with somewhere else to be. Yet his presence had commanded without any effort on his part. Even the air in the tent seemed to follow his lead and go out the door with him when he left. Something about him seemed to anchor the rest of his team, too, as if he were their power source and compass all rolled into one. Ky called it quits. Seth stood to follow. Eric stopped chatting.

And yet Hunter wasn't the designated leader. That position went to Eric Reynolds, The TEAM's agent-in-charge, and the only one Hunter seemed to respect. Sometimes. It was surely not respect glowering on his face tonight. No. It was more like what he'd given her out there in the jungle when she'd recognized him. *That look.*

After Ky and Seth had headed to their camp, Meredith begged off the strategy meeting Teague wanted to hold and went to the shower. Being trapped in an ActiveCamouflage System for any amount of time in jungle heat was miserable. She needed to mention that performance shortfall to Jed. The suits needed internal cooling.

The two youngest on The TEAM, Ky and Seth, made her smile. Both were more timid than Hunter. Eric, on the other hand, had no problem flirting. He was a charmer, a real dark, tall, and handsome type. Only Hunter had played the disinterested alpha, the warrior with no need of anything or anyone.

The flaw to the war games was that Agent Reynolds was also the MI mole. He was there to train the MI agents how to detect a trained sniper, how to track a lethal shot to its source and thus take out highly trained enemy combatants, which in this case, were his own men.

No one was supposed to know this little radioactive nugget of inside information but her boss, Teague. Meredith only knew because she'd overheard Teague on the phone in the MI research facility lab when he'd thought he was alone. That would teach her for working late hours without permission.

The moral implications of the deceit felt like an ethical breach between Eric and his men, and yet she understood the reason behind it. The lion didn't need to know whether the wounded gazelle was armed and fully capable of escape—or assault. So, she kept the information to herself. After all, Hunter Christian was that lion. Why would he need an advantage?

Gathering her cosmetic bag where she also kept her concealed handgun, a change of clothes, an LED flashlight, and her extra-large can of bug spray from the MI tent, she headed for the shower. Positioned across the clearing from their four-man tent, it gave her the only opportunity for privacy from her all-male team. Which was good. She didn't need more problems.

"Hey, Meredith," Eric called when she rounded the tent. He looked pleased with the four ACS_1 suits on their hangers draped casually over his shoulder and the ruggedized rolling crate that contained the rest of the ACS gear in his other hand. His team was bound to win in the games tomorrow, but she looked forward to the challenge. It gave her another chance to shoot Hunter, and baby, she meant for him to go down first. Just the thought added a zip to her step. *We'll see who's Sally.*

"Hey, Eric. You're leaving early? I thought you and Teague would talk strategy all night."

He shook his head. Eric stood a good foot taller than her, with dark hair a woman might want to rake her fingers through just to see how soft it was. Mussed and sexy-looking from the battle, the guy was as hot as any guy from *Thunder Down Under*. Well-muscled from his shoulders to his thighs, all he needed was to strip his shirt off and don a black bow tie. How come none of her teammates radiated the testosterone levels these guys from The TEAM did?

"I just collected our gear for the morning. By the way, you did real good today. Have you had weapons training in a past life I should know about?" He lifted his left brow in a deliciously evil spike that sent a quiver of pure lust up her thighs. Whoever his wife was, she had no business letting him out of her sight. Eye candy nothing. He was—hot.

"Concealed-carry," she admitted. "There was a time I needed it, so I took a self-defense class and bought a gun. I learned about gun safety and how to shoot."

His brows lifted and that was another thing. Eric had the loveliest eyebrows. They almost looked as if he'd plucked them. His coffee brown eyes sparked with male interest in the dim light of propane lanterns. If she was looking for action, he might be worth considering. She'd always found dark eyed men hard to resist. Hence her fatal attraction to Hunter. He had the same color eyes, only his were iced coffee to Eric's hot fudge.

"An ex-boyfriend?" Was Eric trolling for an easy hook-up or genuinely concerned? Men were hard to decipher, each a different puzzle and most not worth the time or effort it took to unravel them.

"Ex-husband," she confessed.

"Ah. Nasty divorce then?" Real sympathy radiated off of him, setting her mind to rest.

She let her grimace answer for her. There was no need to go down memory lane again.

"Me too," Eric admitted, the sparkle in his eyes dimmed. "Any kids?"

"Just one. Courtney. He's three."

"And I'll bet he's the apple of your eye."

"How about you?" She dodged the subject of Courtney. The day she struck up another relationship was a long way off. When and if it happened, the man would have to walk on water and worship at her feet before she'd take that kind of chance again. He'd have to love children, and he'd better be damned devoted to her, too. Until then, talking about Courtney with potential suitors was off-limits.

"No," Eric said, a little too quickly. He ran a hand behind his neck as if he'd suddenly developed a pain. "You ever heard the country western song about unanswered prayers? It was written for me."

"Divorce?" she asked.

"Kind of." He looked away, but not before Meredith caught the sadness shifting across his face.

"Divorce is hard," she said, needing to instill comfort where it might be needed. She'd been down that road, and divorce was a hard one to walk alone. "Yours sounds like it might have been as bad as mine."

Eric turned with a smile she could easily see through. The tease in his eyes was gone. "But life goes on, and like I said, unanswered prayers and all that."

She cut the doomed conversation short. Talking about exes never ended well. "I'd better hurry. It will be too late to take a shower if I wait much longer."

"I'd be happy to stand guard if you'd like," he offered, a glimmer back in his eye.

She almost accepted that gallant offer, but no. A handsome man outside of her shower in the middle of nowhere was the first step down a slippery slope, and the last thing she needed. "Thanks, Eric, but I'm the girl who shot you earlier, remember? I'm pretty sure I can take care of myself."

"You're armed?"

She patted her cosmetic bag in reply. "Always, and not just with lipstick."

He bowed his head in mock defeat. "I stand corrected. Maybe I should be the one asking you to escort me back to my camp."

She let him down easy. "Have a good night, Agent Reynolds. See you bright and early. Be ready to lose."

"You too." With two fingers to his forehead in a half-salute, he turned smartly, the crate bumping along behind him. "Good night, Meredith," he called over his shoulder as he disappeared into the shadows. "Be sure to use extra bug spray. Sleep tight."

Night was coming on fast. Despite the weapon in her bag, she wanted to be inside the tent before it got any darker. She hurried.

Once the shower door was locked tightly behind her, Meredith set her items on the collapsible bench, the flashlight on its side and facing the rear wall for ambient light. She didn't intend to cast any feminine shadows.

With a quick shake, she unrolled a pair of light cotton running pants and a matching long-sleeved T-shirt in lieu of her usual sleepwear. There were insects and mosquitoes aplenty in the jungle. The more skin she covered, the less chance of contracting malaria or garnering any more advances from well-meaning guys. Eight-legged or two-legged, bugs were bugs.

She hung her clean clothes on one of the two hooks next to the shower door and made sure her industrial-strength, extra-large can of insect repellant with plenty of Deet was handy, right alongside the flashlight. The minute she toweled off, she'd smell like a bug bomb again, but, oh well. She'd be stinky, but safe.

Quickly, she undressed and rolled her dirty clothing into a bundle. Turning the water valve on, she stepped into the lukewarm spray of a portable shower's spigot. Nothing felt better than washing away the sweat and grime of a hard day's shoot-out in the jungle.

She smiled at the notion. There she was, on the adventure of a lifetime, in the Amazon no less. How fabulous! It wasn't often a common assistant travelled, much less all the way to the Amazon. She should have been pleased, and she was. Jed was generous with his employees. She didn't know what he saw in her since she'd only worked for him less than a year, but she was thankful for the recognition and this opportunity.

The trip had turned out to be more than she'd expected, and who would've thought a paintball war could be so much fun? *Mental note to self: See if there are any gaming facilities near home in Northern Virginia.* Courtney would love playing cops and robbers with a real paintball gun.

A smile broke out across her face just thinking of that cute little guy. How his father could've walked away from the most darling boy on the planet never ceased to amaze her. Yes, a major job opportunity was a big deal. She got that, but to walk away from your wife and infant son, to berate them because they were holding you back? No way. It had never been about the job. Eddy was just the jerk her mother always said he was.

Meredith planned. The extra paycheck from this fantastic trip might allow her to move into an upscale condo. She hoped. Courtney deserved so much more than their tidy, but tiny townhouse in Falls Church. Virginia. Poor kid. He might be fatherless but he was not out for the count, and neither was she. No two ways about it. This was her second chance at a good life, and she intended to make the best of it.

Shampooing her head brought instant relief. There was something about the fragrance of lavender shampoo that soothed like nothing else. She rolled her neck. The crème rinse worked the same as the shampoo, relaxing the tangles of her thick blonde curls while it filled the small enclosure with fragrance from home.

Heaven. This was nothing short of pure heaven.

The water ran cool for a second, then turned hot as if someone had kinked the hose. Darn. She hurried to finish rinsing, determined not to be the butt of any misguided guy humor on this trip. Could someone be out there? Had The TEAM agents come back to play a little game of their own? A midnight sortie? A panty raid? Men! Give 'em an inch and they'd take a mile every time. All sorts of terribly juvenile options zoomed through her mind. Knowing those guys, it could be—

BLAM!

Meredith ducked to her knees on the slatted wood floor, her heart pounding. *Not funny, guys.* That sounded like a gunshot. Was it? Frightening the only woman on the team wasn't how to treat a fellow employee. Yes, she was all about being a good sport, but—

Blam. Blam. BLAM! Three more shots, and she was mad if those guys thought they could scare her into running out of the shower like some brainless college co-ed. They had another thing coming.

Hurriedly, she turned the water off and brushed a towel over her body just enough to be able to pull her bra on. She scrambled into a pair of matching boy shorts as fast as her trembling fingers would allow. These guys had their nerve. Whichever team they were on, they were not going to intimidate her, but they *would* get an earful.

"You got 'em all?" an unfamiliar man's tense voice called from across the camp.

Who is that? Gulping back the suffocating terror climbing up her throat, she very quietly doused the flashlight and removed her revolver from her cosmetic case. This was no game. Those gunshots were real. She listened, her ear to the door and her knees shaking.

Heavy footsteps pounded alongside the shower. "Only saw the three." Another male. Neither familiar. Definitely not her guys or the guys from The TEAM.

"Burdette ain't gonna like this. Did you at least nail the woman like he wanted? She's the only damned reason we're here."

She lifted her fingers to her mouth. *Nail the woman? Me? As in... r-r-rape me?*

"I can't shoot what I can't see."

"Shit. Where'd she go?"

"How the hell would I know?"

"You tell him then."

"I ain't telling him nothin'. Burdette's an ass. Let him think she's dead for all I care."

The men's footsteps faded, but it sounded as if they'd stopped at the MI tent.

"Hey, Jonesy," one of them called out. "Come look at this guy. He's still alive. See if he knows where she is."

Very quietly, Meredith unlatched the heavy-duty plastic shower door enough to peer around it without drawing attention to herself. The soft glow from the two LED torches outside the tent door revealed two men in identical black pants and shirts standing over another man on the ground just outside the door to the tent. Her lead. Her friend. Teague Horton. What were they going to do with him?

One of the guys crouched, the barrel of his rifle poking Teague's bicep. "Where's the woman, tough guy? You send her someplace safe? You know we were coming for you?"

When Teague groaned, the man gripped her boss's chin and jerked his face upward. "I asked, where's Flynn? Don't be a hero. You talk, I'll kill you fast. You don't, I'll leave you for bait. There's plenty of animals wouldn't mind dragging your sorry carcass off for dinner."

Let him go, you jerk. Meredith lifted her pistol, the saliva gone from her mouth and lips. She'd practiced plenty at the indoor range she frequented, but this—this was real. Still on her knees, she cupped the weapon with both hands and took as careful aim as possible, her whole body shaking.

"Look at me." The guy slapped Teague's face, knocking his head side to side. "Focus, Horton. Don't go dying on me. I need the woman who came with you. Where's Flynn? She shacking up with them other guys down by the river? Is that where she's at?"

When Teague groaned an answer, the guy punched him. "Speak up."

Meredith lined the one still standing in her sights. The other was crouched too close to Teague—she couldn't take the chance she might hit him. Her pocket-sized pistol came with an accurate laser scope on the top rack. She'd always expected her ex to surprise her in the middle of the night, so she'd prepared well and had intended to surprise him right back. Now maybe she could save Teague's life. Planting her butt firmly against the doorjamb, she sucked in a trembling breath and—she fired.

Both men turned in surprise, but the one standing dropped to one knee. She'd hit him! He extended his injured leg and cried, "There she is! Git her! The damned bitch shot me!"

She fired again before either could shoot back, her brain pinging with adrenaline. Where were the guys from The TEAM? Couldn't they hear the racket? Were they dead, too? Was she the only one left?

The uninjured guy pulled his buddy off the ground, spraying the shower with automatic fire as he backed away, his aim going too high to hit her. She ducked lower, one knee bent, the other straight, and one hand to the dirt. At the same time, the injured man's knees buckled, and, when he fell, his buddy's rifle tilted upward. Meredith pushed up from the ground and fired two more rounds. If she couldn't kill them, she could at least force them to run for cover and leave Teague alone.

It worked. The first guy backed out of the camp, dragging his wounded partner and cursing all the way. "You think just because you got a gun you're untouchable? Think again, Flynn. We'll be back, bitch."

Meredith ran to Teague. Sweat glistened off his handsome face, but his chest was wet with blood. His bicep, too. "You're hurt," she cried like he didn't already know, running her fingers along the wound in his shoulder, hoping the round had gone through.

"Meredith," he rasped. "Run. Hide."

"No. I'm not leaving you."

His gaze filled with pain and tenderness. "Have to. Go. Save yourself."

"No, I can save you." She looked up to the sound of thundering footsteps pounding straight for her. Lifting her pistol again, her hands shaking, she aimed high and prepared for the worst. But it was Hunter who burst into the clearing, his belt flopping loose at his waist, his ink-covered chest bare and glistening in the lantern light, his rifle pointed in her direction. As soon as he saw her, he averted his aim. "What the hell happened?"

She pointed the opposite direction. "Two men. They went that way, but they—"

He rushed to her side and knelt, his hands instantly on the hole in Teague's chest. "Hang on, buddy."

"No." Teague grabbed Hunter's wrist. "Leave me. Save her. They'll be back. They want her, not me. Run. Hide."

Hunter shook his head. "Not going without you," he said gently as he shouldered his rifle. "Hang tight. I'll get you ready to travel."

Without a word, he pushed off the ground and ran into the MI tent. Meredith's gaze swept over their camp. She hadn't noticed until then, but the place had been ransacked. Cots were overturned. Their supplies scattered. The backpack she'd brought with all of her clothes lay inside the tent, her things pulled out like trash on the floor.

So where was everyone else? Lyle? Dan? Ky and Seth? Eric?

Hunter was back in seconds with one of the MI medical kits. "Sorry," he told Teague, "but you're not dying on my watch." Ripping Teague's shirt open, he laid his chest bare. Blood seeped out of the bullet hole.

"Give me all the cotton packing," he ordered Meredith. She already had it in her hands, and handed it over. With his thumb, he jammed a thick wad of the packing directly into the wound to the side of Teague's left nipple.

He arched his back and groaned. Tears ran down the sides of his head, and she wanted to cry with him. "Stop," he groaned. "Just take her and go."

"You're hurting him," Meredith cried. Hunter seemed so—angry. Did he mean to hurt Teague?

"Cry later. Pressure bandage now," he snapped, his palm up, his fingers curling. "Now!"

She scrambled to obey, ripping the bandage out of its sterile wrapper, but just as fast as she handed it over he demanded, "Another!"

She couldn't move quickly enough. His brows narrowed into a vicious *V*. He snapped his fingers for another while her friend writhed beneath the relentless pressure of Hunter's other hand, and Meredith wanted him to stop hurting Teague. Tears flooded her eyes at the merciless way he worked. He didn't let up. Not for a second. He'd become a demon, growling when she wasn't quick enough. "Damn it, keep up!"

Teague gasped in pain.

"Give it to me," Hunter barked, his brown eyes gone black, devoid of compassion and his lips twisted with cruelty.

"I am," she shot back at him, nearly tossing the bandage. Icy coldness shuddered off of him. "How many more do you need? I've only got three left."

He didn't answer, just leaned into Teague with one hand clasped over the other, compressing the wound in the poor man's chest. Hunter's thick biceps bunched. The veins on his muscular arms stood out rigid in the dim light, bringing that snake tattoo back to life. Beads of sweat turned to trickles at his temples, dripping down his chest and into the deeply carved rift between his pecs. His chest heaved. "Sorry, Horton, but you're not letting go. Hold on, damn it. We've almost got this licked."

Meredith sat back on her thighs, exhausted and ready to assist but unable to do what Hunter seemed determined to do. If sheer willpower alone could save Teague, Hunter had it in spades.

At last, the clingy bandages held. The blood seeping around the bandages slowed to a trickle. Hunter eased up on his patient, but Teague was out cold by then. Meredith let out the breath she'd been holding in one trembling sigh.

Hunter turned on her, recrimination raking over her nearly bare breasts and her abdomen to parts below. To her underwear. "Are you hurt?"

She shook her head and raked a handful of her hair over her shoulder, fully aware what she must look like. When she didn't speak, he grasped her chin with two bloody fingers, anger fierce in his eyes. "Merry, look at me. I asked you a question. Did they hurt you?"

For the first time, she noticed the glint of sweat shimmering on the eagle, globe, and anchor etched over his sternum, its wings unfurled in majestic, colorful detail, surrounded by profane words against Jihadists and Al Qaeda. Against betrayers and liars. The man was a walking USMC declaration of "up yours."

The snake that ended with a silent hiss on his middle finger extended in writhing circles up his arm, evolving into a sleeve of detailed scales up and over his shoulder as if he were the snake. A skull with dripping teeth marked his other bicep.

Meredith lifted her chin, determined that Hunter Christian couldn't scare her. Not him. Not her friend. "No, I'm fine. I was in the shower when I heard shooting. I shot the one guy—"

His nostrils twitched. Angry dark eyes drilled into her. Hostility shuddered off of him in heated waves she could almost feel as sarcasm poured out of him. "You shot one of them? Did you kill him?"

She understood then. He'd thought because she was mostly undressed that she'd been assaulted or nailed, to use those assassins' crude descriptor, or—could he be thinking she was hooking up with one of her teammates? How could he think *that*? Of her? Did she look that desperate?

In the long run, it didn't matter. She had more pressing things to worry about—like staying alive. "No. I heard shooting. I just thought it was fireworks, that you guys were trying to scare me, but when I opened the shower, I saw two men with rifles." She spared a quick glance at her destroyed camp before her gaze came back to rest on Teague, his face white and his breathing shallow. "Where's Lyle? Where's Dan? Why didn't they come help us?"

"Dead," Hunter said bluntly. "Both took one to the head. Other side of your tent. Looks like they were executed. What'd the shooters say? Did you hear anything?"

"Yes," she remembered then. "They were looking for me. Somebody... Mr. Burdette, I think they said, sent them to get me. W-w-why me?" She hated the weak question the moment she voiced it. It made her sound selfish. Everything wasn't always about her, but had these men died because of her?

Hunter pushed off the ground instead of answering. "Let's get somewhere safe." Striding into the tent again, she caught sight of another tattoo up high on the back of his shoulder. A man's boot print. The snake she got, but this was weird.

He returned quickly with one of the four cots. All four legs had been broken off, making it sturdy enough to hold a man's weight. With his rifle still at his back, he aligned it alongside Teague. "Slide this under him when I lift."

Meredith hurried to obey. As Hunter logrolled Teague to his side, she pushed the cot as far beneath her boss as she could. Gently, Hunter eased Teague onto the vinyl webbing. Instantly, they were mobile, and Hunter was on the move again, collecting what, she didn't know, from the tent. Her team had been murdered or were half-dead, and her head was reeling. Who could've done this? Why?

She pushed a hank of wet hair over her shoulder and went in pursuit of Hunter. When she caught up with him, he was halfway out of the tent pulling one of MI's wheeled, ruggedized supply crates. More than four feet high, the three-by-three container protected part of the team's supplies, foodstuffs, and the drinking water for the duration of the beta test. Hunter passed the retractable handle grip off to her the moment he spotted her. "Bring this with you and keep up."

She balked, her palms lowered to indicate her obvious state of undress in case he was blind and as rude as could be. "I can't go like this. At least let me get dressed."

Without answering, he turned on her, and headed back to Teague, loosening the belt from his waist as he went. "Then do it. We don't have all night."

What a total jerk. Before she called him on his atrocious attitude, loud, angry voices filtered through the jungle behind her. The killers were back.

"Move!" Hunter hissed, his rifle aimed toward the jungle.

Instead of wasting time explaining, she ran to the shower stall, yanked open the bullet-riddled door, and snatched her cosmetic bag and clothes. Fear climbed up her back, urging her legs to move faster.

"Don't let her get away this time," came that same stranger's voice, closer now.

"I say we kill her and be done with it," a different man's voice added. "The bounty says dead or alive, don't it? If Burdette wants her breathing, he can come out here and find her himself."

Flashlight beams zipped high and low, casting scary shadows everywhere. Meredith ran back to the male security Hunter offered, scared to death. But she ran too fast. Tripping over an errant root, she stumbled to her hands and knees at his feet, skinning all four points of contact with the compacted earth and tossing everything she'd just risked her life to save onto the ground.

Growling, Hunter latched onto her elbow, pulling her up like she was nothing but a ragdoll. Disgust poured over his face when he spied her pink cosmetic bag near his boot. "We don't have time for this bullshit, damn it. Move your ass."

"I-I am," she stuttered. Too rattled to think, she left everything behind and ran with him. Once under the cover of the jungle, Hunter again shouldered his rifle and dragged Teague while she struggled with the supply crate, tugging it over roots and rocks, twisted weeds and sharp grass. When the path narrowed, he nodded for her to take the lead.

Somewhere along the line, he'd used his belt to secure Teague to the cot, but damn. The fear of being shot or assaulted screamed at her to leave the bulky crate behind and run. But she didn't. Teague and Hunter needed these supplies. Shaking with outright terror at what would happen to her if she were caught, Meredith remained obedient to Hunter.

Catcalls and hoots of derision echoed behind her. Those thugs were back in her camp, not bothering to lower their voices. One mocked, "Wherever she is, she's stark-assed naked. Shouldn't be too hard to find her now."

She cringed. They'd found the clothes she'd left behind when she panicked, damn it. She needed them. Her bug spray. Her anti-itch cream, too. Even moving as quickly as she was, insects were biting every inch of her exposed flesh, and she had a lot of it.

Hunter tossed an aggravated glare at her when she risked a furtive look over her shoulder. "I said keep moving."

She did, the terror of him being shot from behind adding speed to her sore, bare feet. "It's too dark. I can barely see. Where am I going?"

"Veer starboard," he ordered grimly.

When she looked both ways, wondering which was starboard, he snapped, "To your right."

Okay then. He didn't intend to head back to his camp, which she'd expected. Instead, they headed off the beaten path and into deeper, darker, thicker brush and long hanging liana vines. What she wouldn't give for her flashlight.

The sound of angry men's voices faded, and she was running blind. Only the slap and whip of sharp stalks and stems against her bare flesh and Hunter's pants made any sound. And, oh yeah, the buzz of those insects, and all the sinister noises that lurked within the pitch-black shadows.

"Why aren't they chasing us?" she asked in a whisper.

Hunter didn't answer, just kept dragging the litter, grunting when it snagged on the same roots and tangles biting into the soles of her feet. Meredith didn't speak again. He gave the orders, directing her when and where to turn. She obeyed, wondering how he could see when she couldn't.

At least the ruggedized supply crate had balloon tires that made it easy to pull. Hunter had the heavier load, the trailing poles of the cot digging into the ground. She had to give him credit. He'd turned into a machine, a beast of burden, pausing only to force his load over any impediment, jostling Teague with every step but moving relentlessly forward.

"Stop," he finally murmured, weariness in his tone.

She set the container flat to its bottom, breathing hard and unable to see where they were. How Hunter knew where to stop, she had no idea. The man must have natural night vision.

Her heart still pounded, but gradually, she detected what looked to be twelve-foot-tall stalks of bamboo. Silvery shades of moonlight glinted off the knife-shaped leaves as a slow breeze twisted through them. At last. Some place to hide.

He assumed the lead. The tall plants bent easily to the battering ram of Hunter's bare, broad shoulders and his muscled chest. If they didn't move, he slowed enough to shift them out of his way, but carefully. He didn't break them; just bent them to his iron will as he forged a path.

Once he'd gone several feet into the grove, he eased Teague to the ground, then flattened a six-foot-wide landing for them to stand in. He motioned her into the center of their bamboo shelter. "We'll be safe here."

Good thing, too. Her hands were blistered from the container's handles. Her feet felt as if she'd walked over hot coals, and she needed to catch her breath. She parked the container to the side, angling it into the bamboo to give Hunter enough room to settle Teague to the ground without setting him on bamboo stalks.

The thick patch she found herself in seemed thick and wide—in the dark. Meredith scrubbed her palms up and down her biceps, worried she and the guys were still easy to find. Having Hunter there with her helped. The rifle at his back gave her some measure of security, too. But bamboo was just a bunch of plants and bullets could still reach her. Those men, too.

Once Teague was settled, Hunter dropped his hands to his knees, breathing hard. He glanced up and down Meredith's bare body again, one corner of his mouth hitched upward. Shaking his head, he faced the ground again.

She bit her lip to keep from saying something that wouldn't have been kind. So what if she was still in her underwear? There hadn't been time to grab her clothes once she'd dropped them. She slapped a cloud of biting gnats away from her face. The insect life in this darned rainforest was eating her alive. But that was the least of her troubles. Something else was abundantly clear. And wrong.

She was afraid to ask. "Where's Eric? Where are Seth and Ky?"

CHAPTER FOUR

"They're gone," Hunter replied as calmly as he could. It was nice she'd finally noticed his team had taken a few hits too. That this disaster wasn't all about her. That he was the only man left who hadn't been shot or was missing.

"Where are they?" Meredith all but shrieked.

What'd she think he was, a clairvoyant? "Will you keep it down? They never came back to camp. I thought they were with you."

Despite their precarious circumstances, he couldn't seem to control his snarky attitude. He jerked a thumb-sized flashlight from his pocket, but leveled it to the ground before he flicked it on. They were deep enough in this grove of bamboo to risk the dim light it offered.

"You had a light? All this time, you had a—"

"I couldn't use it until we got far enough into the jungle, now could I?" He tapped his forehead. "Think, why don't you. The light would've lead them to us."

"B-b-but... but..." She stood there, her eyes wide and brimmed with tears and, damn it. He wasn't going to fall for her again.

Setting the flashlight on its side near Teague, Hunter squeezed the bridge of his nose between two fingers, trying like hell to stave off the avalanche of feelings that always came with thoughts of Meredith. His head pounded like a mother. He really needed a cigarette, but he'd left camp without them, and he didn't want to quit smoking now. Not like this.

Meredith Flynn, the girl who'd gotten away, was doing it to him again. Making him care when he didn't want to have an ounce of feelings for her. And him without a nicotine hit in sight. Damn.

She slapped at the clouds of mosquitoes. Angry with her or not, he couldn't help the protective urge that lifted its foolish head at the sight of her standing there, her knees knocked together, stray strands of sodden blonde in her face, and waving her hands like a little girl.

Hunter leaned his rifle beside the supply crate. "Did you guys pack bug spray in your kits?" he asked, unsnapping the lid off the crate, and wishing it was TEAM issued, not MI. Then he'd know exactly what supplies he had—and what extra weapons.

Her eyes widened. "Oh, right. I almost forgot."

He grunted and shook his head. Typical civilian answer. *I forgot*—said no Marine—ever! Whoever'd packed the MI container was smart, though. Several aerosol cans of insect spray were handy. He snagged one and slapped the container's lid shut.

"Turn," he commanded. Uncapping the can with his thumb, he sprayed Meredith's long legs with the life-saving industrial-strength Deet. Cargo pants were a godsend in more ways than one. At least he was half-covered while those skimpy things she called underwear were working his last nerve. Even in the dark glow of the flashlight, he was drawn like a moth to the nicely plump ass presented to him now, dotted with bug bites or not.

"Stop looking at my butt."

"Then stop sticking it in my face. Bend over."

That got her dander up. "Why should I?"

"Because I wanted to see if you were dumb enough to do it." He stood, taking one more long spray up the crack of that taut satin-covered ass, then up her spine just to prove he could.

She shivered and wiggled as goosebumps lifted under the chill of the alcohol in the aerosol. Pivoting on the balls of her bare feet, she faced him, her chin-lift hard to miss.

Before she get a word in, he barked, "Spread your arms, close your eyes, and shut your mouth." Hunter barely gave her time to seal those baby blues up tight before he initiated another long sweep from her open palm, across her chest and under her neck on his way to her other arm. She winced. All those razor-sharp cuts from the copious blades of elephant grass and brush they'd run through had to sting. Bare skin had no place in the jungle, yet there she was, her delicious body on the menu for every bloodthirsty insect within a hundred-mile radius.

Hunter licked his lips, remembering her mouth and the sweet taste of strawberries and honey that came with it. Of moonlight and better days. They'd never taken that final jump into bed though, and for that one smart decision—or lack of one—he was damned glad. She was no lover. Just a girlfriend.

"I dropped my clothes," she muttered out of the side of her mouth at him, her eyes still squeezed tight. Like he didn't know she was nearly naked?

"I said shut up." Hunter leveled a shot of repellant at her chin to enforce his command. When her lips were sealed again, he covered the rest of her with a repellant as well as a good dose of manly appraisal over her very desirable 38Cs. Her skimpy black bra looked more like a corset with tiny white ribbons crisscrossed from cup to cup and a cute little bow tied in between. Women. They always wore sexy stuff under their clothes.

Carefully, he doused her flat stomach before he gave her hips and thighs a good application. And inspection. The front of those boy shorts received extra close scrutiny—just because her eyes were finally closed along with her mouth.

One amusing thing about classy women like Meredith was that everything they owned matched. Must be some unspoken rule. Her bra and panties were no exception, both silky black with vertical silver stripes, stylishly trimmed with white lace. By then he was leaning in. A man didn't often get close enough to taste a nearly bare-naked woman with curves like this one. If he kept this chivalry—or whatever it was— up, she'd be covered with more than just bug spray.

Not going to happen. He snapped the can into his thigh pocket for later use. But when his gaze rolled back to her, her eyeballs were just as rakishly scanning his bare chest as much as he'd been looking at hers. Half-naked men and women were like that, no matter what dire circumstances they were in. They noticed each other.

"See anything you like?" Her nasty sarcasm fit his mood.

"Nope." It felt like they were always squaring off in the battle that had never taken place. Maybe they were.

"Where's your shirt?"

"I was in the river when the shooting started. Guess it's still hanging on the branch where I left it."

"Why were you in the river?"

"I took a swim before bed." Why'd she care?

"Were you naked?"

She would ask something like that, but damn, she could read him like a book. "So what if I was?"

A small smile tugged at the corners of her mouth. "So, you went into a river full of piranha and saltwater crocodiles without clothes for no good reason other than to take a midnight dip? Don't you guys have a shower at your camp?"

"I prefer the river, and there were no—"

"But there might have been. What the heck, Hunter? What were you thinking? You could've been hurt!" She stamped her right foot in that petulant way of hers, scolding him like she had a right.

Something unfurled in his chest, fluttering against his ribs like it wanted out. Might have been his heart. This damned woman still worried about him. Who would've thought?

She kept going. "You've seen the movies. What if giant snakes were swimming in that water? You never know. Don't you ever do that again."

Speaking of snakes…

The silver whisper of a spiraling shadow just beyond her shoulder caught his eye. Long and lean, the slippery fellow must've decided to investigate the warmth emanating from her hot, agitated body. In one quick step, Hunter pulled her forward into his chest, his right hand extended behind her to change that crafty snake's mind—or the shape of its body.

"What are you doing?" She pushed halfheartedly away, her hands planted firmly on his pectorals. Her breath hitched, but she didn't seem too determined to leave. Her fingers massaged where they'd landed.

"Nothing much," he lied, focused on her so as not to cause any alarm. Meredith had a deathly fear of snakes, the last thing he needed to deal with tonight. One loud bloodcurdling scream would bring those murderers running.

Thank God, those baby blues seemed fixed to his chest. "You have a lot of tattoos."

"Yes," he ground out, more focused on the incredible strength of the undulating serpentine in his grasp than what Meredith thought of his ink, but still. Those dainty fingers of hers were a hefty distraction he didn't need.

She smoothed a fingernail over the USMC symbol. "I never knew you were interested in joining the Marines."

"I wasn't." He groaned. The damned winding thing now attached to the end of his arm was determined to live. He was just as determined it wouldn't. Its forked tongue darted at Meredith when his fingers clenched below its broad, flat head, tight enough to strangle it.

"Hunter. Let me go," the lady protested, kind of, her hands still soft and gentle on his chest. Her fingers roved over his nipples, tantalizing the hell out of him and hardening his body.

He hung on tightly, inadvertently to her as much as the snake, but holy hell. How blind was she? Oh, wait. She still had typical Meredith tunnel vision. Everything was always about her.

Reptilian muscles contracted around his wrist and forearm, writhing beyond her view and squeezing his arm while she studiously examined the tats on his chest.

Her extra warm body relaxed while his stiffened with the life-or-death struggle he was caught up in, but damn it. Poisonous or not, he wouldn't let this thing near her.

The muscles in his arm trembled with the exquisitely tough battle of holding it away, while holding her in his other arm. Her fingers turned to silky acceptance instead of another rejection. She snuggled into him, her head under his chin like a lover. All that damp hair of hers spilled over his chest and curled around his arm.

"Oh, Hunter. I knew you still cared."

Give me a break.

Like a vacuum with a mind of its own, his nostrils sucked her feminine essence back into his soul. Sweat. Flowers. And Meredith. He was going down fast. This snake had to die. Instead, it opened its mouth wide behind her head, either to hiss or because it was dying. No sound came out. Just two long, dripping fangs.

If the damned thing had been any bigger, it might have had a chance. As it was—

He groaned, his arm growing numb.

"I missed you." Her lips brushed along his collarbone, her fingers tripping over his bare neck, lighting him up. Electricity sparked, a high-voltage arc that had no business surging between them. A different kind of thunder commenced inside his ribcage, one he'd not expected nor wanted to feel after all these years. Why the hell now?

With one big shudder, he wrapped his left arm protectively around her while, with the other hand, he broke the snake's spine with one quick snap. Grunting, he flicked the still coiling reptilian body away.

Meredith finally looked over her damned shoulder. Of course, she did what she did best—overreacted. Shoving off, she turned into a prancing pony, squealing and standing on her tiptoes as if she could keep both bare feet off the ground at once—like that was humanly possible.

"A snake! A snake! You killed a snake! Right behind me! You killed a snake! Oh, my God!"

"Shhhhh," he cautioned, glancing over his shoulder. "For hell's sake, keep it down."

"B-b-but... you killed a snake. There was a snake behind me and… and now it's dead and… Oh, my God, Hunter! You killed a snake!"

No shit.

Her legs were straight, but Meredith bent over, holding all that blonde hair out of her eyes in one hand while she sputtered over the still twisting, dying reptile. And didn't his blood run hot at the sight. She'd always been his dream girl, but seeing her in this particular position, with her butt sticking out like it was, didn't do a thing to keep the blood supply in his brain.

Damn. He'd smack that ass just to see her jump, but she was hyperventilating like a silly high school cheerleader. Standing beside her like he was, his attention shifted automatically from her sexy backside to her voluptuous and very revealing bosom. Her sexy bra did little to support or cover those fine, full breasts, jiggling and within reach. With her fingers fanning her cleavage like they were and her legs still spread apart and stiff, holy shit. He was losing ground fast.

"B-b-but," she sputtered again, still bent over, still hyperventilating, and still driving him to the edge of crazy.

Precisely. *Butt*—as in the very delectable derrière of the woman he'd once lost his heart and soul to. Also, as in— but—she was married. He turned his back on her, needing to get his mind on track before the rest of his blood supply went south. "It's dead. Get over it."

She straightened, her arms crossed, and her chest, heaving like the drama queen she always was. Women. She'd just shot a guy and survived an attempt on her life, yet she was afraid of a little snake? That thing was just a baby. Wait 'til its mama showed up.

Sharp blue glaciers stabbed him like icicles. Her lower lip quivered. "You weren't hugging me, were you? That's not why you pulled me into your arms, was it? It didn't mean anything. You were killing a snake." She made it sound as if he'd betrayed her instead of saved her.

"It was that or let you get bitten."

"B-b-but I thought—"

"You thought wrong." He verbally slapped her down and turned his back on her because he couldn't tolerate the sight of her succulent, heaving breasts anymore. Teague needed real help, and by then, so did Hunter. He adjusted his, umm, physical situation, before he could crouch beside the MI lead agent. Let Meredith think what she wanted. Did she even know what she was doing to him in that get-up? He could barely catch a breath and his pants had gotten tight. Damned tight. He parted his knees to free up some space.

"You used to be kind and thoughtful and... and sweet," she whispered, her voice all breathy and sexy.

"I used to be a lot of things." He shrugged her off and busied himself examining Teague's vitals in order to get his brain out of the gutter. The MI lead agent had grown deathly quiet during the hurried retreat from camp, but when Hunter pressed his finger for a neck pulse, he felt a strong and steady beat. Teague might be shot, but he wasn't at death's door. Not yet, anyway.

Hunter pushed off the ground for more medical supplies.

Opening the crate brought Meredith to his side. "You called me Merry."

So what? He'd been scared and had let his pet name for her slip. The endearment had gotten away from him before he'd had enough forethought to call it back. So what? It wouldn't happen again.

"You're still mad at me for marrying Eddy."

"No, I'm not." He turned away with a sealed canister of antiseptic wipes, a bottle of painkiller, and his heart locked tight. "Drop it."

She followed. His nose twitched when the scent of her filled his nostrils. Sweat. Fear. A touch of flowery fragrance. But mostly, the smell forever ingrained in his soul, the uniquely sweet scent of Meredith's lush lips and her satiny skin and...

Shit! Fighting for control, he ripped the foil seal from the can of wipes and took a deep whiff of antiseptic vapors to block the memory. She'd had her chance. Teague needed attention now. Not her. Never again her.

Meekly, she took the can from his hand. "I'll do that." Without asking permission, she knelt alongside Teague and administered to her wounded companion, wiping his brow.

Hunter pulled a bottle of water out of his gear bag and twisted the top off. Teague didn't need cleaning as much as a drink. Easing one hand beneath the unconscious man's sweaty neck, Hunter placed the bottle to his mouth and poured a trickle between his lips. Automatically, Teague swallowed. Good sign. This guy just might make it after all.

I hope I do.

CHAPTER FIVE

Now that they weren't running for their lives, Meredith risked an appraising glance at Hunter out of the corner of her eye. No socks, just boots. Loose laces. All the signs of a man who'd run to her rescue just like he'd said. Then why was he so angry?

Her gaze lingered longer than she planned because, well, this was Hunter. The man she would've given her heart, mind, and soul to once upon a time. They'd never gotten physically involved and she wished they had. Maybe everything would've worked out differently.

The man was a study in geometry, all angles and all of them squared off with sharp corners, from the fierce brows on his forehead and that jaw he kept sticking out at her, to his massive chest that looked more like two slabs of chiseled marble. He'd either pumped iron one heck of a lot since the last time they'd seen each other, or he'd done steroids.

His massive shoulders and arms were streaked with welts. All needed to be cleaned, some stitched. A dusting of dark hair shadowed his chin as well as his tanned and glistening pecs. Numerous tattoos covered his thick chest, biceps, and arms all the way to the backs of his fingers.

At first glance, he didn't look a thing like the cute guy she'd known in college. If she'd seen him on the street, she would've walked on by and been none the wiser. There was no trace of humor or softness, no evidence of that dark blond hair neatly parted on the right and combed like he was always ready for church. Cynicism had replaced the sweet, wide-open smile she'd fallen in love with. Black ink, scars, and a deep bronze tan covered the once fair-skinned body. Maybe that was what happened when men became soldiers. Maybe they grew darker from the inside out from all they'd seen and done. Hunter certainly had.

The first time she knew he'd gone off and enlisted was the day after Christmas when she'd run into his mom at the grocery store. Meredith hadn't been feeling so good herself that morning. She'd needed something to settle her stomach and her head, but Mrs. Christian had kept dabbing at her teary eyes.

One friendly comment led to another until the truth spilled out, and then Meredith was sick at heart. She'd wanted to cry. Hunter had always talked about running off to the far ends of the Earth to live the adventures of Kipling and Hemingway, Melville and Dickens. He'd wanted to see the world, but badly enough to join the Marines? It had been a devastatingly mindboggling development in the drama her life was then and so not like him.

Hunter was no fighter. He hadn't even done ROTC in high school or college. He didn't like guns. Heavens, he hadn't owned so much as a pocketknife that she knew of, much less a rifle. He was her best friend, her confidante. She'd wanted him as her lover. Her only. But then along came Eddy, and Meredith had swallowed her foolish college dreams the same way she'd swallowed so many other dreams—with one hard, disappointing gulp.

Shifting to her feet, she scanned the dark jungle around her. For the moment, they were hidden. She felt safe until he spoiled it.

"I'm leaving."

Her heart began to race. "Why?"

"I need to find Eric and the guys. Teague's still out. You'll be okay until I get back."

She bit back her next question. *Why does he think his guys are alive when mine aren't?* "W-wait," she stuttered. "At least let me spray you with insect repellant. You'll… you'll need protection." *And I don't want you to leave.*

His lip curled. "No, I won't. Stay here. I won't be long."

She gulped. She'd be alone in the jungle with a wounded man.

"You've got a gun. Use it."

Her mouth dropped. She had a gun, only—

Dark brows angled to a severe and incredibly sexy *V* when his eyes darted from the crate to her feet and up to her face. He took a menacing step toward her, his lips thinned, his teeth bared, and his fists clenched. "You said you shot one of them, right? You had to have a gun to do that."

"Yes, but it's... it's..." She looked to her side and back to Hunter, glowering like a storm cloud over her. Dark. Ruthless. Bursting with electricity that made the hair on her arms stand up. She couldn't help the magnetic pull between them, the way her fingers itched to soothe those hard edges, to gentle that hostile male's perpetual temper. "I don't know where it is right now. I must've left it behind when I dropped my stuff or maybe when—"

"You what?" snapped out of him.

She raised her palms to placate him. "I had it when I tried to help Teague, but then you showed up, and I must've set it down, and I—"

"You left your damned weapon behind like a—"

"Go ahead. Say it. Like a woman," she bit out, shaking but not going to put up with his perpetual nasty attitude.

"No. Like a damned girl scout!" he hissed, his pupils gone flat and merciless. Cruel. His fingers clenched and unclenched at his sides. "You of all people should've known better. We need all the help we can get, but no, you trot off and leave your piece behind like it's nothing but a tube of cheap lipstick. Shit, Meredith. What were you thinking?"

She lowered her head in shame and took it. Okay. He was right. She knew better than to forget where she'd set her weapon. It was an unforgivable rookie mistake, and one she'd never made until this night. Her concealed weapons instructor would shake his head in disgust if he were here. She practiced gun safety religiously at home. Honest, she did. Her pistol always went into the holster at her back when she was carrying or into the lockbox when she wasn't. No ifs, ands, or buts. And even at three, Courtney knew to never touch Mama's gun, not like he could've reached it. She kept the lockbox on top of her six-foot tall bookshelf in her living room.

"It's just that everything happened so fast. I was trying to help Teague, but then those guys came back, and I'm... I'm sorry." Useless tears threatened. Meredith turned her back so Hunter wouldn't see, but then she got mad. "I'm sorry, already!" she hissed, facing him again and resorting to defiance instead of apology. Let him be mad. Wasn't he always? She was pretty mad at herself, too.

He paced in a wide circle around her and Teague. Once. Twice. The third time around the circle with the bamboo enclosure, he blew out a deep breath and stuck one knee to the ground at her side, the other cocked, and a clenched fist on his kneecap. "I took off in a hurry, too. I'm not angry with you for leaving the pistol behind. I'm just pissed we're in this predicament to begin with. Whoever's trying to kill us is still out there, and they're well-armed."

That helped. She lifted her lashes and risked a look at him. Genuine light shone in his eyes. "I really am sorry, Hunter. I got so flustered. I've never shot at anyone before, and—"

"Forget it." With one quick motion, he lifted his rifle from beside the supply crate and handed it over. "Keep this with you until I get back. Don't set it down, got it?"

"Okay." She accepted the compact weapon, resting it across her knees so he wouldn't see how badly her hands shook, or how much he'd gotten to her. "Do you have another? A pistol maybe?"

He scowled. "Don't worry about me. Have you ever shot one of these before?"

She swallowed hard. "Yes. I've used a rifle at the shooting range, but what will you use? You're unarmed."

Another scowl. Another snark. "Marines are never unarmed. Remember that." He wiped a hand over his face before he stared her down again. A puzzled frown shifted across his brows, as if he were trying to decide if he could trust her. "Listen up. When I come back, I'll give you a signal. Hotel Charlie. That way you'll know it's me. Answer back with Mike Foxtrot, you got it? That way I'll know you're still safe. Whatever you do, don't let anyone get close without that code."

His gaze had become a steel trap she couldn't tear her eyes away from. She nodded, her throat gone dry, unable to speak. Secret codes. Assassins on the prowl. *Wow.*

"Keep quiet, Meredith, I mean it. If you hear footsteps or anyone rustling through the bamboo without giving the Hotel Charlie signal first, shoot to kill because it won't be me."

"But it might be Eric or the guys. I could let them in, right?"

Dark lasers pierced her gaze, stabbing straight to her heart. "I doubt you'll see them. Be tough. Keep your head, and let whoever's snooping around come to you before you open up and fire. Can you do that?"

She nodded vigorously. "Hotel Charlie. Mike Foxtrot. Our initials. Got it."

That seemed to do the trick. Hunter took a deep breath. His Adam's apple bobbed. "Now you're talking. Good girl." He tapped her thigh just one time with the tip of his index finger, his focus already on the jungle behind him. "Take care of our guy. I'll be quick." With a quick shove, he was off the ground and gone. The jungle silenced except for the muffled clatter of bamboo canes as he walked away in the dark.

"Wait," she called out to him. "At least take the flashlight."

But he was gone. Meredith pulled the rifle strap to his weapon over her head and positioned it behind her back with the barrel pointed down, as she'd seen him do. Teague needed her, and she needed both hands to help him.

Since he was drenched in sweat again and still dirty from everything he'd lived through, she took the time to clean him, using several wipes. Over his face and down his neck she went. Very gently, she cleaned the blood off his chest and away from the bandage Hunter had applied. Teague never made a sound, but he was breathing easier. Her nerves settled. Service for another was a welcome diversion.

Wrapping the soiled wipes into a tight bundle, she lifted to her feet and inspected the contents of the supply crate. Stocked with bottled water, a portable water filtration system, MREs, energy bars, more insect repellant, several sealed plastic boxes, and another medical kit, as well as a single olive drab sheet, the container was a rolling godsend. She deliberated over cutting a hole in the center of the sheet and using if for a poncho, but no. Teague might need it more. She couldn't risk his recovery for vanity. Still, a change of clothes would've been nice. A shirt. Pants. Shoes. All of those little things a person took for granted.

Her fear subsided as she realized she wasn't completely without means or protection. When Hunter came back, all would be well. Hopefully, he'd have his guys with him. She doubted it with her men murdered, but he had to try. She would have.

Tucking the soiled wipes into a loose piece of plastic, she stuffed the garbage into the container before securing the lid again. The first rule of every good camper: *If you bring it in, you pack it out.*

"Meredith," Teague rasped, his eyes mere slits, a line of spit eking over his stubbled cheek.

"I'm here," she said as she knelt at his side and took his hand.

"Lyle? Dan?"

"Shhhhh. Don't talk. You need to rest."

"I need answers."

"They're dead," she admitted softly. "I'm sorry."

"Who? How?"

"I don't know." Meredith stalled telling him everything for fear he'd think he needed to defend her. "But Hunter's alive, too. He's gone back to camp to find his men. He'll be back soon."

"Ky? Eric too?" Teague rolled his eyes and groaned. "Everyone?"

"I really don't know, but you need to rest. We can talk about this later."

He inhaled a long, shuddering breath. "There's something... you need to know."

She edged her knees in closer, squeezing his hand gently to her breasts. "What, Teague? What do you want to tell me?"

He squeezed back with one hard clench that didn't last but seconds before his grip went limp. "There's more than one," he whispered weakly, his strength fading.

She leaned closer, her ear to his lips. "More than one what?"

His voice dropped lower. "Eric knew. There's more than two."

She smoothed her hand over his forehead. Teague was on fire. His words made no sense. He had to be delirious, and yet his sentences were not the garbled rant of a crazy man.

"What are you talking about, Teague? One what? Two what? What did Eric know?"

"There's..." He coughed up a clot of dark red. "Meredith, there's..."

Meredith snatched up another wipe and ran it gently around his mouth to remove the blood. His eyelids flickered shut. Instead of providing another piece to the puzzle, Teague drew in a long wheeze that ended in a hissing sigh. His head lolled to the side. His features relaxed as the wrinkles of anxiety faded.

"I don't know what you were trying to tell me, but you need to rest now. Maybe when you wake up, you'll feel better. We can finish this conversation then," she whispered.

Because there wasn't anything else to be done, she methodically finished wiping him down, then sprayed him with insect repellant and covered him with the sheet. She stayed beside him in their dark little hideaway, her arms wrapped around her knees, hoping the trail of busy ants several feet away didn't deviate from their single-file formation around the supply container. They were big, their bodies shiny in the dim light. She didn't have enough bug spray for an ant army.

At last she turned the flashlight off. The jungle night was dark and deep around her. A bird squawked in the canopy overhead, but other than that, her bamboo fortress remained silent. Gradually her eyes grew accustomed to the dark, enough that when a centipede as big as her hand decided Teague was in its way, she brushed it aside. Her ears strained for the sound of Hunter's return. A footfall. A rustle. Anything.

But nothing answered.

So, she analyzed her predicament and thought hard. She had distinctly heard the murderers in the MI camp say that some guy named Burdette wanted her dead. Why would anyone want her dead? Maybe her ex, but that seemed a fantastical stretch of the imagination. There were times Eddy had been rough with her, but he wouldn't kill her.

Besides, he was back in Maryland or Virginia. She didn't know which at the moment, but wherever, he was most likely still living the high life. For a guy who'd barely finished college, he'd certainly thrived at what he did best. Hunting failing businesses down. Coercing financially depleted small business owners to sell at bargain basement prices, and just generally ripping them to shreds until they gave in and gave him what he wanted—everything.

But what good could her death possibly offer him? Eddy was already filthy rich. Their only remaining link was their son, Courtney, and oddly, Eddy had always maintained a decent, though distant, relationship with that little boy. He'd kept up with his child support payments, if only because his timeliness gave her no reason to go after him in court again. He hadn't once considered joint custody.

No one else came to mind. As far as she knew, her coworkers liked her. She had no male friends in her life. There was no jilted lover in her past. Pulling her legs in tighter to her chest, she leaned her forehead to her kneecaps. Always the popular girl since kindergarten, it was hard to imagine anyone disliking her enough to want her dead.

A sudden gasp from Teague jerked her out of her reverie. She rolled to his side. "What can I do for you?" she asked, her hand on his forehead.

His fever warmed her fingertips. Easing off her knees, she retrieved a bottle of water. The man was on fire. She needed ice, not lukewarm water, and he needed a doctor.

"Flynn." His voice grated. "Why are you still here?"

"Because you are," she replied evenly. "Now rest easy and—"

"No." He grabbed her wrist, his breath hot in her face. "You need to run. Now."

"Why would I leave you like this?"

"Because..." He sucked in a rasping breath. "There's... there's three."

His body went limp but his vehement declaration stopped her heart. "Three what? Teague, wake up. What are you talking about?"

Meredith froze, sure she' d heard the crunch of a heavy footstep outside the bamboo.

CHAPTER SIX

Efficiency—another mark of the sniper. Right behind sharpshooter eyes and cold heart.

Hunter moved quickly now that Meredith and Teague were hidden safely behind him. He'd come full circle to his camp, or at least where it had been. One of the LED torches still stood where the tent door used to be, the other busted in the dirt. Smoke now seeped from the remains of their heavy-duty nylon tent.

The place was deserted. Whoever'd been there had destroyed both camps, forcing any TEAM or MI survivors into the dark jungle. Like McCormack's men, his guys had been dropped off in this god-forsaken jungle with three rigid containers on wheels full of enough supplies to last the week. All of those containers were missing. What the hell did those murderers want? What were they looking for?

Kicking through the burning debris of his tent, he found the extra backpack that had served as his pillow. No Marine kept just one weapons cache. Jerking the bag out of the charred debris, he dusted the scorch away and lifted the flap. None of the rounds inside had cooked off. That meant the fire hadn't been hot enough. Whoever torched the tent didn't use an accelerant. Good deal.

Removing his knife and its holster from the mesh pocket inside the pack, he dropped to one knee and strapped the knife onto his ankle. His extra shoulder holster and loaded pistol went over one arm next. All spare magazines went into his pants pocket along with a pocket pistol. Armed once more, he stood, alert and ready for war.

He seethed looking over the blackened shapes his buddies' cots had been reduced to, tough. A pair of wire-rimmed sunglasses caught his eye. They were dirty but not broken. Ky's. Hunter stuffed them into his shirt pocket on his way to where Eric's cot had been. There was a scorched metal box the size of an iPad on the floor. Two pictures and a folded letter fluttered out when he picked it up.

Hunter crouched to retrieve them. The larger photo was a slightly scorched family portrait of Eric with his parents on graduation day from boot camp. Damn, look at him. That goofy young man grinned from ear-to-ear. His parents looked just as proud.

The corners of the other photo, that one of a dark-haired girl, maybe ten or twelve, were dog-eared and burned. Hunter peered closer. That little girl sure resembled Eric. A lot. Same dark eyes. Same smile. Lots more dark hair, and longer, but yeah. She was a mini version of Eric.

Hunter flipped the image over. In neat, childish script, *Love you, Daddy* scrawled across the back. A line of three red hearts with arrows through them underscored the sweet sentiment.

Interesting. Eric had a kid? He'd never said a word, never once let on he'd been married or had a girlfriend. *Holy shit.* More interesting was the man's ring and the brass key, both stuck to the bottom of the box with a strip of now-melted tape.

Hunter secured Eric's private belongings back in the box, and stuck it inside his gear bag with Ky's glasses. Let the man keep his secrets. One last scan of the area verified everything flammable had burned, including his few extra clothes. Rising to his feet, Hunter made Eric, Seth, Ky, and that pretty little girl a promise. He would find his men. God help whoever stood in his way.

He'd no more than shook off the dire assessment when flashlight beams pierced the jungle opposite where he stood. A single shot ricocheted past him. Instead of returning fire, Hunter ducked into the cover of vines and brush to wait on the advancing idiots. He had Meredith and Teague to think about. He couldn't engage until he knew for certain what he was up against and he wouldn't lead these guys back to her.

Two black uniformed men advanced warily into the clearing, both with compact rifles. The narrow-beamed flashlights on their helmets announced exactly where their heads were. *Un-fuckin'-believable.* Hunter could've sniped them right there and then, both headshots. They'd certainly made it easy, but he restrained his itchy trigger finger and hunkered low to watch and learn. There were too many unanswered questions.

The duo walked through the camp like they owned the place. "You get him this time?" one asked, sounding as if he could've cared less.

Hunter cocked an ear. *Him who? Me?* These jerks couldn't be talking about him. They hadn't cleared the dense brush opposite his camp when they'd fired and he was fairly certain they hadn't seen him. Were they idiots?

"I'm not even sure it was the same guy. Might've been that woman or one of them monkeys. You know how big they are."

"Next time, use your night-vision goggles," the first badgered the other. "Monkey or man, kill the bastard."

"How d'you expect me to do that when he's like smoke?"

"Smoke, my ass. If it was him, he's a grunt like the other two we put down. Shoot him and be done with it."

Hunter's ears perked up. These guys had killed two of McCormack's men, but it didn't sound like they'd killed Eric, Ky, or Seth. But who was like smoke? They couldn't be talking about him. He hadn't run into these guys until now. Hope flickered to life that Eric and the guys were still alive.

The guards weren't forthcoming with any more info. The one kicked his way through the camp. "Ain't nothing here. Come on. Let's fade to black."

When the two turned back the way they'd come, Hunter followed. They made that easy, too. The whole concept of 'fade to black' was stealth and silence, neither of which these guys seemed to comprehend. They made enough noise for a dozen men, and their flashlights might as well have been flashing neon signs proclaiming their exact location to the whole world.

Hunter kept close enough behind them to reach out and touch. Or kill.

"You still thinking what I'm thinking?" The big guy in the lead spoke over his shoulder.

"Might be." The fat bastard behind him chuckled as they tromped along the trail between The TEAM and MI camps. "Depends on who gets to the woman first. Just so you know, I don't share."

Her. Meredith. Hunter's jaw tightened. *Touch her and I'll gut you like a pig.*

"Yeah, but I hear she's a real spitfire in the sack. Likes the whole bondage thing. Whips. Chains. Cuffs and collars. I'd like a piece of that ass." Big Guy sounded as if he'd been talking to someone who had an ax to grind with Meredith. "Always liked a woman who can take a beating and still deliver like she means it."

"Hell, I got a belt. Fact I got two. I'll loan you one. Let's see who can make her cry, open up them long legs, and—"

"Shut your pie hole." Big Guy stopped and pointed to the drag marks the cot had made. "Look here. Tracks."

Fat Bastard shoved around Big Guy to take a look. "You think she went this way?"

"She did if she's dragging the Horton fella. Come on. We take him down easy and then she's ours. Let's go get some of that ass you're planning on whupping. Least ways, I can watch." Big Boy lifted his rifle up against his cheek, aimed it forward, and took one step on the trail that led directly to Meredith.

Hunter's gut clenched at their brutal plans for that petite but feisty woman. Who had they been talking to about her? Who'd been lying about her? Hunter might be angry with Meredith, but she was no tramp and she didn't do bondage. He knew it to his soul, damn it.

"Don't shoot her before we play with her," Fat Bastard whined.

"I ain't gonna shoot her, but I ain't taking chances, neither. She's a tough bitch. Don't forget, she shot Jonesy."

"Yeah, but..." Fat Bastard smacked his lips. "I like 'em tough. It ain't no fun when they're beat up and they just lay there and take it neither."

Hunter could take no more. Silently closing in on the pair from the rear, he raised his USMC knife. It allowed him to be silent and deadly when he had dirty work to do.

It took less than five minutes to dispatch the bumbling degenerates. Fat Bastard went down with his throat cut from behind. Big Guy took a little longer, but only because he thought he had a dog in the fight. Turned out he didn't. One lightning kick to his throat ended that misconception.

All business now, Hunter collected their weapons, flashlights, and searched their pockets. He found no wallets or identification, but both carried concealed knives, matching stainless steel holstered revolvers—both .44 Magnums, five-inch barrels. He checked the chambers. Five rounds each, and nearly full ammo packs of 454 Casull on their belts. Between the handguns and the basic-but-deadly tactical carbines they'd been toting, these guys were armed to the gills.

On top of the guns, Hunter found identical key fobs in both men's pockets, and a garrote in Big Guy's back pocket. Fat Bastard's vest concealed a set of brass knuckles and a cigarette lighter, along with three foil-wrapped condoms. More interesting was the full syringe in his shirt pocket. Hunter held it up to the light. It wasn't one of those jet-injector hypos like they shoot you with during your USMC physical, just a regular needle and vial hypo with a finger plunger. *What the hell is this?*

Checking Big Guy more thoroughly, he found a similar hypo along with a vial of liquid. Again, he paused, holding the lime-green stuff up to the beam from one of the assassins' helmets. These guys were common thugs, not even decent military-grade, probably boot camp washouts. Why were they packing pre-filled hypodermic needles? Were they all on drugs? Could it be an antidote for spider bites maybe? Snake venom? Exactly who were they after? Just Meredith? The ActiveCamouflage System? Corporate espionage might be behind all this, but Hunter had one of his gut feelings.

He just didn't have all the puzzle pieces to go along with that feeling. Hurriedly, he stashed both capped hypos and the vial into one of his many cargo pants pockets and let the mystery go for now. The flashlights were small enough, they fit in another pocket. Going one step further, he pulled Big Guy's shirt and boots off. They might be a little large, but Meredith needed something to cover that sexy body of hers before Hunter did something really stupid. He couldn't handle the continual sexual assault on his eyeballs.

Stripping Fat Bastard's bloody shirt off next, Hunter shrugged it over his bare shoulders and buttoned up, intending to wash it in the next puddle he came across. Wearing a dead man's clothing wasn't his favorite thing to do, but he needed cover. The bugs were eating him alive. He should've let Meredith spray him down, but his pride got in the way. Marines never asked for help. They were the ones who gave it.

"Lance? You there?" a disembodied voice crackled at his throat, startling Hunter out of his egotistical rant. Was it possible? Sure enough. He pulled the shirt off to inspect it and found the smallest walkie-talkie he'd ever seen fastened to the underside of the collar. Unclipping it, he examined the feather-light device. No wonder he hadn't noticed it. The thing weighed less than a ballpoint pen.

Deliberating for all of one split second, he retrieved the other shirt and pulled the walkie-talkie off its collar, too. Walkie-talkies of this grade surely included GPS locators. Someone would come looking for Big Guy and Fat Bastard and he meant for them to be found. It was time to make a point. A very deadly point.

He set to work with that extra sharp blade of his, working over four bamboo stalks. That's all he needed. He didn't have time for more, not with Meredith on her own. Once done with the stakes he'd made, he shoved them at just the right height and angle across from the bodies. Not only did he intend to humiliate the naked remains of these two guys he'd killed by leaving them for the jungle nightlife, he meant to strike back at whoever was behind this hostile takeover. Whatever jokers came looking for Big Guy and Fat Bastard wouldn't notice the bamboo spears until it was too late.

Hunter knew his history. During the Vietnam War, both Viet Cong and Americans had resorted to using booby traps with punji stakes to surprise their enemies in the dense jungles. Bamboo could be deadly, and simple vines could be rigged as trip wires.

He worked swiftly. Finally done and sweating, he strapped the walkie-talkies to the sharpened stakes. He stretched the trip wire vines extra tight, so, with one wrong step, the stakes would spring forward, and any would-be rescuers would never see what hit them.

Hunter chuckled at his dark humor, but he wasn't going down without a fight. Wrapping the spoils of war into one bundle, he beelined back to Meredith and Teague. Stopping short of the hiding place, he cupped one hand to his lips and whispered, "Hotel Charlie."

Meredith didn't respond.

He cocked his head to listen more carefully and repeated the signal a scant bit louder. Still, no 'Mike Foxtrot' came back to him. Only silence. In five swift steps, he was inside the grove. She was gone, damn it. The litter and everything else, too.

A single gunshot pierced the jungle from the direction of the MI camp, and Hunter couldn't get out of that bamboo hideout fast enough. The enemy was on the move. He let his senses reach out into the jungle to pick up the slightest sounds of a woman dragging a heavy load. The slightest sigh or shadow. The smallest scent. Anything.

Opting against using the flashlights he now possessed, he searched for tracks in the dark, ruts from the heavy travois he'd turned the cot into. They were easy to find. She'd left a trail anyone could follow. Where was she going?

One more shot echoed behind him, and he pressed forward. Running on instinct and a healthy dose of fear, Hunter literally turned into a walking radar dish, willing himself to receive input from all directions. He tuned the world out and tuned in, his only mission that one particular sound in front of him. That quiet murmur. When it stopped, so did he. His nostrils flared. He'd caught a whiff of some flowery scent. *Meredith.*

Advancing cautiously, he angled his broad shoulders between branches and shrubs. At last he found her crouched behind a fallen log twice her size. He'd almost missed her. She'd covered herself under a layer of leafy branches, but the sharp line of his rifle in her hands gave her away. Stealthily, he approached her from behind until he was close enough to touch. He knelt, placing one hand firmly on her upper arm and whispering, "Hotel Charlie."

She nearly jumped out of her skin, which would've been a neat trick since that was about all she had on. "Darn it, Hunter, you scared me," she hissed, lowering her weapon, scanning the shirt splashed with someone else's blood that he was wearing.

"Why'd you break cover?"

"They came." She clutched his wrist, the whites of her eyes showing. "I heard them. Two. Maybe three guys. I think they were the same ones."

"I've seen two of them," he whispered back. "We won't be seeing them again, but there are others. Let's move. Where's Teague?"

She pointed wordlessly to a truck-sized rock sticking out of the ground several feet away. "I hid him over there. No one will see him in all those roots."

He glanced at the massive banyan tree with its army of columnar roots entrenched along its trunk. "Good thinking."

"Did you find any of your guys?"

"No, but I've got a shirt for you to wear and another couple more guns. Some ammo." He tucked his pistol into the palm of his hand and extended his other hand. "Give my rifle back."

Just as he took it out of her hands, a sudden movement starboard caught his eye—and then his heart. The blackest panther had just dropped soundlessly from the tree branch Teague lay beneath, no doubt lured in by the scent of blood.

Hunter barely had time to aim. His shot went wild. So did the cat, but now the whole world knew where they were. He pulled Meredith to her feet. "Time to go."

Easing her branches aside, she peered both ways before she stood. It was a small thing, but the innocent action made Hunter very aware just how unskilled she was at covert operations. She was a woman, a very feminine woman in the wrong place at the wrong time.

With her elbow firmly in his right palm, Hunter shoved his rifle over his shoulder before he secured Teague's cot again. But damn, Meredith surprised Hunter again. The damned rolling crate stood alongside Teague's litter. How had she managed that?

CHAPTER SEVEN

Meredith kept an eye on Hunter. He seemed different, radiating a feral energy that fit the tempo of the jungle more than that of the civilized world. He was like that panther, wild and lethal, intense and abrupt. Cold. Deadly. What happened while he was looking for his men?

"How's Teague?" He broke the spell.

"Feverish. Still bleeding. We need to change the bandage."

"Not now. That shot will bring trouble. We need to keep moving."

Warmth radiated off his body as they walked side by side. The path turned wide with fewer trees, the ground clear of shrubs. Vines and roots still snared the container and the litter as they hurried, but they were able to move quicker. Some kind of fungi glowed in the dark and the tree roots seemed more like giant fingers stuck into the ground, anchoring the massive giants as their branches reached high into the canopy.

A rustle in the brush behind them turned him around. He set the litter to the ground, and, without a word, charged the intruder before she could be sure it wasn't Eric or the guys.

A struggle ensued, and Meredith was witness to two lethal fighters squaring off in the dark. The intruder grunted. Hunter cursed. They backed away from each other, both gripping long, serrated knives.

"Who are you?" Hunter hissed, his rifle still at his back.

What was he thinking? "Shoot him," Meredith whispered. "Use your gun."

"Your fucking worst nightmare." The guy hefted his blade from one hand to the other. "You killed two of my buddies back there. I'm here to return the favor."

Hunter stuck his chin at the intruder. "Why don't you step on up and die trying?"

Typically, he charged the short distance, his head lowered and his shoulder angled. He met the intruder with thunder, swinging out with fists and growling profanities. Two blades glinted amidst the flying tangle of men's arms.

Hunter feinted to his left, but quickly lunged right. The other man kicked out with his boot, but Hunter had gotten in too close for that strike to be effective. He crashed both fists to the sides of the guy's head and the man fell groaning to his knees. Hunter gave him no quarter, just landed a solid kick to his throat and down the assassin went.

Meredith's heart beat high in her throat, but she couldn't look away.

Hunter jumped on the guy's torso, his knee in the stranger's gut and his hands at the man's neck. Choking and his eyes wide, the guy gripped Hunter's forearms, trying to break the hold. The cords in Hunter's neck stuck out. Muscles all the way up his arms bulged, the veins on his forehead, too. The coldest shadow darkened his face, and Meredith knew he was killing his opponent.

And then she understood. He'd deliberately chosen his knife over his gun. It was almost as if he'd needed to feel his enemy's life seep out of him, as if Hunter needed the risk, the challenge of close-up battle. As if he courted—Death.

At last, the intruder's eyes rolled back in his head and his body went slack. Her heart fell to the forest floor. He didn't twitch or hiss or do anything she'd expected a dying man would do.

Hunter bowed his head, his hands to his knees, and still straddling the dead man.

She saw it then—the knife handle protruding from Hunter's chest. She flew to him. "Hunter!"

When he lifted his head, the cold disgust in his eyes raked her up and down, halting her in her tracks. "Don't touch me."

She froze at the deadly chill in his voice, but in case he didn't know, she whispered, "B-but you're hurt."

A glint of surprise shifted over his face when his chin dropped as he took in the blade. Without a word, he jerked the wicked thing out and tossed it aside. The man needed help, but he didn't wince or gasp or... or anything.

Once again, she shifted closer—until he straightened. A stranger she no longer recognized glared back at her. His upper lip lifted into a half snarl like a wolf protecting his kill. She lifted her fingers to her lips at the feral beast on his knees. This wasn't her friend. Not anymore. Hunter's pupils were devoid of light, and the handsome face she'd wanted to caress now seemed chiseled in marble. Cold. Relentless. *Dead.*

The hardened warrior had returned. Without a word, he shifted off to one knee and began disrobing the man he'd just killed. Swiftly. Efficiently. Like he'd done this many times before. Hunter took everything, right down to the man's underwear. He only paused to roll the man to his side, facing away from Meredith.

Grunting as he pushed to his feet, Hunter held up a plastic syringe. "Do you know what this crap is?" he barked, breathing heavily, blood staining the front of his shirt.

She shook her head, wanting to help if he'd let her. "No. What?"

"Never mind." He tucked the capped syringe into one of his pants pockets, and rolled everything else into a bundle except the shirt. Using the man's belt, he secured the bundle and turned to her again, his top lip lifted in a sneer. "Are you so desperate you're into M&Ms?"

"Am I what?" she asked him right back. "How can you ask about candy at a time like this?" *What a stupid question.*

"I didn't ask about candy. I asked you... hell." He rolled his eyes, annoyed at her for what she didn't know. "Never mind."

Oh. Now she felt stupid. Did he mean S&M, as in sadomasochism? BDSM and all that—stuff? Her mother's ears had automatically registered M&M because—well, that was her life. Heat swarmed her cheeks like a flash fire. Hunter must think she was an idiot, but still. What did S&M have to do with anything?

Intensity shuddered off Hunter, so Meredith kept her distance and stayed with Teague. He, at least, seemed stable, but she checked on him anyway. Hunter didn't look at the dead man's body again; she couldn't stop. Her eyes seemed unable to look away. At least as tall as Hunter, he was thicker around the middle. Even in death, his fists, as big as hams, were clenched tight, yet Hunter had taken him down swiftly. Almost easily.

Reality shivered down Meredith's spine. Frightful awareness blanketed her shoulders with a chill. Hunter had murdered this man, and he'd done it quickly. Efficiently. With blood on his hands. Like he knew precisely how to end a life. She rubbed her arms to ward off the bleak tendrils winding into her soul. Hunter Christian was a killer.

Rummaging through the brush, he retrieved the dead man's knife that he'd tossed aside at the start of the scuffle. It joined the rest of the gear on the litter alongside Teague's legs. Hunter tossed the dead man's shirt and boots to her. "Here. Put 'em on."

She turned aside and let them drop to the ground, not wanting to touch anything that belonged to the dead. "No thanks."

"Do it," he ordered, pointing to the bundle at her feet. "He doesn't need them. You do."

"But he's d-d-dead."

"So?"

But you killed him, and the shirt smells bad, and I... I don't want to. She faced him, almost afraid to look into his eyes. How could he be so heartless?

Hunter's brows narrowed. His upper lip twitched, and she got the point. He thought she was defying him, which she was. Kind of. Mean Girl seemed to have taken a time-out just when Meredith could've really used the burst of confidence. She'd never known she had a stronger, meaner side to her until Eddy had taught her the ropes of living with a total jerk. Too bad Mean Girl didn't always show up when Meredith needed her.

She looked down at her dirty, bloodied feet. What a mess. Her French pedicure had been reduced to grime, stubbed toes, and cracked nails. Walking barefoot through the jungle wasn't easy. There were thorns aplenty, and she'd found every last one of them. Her feet hurt. There wasn't a part of her body that wasn't scraped, scratched, or bitten. But could she reduce herself to stealing from a dead man?

"Put 'em on," Hunter ordered again, his tone a soft whip of contempt. He'd already put on another guy's shirt, which looked worse with the blood pouring out of his knife wound. "I'll not ask you again."

Or what? You'll kill me, too? She didn't understand. If he'd just let her help, this despicable thing he wanted her to do might not seem so abhorrent. She ached to help him, to doctor him. Why wouldn't he let her near?

Ugh. She complied, sliding her feet into the dead guy's over-sized boots. They were too large and better than nothing, but the shirt? No way. Just the thought of a dead man's shirt against her skin pitched acid up her throat. Wearing his boots was bad enough.

"Are you ever going to do what you're told?"

Meredith looked up to that same angry scowl. Out of the blue, Mean Girl was back from her break. "Are you always going to treat me like I'm stupid?"

Without asking, she picked up the shirt and ripped a piece of the hem from it. Folding it into a makeshift bandage, she marched up to her angry, very stubborn companion. Before Hunter could open his big mouth to pitch another fit, she latched onto his massive forearm and stuffed the rag down his shirt, pressing it firmly to the hole in his chest.

He rolled his head back and hissed.

"You can growl all you want, but you need help. Now shut up and let me." She knew how to order people around, too, darn it.

It was hard to miss the way her fingers didn't quite circle his arm. The way her heart pounded at her audacious nerve. The way the merciless glare of a war-hardened soldier stole the breath from her lungs. She nearly wilted, but this man needed help. He'd just saved her life twice, and yeah, he'd killed someone, but he'd done that to save her. He wasn't just a cold-blooded killer. He was Hunter Christian, and he used to be her friend, and someone needed to save him for a change.

He kept glaring. She kept the pressure on his chest whether he liked it or not. Man, he was one stubborn jackass. She had to be hurting him, but other than that initial hiss, he didn't react, didn't even flinch a muscle or blink one evil eye. And for sure he'd never say thank you.

But that wasn't what she wanted, was it?

Meredith bit her lip at the hard man beneath her touch. What had happened to the tender, fun-loving person she'd once known? This Hunter was gentle one moment, but off the charts angry the next. He hadn't always been like this. He'd been one of the nicer guys she'd known while growing up, prone to excel in English Lit and poetry, never gymnastics, and certainly not ROTC. She never would've figured him for USMC material, not in a million years. An artist maybe or an author, possibly a teacher, yet there he was, an ex-Marine, hard as stone, and ready to die for everyone else. Worse, ready to kill.

He glowered an intensely sexy frown that sparked her female libido, as close as they were to each other. The boy she'd once loved was gone and only the all-male version remained. How could she not notice the fire in his dark eyes, the way his brows arched as if he expected her to cower, to be afraid of him? She wasn't, not really. When he glanced down at her hand inside his shirt, his long, thick lashes fluttered over his rugged cheekbones that seemed more stone than flesh. Heck, even the black stubble on his chin radiated pure testosterone, but she was sure the boy she knew was still in there.

A tsunami of desire for that Hunter swamped her common sense. Out the door went logic, and in came one ragged, scruffy feline on the prowl. She leaned toward him. He didn't budge, just let her approach like he was approachable, like she couldn't get through the wall he'd built no matter what she tried.

But try she did. "What happened, Hunter? You used to be so different. Why the change? What—?"

"I got smart." The cleft in his chin was more pronounced in the dim light. "What the hell do you care?"

His vehemence took her breath. "I'm just surprised. You used to be so—"

"Trusting?" He brushed her hand aside and ripped the bloodstained cloth out of her hand. "Forget it." Tearing off a smaller strip of the cloth, he wadded it into a golf-ball-sized plug and shoved it into the hole in his chest with his thumb, staring at her the entire time. Not once did he blink from the pain, and it had to hurt. He just kept plugging that hole, stabbing the wad in deeper until he'd staunched the blood flow. Just stared her down until she could take no more.

Her resolve crumbled. There was a time in her life when she'd had to learn to stand up for herself, but this was different. Eddy had hurt her for sport. He'd thought it was a game. Hunter was something else. He seemed to be carrying a deeper pain than that knife wound.

"Hunter. Please. Talk to me. There's just you and me. We've got a long road ahead of us. We need to be able to at least talk. Tell me what happened. What changed you?"

The darkest eyes flitted to her fingers where they still clutched his forearm. He couldn't have hurt her more if he'd slapped her.

She let go.

CHAPTER EIGHT

"We're going to end this one way or the other. Move it. We need to get to the river."

Did she not get the point? Hunter was tired of running from whoever was hunting them. It was time to hit back at the enemy, and hit back hard. If the guys chasing them thought those bamboo booby traps he'd left behind were brutal, they had no idea what brutality was about. The best defense was a gawddamned hard offense, and he intended to be as offensive and brutal as he needed to be. *Never piss off a Marine!*

As far as choosing his knife over his gun with that last guy? Hunter rolled the cramp out of his right shoulder. Sometimes a guy needed the hard and dirty way of settling up with a dirtbag.

"But why would anyone do this to us? To me?" she asked, a definite whimper in her voice as they prepared to trudge through the jungle.

God, he needed a cigarette! She hadn't moved an inch. Her hand wasn't even near the container's handle like she intended to snap to. He rolled the clawing pinch out of his neck, then flexed his shoulder because the grip of aggravation was still there. Every word out of her whiny mouth worked his last nerve.

Why no longer mattered in this fight to the death. Couldn't she figure that out? Jesus, it wasn't hard. Only *who* mattered, and Hunter had an appointment in the near future with that asshole. As soon as Meredith and Teague were stashed somewhere safe again, he meant to backtrack and hunt every last one of those bastards down.

"I said move out," he growled, tired of explaining what would've been obvious to anyone with a brain.

"No," she said stubbornly, and he understood. Really, he did. Meredith was a born drama queen and probably tired of walking in the dark. No, wait. Maybe she'd broken a nail helping him neutralize that last bastard. No, wait again. That wasn't right. All she'd done was stand and watch and snivel while he'd fought hand-to-hand for both their lives. She hadn't even picked up a branch or a rock to knock the guy over the head like another soldier would've done. Obviously, she wasn't dressed for this kind of an outing. She wouldn't even put on the shirt he'd given her. Or maybe it was the boots, just not her style, and she needed to—shop!

He lifted poor Teague's litter, nothing but disgust on his mind. Yeah, he could've ended that fight with one shot. He had a gun, but sometimes revenge required a man to get his hands dirty. Hunter started walking. With or without Meredith at his side, he had a mission to finish. If she thought he was going to get weepy-eyed because he'd gotten into a little knife play, guess again. As long as nothing major had been severed and the bleeding eventually stopped, Hunter did what any jarhead would do in his circumstance. He kept moving.

"I thought we were going to the river?" she called after him.

"We are."

"Well, the river was near your camp, the last I remember. We're miles from there."

"There are no waterfalls there."

"So what? Why do we need waterfalls? And what is your darn problem?" She was the one doing the barking now, and she still hadn't moved one step.

Hunter rolled his shoulders before he turned to face her. Fine. If she wanted to fight, he was ready to accommodate. God knew he'd had plenty of time to think about this moment. The litter went back to the ground, and Teague with it. Hunter stalked back to Meredith, ignoring the pain in his chest but not the hemorrhoid in his butt named Meredith! "You really want to have this discussion now? Here? When we're running for our lives?"

Her chin lifted. "Why not?" Her hands came to rest on her hips, which, oh, by the way, were mostly naked. Damn her. She should've put that shirt on like she was told. Meredith never had learned to listen, and now she sure as hell wasn't playing fair.

"What's wrong with you, Hunter Christian? You used to be nice, but you've had a chip on your shoulder from the first minute you saw me," she informed him like he didn't already know, her hands on the curve of her shapely hips. "Heck, you should've seen the look on your face when you found out it was me under that helmet."

"Visor. Remember?" He tapped his temple to make his point crystal clear. "I didn't know it was you, or did you get scared and forget that, too?"

Her eyes nearly bugged out at his perfectly aimed hit below the belt. Yeah, she knew he meant the gun she'd *lost*. Who was that stupid they forgot where they put their weapon in the middle of a fight? *Apparently, Meredith!*

"Give it a rest, Christian. You had to have seen the roster before you came on this operation. You knew I'd be here. How many Meredith Flynns do you think there are in the world?"

"What damned roster? Why'd you have to come on this little vacation?"

"Because it's my job." She had a cute way of sticking her chin out when she emphasized certain words like *job*. "Teague asked for a four-man opposing team, and Alex Stewart sent men. Teague and I didn't care who they were."

"You married him!" Hunter roared, the truth finally out in the open where it belonged.

"Him? Teague? No I... we're not... Oh... him." Meredith took a half-step back, her fingers to her open mouth. She blinked as if he'd just shared a piece of news she'd never heard before. *Like hell.* She knew what she'd done the day she'd stepped all over Hunter's heart on her way to good times with Welch, the richest freshman in college.

"You left me without saying a word. You ran! Not once did you think to call or explain why that good-for-nothing was suddenly your man of the hour. Not you. Not queen-of-the-ball, everybody-loves-me Meredith Flynn. Oh, no. I thought we were moving in together. After all we'd said, I thought we meant something to each other. I thought we were solid!"

"But I... I..."

"But. You. Lied! All the shit you said about loving me was nothing but lies. You never meant any of it." He wiped his lip with the back of his clenched fist, angry that he was out of control, and that he needed to hit something. She had yet to offer one solid line of defense.

Overhearing Big Guy and Fat Bastard's bullshit earlier had only stirred everything up again. Hunter had loved Meredith with all he had. They were an item, at least, he'd thought they were. But she'd had money back then, and he should've seen it coming. Birds of a feather and all that crap. She and Welch ran in the same circles, and so did their parents.

Hunter was born a nobody and would die a nobody.

Swallowing hard, he forced himself to calm. A little. "I don't care how you live your life, but I'm not a fucking doormat for you to traipse over on your way to fame and fortune. You've got your rich boy. Go back to him. Leave me alone."

"You left me," she whispered so softly he almost didn't hear her. "You joined the Marines after Christmas, and I talked to your mother, and, Hunter, you never said a word to me—not even goodbye. You just… left."

"I left you?" He was back to growling. Everything about her made him so damned angry, he couldn't think. "You were wearing his ring, remember? How could I stay? And why? So you could rub it in my face every time I saw you? So I could watch you walk down the aisle with the jerk who'd kept track of every cheerleader, co-ed, and wannabe that he banged? Did you think you were something special to Welch? Did you think he cared for you more than I did? Is that why you slept with him?"

So there. Yes, Hunter knew what had happened after the homecoming game, after the big drunken orgy at Welch's apartment, the apartment Welch's parents had paid for so he could live the high life while other kids worked two jobs to get through college. Hunter knew about Meredith's pregnancy. Hell, the whole school did. If she'd just have told him and not let him find out through the San Diego Southern University grapevine. If she had half a spine.

His anger ratcheted higher. If Welch had been there in the jungle with him, Hunter would've taken him apart.

Meredith pursed her lips, framing the smallest *O*. A bleak shadow deepened the blue of her irises to gray, but Hunter kept letting her have it, every last fermented drop of the bitterness he'd stored in the wine cellar of his heart for far too long. "Why shouldn't I have left? I needed to get the hell away from you." He snapped his fingers. "The Corps made it happen, and you know what? It felt gawddamned good."

Meredith blinked with that doe-eyed look of hers. She lifted her chin, her lower lip trembling. "But Hunter—"

"Don't but me!" He couldn't tolerate any more lies. "It's too late. You're married. Stop waving your ass around like you're not. I saw you with Eric. Shit. You're the last thing he needs in his life. And stop coming on to Seth and Ky. They don't need the likes of you screwing them like you did me!" Now he'd stooped to mean and nasty, not his forte. Eric, Seth, and Ky might have been dead for all he knew. He had no right drawing them into this fight. He shut his mouth before he dishonored his friends further.

"But Hunter—"

He jerked a palm up to her face. "Stop, Meredith. Stop trying to explain. I gave up on you long ago. Don't think you can wave your tits at me and I'll give in. I've been there once. I gotta give it to you..." He paused long enough to suck in a long, deep breath that didn't come close to easing the angst in his gut, or the guilt he felt for unleashing on her like he had.

Yeah, not one of his finer moments. "I learned a lot the day you walked out on me."

"Like what?" she asked, her voice suddenly as calm as a summer morning, something glimmering at the corner of her eyes. She wasn't angry. She hadn't come back at him, not once. Was she... *could* she in any way be as filled with regret as he was?

He stopped in his tracks, cocked his head, and glared at her, needing to understand what had just happened. The tiniest inkling of suspicion whispered at the back of his hard head that maybe he'd missed something. That maybe she'd trapped him all over again. Hell, no. Not this time.

"That all women lie," he spat. "They play a guy like the trusting fool he is, they get what they want, and, shit. I don't have time for this." He stalked back to Teague. "Move out."

"No."

He froze, clenched his fingers into fists, and counted to ten before he returned Teague to the ground and whirled on her with deadly deliberation in his heart. It was time she knew who she was dealing with. Nose to nose, he ordered her one last time, "I. Said. Move."

She lifted her chin, daring him like she had a choice. "And I said—"

"No! Fuckin'! More!" Hunter bellowed. He meant to do nothing more than get in her face and intimidate the shit out of her. Like a Marine Corps drill sergeant. Like the demon he truly was. She should be scared of him, damn it!

It almost worked. He'd backed her straight into the nearest tree and cornered her, his hands on the trunk near her shoulders. She was caged with nowhere to run, and he'd catch her if she dared try.

Finally! The perfect level of shock and awe blossomed in those dusky, baby blues. He sneered his dominance and took hold of her chin, the pad of his thumb forcing her face up so he could rain holy shit down on her.

She knew it, too. She'd stepped too far over the line this time. Meredith Flynn was in for an overdue and damned good butt-chewing, and he was just the man for the job.

Until everything went to hell.

He's going to kill me.

The panicky thought no more than quivered through her mind when he was breathing hard in her face, his heaving chest brushing up against her breasts, inciting a fire in her blood. The manly scent of spearmint and tobacco filled her flared nostrils. Darn, but he'd never been this mad at her before. This fierce. This hot. This—sexy.

She pulled her bottom lip into her mouth and bit down on it. He noticed. His nostrils flared. His eyes darkened to pure black obsidian. Before she could catch a decent breath or come up with one word of warning that he'd better back off, he lunged, and his overheated mouth crashed into hers. It hurt. He'd hit her teeth and lips too hard and—not hard enough.

Desire for him flamed to life.

Angrily, he deepened the kiss, his tongue forcing her lips apart, and his hand framing her face. She melted. Molding her body to his, she let him enter her mouth. Let him take whatever it was he thought he needed so badly that it incited a moan when he took it.

His lips, his tongue, the hard shaft of steel at her belly, all of it—she absorbed every startling part of him into her soul with a rampant hunger she hadn't known she possessed. The scruff on his cleft chin grated over her lips, tenderizing her skin, but along with it came a fire in her veins. She burned for him, wanted every last breath of his.

Please, more.

Hunter growled, his tongue demanding harsh possession of her mouth, tangling with hers, his fingernails stroking down her arms and up again, demanding she respond. And she did, arching against his hard body, riding his thigh, her fingers knotting of their own volition in his hair. She held him tight, pulling him into all she had to give and all she needed. Two could play this game.

Raw feral need crackled from him to her. Her toes curled. She felt them inside the humongous boots on her feet, but worse, her entire body responded to his devouring mouth, his fingers raking down her back, demanding utter compliance. At last he clutched her almost bare ass. He lifted her off the ground and strapped her onto his hips, but she wanted all of him. Her body hugged those angular male hips, molding her innermost core to his bulging zipper.

Heat filled the empty place between her ears because she'd lost the ability to think. No logical reason to push him away came to mind, not even after all the accusations he'd hurled at her. Not after the hurt she'd seen in his eyes.

She clutched his shoulder blades. All ten nails dug in hard and fast, holding him as tightly as he gripped her. *'Please, don't do that,'* never entered her very focused mind. Only,

'Yes, take me. Take me. Now.' She knew what she wanted, and she wanted him.

The taste of Hunter filled her mouth. The smell of him filled her nose. Meredith writhed, needing his body inside of hers. The fire was wild and the fuel was—Hunter.

Closing her eyes, she lost what was left of her tattered heart to Hunter Christian, the only man she'd ever loved. This joining had been a long time coming, and it had happened fast. One minute they were fighting like mortal enemies, the next they were hanging onto each other for dear life, on the verge of being bound to each other for time and all eternity. The ground vibrated beneath her, and all she could think of was Hunter filling the emptiness in her body and heart. She moaned, ready to comply with whatever he demanded next. However. Wherever.

Desire had never tasted sweeter nor felt so painful, but that wasn't the Hunter she knew, was it? As hard as he had crashed into her, as urgently as he clutched her backside, she knew in her heart he was already leaving. Already running away. Like last time. Again and again and again. She held on tighter, intent on giving her all if it would just help him decide to stay.

Don't go. Hunter, please don't go.

But just like that, he did.

Hunter released her, letting her slide down his thighs to the ground. The heat between them cooled and dissipated, her heart with it. She could barely draw a breath.

Blown away by the sheer passion of the last thirty seconds, she saw stars when her feet touched earth again. Her body leaned instinctively toward his, bereft of the fire it needed to live. To love. She'd been left needy and hollow, aching for the feel of him inside of her. Every nerve burned with raw and desperate unquenched desire.

Taking a full step back, he let go of her hands and severed the connection. He bowed his head and blew out a ragged, "Damn it to hell."

With his hands to his knees, he didn't look at her, and it was just as well. She wasn't sure what he'd see.

"Son-of-a-bitch." He cursed the dirt between his feet, huffing great heaving breaths.

Meredith leaned into the tree behind her, weak-kneed and content to let it hold her upright. At least the experience had moved him as much as her. She latched her fingers to the bark of the mighty trunk; afraid she'd fall if she let go. There would be no apology for what she'd just done, no explanation, and no need for either. Just heaving breaths. Just lingering embers that, with the least provocation, could flame back to life if he cared to so much as breathe on her. If he cared at all.

Nothing—*nothing*—in life had prepared her for this insatiable hunger for Hunter Christian. Why were they only now discovering this about each other now? Why not—then? Why not before she'd thrown their one sweet chance away? Everything might have turned out so differently, if only—*if only*—what?

She knew the answers. So did he. If she hadn't gotten pregnant. If she hadn't erred when she'd decided the baby's father deserved a chance to prove himself a better man. If she hadn't kept the secret from all her friends as long as she had. If only she'd admitted the truth—that she wasn't the good girl everyone thought she was. If Hunter hadn't run off to war without giving her a chance to explain.

Too many foolish decisions stood between them. Her head reeled, filled with doubt and awe and wondering. "We need to talk," she whispered hoarsely, surprised she could speak at all. He needed to know the entire truth, not just what he thought he knew.

"No. We don't." Without another word, he straightened and turned away. Hunter lifted the litter, and, his head low and his shoulders tight, he marched into the jungle, no doubt expecting her to follow like the arrogant man he was. The only difference was that this time, she couldn't. With one soul-rending kiss, this angry man had just claimed her and deserted her at the same time.

CHAPTER NINE

Son-of-a-bitch!

Hunter spat. He couldn't contain his disgust with himself. For the first time in forever, he'd done the unthinkable. He'd fulfilled a dream and shattered it at the same time, like some hot-blooded prick out of high school who finally gets the girl of his dreams, and why? For what? Meredith obviously had no clue what she'd meant to him or she wouldn't have stood there and taken one for the team.

And yet they'd cared for each other once, hadn't they? Hell, he didn't know what was real anymore. She had him so mixed up he couldn't focus when she was around. And that damned underwear! Why couldn't the woman ever do what she was told?

Of all things, Elizabeth Barrett Browning's love poem for the ages came back to him. *"How do I love thee?" Let me count the fuckin' ways! Dressed. Half-dressed. Naked. Upside right. Upside down. Any and every other damned way in between. That's how!*

Add to that angst of the stupid college jerk he used to be, the one who'd thought she could actually fall for a geek who'd loved English Lit as much as she did. He was the dumbest dumbass on the planet. A smoke right damned now would help, but did he have one? Shit, no.

Every stalking step away from her became an exclamation point to his internal rationalization. She was the one who'd broken it off. She was the one who'd run to Fast Welch the first chance she'd got. She was the one who'd never looked back—not like Hunter had given her much of a choice. The Christmas night he saw her ride off with Welch was also the night he turned his pitiful excuse of a life around. He'd gone home with one purpose only—to change. And change he had.

By midnight, all his lost saints had been boxed in cardboard and on the curb for Goodwill, never to be seen in his hands again. Nothing had been sacred that night. Not Homer's *Iliad*. Not Steinbeck's *Grapes of Wrath,* or Hemingway's *For Whom the Bell Tolls*? Out they'd all gone, out of his life in one angry fit of never turning back.

With the slate wiped clean, the next morning he'd said goodbye to his folks and marched down to the local USMC recruiting office. His dreams had been destroyed. Why not erase his past life along with them?

Stupidest thing he'd ever done. But he'd learned every other lesson the hard way. Why not that one?

Not one for much upper-body strength the day he'd joined the Corps, he'd learned. By the end of boot camp, he could pump fifty just because some loud-mouthed SOB of a drill sergeant told him he could and would. Not one for endurance, Hunter had learned quickly about perseverance and packing more than one hundred pounds of gear. Not only that, he could do it in the dead of summer in full uniform while dragging another soldier who'd passed out from the heat.

Like any good jarhead, Hunter kept moving. There was no way to plan a decent offensive strategy with thoughts of Meredith muddling up his brain. And damn. Teague had gotten a lot heavier as the night grew shorter. Daylight would soon hit the eastern horizon, but damned if Hunter knew which way was east after a night of running.

It didn't help that the litter was loaded with the ammo and gear from the three enemy assassins, either. Hunter doubted he could strike back in the middle of the night, and there was no way they could make the river before morning. Sleep was a luxury he couldn't afford, but Meredith would need it. Soon.

Damn. Hunter had never been so undecided. He had to get his act together or none of them would survive this night. At least she'd chosen to pick up those supplies and stick close. She was afraid. He read it easily in her body language. Gone was the cocky girl who used to throw her pom-poms in every jock's face who looked her way.

Now, if he could only shake the taste of her mouth off his lips.

Focus, Hunter. Stop looking at her.

Easier said than done.

If you always do what you've always done, you will always get what you always got.

Meredith's mantra hadn't failed since she'd relied on it for impetus to get out of her failed marriage. She depended on it now. Whoever came up with that saying was darned smart. There was more to life than putting up with abuse and neglect day after day. She'd proved it to herself before. She could do it again.

Meredith followed Hunter's broad back, dragging the supply container, sure he knew she was there although he hadn't made direct eye contact. No. That would be civil communication, and heaven knew he wasn't that kind of gentleman anymore. But he used to be. She'd seen a glimmer of that guy she used to love when he'd come rushing to her rescue earlier. Only now?

What had she been thinking? That he cared? *Get over it, girlfriend.* Mean Girl was back with a vengeance. It was just one kiss—not like he'd swept her off her feet or anything truly earth shattering. And it sure wasn't like she couldn't live without a man in her life, another thing she'd proved to herself the hard way. Men were the bane of her existence. Well, she'd show them. Him. Hunter.

What did he think she was, anyway? Kiss her like a lover one minute and push her away the next like she was some disposable tramp? Like she was easy? Desperate?

Her tongue rolled over her bottom lip at the thought of him and the heat in that kiss, that incredible kiss. *Whoa.* He had kind of swept her off her feet now that she thought about it, and slamming her into that tree was a darned hot move straight out of *Fifty Shades*. He'd turned her on before she knew what he was doing. That kiss told a story all its own. Did he have a clue how handsome he was when he was angry, yet how gentle he'd been? How carefully he'd held her in his arms?

Her eyes drifted over that square set of shoulders up ahead and the dark line of sweat down his back. Clueless or not, the man had a nicely muscled backside. Heck, he was nothing but muscle from the back of his neck to his calves, and no matter what, he just kept going, dragging Teague over roots, through brush and grass, over dirt and jungle paths. The man was a machine—with two of the softest, sexiest lips she'd ever tasted. Kind of sweet. Sweaty. Prickly. But oh, so warm and tender, a hint of smoke and mint and—Hunter.

Oh, for heaven's sake, it was just a kiss and a quick grope—only it no longer felt like just a quick anything. Her backside still burned where his fingertips had gripped like he was hanging onto her for dear life, like he could shred the thin layer of silk between him and her without any effort. Like he didn't want to let go.

The thought sent a shiver racing across her shoulders. She smoothed one hand over her rump. Every muscle inside her clenched with the need for him, wept for the closeness, the rub and roughness of his all-male and very delectable body. His hands. His lips.

No way! I don't want Hunter, her inner Mean Girl screamed. *He's the one who lost control. Not me. Well, okay, so maybe me for just a second there, but... no way!*

Meredith watched him march ahead of her, every step sure, every rippling muscle employed to save Teague's life. Her chin stung from the harsh but oh-so welcomed assault. Bruised and swollen lips testified to the depth of his feelings. And hers.

No! No! No! It wasn't me. He lost control. I only reacted. I only kissed him back because I had no choice. I only... only—really want him to do that again.

The fact remained. This time he'd lost control of that tough guy persona that he seemed determined to shove in her face every chance he got, but deep down inside where it counted, he might just want her as much as she wanted him.

I do not. No, no way.

CHAPTER TEN

Casting his gaze upwards, Hunter studied the trees with the best branches for climbing. Since striking back at the enemy was out of the question for the moment, he opted to hunker down and camp until dawn. Up high in the branches seemed the best place for Meredith, though. Out of sight and out of mind.

Stopping at the base of a wide tree with long branches, sprawling roots, and a good cover of leaves, he eased Teague to the ground. "Rest easy, buddy. We're making camp."

Instantly, Meredith released the supplies and was at Teague's side. "I meant to tell you before. He talked to me when you were gone earlier tonight."

That was unexpected news, although it wasn't like Hunter had given her much time to share anything before but her—lips. He activated one of the larger flashlights, again leveling it where it would only offer muted light. His eyes drifted to her mouth. He'd left her lips swollen. Red. Lush. His all male mind drifted to other parts of her anatomy that he'd like to leave just as swollen and—

"Did you hear what I said?" Her hand clamped his forearm. "Teague woke up and he talked to me when you were gone."

The tip of her tongue moistened her bottom lip and—*damn it! Focus!* "So, what'd he say?"

"I'm not sure if he was delirious or not, but he kept trying to warn me. Something about there's one, there's two, Eric knows something, and there's three."

"Three what?"

She shrugged. "That's the thing. I don't really know what he was talking about, but it was the way he said it, like it was urgent, maybe top secret."

Hunter concentrated on her eyes to keep his mind off her mouth. That didn't help. Even in the dark he could see the honest concern glistening there.

"I ran into two other guards," he admitted, needing to tell her that story before he lost track of it.

She grimaced. "Are they dead, too?"

She might as well have slapped him in the face. That spoiled the after effects of the kiss once and for all. He rolled his right shoulder and changed the subject. "It's too late to get to the river tonight. You're going up into the tree."

"No, I'm not."

He bit his tongue. If she were a female soldier, she'd shut up and do what she was told, but no. He'd gotten stuck with a rich little cheerleader who thought the entire world lived to kiss her privileged ass. "You go up. No discussion. You'll be safer topside, and that—"

"But I'd rather—"

"And THAT way..." He dared her to argue one more time. "I'll have one less person to worry about down here on the ground. You can take a pistol up with you and cover both of us. No one will be expecting you up there."

"I'm not going up there if you aren't." She pursed her lips and turned, tending to Teague, her fingers to his brow as if Hunter had suddenly disappeared.

"Listen here, Meredith," he spat her name, his need for nicotine getting the best of him. "There's only room for one boss in this outfit, and you're not it!" he shouted, pointing to the limbs overhead. "Get your ass—"

"No! I'm not going up any tree!" She jumped to her feet too, nearly stumbling because of her big boots. "You listen here, Hunter Christian. You think you can intimidate me because you're bigger and badder and you bellow louder? You think I'm scared just because you give me the evil eye all the time? Well, I'm not, so save that bullyboy routine of yours for the next wimpy guy you run into, because it's not working on me. You're not a bully!"

Hunter could honestly not think of one thing to say, so he glared. Most guys thought he was nothing but an ass. What the hell had happened to this pushy little girl? One minute she was batting her eyes and sexy as all get out, but the next she damned near sounded like his drill sergeant. What was a guy supposed to do?

She kept coming at him. Her finger stabbed his chest opposite where the knife had left its mark. Unprepared for her touch, he winced. "And another thing, Bucko. Stop with the gung-ho, Rambo stuff. I am not one of your guys. I'm a woman, and you will treat me accordingly. I'm going to make mistakes. Deal with it. So what if I lost my weapon? It happens."

Bucko? Did she seriously just call me Bucko? He shook his head at the rest of her profoundly incorrect statement. "No, Meredith, it doesn't happen. A Marine never—"

"I am not one of your Marine buddies!" She squeezed her eyes shut and shook her head. Blonde tangles trembled over her shoulders. "What did I just say? You don't get it, do you?

You're all I've got, and I'm all you've got. Hate each other or not, we've got to work together if we want to survive."

She ceased her attack to rake her fingers through all that hair. He couldn't help himself. She looked like a beautiful lioness with her mane wild and free, so damned fierce and mad, her chin sticking out, her lips asking for another kiss. And that was the problem. He didn't hate her. God knew there was a time he'd wanted to. He'd sure as hell tried. He just never could.

"Anything else I can fucking do for you, your highness?" he bit out to break the spell.

Her chin jutted out. "And that's another thing, Hunter. Stop swearing at me! Everything out of your mouth is just plain demeaning and ugly, and I'm... I'm sick of it. You're not in the Army now, and I never was. You will treat me like a lady from now on or there will be consequences. Do you hear me?"

She stabbed her index finger in his face, and his stupid male heart four-wheel-drifted to a screeching halt, wishing she'd do it again. He wanted to suck on that pretty little finger, maybe wipe the snarl off her mouth with his lips while he did it. Hot damn, she all but glowed she was so angry, and he was falling head-over-heels, not able to catch his balance.

But he couldn't let her uppity commands go unchallenged. "At least get the service right. I was in the Corps. They're not interchangeable like Tupperware lids." He gave her his best USMC stare down. "The Marine Corps. Ever heard of 'em?"

"I don't care. Stop cursing. That's the point!" Her voice ratcheted higher with every word. "If you can't say anything nice, then don't say anything at all." Her lower jaw jutted forward like she meant to look mean. It wasn't working for her. All it made him do was want to bite that full lip before he jerked her into his face and kissed the hell out of her. Every finger clenched to take hold of that hard head of hers, to hold her tight, and kiss her into oblivion.

But he didn't.

"Fine," he hissed, because a more manly declaration would've been too coarse for her *delicate ears*.

"Fine," she hissed right back at him, her swagger on.

They stood locked onto each other's radar like Wyatt Earp and Ike Clanton at the OK Corral, only Ike was incredibly sexy, sweaty, and wearing the skimpiest underwear. And boots. No gunslinger had ever—*ever*—looked so hot. Her chest heaved. Those luscious, pillowy breasts were peaked and pointing straight at him. Beckoning. Begging for a nip of his teeth.

She bit her lower lip, pulling it into her mouth in that cute way she had, and—

Meredith damned near bowled him over she crashed into him so hard. He groaned but took the hit, scooping her into his arms, his hands on her ass, want to or not. *Oh, what the hell.* Who was he kidding? He wanted her in his arms, and he wanted a whole lot more.

They staggered backward a full step before he caught his balance. The hoarse female sounds coming out of her throat didn't help. All that urgent moaning and growling did was make him want to please her in every way, shape, and position no matter what that knife wound in his chest was telling him. This was no helpless little girl in his arms. This was a woman who knew what she wanted. This was—*a married woman.*

Shit! He pulled away from her at that annoying fleeting reminder, really, he did, but she was having none of it, not with her fingers hooked around his ears like they were. She'd turned them into handles, pulling him forward and steering him back to her mouth like he'd better damned well obey. Any hesitation on his part was met with a grumbling course correction that brought his lips back in line with hers.

And just like he remembered, Meredith's mouth was hot, sweet addiction. His body responded, hardening to steel that would soon shred those silky black panties out of his way if she didn't take them off.

Lifting one foot off the ground, she hooked both arms around his neck and climbed on board, anchoring her leg around his hip like he was a stepladder. Once more, he adjusted his stance, widening his thighs to make it easier for her to catch hold and hang on.

Damn, he was losing ground fast. Some damned loud-mouthed bird squawked far off in the distance. It might be one of those alerts that birds made when a predator was afoot, but she kept rubbing her core against his damned zipper and he forgot the bird and whatever might be hunting it. Was she trying to knock him over? Okay. He got the hint. She meant to go to ground. Good thinking. Horizontal always worked better than vertical.

Easing one hand to the ground behind his back, he took her down with him. So much feminine bare skin presented itself for his touch and taste. Everywhere his hands and mouth strayed felt silky and soft, lush and tempting. Pushing the cups of her bra down brought both plump breasts to his mouth level. Fire flamed the last shred of logic in his head away.

When she arched her back and whimpered, it was all the invitation he needed to take one succulent nipple into the heated cavern of his mouth. A long dormant hunger roared to be satisfied. He wanted to swallow her whole, bite her, eat her up, and never let her go. This wasn't the time for tenderness and savoring. His right hand slid down her bare back to the soft swell of her ass, and she was putty in his big hands, hot, taut putty that held a universe of pleasure and pain within easy, tempting reach.

His fingers easily breached the silk panties, smoothing over one spanking hot cheek on his way down to her core. He'd always dreamed of this moment when he and she... when he and she...

She's a married woman.

Shit!

"No." Of all things, Hunter never expected to say that word to a turned on and incredibly hot female who was doing a helluva good job breaching his belt and zipper all by her lonesome. Her demanding fingers stroked his ears, tugging him to turn into her pushy mouth again.

Okay, I can do that.

He tasted, his tongue probing deeper, and every ounce of him demanded the sustenance he craved. His taste buds wanted more of her sweet mouth. His heart couldn't resist the seduction of imminent satisfaction. There was no way he could get enough. Eat her up. All of her. Drink her in, every last bit. Only...

She's married.

Her fingers slid beneath the waist of his pants. "Meredith. No," he breathed as he lifted his palms up and off her steaming-hot ass and planted them firmly higher on her back where they couldn't wander. "You're..."

"But Hunter," she whined, rubbing her nose up his jaw to his ear, framing his face in the tenderest embrace of silky-soft fingers, another feminine assault in progress.

He closed his eyes at the sultry plea in her voice, the enticing promise of the best sex of his life in his ear. He very nearly succumbed to the very sensual temptation of all that sizzling bare skin. Her breath mingling with his. The honey-dipped taste of her tongue and lips, but...

She's married, dumbass!

"No." With strength he didn't know he had, Hunter eased her off of his lap and moved her to his thighs, fighting for restraint to do the honorable thing. To retreat. To protect her. If he didn't get hold of his senses right there and then, there'd be no stopping either of them. And stop he must, because Hunter Christian might be a lot of things, but he didn't use nor abuse women. He didn't lead them on, and he didn't make promises he didn't intend to keep. His mother had taught him right. *If you want to dance, you have to pay for the music.*

And a smart man never danced with a married woman.

He swallowed hard, trying like hell to get the hot blood pounding through his veins to cool down. There would be no dance, and the only music he'd ever paid for was never this good.

With a petulant huff, she rolled to her side, taking all that luscious fire and heat with her. He could barely breathe, so he brushed both palms to the earth to scrape the satiny feel of her skin off his fingers. It didn't work. He dug his fingers into the compacted dirt, willing the taste and feel of her away but wanting to strap her luscious body back onto his hips. Shit. He couldn't think of anything but how much he'd needed her for years. How all those lonely nights could be wiped away. All that self-loathing...

If he weren't an honorable man.

If he could forget.

But he wouldn't.

Meredith lay beside him, her back to him and panting as heavily as he was. "I'm sorry. It's just that... I thought... I mean..."

He gulped. Every minute with her seemed incredibly backward. A woman telling a man she was sorry for taking things too far? A man refusing a sexy woman's advances? How weird. Maybe she was right. Maybe they did need to talk.

He reached for her hand. "I think maybe it's time we set—"

She sniffed, batting him away. "No, Hunter. I get it." Pushing up into a sitting position, she adjusted her bra, covering herself. She glanced at Teague, still out cold where they'd left him. Her eyes glimmered in the dim light.

Oh great. I've made her cry.

She pushed that adorable backside of hers up off the ground and went straight to Teague. Instead of checking him, though, she rummaged through the bundles of men's clothing on the litter beside him. Hunter felt like an ass, but he couldn't ignore the view. She must work out. That ass inside those skimpy panties that were low enough he could see the upper crack of her backside, was taut. And tan lines. *Holy shit.* What had he signed up for? Murder? Mayhem? Hot steamy sex? Sounded more like a bad B movie instead of an operation on foreign soil gone sideways.

Rising onto one elbow, he searched for a way to diffuse the cold war while his body calmed. All he could do was watch; there was no getting to his feet. Not yet. Not with that backside still on display and the baseball bat in his pants.

Somehow, their roles had reversed. She was mad. Still, the ring on her finger made it clear. He should've never allowed this second moment of passion. Hunter didn't play with another man's wife, even if the other man was a jerk and a liar from the ground up. Welch was Meredith's choice. Her problem.

Giving the dead man's shirt one final shake, Meredith sniffed, shuddered, closed her eyes, and put it on. Finally, the fabric did what Hunter had wanted all along. The filthy black shirt hung to her knees and covered her body, only it didn't make a damned bit of difference after all.

He wanted her just the same.

"Can you help me change Teague's bandage? Please?" she asked without making direct eye contact, her voice tight and fragile as if it might crack.

"You bet." Finally under control, he scrambled to the supply crate, retrieved the medical kit, and knelt alongside the litter. Poor Teague was covered in sweat and still out of it, which was good. He didn't need to witness what had just almost happened between the two people who were supposed to be saving his life.

As much as Hunter strove to be gentle, he knew what a bullet hole felt like. Silently, they worked together. Meredith made a good nurse. She took care of the little things, like cleaning Teague's face and mouth, wiping him down with a cool, damp cloth, even rinsing his hair while Hunter removed the saturated packing from Teague's chest, repacked the wound with another homemade wick, and rebandaged it. He forced a drink between Horton's dry lips, then ran a quick hand over his own head. It seemed like days since he'd been submersed and relaxed in the river back at the TEAM camp.

"You're next," Meredith stated, not asked. By then, Teague was semi-clean. His bleeding had slowed, but the bullet was still inside of him.

"No, I'm good," Hunter answered, but when he stood, she stood too.

She was all of five-feet nothing, and he towered over her. He gave her his best USMC stare, the kind that was supposed to intimidate his enemy, but she didn't back down an inch. Her moment of weakness seemed to have passed. Bossy Meredith was back in action. "I'm not asking, Hunter. Sit down and let me look at that knife wound. You can't save the rest of us if you get sick with infection, can you?"

She made sense, but how was she working him like she was? One minute scared, the next tough—all she had to do was throw in a good dose of lust and his head was spinning.

Another man wouldn't play these kinds of mind games. Guys were the same from sunup to sundown, steady and not prone to temperament, the ebb and flow of tides, or stormy weather. They bucked up and they marched on. They obeyed orders, but Meredith? She was complicated. He could smell it in her. Sweat and sass, fire and ice. Worse, try as he might, every last nerve of his seemed to be in league with her. For lack of a stronger, harsher word he'd normally use—sheesh! She was the one made of smoke, not him.

Fine. He sat cross-legged beside the litter.

Fine. Without asking, she knelt beside him and unbuttoned his borrowed shirt. He looked away and let her do her thing, let her murmur when she saw how sore that hole in his chest was. How bloody. The damned knife wound did hurt, and their tumble hadn't helped, though he'd never admit that to Meredith. He'd had worse wounds. On a scale of one to ten, this was probably a solid five unless it got infected. He'd had a couple of eights before. Lots of fours. Ten was dead. That wasn't going to happen.

She leaned in closer to examine the mess. "Oh, my," she breathed, all the tenderness of an angel come to life and just that fast, he was lost again. His nose flared, seeking after the fragrance of shampoo in her hair. Blonde tendrils brushed over his clenched hand. Was she doing that on purpose, teasing him with what he'd declared he wouldn't do with her? Was she daring him? Tempting him?

Hunter stilled. He dared not move. She had the softest, sweetest touch his skin had ever felt while she doctored and cleaned. Her fingers whispered like angel wings over a weary man's ragged skin instead of hurting it. Every inch of him wanted her back in his arms. Every depth of his tired warrior's soul called to take her, to mate with her, to bend her—to love her.

He was a better man than Welch. Hunter knew it to his soul, yet he closed his eyes to silence the crescendo of rising need in his loins. On a scale of one to ten, he was fast on his way to fifteen and losing control.

She scooted her butt closer as she wiped the area just under his collarbone clean. It stung, but then she made it worse. Without asking, she surprised him when she flattened her palm to the middle of his chest and pressed him easily to his back.

That hand. Those strong and very tender feminine fingers. It had been years since a woman had touched him like Meredith just did. Hell, it had been years since he'd let any woman close enough to touch him at all.

He watched the motherly emotion play across her pretty face. She seemed determined not to meet his eyes—probably a good thing. Rotating her waist, she turned from the first-aid kit at her right, then back to him as she carefully cleansed the wound. She helped herself to a thick layer of cotton packing and gauze. She doctored, and she—cared.

His chest didn't hurt any longer. Not a bit. Okay, maybe a little, but the gentle touch of her fingers on his skin was an unexpected balm that seeped all the way into his very cold heart. A woman's touch healed so much more than medical care could.

He caught a glimpse of her long legs peeking out from beneath the shirt again, her knees bent, her boots tucked under her butt, and the last of the pain went away along with his last shred of self-control. At least her lush, warm breasts were covered. *Like that helps.*

Hunter closed his eyes and willed himself back to the blast furnace scorch of the Iraqi desert, to the frigid North Pole, anywhere but there in the jungle beside her. He knew what lay beneath that damned dirty shirt—a smoking-hot body in the cutest damned bra and panties, yes. But more? The woman he would always love, but could never have.

She pressed in closer, her hip against his, and he stiffened, fighting the urge to lay her flat and field strip her down to her barest, most intimate bits and pieces. "Am I hurting you?" she asked, finally looking down at him, blonde corkscrews dripping over her shoulders like a centerfold bombshell straight out of *Playboy*.

He shook his head, which she mistook for a man in too much pain to speak.

"I'm sorry if I was too rough," she murmured, the tip of her tongue slipping over her lush lower lip when he wanted it slipping over him. Anywhere. Anytime.

How did women not understand how the male mind worked? They should since they were why men went to war, pillaged and plundered, raided foreign countries, and drove themselves stark raving crazy. His body had perked up and instantly, his predatory thoughts sprang back to life, painfully obvious, at least to him.

Her glance shifted downward to his zipper. And now she knew.

"Stop," he rasped before he got any harder.

"No, Hunter. Not until I've finished bandaging this wound. It's deep, and I—"

He latched onto her wrist, halting the most incredibly tender nursing he'd ever endured. "Please, Meredith, for God's sake, stop."

She trembled, her neck muscles constricting as she swallowed. "But you need stitch—"

"No." With a groan, he rolled to his side away from her and faced the litter. Teague rested peacefully beside him— Hunter—the weakest man on Earth. The deepest feelings of his heart spilled out of that wound in his chest to the jungle floor. She just couldn't see them. She mustn't.

Meredith's soft fingers on his bicep didn't do anything to strengthen his resolve. "I'm sorry I hurt you before," she whispered, a catch in her voice. "I only wanted to help. I hope you know that."

God, I know! He just didn't know which pain hurt worse anymore—the one in his chest, the one in his pants, or the one breaking his heart.

CHAPTER ELEVEN

Damn him. Who does he think he is anyway? Vin Diesel? John Wayne? Superman?

Hunter's rejection was the last straw.

Slowly, Meredith sliced the papaya-like piece of fruit she'd grabbed on their way through the jungle. It was nourishment, and she needed something in her stomach after a bad night of run-and-hide.

Her heart turned to Courtney. He was the only reason she'd come on this beta test. Jed McCormack took care of his new employees. He reached out and nurtured them, and darn it, very few strayed once they were part of his MI team. A genius at inspiring loyalty, he paid his people well. The extra cash from this out of country mission would go a long way toward a better life. If she lived to get out of this country...

A leaf fluttered from up high, drawing her attention to the supply crate. Once again it had proved indispensable. Not only did it hold a set of knives and eating utensils, but the medical kit contained sterilized scalpels and antibiotics, too. That meant surgery for Teague the first chance they got—Hunter, too, if he'd ever climb down from his high horse long enough to let her help him. Maybe she wasn't a doctor, but she could do more than just wash and bandage. That knife wound had to hurt...

Dashing the darned tear out of her eye, she took another bite of the sweet juicy fruit. What did he want from her, anyway? Obedience and a salute? He acted like he couldn't stand for her to touch him, the ass. Had she misread him that badly? Ever? Had she missed all the signals? *Guess so.* She hadn't kissed a man since her divorce from Eddy, and not much before that disaster. She hadn't dated. Maybe she was out of touch. Maybe she was the stupid one in this jungle tonight. Gah!

Her problem was the raw virility shuddering off Hunter. Every breath he took, every move he made attracted her heart, mind, and soul like no other man had done. Even with that knife in his chest, she'd seen nothing in him to indicate weakness or indecision. He was more machine than man, now trained in the art of warfare and killing instead of sonnets and lyrics. Had he lost his heart along with all the lives he'd taken?

She dashed another tear and resolved, *'No more!'* He could hate her all he wanted. There was no way she'd let him die. No way. Hunter Christian was her ticket out of here, and that was all he was. Yesterday was yesterday and it was done, darn it. She snapped off another piece of fruit and ground it to pulp between her teeth. So there!

He'd taken up post at the base of the tree where the roots flared into the soil like the thick bars of cages. Their resting place wasn't much of a camp. No fire. No sleeping bags to curl up in to keep the bugs away. No mosquito netting.

Hunter's head pivoted as he continually scanned and studied their surroundings, but not once had he looked her way. Not enough to really see her. She would know. Her traitorous eyes continually strayed for a sideways glimpse of any part of this harder-than-hard man. Her nostrils flared, hoping for a hint of his sweat, his blood, any scent that might waft her way. Maybe spearmint. Maybe tobacco. All of her senses were somehow magnetized, seeking him out, reaching for everything and anything that had to do with his body.

He hadn't had a cigarette since this exodus started and maybe that was his problem. He was experiencing nicotine withdrawal. Well good. It served him right.

He'd pulled a handful of vines in a pile beside him, probably needing something to keep his fingers busy. Well, fine. Let him play with vines. Meredith focused on the piece of fruit in her hand. Tough and coarse, she hadn't eaten anything like it before, but it had to be edible. She'd know soon enough if it weren't. She'd eaten two slices and her stomach had yet to rebel or offer a twinge of distress.

Glancing sideways one last time, she locked eyes with the two-legged predator in camp.

Hunter.

Like him or not, he might be hungry. That would also explain his rabid behavior. Lifting her hand, she offered the slice of fruit in her hand, fully aware how her foolish feminine body responded to him of its own accord. Every part of it salivated at just a glimpse of his handsome, rugged face, despite its perpetual scowl. Her nipples hardened like pebbles rubbing against the silken pressure of her bra. She'd love nothing better than to tear it off and be rid of it. Push-up bras were torturous after all these hours, but she didn't dare. She didn't need her breasts loose and swaying beneath the cotton shirt or her nipples drawing his attention to her.

She wanted so much to hate Hunter the way he seemed to hate her, but even her fingertips begged for one more chance to rake through his hair again. Nearly as black as night, she wondered where the blond had gone. Had war turned him so dark inside that it changed his hair color, too?

With all the ink covering his arms, shoulders, back and chest, he was Hades come to roam Earth, dark with anger and wrath, ready to plunder and pillage. Every nerve in her body escalated to DEFCON Delta, then higher the longer he stared at her without speaking. Could he read her mind? Did he know that with one beckoning curl of his little finger she would run to him despite his rejection? Her tongue slipped between parched, parted lips at the thought. *Give me a sign, Hunter. Just blink, for heaven's sake, and I'll be right there. At least, let's be friends.*

At last she broke the contact, the heat in his stare too much to bear, the unrequited tenderness in her heart too much to endure. The poor thing pounded loud enough to raise the dead. She'd become prey, but she didn't want to relinquish her control again. Not to him. Not to anyone. Let him go hungry. She'd dealt with enough asses in her life and lived to tell about them, too. No more.

"Give me a piece," he ordered, begrudgingly as all get-out, but finally breaking the silence.

She did as he asked, cutting the last of the fruit in half and giving him the larger, fresher piece. He accepted the offering without a word of thanks, and like the idiotic female she was, encouragement flickered to life in her heart. She'd done something to help him. It was a small thing, but—it was something.

Mean Girl roared to life. *You. Are. Such. An. Idiot!*

Hunter lifted the fruit to his mouth and took a big, juicy bite. He grunted as a trickle of juice dripped out of the corner of his mouth and down his scruffy chin.

She couldn't look away. Her throat constricted and her tongue lapped her bottom lip. Just once. What would that dribble of juice taste like if she climbed into his lap and licked it off his skin?

As if he'd read her mind, Hunter ran the back of his hand across his chin and wiped the temptation away.

Her lashes dropped, hiding her wayward reverie. She hadn't meant that slice of fruit as a peace offering, but his acceptance of it felt precisely like a truce. Of sorts.

Her tongue touched her lip as if she could taste that single drop from where she sat. Hmmm. A mouthful of Hunter...

Yeah. I'm an idiot.

Meredith snored. She was quiet about it, but she did snore.

Hunter glanced over his shoulder. He'd lost the war to get her into the tree and that was okay. There she was, her back against Teague's litter and her head on her outstretched arm, sound asleep with her mouth half-open. She'd swept her hair back and off her face. Her other arm rested on her bare thigh, her hand cupping the cheek of her ass, lifting the long shirt out of her way in the process. She was a sight to see with one knee bent and the other straight. Meredith looked like a sexy little girl. Innocent. Peaceful.

He had to give her credit. Grabbing some fruit for the road was smart. Fruit wasn't exactly his choice of meals, but hey—it would do for tonight. Maybe tomorrow he'd skewer a monkey or something. Roasted meat would be better for all of them, and if Teague woke up, he'd need solid food to heal.

But that get-up she was still wearing drove him crazy nine ways to Sunday. At least she'd listened and now had boots on her feet. Yeah, they weren't the best fitting, but they were a damned sight better than nothing.

But that shirt? She might as well be naked for all the good it did him. The girl had tits from here to eternity. More than a handful, but not sloppy. No. Meredith was in fine physical shape. Firm. Taut. Athletic. She worked out. It showed. Yeah. Those kinds of tits. There was a day when he'd called them breasts, but that day was in the past with the gentleman he used to be.

Closing his eyes, he willed the feelings of his heart to cease. How was he going to survive the rest of this screwed up operation if he couldn't deal with one night in the jungle with her? Hunter honestly didn't know.

She'd changed. A lot. She'd decimated the cheerleader memories he'd held of her with the way she'd manned up and towed that supply crate without complaining. She'd dragged Teague to safety when she'd needed to, she'd doctored him, and she'd even shopped in the jungle for fruit along the way. She was stronger.

Maybe her marriage to Welch had been a good thing. Hunter didn't see how it could be, but who was he to judge the dynamics between husbands and wives? He'd never been married—had never entertained the notion after she'd run off and left him. Why compound the problem by marrying someone he couldn't love the way he'd loved Meredith?

A hush fell upon the jungle. At last the thing in his hands was done. Now was as good a time as any. Hunter shook the vines out and tied the ends together with a quick, tight wrap of another vine. Securing the contraption of interlocked ropes between two nearby tree trunks, he tested it with his weight first. The trees bent and creaked a little when he lowered into it, but not much. The vines were strong. They held. Good enough.

He'd started playing with the woody vines because his cigarette-deprived fingers needed something to do. Now he was glad he had. The primitive hammock would support a woman as light as Meredith without any trouble.

With his knife in his hand, Hunter sliced the sheet covering Teague into halves. The man seemed to be holding his own, but traveling had to have been hard on him. Hunter got him to swallow another mouthful of the bottled water from the supplies and vowed to get him to safety once the sun came up, at least where he could remove the bullet still buried in his chest.

The next part would require every last bit of Hunter's already shredded willpower. He sheathed his knife and quietly, he knelt beside Meredith where she lay. The poor thing was exhausted, and yet she commanded his heart as she always had. He'd been smitten long ago by the joyous light in this woman. Even there in the dark of a sweltering jungle night, all that blonde hair on the ground around her gave her the aura of an angel. When he traced a gentle fingertip down the edge of her jaw to her chin, she sighed a breathy, girly sigh and scrunched up her nose.

Hunter lifted her from the ground to his chest. She came easily into his arms, her hand splayed innocently over his heart. He smoothed the dirt and leaves out of her messy tangles. He closed his eyes and wished the troubles of the world away as his nose dipped into her fragrant tresses. A hint of flowery shampoo lingered. That was his Merry, a breath of something good and sweet.

Waking in the morning with her in his life and in his bed could heal him. He knew damned well it could. He might see the rainbow again instead of the storm clouds. He might finally be able to leave the darkest parts of his soul behind and see beauty in the stars at night. He might once again be the man he'd left behind in that one immature, foolish decision he'd made long ago.

"Hunter?" she asked, all dreamy-eyed and angelic. "Is that you? Are you, umm...? Are we, umm...?"

"There is no *we*, Merry. Shush," he whispered. "I'm just going to spray you with repellant. Go back to sleep."

"Hmmm," she breathed, already asleep in his arms. "S'gonna be okay."

"Good night, Meredith."

"G'night," she mumbled groggily, her nose pressed into his shirt.

He bowed his head in humility and wonder. This woman had always been his Helen of Troy, his Juliet, his Desdemona. Hell, she'd been his Eve, his only true love, and his most wicked temptation rolled into one. She, a married woman, was the ultimate forbidden fruit.

But for this one moment, holding her in yet another warm embrace, Hunter couldn't bring himself to pull back—the feel of her against him was so tender. He wished he were a stronger, nobler man even as he closed his eyes and pressed a fervent kiss to the satin of her forehead.

There he was on bended knee and holding all his lost dreams. His hungry soul drank her in. His starving heart believed yet again. Whatever fate lay in store for the two of them, it would end or begin in this god-forsaken jungle a couple of thousand miles from home. All he had to do was keep her safe, like that was no small feat.

In humility, he pledged his honor and his pride, as battered as they were, to the task. No Marine had ever pledged more.

If he were a smart man, he would've left her lying on the ground. He would've never picked her up. He would've kept his distance and walked away, but no. There he knelt, a foolish man forced by unrequited love to walk alone, his heart slowly being consumed by the feminine wiles of the gentle lady in his arms. God, he wanted her to stay.

But she couldn't, and he wouldn't want her to be a vow-breaker. Marriage was a sacred covenant. With a blur in his eyes, he broke the heartfelt kiss, and, lifting her gently so as not to wake her, he transferred her to the hammock. The tree branches didn't squeak when he nestled her into the bed of vines. Cautiously, he removed the men's boots from her feet and set them within reach for the morning.

Ah. Her heels and toes were red with blisters, yet the poor thing hadn't uttered a word of complaint. Damn, she needed decent socks and properly fitting footwear, not some dead guy's boots. It was a wonder she hadn't limped. She should have.

Hunter ran a quick hand over his face. Standing over Meredith and holding her slender, ravaged foot in his big, callused hand, the difference between them seemed an insurmountable chasm. She was Beauty, and he the veritable

Beast. Her life was meant for balls and gowns, champagne and lace, his for the deadly art of war and the never-ending solitude that went with it. The ugliness of death. Someday she would be a mother, a giver of life, but he would forever be the taker. The sinner. The shadow that wasn't worthy to stand in her light.

He cast a mist of aerosol repellant over her, making sure to cover her feet. It had to sting, but she didn't budge. Wrapping her in the cocoon he'd crafted for her, he returned to his post, his back to the tree, his eyes on his ragged camp.

Hunter blew out a sigh of resignation. What he wouldn't give to slide into that hammock beside her and hold her until morning broke. Just once. But he didn't. He wouldn't. He was her sentinel, her last line of defense. Not her lover. His sin now was that his heart had begun to melt.

But she must never know.

CHAPTER TWELVE

Such a racket! Meredith had never heard so much chattering, chirping, or whistling interspersed with the loveliest melody this early in the morning. It was amazing. She peeled open her tired eyeballs and stared at the treetops, enthralled with the spectacle of color and music. Courtney would love this.

It dawned on her. She wasn't on the ground. There were no bugs on her as she'd fully expected.

Fingering the light covering on her body, part of the sheet she'd given Teague, she stretched in one long, languorous muscle-rousing stretch, her arms over her head before she rolled to the ground. Her feet were bare. She felt—good. Tired, but good.

Teague lay quietly in his litter, his chest lifting and lowering in steady rhythm, his face clean and his hands folded on his belly. One of Hunter's boots extended from the edge of the tree so she knew right where the grouch was.

She pushed the vine hammock backward and let it swing. So, this was what he'd been making last night. How thoughtful. She wiggled her toes to brush the ants off her feet. Maybe there was hope for him.

Morning had truly broken out in the most amazing chorus she'd ever heard. Birds were everywhere, but the music had to wait. She needed to pee in the worst way. Grimacing, she pushed her feet back into those awful boots for another day of toe-pinching, heel-burning travel, and she tiptoed away from the men to take care of business behind a not-too-distant patch of leafy fronds.

Crouching there in the ferns, she surveyed her domain. The spectacle of the new day was everywhere. Tiny bejeweled hummingbirds zipped and raced overhead on their search for enough fuel to top off their high-octane energy. Electric blues flashed through the emerald shades, followed by brilliant flashes of reds and even more brilliant yellows. Oranges striped with indigo caught her eye only to be replaced by shimmering iridescent jewels on wings. And that was just the birds.

Rising to her feet, she secured her underwear, but she couldn't stop looking. Or smiling. All of nature was alive, and it was beautiful. Clouds of tiny insects lifted from the curly fronds of six-foot-high ferns. A huge blue butterfly drifted overhead, the most elegant creation she'd ever seen. As she strolled back to camp, she noticed tiny tree frogs were everywhere, all adding to the noise.

"Lovely, isn't it?" Hunter asked softly from where he leaned against the tree, his ankles and arms crossed.

"This jungle is the most amazing thing I've ever seen." She shot him a cautious look, nodding toward the hammock. "That was a nice way to wake up. Thanks."

He shrugged. "You needed to be off the ground and away from the bugs. No big deal."

But it was. "I mean it. Thank you," she said, very aware he'd also been the one to put her into that bed. Maybe some part of the man she'd once known was still in there. "Did you see all the frogs? There are so many different colors. And they're cute."

"No pets," he teased, and she had to look twice. There he was again, that other Hunter she used to know. The one she missed. Would she ever figure this guy out?

By then he was on his knees, tending to Teague, so she enjoyed the view of morning in the jungle, feeling she might survive after all.

After they breakfasted on the remaining fruit, their journey to the river continued. Hunter dragged the heavy litter while she commandeered the supply container. It was slow going, but Teague's forehead had felt cooler when she checked him, and Meredith was encouraged again. Hunter didn't hate her. She was sure of it.

But then he spoiled it. "Whose bright idea was it to beta test the ActiveCamouflage System in South America? Why Brazil?"

"Probably Mr. McCormack's. He's the only one savvy enough to get around the current administration. Why?"

"But why this country?" he persisted. "What's this place got that others don't?"

She shrugged. "Jungles?"

He didn't say another word for a few minutes, but then he made it worse. "Whose idea was it not to allow us guys on The TEAM to use GPS or sat phones while we're here?"

"Mine," she answered promptly. "Neither team had the choice. GPS and sat phones can be tracked. It might've thrown the results of the beta test. Someone might have used them to contact someone for help. We wanted this to be purely human against the ACS."

"You suspected us of cheating?"

"No." She shook her head to emphasize her words. "But we needed established absolutes to insure the credibility of the test. No GPS for either team was a given from the start."

"Who came up with the idea of war games in the first place?"

"Why does it matter?" She didn't like his tone of insinuation.

"Who stands to gain if MI's ACS_1 doesn't come online as scheduled? Who's Jed McCormack's biggest threat? His competition?"

"That would be any defense business with a competing interest," she said, still careful to stick as close to prickly Hunter Christian as possible. His questions raised her ire, but she had to give him leeway as she dragged the supply crate. He was only asking the same questions she'd be asking if she were in his place. She turned the tables on him. "Who do you think is trying to kill us?"

"Why don't you tell me?"

"Wait. You don't think someone on my team had anything to do with these murders, do you?"

"Who else knew we were coming here? Seems to me your office has a leak. Someone's been talking to the wrong people."

"What about your office?" She sent a volley right back at his arrogant head. "My team was solid. Besides, they're all dead. Or did you forget?"

That ought to have shut him up, but it didn't. "Well, someone sure talked, and it wasn't us."

"What about your guys? I haven't seen their bodies yet?" She cringed the moment those words came out of her mouth. She didn't want to see any more bodies, especially not Eric's or Ky's or Seth's. It was bad enough her friends were dead. "I'm sorry, Hunter. I didn't mean that. I trust you guys. Honest."

"But think about it," he insisted, ignoring her hasty insult. "Who else had inside information on this op? Who knew exactly where your team was camped for the night? Who else could've done this if not someone inside McCormack Industries? Someone who knew where and when to strike?"

She raked her fingers into the tousled hair that had fallen into her face and shoved it over her shoulder. Darn him. He'd made her mad again. "Are you accusing Jed?"

"Are you accusing Alex?" He took it up a notch, and she wanted to knock him off his high horse at those very stupid accusations. Jed and Alex were impeccably honest. Their agents too.

"Just where do you think Seth, Ky and Eric are?"

"Dead," he stated. "Damn it, woman. Will it make you happy to finally see their bodies, too?"

She stopped walking. Given the choice she'd head in the opposite direction, but she had to keep up with this rude, unpredictable guy or die in the jungle.

Suddenly, Hunter rested the litter to the ground and took a menacing step back to her. The minute his arm reached out, she dropped the handle to the supply crate. She flinched, her palms up, anticipating a slap for having made him mad. It never came.

He'd reached completely behind her. And then it got worse. A shiver thundered through her body when the twenty-foot long twisting body of a hissing snake came into view. Without thinking, she leapt behind Hunter while he wrestled the pulsing, slithering thing, his big hands fisted and clenched tight beneath the striped, arrow-shaped head, the snake's tongue darting out to taste the back of his hands, its fangs bared and dripping and—

It looked at her with its milky blue yes, the eyes of a devil.

A full-body shiver raced up Meredith's spine, making her wiggle. Frightened, but needing to offer encouragement, she rested her palm to the center of Hunter's sweaty back, careful to keep an eye on that evil creature and her body well out of its range.

Monstrously thick coils circled Hunter's wrist, winding up, concealing the tattooed snake on his forearm, the tip of a real serpentine tail whipping the air, searching for purchase on its victim. He grunted under the constrictor's assault, beads of sweat dotting his forehead, trickling into his eyes, glistening into rivulets down his neck. And still he fought.

Meredith stifled her scream, wanting to help, but this snake was so big, its body as thick as the tree branch it had slithered down from. Creamy gray with reddish-brown diamond saddles over its spine, the creature's skin devolved into darker reddish-brown scales near its tail, that grasping tentacle that had just wrapped itself around Hunter's chest. Squeezing even as it shifted lower to his waist. Clenching. Spiraling, every scale a living, undulating muscle of death by suffocation.

"Shit," Hunter wheezed, his face contorted with the struggle of man against this behemoth.

Another violent shiver wriggled up Meredith's spine. She stamped her feet at the injustice of their situation. The whole damned jungle was trying to kill them!

With another growl and a grunt, Hunter let out a mighty roar as he snapped the neck of the beast. Unwinding its writhing body from his torso, he slammed it to the dirt. The dying snake's body kept squirming, twisting, and thrashing while Meredith rubbed her biceps to calm the gooseflesh climbing up her body. This snake was so—big!

Hunter dusted his hands to his thighs, inhaling deep breaths, his chest heaving. "Snake," he wheezed, his tone casual while her insides quivered.

"I know," she whined, but then she gulped. He hadn't meant to hit her. He'd saved her life. *Whew.* Again. What a relief. Okay, so any moment now, her heart should stop beating like the whole damned percussion section of her college band. Any minute now, she would recover. Any minute now...

The dying snake squirmed, but judging by the sharp right angle of its head to its body, it wasn't going anywhere except into another predator's stomach. She rubbed a nervous palm over her mouth, unable to take her eyes off the serpent, her heart still pounding. It was big enough; it could've eaten her. All that writhing and squeezing could've been around her neck or her chest. It could've squeezed her to death. Swallowed her whole.

"Did you seriously think I was going to hit you?" Hunter asked, when he could finally breath, his gaze scrolling from her fingers digging into his forearm to her face. "Back there? Did you?"

"Umm, no. I just, umm..." She pulled her hand away from the warmth and strength of his arm. How embarrassing. She hadn't remembered grabbing hold of him.

Meredith gulped down the acid in her throat, not sure how much of her failed relationship with Eddy she wanted to reveal, but yes. For a split second there she'd most certainly thought Hunter would hit her. He'd gone all Rambo on her last night in the dark. Then they'd kissed. But still. He was bigger and meaner than she was. Angrier.

"I don't hit women, Meredith," he said earnestly, sincerely. He cocked his head, leaning down to peer closer into her eyes. "I don't hurt children, animals, or old folks either."

There was no way to lie. She swallowed hard. Her lashes lowered, hopefully before he'd caught one glimpse of the truth she'd buried or the man she'd run from.

"Is there something you want to tell me?" he asked, his tone pitched with genuine concern. And there he was again, the gentle man she used to love. This Hunter she knew, and she wanted him to stay.

She lifted her chin. The utter darkness of his eyes had lightened to a dark coffee brown with caramel sprinkles. Just as she'd remembered. She took a deep, cleansing breath, not afraid of Hunter Christian. Not him. He'd never hurt her.

"But I do kill snakes, the two-legged kind and the kind that slithers on its belly," he growled.

She faced him stoically, wanting to share but not quite sure if she should. Did he mean Eddy by that two-legged comment? Did Hunter have any idea what she'd lived through?

He must've read her unwillingness to share. With a soft snort, he resumed the role of beast of burden, lifting the litter, and away he went.

She scrambled to keep up, dragging the wheeled container behind her. Hunter just kept going, with a hole in his chest no less. What was this man made of? Titanium?

The silence between them stretched until it hurt her heart. Meredith needed to talk about the thing that had very nearly happened with the snake, and also with Hunter reading her mind like he had. Did it never go away, that startle reflex a woman developed once she'd been slapped and punched in the face by a man? By her husband, the man who was supposed to protect and respect her?

She needed to vent. Oh heck, she needed Hunter to wrap his big strong arms around her and tell her he'd keep her safe. That would be a nice change. Eddy never had. He liked to strong-arm her, though. His idea of fun always turned to torture, then sex, brute-force, humiliation, and pain. When she'd cried for him to lay off, well, things had gotten worse. Too late, she'd discovered Eddy didn't like being told what to do. Or asked.

She had a definite attraction to Hunter, but was he any better than her ex? She'd seen him kill a man without remorse, and now a giant snake, an adult-sized boa constrictor. The gentleness in him seemed disposable, a tool he pulled out of his gear bag when he needed it, and just as easily stowed it once it served his needs. Eddy could be like that—sly one moment, cruel the next.

After hours of walking, her feet were miserably sore again, and she needed another rest, but she wouldn't give Hunter the satisfaction of telling him so. No. Let him think of it all by himself. That was obviously what he was best at— dreaming up a world of corporate lies and deceit. Yet the fact remained. Someone had to have shared the whereabouts of this top-secret ACS$_1$ prototype test. Why else would a stranger named Burdette be looking for her?

Hunter stopped in his tracks so suddenly that she almost ran over the litter with the crate. He made it worse when he sidestepped and she ran smack into his back. Wow. The man was made of steel. He didn't budge, but she nearly fell backwards from the impact. To catch herself, she latched onto his belt and peered around him.

"What now?" she asked quietly, afraid she might disturb another assassin or something just as deadly. Like a snake.

Hunter held a fisted hand up, one finger extended forward.

She looked closer, not seeing what he wanted her to see. "What?" she asked again, still looking for a twining, twisting serpent amongst the variegated-green dangling vines.

"Fence," he growled.

Fence? Oh, now she saw it. The crazy thing looked like the one out of *Jurassic Park*. The network of coils and conductors had to be twenty-feet high. How could she have missed it? Oh, wait. She'd been looking for shiny, slithering snakes—that was how.

"What's a fence doing in the middle of the jungle?"

Of course, the big, strong, silent type beside her didn't answer. Instead, Hunter crouched to one knee and selected a short piece of a wooden branch from the ground. Tossing it into the wires, the wooden missile evaporated in a spray of sparks, smoke, and crackle. Wow. The fence wasn't only electrified—it was darned electrified.

"What are they trying to keep in? The panther?" Meredith asked.

Hunter straightened, his eyes searching the jungle behind her. "Us."

CHAPTER THIRTEEN

Just damned great. A bungled op. A half-naked woman. Murderous guards on our trail and now a fence? Could this mission get any crazier? What the hell's going on?

"How do we know who built it?" Meredith asked, her hand shielding her eyes from the morning sun.

"I don't care who built it. Move out," Hunter ordered. With no way forward, he did the only thing he could. He turned the litter around and retraced his footsteps, needing to get Meredith and Teague to safety before Fat Bastard's buddies caught up with them.

But damn, all the worst case scenarios pinged in his head. Why an electrified fence? Why here? Precisely how large was the confinement area? Was he caught inside or outside of it, or was something else going on that neither the MI nor TEAM guys knew about? Worse, were they being herded in a specific direction?

That was what he'd be doing if he'd meant to trap his enemies. Brushing them into a narrowing chute to their doom was a damned good idea. Hunter wished he'd thought of it, but if that Burdette guy thought he had Hunter trapped, the guy didn't have a clue what a pissed-off Marine was capable of.

But Hunter also knew Alex and Jed had both vetted this specific jungle area of Brazil before they'd agreed to perform the beta test here. They would've spotted the fence then. Whoever'd built it had money, but Hunter had his doubts that guy was Burdette.

Blam! Pop! Pop! Pop! Gunfire erupted in the jungle ahead and Hunter launched himself sideways to shield Meredith. The container tipped to its side when she dropped to the ground with him sprawled on top of her. Teague groaned, the first sound he'd made in a while. A flock of noisy birds lifted out of the jungle trees, and instantly, Hunter's gaze raked the dense cover of trees and vines for sniper hides in the trees.

Shit. He'd been distracted, and now they were in danger. They could very well be caught in one of those narrow chutes intended to push them into a kill zone or a trap.

Hunter sucked in a breath and turned into the USMC radar dish he should've been all along. Tree trunks lifted above the brush and smaller trees, but no sniper hide revealed itself. The steady chatter of monkeys confirmed the feeling in his gut. None of the three men he'd come across were black ops material. They weren't smart enough to have preplanned something as simple as a raised platform to shoot from.

His nostrils flared as an oddly sweet, but rank, odor drifted along the moist jungle floor, bringing with it the oppressive aroma of decay. Animal decay. Something damned large had died nearby. It was time to move.

He would have, except he finally noticed where he'd landed. On Meredith. He found himself crouched over her, one leg extended the length of her body, his elbows dug into the dirt alongside her arms while, unfortunately, his other knee had landed between her legs, right up against her delectable, feminine hot spot. That son-of-a-bitch karma had done it to him again.

Her hand brushed against his chest even as he looked down into two pools of worried blue. "Don't be afraid," his big mouth said. "I'm here. I won't let anything happen to you."

She blinked and nodded, her palms firm almost as if she thought she was keeping him from falling. "I really do know that about you, Hunter."

Another two shots snapped his head up. Whoever was out there didn't seem to be after him or Meredith. Not yet. The racket was headed in the opposite direction. Maybe this wasn't the trap he'd thought it was. He dropped his chin and faced the lovely lady beneath him again. "Let's get out of here."

"Okay," she breathed, her tongue tracing her bottom lip.

He had to move before his body sprang to stiffer attention. Angling his rifle into his left arm, he pushed off the ground and offered her a hand up. She came easily, but he didn't offer her the comfort he wanted to. This was no time for hugs. They had some rugged ground to cover.

They weren't far from river country, home to some of the steepest terrain and highest waterfalls on the continent. Deeply forested and full of peril, it was their only chance to elude the men after them. Hunter began to doubt his first take on that gate. No one could've built a fence big enough to contain the mighty Amazon with all its tributaries, could they?

Jumping to conclusions could get a guy killed, so he went with his gut. The river was still their best option. After righting the supply crate and making sure Teague was good to go, Hunter shouldered his load and once again turned back the way they'd come. If lucky, he could leave Meredith and Teague somewhere safe along the riverbank while he returned for his guys. If unlucky? Well, damn. Things would get tougher. He shrugged the pinch out of his stiff neck and marched on.

"What's the plan?" Meredith asked timidly at his rear.

"Find out who's behind this," he answered patiently. He'd seen the fear in her eyes before. This nightmare had to end.

"How are you going to do that?"

He rolled his eyes, which she couldn't see because she was still behind him where she belonged. Marines charged into battle, that was how. If she was as smart as she thought she was, she'd know that about him by now.

Intent on getting her someplace safe, he darned near ran over the corpse. Make that corpses. *Holy shit.* Hunter stopped just short of the depression in the ground at the tip of his boot. Flies buzzed in one huge black, crawling sheet over the bodies. *So this is where those smells came from.*

Oomph. Meredith bumped into his back. "I'm sorry."

He held up his fist for silence, but the dammed woman kept apologizing. "I got off the track and I wasn't watching—"

"Shhhhh," he hissed, pausing over the carnage. Two of Meredith's team members lay sprawled in between two other bodies, all in rapid decomp. Animals had been at them. Fingers and toes were chewed away. Eyeballs were missing. He recognized Lyle's bald head. The mop of curly dark hair on one corpse might be Eric's. There wasn't enough left of the face to be certain.

Oh, God. Eric. Hunter's throat went dry. If he ever needed a smoke, it was then.

What would anyone hope to gain by this atrocity? Besides the defense contract, if that truly was the motive, why go to the extreme measure of killing everyone involved in the beta test? What purpose did that serve?

Meredith's ragged gasp brought him to his sense. She stood at his right elbow with her hand to her mouth and her eyes wide open, staring at the bodies. "It's… it's Lyle," she moaned, pointing at the horrific scene.

"Don't look." Hunter stepped in front of her to block the view, cussing internally that he'd allowed her to see it. This was a dammed ugly sight, and she was no soldier. It was bad enough for a guy who'd seen it all, but a woman? He laid a hand to her shoulder and turned her to face the opposite direction.

"Is that Eric?" she asked, blinking through tears.

"Maybe," he muttered, not wanting to think of his friend like that. "Come on. Let's get out of here."

She acquiesced quickly, her face ashen and tears clinging to her eyelashes. They'd gone no more than another twenty yards when he heard the sound of boots coming toward them. Lowering Teague's litter into the dense brush, he motioned Meredith to stash the carton, then tugged her into the shadows with him. The only problem was she landed with her back to his chest.

Damn. He didn't mean to grab a handful of her breast in the process. Hunter dipped his nose into her hair, blocking the stench. The poor thing trembled, and he felt bad for being so thoughtless of her tender nature. This operation had to be hardest on her. Contrition for being a selfish man flooded his heart. He needed to back off and he knew it.

The assassins didn't seem worried about being overheard. The two men headed straight toward him and Meredith. Well, good. He was maybe a little distracted by the very feminine ass rubbing against him, but willing and able to take them on nonetheless.

If only he could think a little clearer. Meredith melted into him, her butt against his groin, and it was all he could do to focus. She was soft and warm. His body responded involuntarily with all its pent up angst, and of course, she was bound to notice the *flashlight* pressed hard against her backside. Any woman would. Years of abstinence didn't do a thing to calm the effects of a good-looking woman in too close proximity.

Damn it. Not now.

The adrenaline coursing through his bloodstream didn't help, not with two assassins only feet away. He held his breath and willed Meredith to do the same. Oddly, she did.

The assassins stopped directly in front of their leafy hideaway.

With Meredith plastered against him, the tiniest thing in the dead-cold center of his heart unfurled once more. Warmth blossomed inside him.

"Why are we still out here in this crap shoot?" Assassin One asked the other. "Nothing's going on."

"To finish the job," Assassin Two declared hoarsely.

Hunter cocked his head, hoping to think better. Instead, his nose landed deeper in Meredith's hair, a sweet smell no matter what the circumstances. A good sniper shouldn't have to deal with so much pleasant distraction.

"Damn it, they're not here. For all we know, the big cats got the last of 'em last night. We're wasting time. Them two are already dead. They've got to be."

"No," Assassin Two replied. "We would've found body parts. Blood. Clothes or something."

"Not if them big cats dragged the bodies up into the trees."

"Panthers don't do stuff like that."

"Sure they do. They're all the same, only these bad boys are pitch black," Assassin One argued. "Don't you know anything?"

Very aware of how close these two murderers stood to him and Meredith, Hunter opted for the best defense. *Nothing.* He cocked his head and listened instead.

"All I know is this job isn't what I signed up for." Number Two had stopped with his back toward Hunter and Meredith. The short-stocked rifle snug under his arm turned with him as he scanned the jungle at his left and then his right. "Burdette thinks just because he's paying us that we're going to do everything he says. I got a problem with that kind of thinking. I'm all about making a buck, but I've got my standards."

Assassin One cocked his head sideways and shot Number Two a quizzical look. "You got standards? Like what?"

"Like I don't like killing unarmed people, for one thing. I don't like draggin' bodies up here, neither, and I don't much like what he's doing to that other guy. It ain't right. He might have been military, but he would've talked by now if he knew where she was."

Hunter's ears perked up. *What other guy? Who should've talked by now?*

Assassin One pulled a pack of cigarettes out of his shirt pocket. "Let's move. I need a smoke, and this place stinks. We're downwind from the dump. Come on."

Before the men had time to move out of range, Hunter eased Meredith to his left side, immediately freeing up both hands. That was all he needed in order to work without making a lot of noise. He crept forward until he was in Number Two's shadow, and, with one quick twist, he snapped the guy's neck.

Assassin One responded with a lightning-quick weapons-up, but Hunter was quicker. One fast sideways kick connected with the man's Adam's apple, crushing his larynx and dropping the guy to his knees. The man gurgled on his way to the ground, his eyes wide with the knowledge he was slowly suffocating to death. Hunter stuck his boot in the guy's back and rolled him over so Meredith didn't have to watch him die.

Good work, Christian, Hunter told himself, proud to have struck a blow for survival. He knelt and quickly began the prerequisite disrobing of one's enemies. Both bodies were stripped in record time. Again, the dead men were armed with the same hypos and vials of the lime green fluid he'd found on the other three men he'd killed. He tucked them into his pants pocket, intent on having them analyzed the moment he got back to civilization.

After he stored their clothing and miscellaneous gear alongside Teague, he draped their rifles over his shoulder and removed the batteries from the walkie-talkies concealed in their shirt collars.

It took a few minutes before it registered that Meredith hadn't moved or made a sound. He twisted his neck to see what she was doing. Their eyes locked, hers wide with horror at what she had just witnessed him do. Both hands covered her mouth. Ashen now, the soft, compliant women he'd just held in his arms had turned rigid with the most condemning glare.

He finished his work and pushed up from the ground, not caring for one second what judgment might be running through her head. He was back in warrior mode, his gentle thoughts for her stowed. *This is war, and war is damned ugly. Get the hell over it.*

"Who are you?" she hissed.

"The man who's going to save your sorry ass so you can run back to Fast Eddy, that's who," he hissed right back at her. "Now buck up. Get moving."

"Why would I—? Do you have to kill everyone you run into?"

He bit his tongue and stowed his sarcasm. That stupid question deserved no reply. The only thing keeping her alive was his ability to end her enemies' lives and do it quickly. How hard could it be to connect those dots?

As per his usual method of dealing with feminine confrontation, Hunter turned his back on Meredith and left her with a decision to make. She could follow and keep driving him crazy or she could stay with the dead men. Leave or not. Live or die. Up to her.

He secured the litter in his blistered palms and began what he hoped was the final leg of the journey to the river. At least, there'd be two less predators in the jungle tonight. *Good riddance.*

CHAPTER FOURTEEN

Meredith couldn't process what she'd just witnessed fast enough to know what to think or what to do next. Every step with Hunter seemed to lead to death and destruction. He'd just murdered two men right in front of her, and he'd done it swiftly, without hesitation or remorse. Within seconds, he'd methodically stripped the bodies clean and left them at her feet. Like trophies. Or a morgue.

Her feet wouldn't move. She couldn't make them. Awful smells wafted upward, filling her nose. Her head and her stomach roiled. She squeezed her eyes tight against the sight. The smells. The sounds. The awful look in the men's eyes when they died.

He killed them.

Hunter's butt disappeared into the jungle beyond the murder scene, the litter jostling behind him. Only this time was different. To follow she'd have to step over one of the still warm bodies, dragging the supply crate, too.

I'm supposed to follow him? But he's no better than they are.

Her legs refused to obey. There was no way to make them. She was turning to stone and Hunter was leaving. Again and again and again. That was all he'd ever done. Leave her when she needed him most. Walk away and never look back. Only now...

The jungle stilled.

He really was gone this time.

The thick blanket of insects from the corpses droned in an unrelenting buzz. Just the thought of what all those bugs were doing to the bodies sickened her. Bile crept up her throat. She didn't dare breathe, the stench too nauseating to pull into her lungs. A wave of dark shadows swarmed up from the humid jungle floor, bringing another wave of odors she'd rather not inhale nor remember. The jungle shimmered into a mirage of sickening pea green and gaseous putrid air.

Even Mean Girl trembled as darkness swirled around her.

Stupid woman.

Hunter had banked on making it to the river to save his life, not to mention Meredith's and Teague's. Rivers overflowed and when they did, they created eddies and swirling pools of calm in their wake. They eroded rocks and boulders. If they were strong and turbulent enough, they hollowed out sandstone and granite into hidden caves where a man might find a safe place to hide. This mighty Amazon has been working that miracle for millennia. Surely there was a cave behind one of the many waterfalls along the river.

What he hadn't counted on was dragging Teague while he carried Meredith. Still, she wasn't that heavy. His palm on her ass was pleasantly splayed over both cheeks, soft and warm, nicely rounded. She was a fit woman, not flaccid and flabby. A misguided thought skipped through his mind. *How many babies has she had with Welch? One? Two? They must be ugly kids with him for a father.*

She moaned, both arms flopping down his back, lightly slapping against his backside as he tromped through the jungle, pulling the litter behind him with one hand and balancing her on his shoulder with the other. Because of her fainting, he'd have to make another trip back to retrieve the supply crate from where he'd stashed it.

But that was what men like him did—their duty. At the start of this operation, he'd planned on catching a lazy day fishing the Amazon after the war games. He'd heard there were red-bellied piranha and armored catfish in the river. Bull sharks and the giant river fish called pacu. Now he just wanted a place to hide.

Meredith moaned and lifted her head. When it dropped against his back, Hunter swatted her ass. "Shh," he ordered, not wanting her to spoil their only good luck. "Be quiet. Stay down."

She didn't move again.

Meredith was right, as much as Hunter hated to admit it. He needed to stop killing every assassin he came across, if only for her sake. Once he got her settled, he planned to interrogate the next joker he came across, but he couldn't do that with her watching.

He found himself being extra careful not to bang her head on passing shrubs or tree branches. As it was, her hair dragged through every branch in his way. It would be one big rat's nest by the time they were safe.

Time was short though. By now, he'd taken out five of Burdette's men. An alarm would surely sound when those last two guys didn't return to camp.

At last, he came to the thunderous river's edge. Hunter stayed to the shadows while he scanned the best way forward. There was no opposite shore at this point in the river, just a solid wall of stone and jungle. A waterfall fell from the top ledge of the stone, but there was no cave behind the sluicing water, only sheer granite interspersed with rock ledges, all stained and smoothed by eons of erosion at work.

It was a long shot anyway. Hunter lumbered onward, but stuck close to the river. The sun beat down. The jungle steamed. Still, he marched. Meredith must've hit her head pretty hard when she fainted. She hadn't stirred since he'd told her to stay down, and he was glad. He didn't need her confirming how stupid this idea was.

If Burdette was behind that fence back there, this area made sense. Between the river, and the sheer wall on the opposite shore, Hunter and what was left of his team were in a controlled area.

It took miles of traipsing the riverbank before he found what he was looking for—a set of three waterfalls, again on the opposite shore. Hunter eased his two burdens to the jungle floor and stretched his back, cracking the ache out of his spine. If this was a waste of time, well, he'd be looking for cover in another stand of bamboo.

The waterfalls roared down the opposing mountainside. East of the falls, the mountain curved into a shallow shoreline. No bizarre fencing came into view and no sign of construction, either. Just a vertical wall of stone. Vines and trees. Monkeys and birds. The usual.

A stretch of rocks and boulders across the river had created a natural dam that, combined with several fallen logs, had enclosed a pool closest to where he stood. When a long silver fish jumped from the still water in the center of that pool, Hunter smiled. Maybe he'd get some fishing in after all.

The rest of the river flowed into two channels, one bucking white water, the other leveling out into spans of slower moving flat water with swelling undercurrents. This wasn't the mighty Amazon, though. Probably just one of the many tributaries that spread like veins and arteries through this stretch of South America.

Hunter made short but cautious work of the distance to the nearest waterfall. The USMC boots on his feet had served him well over the years. Water hadn't hurt them before, and it wouldn't hurt them now.

Careful not to lose his balance, he jumped feet first into the river and sloshed along the gravel bed to the front of the first waterfall. The sheet of water sluicing down that portion of the rock wall hid nothing but a hollow depression, not deep enough to serve as shelter. When the second waterfall wasn't any better, his hopes sank.

Hunter scanned the riverbank in both directions, looking for bamboo. This waterfall was his last chance to find a cave, and he was tired. It was a foolish idea anyway. *So much for Hollywood.*

The river bent at that point, creating a natural corner where the third waterfall faced the second. To his left, the stone wall ended in the river. He'd come this far; he had to try. Still fighting to stay on his feet in the swift current, Hunter bypassed the last waterfall and came at it from the farthest side where the riverbank was dry and sandy. He flattened his back to the cold wall and edged forward along a narrow ledge. *So far so good.*

This last-chance waterfall arced off a stone shelf in the granite face before it tumbled maybe twenty feet into the swiftly moving current. Darkness shadowed the wall behind the falls and Hunter kept going. This portion of the mountain faced north so it was cold and mossy. He splayed his fingers, searching for traction to keep upright. Gradually, the ledge widened into a dirt path, and, *thank you, God*. He'd found an actual hollowed-out divot in the rock that could pass for a cave. Nearly ten feet by ten, it sloped upward from the noisy waterfall, opening into damp and chilly darkness.

He shook the chill off the back of his neck and checked for animals, lizards, or snakes. It wouldn't do to have to fight off the local wildlife on top of the murderers roaming the jungle. Casting a beam from his flashlight into the darkest recesses of the cave, he took stock of their new digs.

Crystals glistened in a myriad of rainbow shards under the focused light. The floor appeared to be relatively dry. The innermost walls were also dry while the mouth of the cave ran with streamlets from the thundering falls overhead. It was noisy erosion at work, and Mother Nature at her best, but it also made for a decent shelter, and he was damned glad he found it. From where he stood, he couldn't see beyond the veil of sliding water. He doubted anyone could see through the falls to him.

Retracing his steps, Hunter gathered his unconscious friends and transferred them to safety. First Meredith. Once across the river, he dropped to one knee inside the cave and settled her onto the driest patch of earth he could find, extra careful to cushion the back of her head as he laid her down.

Then Teague endured a bumpy ride over boulders and logs, but there was no choice. Lowering the litter inside near the mouth of the cave, Hunter turned back to Meredith. She was a little wet, but she should've come to by then.

His heart stilled. For the first time in twenty-four-hours, the world took a break, and it was just Hunter and Meredith in a deep, dark place where they were finally safe. Teague was unconscious. There was no Fast Eddy in the background tapping his patent leather toes to make her jump to his bidding. No cheerleader squad waited for Hunter or her to step out of line with someone not worthy of the in-crowd. There was only nerdy Hunter Christian with the prettiest girl in the world.

My girl.

He stroked the side of her face, his thumb on her cheekbone just below her closed eyes. Meredith hadn't changed a bit. She was still the one and only girl he thought of. Dreamed of. Wanted.

She turned into his touch with a sigh. That old familiar pinch in his heart was something else again. The damned thing never let up, and it had only gotten worse since he'd discovered she was also on this op. He froze, bent over her in a lover's pose. Wanting her with every beat of his tried and true USMC heart. Needing her to the depths of his warrior's soul. Loving her with the most torturous unrequited love in the universe of lovers.

Only he wasn't her lover, was he? How well he knew. Hunter hadn't been good enough for her before, and he wouldn't be now, not after what she'd witnessed today.

Killing those two men was just plain bad timing, but he'd really had no choice. Still, he wished he'd planned better, at least been more thoughtful, more considerate of her. She hadn't needed to see that side of him. Not her. Not ever. Like so many times before, he wished he'd been a smarter man.

"Hunter," she whispered, and immediately, his heart kicked into second gear.

Did she just call his name? Or did he imagine it because he wanted it so badly to be true? "Yes?" he answered hopefully.

"Hmmm," she replied with nothing more than a dream answer.

He leaned into her mouth, wishing he hadn't stolen that taste of her sweet lips before. What a mistake to make after all these years of hardening his heart, stealing a kiss from the woman who'd literally changed his life for the best and the worst in a moment of weakness. Okay, he knew better. He'd been the one who'd made all the worst possible, wrong decisions those years ago, but only because she'd broken his heart.

What a fool he'd been. Hunter slammed the door on his trip down Memory Lane. What was done was done. He sucked it up and he let it go.

Meredith seemed to be sleeping comfortably enough. Lifting off, he distanced himself from her yet again. It was better this way. He pulled another shirt out from the bundle of clothes on the litter and draped it over her shoulders to keep her warm.

The sight of her so peacefully asleep under that shabby covering was more than his heart could bear. He knelt at her side again and cupped her jaw. A thousand questions came to mind. Why had she played him like a fool? Better yet, why had he let her? Worse, how could she have married Welch out of the blue like she had? But worst of all, why had Hunter left?

In all his life, he'd never wanted a woman as much as he'd wanted Meredith. Not then. Not since. Not ever. And yet he'd deserted her as surely as she'd betrayed him.

The breath of her soft sigh caressed the palm of his hand. There was no waterfall crashing into the river outside and no cave—there was only the woman he'd given his heart to long before he knew the cruel ways of men and warriors. So long ago.

Could a boy that young and foolish love deeply? Oh, yes. Stupid boys like him had been falling in love for hundreds of years. A silly verse from his past called to him with, *"What light through yonder window breaks? It is the sun and fair Juliet is..."*

He let the lovely sentiment go unfinished and unspoken. Hunter bent down to Meredith's mouth, aching to be the only man in her life. The man she confided in, and the one she ran to for shelter and companionship. The man she loved and made love and life with. But he wasn't, was he? He lingered a kiss away, but he might as well have been standing on the moon. Life with Meredith in it was never meant to be.

Not for him.

With that well-known pain in his heart, he settled for a single chaste kiss to her forehead, one from which Meredith didn't stir and one she wouldn't remember. She'd never know the love he had carried all these wasted years for her, nor that she was the woman his soul longed for in the way of Shakespeare's tender prose. Despite discarding every outward sign of his once poetic self, Hunter had never found a way to shed the softer dimension of his soul, not even in a hard man's world. There was still a foolish, lovesick poet hidden away in the deepest crack in his warrior's soul.

Yes, he had killed, but that was the only way a kid survived the brutality of war. He'd learned fast. Man up. Get tough or earn the wrath of his squad. Kill or be killed. Yes, he'd been scared more times than he'd admit, but what Marine wasn't afraid when it came time to march out, dig in, and dish out? Yes, he was damaged, but Hunter Christian was still alive and kicking. That ought to count for something, and he knew damned well it did, just not in Meredith's world. She truly was fine Irish crystal, and he just an ordinary brown beer bottle of little value in the grand scope of things.

She deserved better.

Her turned-up nose wrinkled in her sleep. Always one of his favorite features, he longed to tap one finger to the end of that pert nose in the ways of their old camaraderie. He wished she'd open her pretty eyes, awaken, and for once, really see him for the man he was. For the lover he wanted to be.

Pulling his wallet out of his rear pocket, he fingered through the few pictures he'd carried with him on his deployments. His mom and dad on their thirtieth wedding anniversary. His USMC class at boot-camp graduation. And one more. There she was in Technicolor perfection. Meredith Olivia Flynn. *The perfect name for the perfect girl.*

And just that fast, it clicked in his hard head. Flynn? Not Welch? She was still using her maiden name, like one of those new-generation women who maintained their identity no matter how many times they married. Didn't it figure?

He removed the photo from its years-old shrine. Regardless of the tender thoughts he carried for her, the time had come to give the picture back. He had enough unfulfilled expectations to fill the Pacific Ocean. Why keep holding onto something that was never meant to be? Why keep inviting more pain?

Besides, he might not return from this next reconnoitering foray. He wanted her to have it. One last time, he ran a gentle finger down the edge of her jaw to her chin. She sighed in her dreams, her brow knit as if she disagreed with what he was going to do. It didn't matter. She belonged to someone else and giving her picture back would put a stop to any and all wishful thinking.

Gathering what was left of his common sense, he tucked the memory between her fingers and did what he did best. Hunter lifted to his feet and he walked away without looking back. He had a job to do.

CHAPTER FIFTEEN

The beautiful ebony night sky filled with stars, each brighter and lovelier than the next. They sang and chirped, and Meredith was beyond pleased that stars could sound so much like birds. In her perfect dream, all was bright and beautiful. What could be better? Nothing—until two hands reached out of the shadows and latched onto her neck.

She jerked upright, a scream crawling up her throat. For a frightening second, the dream lingered. She smoothed trembling fingers over her throat, sucking in huge breaths. The hands had felt so real, but it was a dream. Her neck wasn't broken. Wherever she was it was dark and damp and noisy.

Gradually, the horror from the dream faded. She could make out Teague's litter alongside her. His steady breathing so close at her side calmed the nightmarish sensation of being strangled away.

Swallowing hard, she took stock of the cave. That Hunter. He'd found one, just like he'd said he would. She leaned back onto her hands. Everything around her was dark and clammy. Only the sand beneath her fingertips felt dry. Pinpricks of light glistened overhead like the stars of her dream. She brushed a leaf away, thankful it wasn't a spider.

"Where am I?" she asked the darkness, hoping Hunter would answer and tell her to shut up. At least then she'd know she was safe because he'd be there in all of his grumpy glory. But the crashing waterfall at the mouth of the cave was the only reply. It also made a loud enough buffer of white noise that could have disguised approaching footsteps or enemy voices. Warily, she pushed to her feet, needing to know where she was, or if Hunter was close by guarding the place. He hadn't left her to fend for herself, had he?

Gathering her courage, she checked on Teague's condition first. His fever had diminished, a good sign, but the rolling supply container was nowhere to be found. That explained Hunter's absence. He'd no doubt gone back for it.

Meredith's innate mothering instinct kicked in. Teague and Hunter would both need food. Maybe, if she were lucky enough, she could find some more of that fruit she'd picked on the run last night.

Cautiously, she ventured forth, scanning the jungle before she stepped around the shower plummeting at the entrance to her hideaway. Wow. Hunter certainly knew how to pick them. This particular waterfall was carved into sheer stone with an overhanging lip that propelled the water away from the entrance and almost made it easy for a person to come and go. Almost. Ducking through the misty curtain at the far end of the natural doorway still left her plenty damp.

Meredith smoothed a hand over her tangled locks and picked out some leaves and tiny bits of other stuff in her hair. The last thing she'd remembered was her knees buckling. What had Hunter done, dragged her through the weeds? That would be so like him.

A sandy shore lined the other side of the river, while rocks and boulders littered the side she stood on. Oh yeah, and that sheer stone wall to her right. Not a fruit tree in sight.

Getting back across the river was the problem. That was where the trees were.

Determined, she stuck to the stony pathway across the river. She slipped into the fast flowing water between the rocks, but she made it. Once there, she took a deep breath. With her confidence restored, she studied her new hideout.

A stone ledge far above jutted out of the dense undergrowth of vines and more vines. The foamy white water projected over that ledge tumbled into swirls of turquoise and teals to crash into a pool of coffee brown nearly at her feet. How lovely. Two smaller waterfalls spilled to her immediate right. The ethereal beauty of this misty paradisiacal hideaway took her breath. It seemed too good to be true, but Hunter had trusted his instincts, and it had worked.

Meredith inhaled slowly, finally able to let a small portion of her tension go. Despite the horrors she'd seen during the last twenty-four hours, this place felt safe. Mist drifted upward from the churning falls, further shielding the cave's entry. Brightly colored macaws flitted from tree to tree and flowers bloomed everywhere, on rocks, trees, and straggly vines, adding a delightful ambience to the surreal place.

A sigh escaped her lips. For this one moment, peace seemed to flow outward from the falls, enveloping her in calm. She stood there, lost in the moment. How odd that Hunter was the one who'd brought her here. Of course, then he'd left her, but that was typical Hunter behavior. He had no problem confronting an armed and dangerous enemy head-on, but a woman? That was when he seemed to give up, turn tail, and run.

Of all the hurts he carried, and he must've endured a lot during his military service, it seemed the one she'd caused when she'd married Eddy had hurt Hunter the worst. Meredith would've given anything to go back in time and change what she'd done.

The anger in his eyes when he'd accused her of leaving him was justified, but she'd seen something else glimmering there, too. He'd tried to cover it with nasty words, but too late. She'd seen the truth. Hunter still cared.

She gulped past the hard knot in her throat. He wasn't alone in that feeling. She cared for him, too. Drawing in a slow, deliberate breath, she exhaled slowly through pursed lips. It was time to find something to eat.

Free at last. Hunter moved quicker once he wasn't encumbered. Now that he knew Meredith and Teague were safe, his mission had been reduced to one urgent goal: Rescue that military guy Burdette was torturing. God help Burdette if that guy was one of the guys from The TEAM. Hunter hated brutality, but he hated it when it was inflicted on one of his friends worse.

But to get to Burdette, he had to search out the enemy camp and get inside. Heading back to what was left of the MI camp, he hoped one of those ACS$_1$ suits had survived the fire. If not, what he had to do next would be a lot more difficult. Maybe bloodier.

Closer to Meredith's camp, his hackles raised as he detected two distinct voices on the trail ahead of him. The

ACS₁ could wait. Hunter backed into the shadows as a couple of guys in uniforms passed by, dragging two body bags. Judging by the bloated size of the bags, they'd found Big Guy and Fat Bastard.

But what about the trap Hunter had rigged for a killer surprise? How could these two jokers hauling the bags still be alive? Hadn't his booby trap worked? Or were these guys too smart to fall for it? He doubted that.

Hunter hung close and let Tweedledee and Tweedledum lead the way. These guys were a joke. They made enough noise, cussing the weight and stench of their dead buddies. No way they were smart enough to avoid the spring-up-and-slap-you-in-the-face bamboo sticks. It might not be Big Guy or Fat Bastard in those body bags after all.

Eventually, a clearing and a camouflaged tractor–trailer rig came into view. Then another. With high axles and wide balloon tires, both rigs appeared capable of traversing rugged jungle terrain by simply crushing everything in their paths. A heavy push bar at the front of the vehicles verified they were more tank than recreational. A generator hummed from the backside of the rigs.

In plain view of Hunter's hidden position, two tents faced each other. Camp chairs and a fire pit occupied the space between the tents. Several more men dressed in the same style of black uniforms as all the men Hunter had encountered came and went, seemingly at ease. Most weren't carrying weaponry aside from a pistol at their hips. None appeared to be on high alert. One lingered at the door to the first tent, peering inside.

Hunter crouched in the dense vegetation to watch and learn. These guys seemed well organized and well-funded. He scanned the perimeter, expecting some level of security for a camp this size, maybe a guard or two on patrol. Nothing. He looked closer, searching for trip wires, cameras, motion sensors, or spotlights. Still nothing. It didn't make sense that an enterprise of this magnitude would leave itself vulnerable to attack.

Suddenly, his spidey senses tingled. A shiver of goose bumps ran up his neck into his scalp. His inner sniper whispered: *Hold still. Don't move. Don't even breathe.*

He didn't. Just scrolled his eyes from side to side until he knew why the instinctual alert. It took a minute to detect the silvery shimmer on the breeze that, at first glance, looked more like a spider web. Even then, portions of it vanished from view. The damned thing surrounded the entire camp like a gigantic sheet of mosquito netting draped from post to post and over the RVs. One moment there but the next it became completely invisible.

He watched it fade in and out of sight. That had to be their early warning system, but what did it do? Hunter settled cross-legged to the ground, needing every last bit of intel these jokers had to offer.

Tweedledee and Tweedledum had dropped the body bags at a framed gate comprised of what looked to be black propylene tubing. Fumbling in his pants pocket, Tweedledee brought up a key fob and pointed it at the gate. The netting shimmered into sight. All of it. Noiselessly, the gate swung inward, and into the inner sanctum he went, dragging his corpse behind him.

Tweedledum followed, complaining at the heat and weight of his load. When the gate closed automatically behind them, the netting all but disappeared.

Hunter pulled one of the many fobs he'd collected during his kills out of his pants pocket. *So that's what this is for.* He pressed the only button on the fob, but the gate didn't respond. Just as he'd suspected. No doubt the entry code had been changed when the first fobs had gone missing. Still, it was an impressive notion, all this high technology in the middle of nowhere. Most of these jokers might be dumber than dirt, but the place was technologically impregnable. Burdette, if he was the brainiac behind this, had to be after MI's ActiveCamouflageSystem. That was the only thing that made sense.

Only it couldn't be. Big Guy and Fat Bastard had known—or thought they'd known—some pretty nasty intel about Meredith. Something else was going on.

Hunter rolled away the pain in his neck that always came with the thought of what those jackasses said about her. Given the chance, he'd kill them again.

It didn't take long before a man in khaki pants and a short-sleeved Hawaiian shirt stepped out of the first trailer, his chin held high. "Has he talked yet?" he asked no one in particular, his gaze on one of the tents.

One guard snapped to attention. "No, sir. Are you sure he knows anything?"

"I'm sure," the important man answered. "Mr. Teach was very specific. Flynn is the key. McCormack's beta test had to be completed by the end of this week to meet a Department of Defense deadline. If MI fails to comply, the bidding reopens to the public. This guy's the only one we've captured so far. He has to know where she is."

That caught Hunter's attention. Flynn is the key? To what? Only one captured? Exactly who did this guy have in that tent, Eric, Seth, or Ky? And why did that name, Teach, sound so damned familiar? Hunter stored it away for later scrutiny. He had his guys to rescue first.

Mr. Khaki Pants lifted his head, his nostrils flared. "What on earth is that foul odor?"

"Jonesy and Clark just got back with a couple more of our guys," the guard replied.

"We don't have time for all that *never leave a man behind* bullshit. They should've dragged them to the dump like everyone else. Teach is getting impatient. He wants results, not bodies."

"Yes, sir," the guard said.

Paralleling the man's walk back to the tent, Hunter stuck to the shadowy cover of the jungle and hoped for a glimpse inside. No such luck. Two flaps shielded the entrance, one overlapping the other. Nothing of the interior became visible when Khaki Pants ducked inside. The guard he'd been speaking with took up residence on a camp chair outside the tent. "Where'd you find these two, Clark?" he asked.

Clark jerked his head in the direction of The TEAM's camp. "Not far from camp two, but the place was rigged, Masters. You shoulda seen it. That son-of-a-bitchin' ghost is a damned devil, is what he is. This is just Hoffman and Bauer. He got them cuz he set up a trap where he killed Stevenson and Daggett. Me and Jonesy still gotta go back for their bodies. It's a mess back there is what it is. After he killed 'em, he stripped 'em naked. Animals been at 'em."

"Shit, Stevenson and Daggett, too?" Masters grabbed the back of his bare neck. "I wondered where they were."

"Yeah, and Hoffman and Bauer never knew what hit 'em. They both got it face-first with sharpened bamboo sticks. We thought they was standing up when we first seen 'em. Only they wasn't. Crap, they was hanging there, impaled like a couple frogs on stilts over Stevenson and Daggett's dead bodies." Clark dragged a hand over his sweaty face. "All four of 'em was already bloated up. I hate the heat of this jungle."

"Damn straight," Jonesy muttered. "We gotta catch this guy 'fore he picks off the rest of us like he did Johnson. He's a mean SOB, the way he leaves our guys out there naked. Damned humiliating is what it is."

Masters pursed his lips, shaking his head and glowering. "I told Burdette to secure the ACS gear before we opened fire on these guys." He kept his voice low. "We're not dealing with regulars. These guys are spec ops. This mess could've been avoided if he'd listened to me instead of pretty-boy, Teach."

There was that name again.

Jonesy grunted. "Reason isn't Burdette's strong point. He just wants the girl. All this other stuff is just one big smokescreen. You know that as well as I do. He's kissing Teach's butt, big time. Thinks bringing Flynn in alive will make him indispensable."

Masters chuckled darkly. "He can think all he wants. Teach doesn't care much for Burdette or Flynn. He'd just as soon see a picture of her dead body than have to deal with her alive."

Hunter's spine stiffened. Whoever Teach was, he needed to die.

"Yeah, well, this ghost guy is pissing me off," Clark growled. "I get my hands on him and I'm gonna throw a barbecue in his honor. Then I'm gonna ram a bamboo stick up his ass and grill him over a nice bed of hot coals. I'd like to hear him scream for a change."

Masters tapped a finger to his lower lip. "You've got to admit that poisoned dart was right out of the guerilla warfare playbook. Johnson never knew what hit him."

Hunter's ears perked up again. Until now, he'd thought Johnson was the man he'd killed after he ran the panther off. But someone was out there using poison darts? Good to know.

Jonesy pushed out of his seat. "You sound like you're on his side, Masters. What's wrong with you?"

"Not at all." Masters lifted a palm to placate his aggravated partner. "I just respect a fellow warrior who's taken the time to understand the game and his opponents. Don't worry. Whoever this ghost is, he's on the losing team. We'll get him sooner or later. He might be smart, but he's outnumbered."

Yeah, by a team of morons.

"Damned right we will," Clark muttered. "Come on, Jonesy. Bring a couple more body bags. Let's get Hoffman and Bauer back to camp so I can take a shower. I stink and so do you."

Jonesy shook his head, his nose wrinkled in disdain. "I say we let 'em stay where they are. They're downwind. No sense dragging more corpses into camp. These two are already stinking up the joint, and they just got here."

"Good thinking." Masters nodded. "Why don't you two park these guys with the rest of the dead? Burdette's right. We don't have enough cold storage to haul everyone home."

Jonesy stuck his thumb in his chest. "Me? But you're the a-hole who told me to go get these guys. Now you expect me to haul them up to the dump? I don't think so."

"But you will," Masters said with authority. "While you're out there, watch for Fergusen and Hansen, too. They should've been back by now."

"Where'd they go?"

"They hauled Wilkinson up to the dump at first light."

"Wilkinson too?" Clark asked in disbelief. "Man, we're dropping like flies."

"Stop whining. It won't take long now," Masters reassured. "We'll get this guy. He'll make a mistake. Trust me. They all do."

"But I got a bum leg," Jonesy complained.

"Yeah, 'cause you got shot by a girl," Clark snickered.

"Give it a rest," Masters growled. "She only creased you, Jonesy. Go with Clark. Make it quick."

Jonesy squared off with Masters, his fists clenched. "No. I'm tired of all this shittin' grunt work."

Masters jumped to his feet. "You heard me. Get 'em out of here."

When Jonesy didn't move, Masters took a step forward. "You got something to say?"

"Nothing that can't wait," Jonesy shot back at him, "but Burdette better be serious about that bonus."

Masters stood down, his fists still clenched. "Don't worry. You'll get what's coming to you. Quiet..." he hissed, glancing over his shoulder.

Hunter knew how to count. He'd eliminated two men at the body dump—no doubt Fergusen and Hansen; two more with the booby trap—Hoffman and Bauer; as well as Big Guy and Fat Bastard who he suspected were Stevenson and Daggett. Plus, he'd ended the bastard who'd stabbed him after the panther attack. Could have been Wilkinson. Hunter didn't care, but he'd only killed seven, none with a poison dart. Genius. Hunter wished he'd thought of that one.

Khaki Pants, aka Burdette, exited the tent, wiping his red-stained hands on a white towel.

"Any luck?" Masters asked politely, his hands clasped behind his back like a well-trained attack dog.

Hunter tensed, straining to hear every last word.

"It won't take long now." Burdette glanced at the tent behind him. "He's ready to talk. Don't take any chances. Record everything he says."

"That's what you said last time," Masters muttered, "only he ain't said much we didn't already know. I've got to be honest—I don't think this game with the tape's working."

Burdette shot a sharp glance past Masters to the jungle beyond the camp. "It will now. His friend is out there. I can feel him."

What tape?

Masters grabbed the back of his neck, rolling his shoulders. "You can, huh?"

Burdette nodded, scanning the perimeter. "Trust me. We're not alone."

Count on it, Hunter promised.

"Mr. Burdette, sir." Masters tipped forward on the balls of his feet. "You might as well know that the men are getting antsy. We've lost eight guys that we know of and three others are missing, but we've only killed two and we've only spotted Flynn the one time. Those aren't good odds."

Burdette stuck the towel in his back pocket as he turned his back on Masters and headed into the first trailer. "I don't give a shit what your men think. I'm not leaving until we find her, alive, damn it. Tell them there's a five-thousand-dollar reward to whoever gets her first, and I'll double it if they bring her back in the next twenty-four hours."

Hunter hefted his pistol up from the holster on his hip. *Not if I get you first.*

CHAPTER SIXTEEN

Meredith heard them before she saw them. It had to be monkeys. Nothing else could make that much awful screeching, howling, and racket. One of them let go of an ear piercing, "Woot. Woot. Woot," as the entire monkey gang descended to the lower branches of the trees across the river.

She couldn't help but smile. Monkeys were smart, and the trees they'd settled in were filled with fruit. Her stomach gurgled. She might just have found tonight's dinner. Wouldn't Hunter be surprised?

The second she thought of him a shiver rippled up the backs of her bare legs and over her butt. She rubbed her arms to warm herself from the chill. Darn him anyway. He wasn't even there, but he'd affected her. How had he gotten under her skin so quickly?

While the monkey gang dropped or decimated every piece of the globe-shaped fruit they touched, she ducked under cover and watched. She knew better than to make her presence known to these noisy marauders, but what a sight. Courtney would've loved seeing these busybodies.

The long-armed force swinging through the branches was pure magic to behold. Agile and strong, the gang moved like high-wire trapeze artists one moment and thieving scallywags the next, stealing fruit from each other as they swooped by on vines. Babies clung to their mothers' backs and bellies while youngsters wrestled each other in midair.

When another shrill howl rent the jungle, the entire gang chattered noisily as they split. One moment the jungle was filled with rowdy simian banter; the next, they'd scrambled out of the high treetops and vanished. The eeriest silence reigned.

Goose bumps lifted on her arms. She glanced over her shoulder to the shadowy jungle behind her, suddenly aware she was as much prey as the monkeys.

Hurry, Mean Girl prodded. *Grab some fruit before they come back.*

Meredith worked up her courage to take that first step. What if this was a trick and the monkeys were waiting for her?

You can do it. Mean Girl could be pretty snarky when she showed up, and pushy, always testing Meredith's faith in herself.

"Maybe," she said out loud, considering how badly she wanted to be a mighty hunter–gatherer. She was on her own and her waterfall sanctuary was all the way across the river. What if she had to run? What if she fell in?

Then don't fall in.

Meredith hurried into monkey land, but she was no more than beneath the trees when she spotted a curtain of pink and purple flowering vines hanging from above. The fragrant vine weaved into the forks of neighboring trees, and she would've liked to sample the pleasant fragrance, maybe taken some of those flowers back to the cave with her. God knew it needed something sweet smelling to hide the smell of wet dirt and sweat.

She would have snagged some of those flowers if the ants in them hadn't made her think twice. Beauty and danger seemed to walk hand in hand throughout this jungle.

Determined to prove useful to Hunter, she gathered the front of her smelly, borrowed shirt into a pouch and collected a weighty armful of fruit. If monkeys could eat it, so could she and her guys.

A creepy feeling that someone was watching made Meredith glance over her shoulder. Nothing stirred but the breeze through those ant-infested flowers and vines. Was she being watched or was she just paranoid? She hurried.

Meredith snagged three more too-pretty-to-be-left-behind pieces of fruit, thankful for the first time since she'd put it on, for her over-sized men's wear. At this rate, she wouldn't need to leave the cave for days. Hunter might even be proud of her. But she'd been exposed way too long. It was definitely time to get back under cover.

Intelligence gathering was a lot like assembling a puzzle with some of the pieces missing. Burdette had at least one TEAM agent inside that tent. Another agent was working outside the wire, the one Clark called a ghost, but the third was missing. It would've been good to know which agent was which.

Hunter crept nearer the gate, tracking Burdette as he climbed into the first trailer and slammed the door behind him. Masters ducked inside the tent. The camp emptied as the corpse detail, Jonesy and Clark, headed out of camp, complaining and dragging Hoffman and Bauer behind them.

Before the gate whooshed closed behind the body bags, Hunter slipped inside the enemy camp and ducked to the rear of the first tractor/trailer rig. Both rigs were large enough to house more mercenaries, but he wasn't leaving without his man. Or men.

Keeping low and out of sight, he skirted the back of the first trailer and ducked between the two parked rigs to crouch alongside the one tent. He checked the other tent, the one Burdette hadn't bothered with, first. Hunter needed to be sure he wasn't leaving any of his guys—or their bodies—behind. Cautiously easing the flap aside with the back of his hand, he confirmed his suspicion. The place was empty but for a couple cots and some gear.

"Why don't you wise up, tough guy? Tell me where she is and I can make all this pain stop." Masters' voice drifted from the other tent, followed by slapping sounds. Groans. High-pitched whines of a man in distress.

Revulsion rankled deep in Hunter's gut. The torture ended now. With one quick slice of his blade, he angled inside the tent and lunged. His arm and knife were at Masters' throat before the bastard could cry for help or inflict more pain on the man strapped to the metal table. A shiny scalpel fell to the floor and—

Gawddamnit! Seth McCray lay stripped to his Jockeys on that table, his wrists and ankles cuffed, and his sweaty body covered in bloody nicks and cuts. He'd clearly been beaten. His face was bruised. Silver duct tape sealed his lips, but his desperate eyes widened when he caught sight of Hunter.

Masters gripped Hunter's forearm in a pathetic try for defense, but didn't the tattoo, SEMPER FI, on the back of his hand, incite a sickening wave of disgust? A USMC brother had been torturing Seth for information, but not allowing him to talk? What kind of bullshit was that?

Revenge flamed to life. Hunter tightened his arm around Masters' neck and walked him to the edge of the table, his knife ready to do the deed. "Unbuckle him, you son-of-a-bitch."

Masters turned politician. "A brother Marine? Well, isn't this a coincid—"

"Unbuckle him!" Hunter hissed, not playing the game. In a lightning fast move, he traded his blade for his pistol. Masters was stalling for time and maneuverability. He'd get neither. "I'll let you loose, but you'd better not try anything."

"Sure. No problem." Smart enough to comply, Masters freed Seth's bloody ankles, but craftily eased a hand behind his back. Predictable move.

Hunter growled. "Go ahead. Pull that blade out of your side sheath or that pinkie pistol out of your pocket. You think I won't fucking blow your head apart?"

Masters' upper lip lifted into a sneer. "You've got balls, I'll give you that, but you, my comrade-in-arms, are outnumbered and outplayed. My men will be all over you the minute you step outside."

"Not if you're going with me, dirtbag. And I'm no comrade of yours. Release him. Now."

"Who the hell are you?"

"Hunter Christian. Corporal out of the Two/Four." The Two/Four being the Second Infantry Battalion, Fourth Marine Regiment, garrisoned out of Camp Pendleton. Second to None. The *Magnificent Bastards. Stick that in your eye.*

Masters grunted. "You're one of them, huh? What if I refuse? All I have to do is—"

"Try me," Hunter purred. "You know damned well what I can and will do. That's my friend you've been carving on. Go ahead. Call your guys. You're a trained killer like me. I'd love to see one of those jerks try to save your punk ass before it hits the dirt."

Enough said. Masters unbuckled the wrist restraints. Slowly, Seth swung his legs over the edge of the table, his knuckles white. Grimacing, he peeled the sticky tape off his mouth and spat. Bloody drool ran over his chin, but he wiped it with the back of his hand. "Hey, Hunt," he rasped, leaning too far forward, swaying like he was dizzy. "Damned good to... see you."

Hunter steadied him with a palm to his bicep. "Stay right there, buddy. Don't move. You're going for a ride." With another wave of his pistol, he backed Masters against the table. "You're going to pack him. Should be easy. You're already an ass."

Seth balked at climbing onboard the man who'd just been torturing him until Hunter nodded toward the scalpels lined up in surgical order on a side table. "If I was you, I'd want a few souvenirs. Take all you can carry. This donkey might need a reminder who's boss."

"Hell, yeah." Taking the hint, Seth grabbed the nearest blade and clutched Masters' neck from behind. "Bend over," he ordered. It took him an unsteady minute to climb on, but then it was his arm around Masters' shoulder, a nice shiny scalpel to his adversary's throat. "Damn it, Hunt. He was going to kill me. Sure glad you showed up."

"It's your turn now, buddy. If he so much as grunts, you end him. Hear me?" Hunter backed away, keeping an eye on Masters.

Seth nodded his shaky head. He'd said the right words, but he was in damned bad shape. And weak. Masters needed more incentive.

"This is how it's going to go down," Hunter explained as he pressed his pistol to Masters temple. "If you so much as make my buddy breathe heavy, you'll wish you died on your last deployment. Understood, Sally?"

Masters' lip curled, and that was a good enough answer.

Hunter nodded to Seth. "Get a good grip. Let's get you somewhere safe."

"Damn straight." Seth leaned heavily onto Masters' back. "Giddy up, asshole."

Masters accommodated his passenger by hooking his hands under Seth's thighs and hoisting him higher to balance their weight. "Now what, genius?"

Hunter pointed his chin to the door. "Now we go home, and if you know what's good for you, you'll make sure we get there. If we run into any trouble, you die first."

Masters grunted, but ducked his head as he stepped out of the tent. As expected, a grumbling roar went up from his men.

"What do you think you're doing?" Mr. Burdette demanded. "You can't—"

Hunter ducked out of the tent, his pistol in Masters' neck. "Back the hell off. Now."

"You gotta let us pass," Masters wisely advised. "He'll kill me if you don't."

By then, several other armed men had gathered, their weapons drawn. Hunter nudged Masters forward, ready to prove his point should one of them try to be a hero.

"How'd you get in here?" Burdette asked, like Hunter would waste time explaining.

Stopping in front of the man who'd thought he was in charge, he snapped his fingers. "Sat phone. Now. I know you've got one. Hand it over."

Burdette complied, dragging a satellite phone out of his belt holster with shaky fingers. "Are you MI or one of those bastards Alex Stewart sent?"

"Bastard at your service," Hunter stepped into the corporate operator's comfort zone to grab the phone, using his body size as an absolute threat, the blunt barrel of his weapon digging into Masters neck. "Did you enjoy cutting on my buddy? My friend? Did you, huh?"

A good foot shorter and at least a hundred pounds lighter, Burdette took a full step back. "I... I..."

"Exactly," Hunter hissed. "You don't have the balls for a face to face fight, do you?"

Just then, Jonesy and Clark reappeared at the gate without the body bags. They obviously hadn't been to the dump. Jonesy snapped his pistol out of his holster, but before he could aim, the tiniest whirring sound zipped through the air. Jonesy slapped his neck as if he'd been stung. His legs turned to jelly as he slid in a half-spin to the dirt.

Clark jumped clear of his suddenly prone buddy, performing a damned near perfect pirouette, his rifle aimed into the jungle. "It's him! That damned ghost is back. He just killed Jonesy!"

Well, I'll be damned. Hunter was as dumbfounded as Burdette's boys, but a genuine smile tugged the corners of his mouth. One of his guys was out there in all that jungle green and he—or they—had his back. He didn't waste the opportunity. Backing away from Burdette's restless army, he kept one eye on Masters, the other on the gate. Clark stood there, his weapon drawn. He was the jumpiest of the rapidly decreasing army of buffoons. The rest seemed frozen in place, unwilling to move lest they risk the wrath of the ghost.

"Open it," Hunter ordered.

Clark kept his eyes on the jungle while he activated his key fob and shoved the gate open. "Git outta here. Hurry. I don't wanna die."

"Remember what I said, Burdette," Hunter growled in parting, his pistol marking the side of Masters hard head. "I can get you anywhere, anytime. Move it, Masters."

Not until they were out of sight and safely under cover did Hunter take the chance. "Eric? Ky?" he called into the shadows.

But no one answered. No glimmer of a possible ACS suit fractured the leafy surroundings, either. Hunter didn't have time to waste. He set a trail for the river. If Eric or Ky were still nearby, they could follow. Burdette's sat phone was an unexpected coup. Once he dealt with Masters, Hunter intended to use it.

CHAPTER SEVENTEEN

"Stewart."

With that one word, Hunter breathed a sigh of relief. He was so damned glad to hear his boss, Alex Stewart, CEO of the most elite undercover operation on the East Coast. "You wouldn't happen to be in the neighborhood, would you?"

"Damn it, Hunt. I've been calling you guys for hours. What the hell's going on?"

"We ran into a little trouble. Lost half the MI team last night. Got two injured men and a couple prisoners." Hunter threw that lie into the mix to keep Masters guessing. For now, he was fairly obedient—not like he had much choice with Seth holding a scalpel to his jugular like he was.

"Prisoners? Two injured? Who's hurt? Better not be one of my guys," Alex growled.

"Seth," Hunter admitted, his pistol still ready for action in his hand. "He's cut up pretty bad, but he's with me. Teague Horton took one in the chest. Don't think it's life threatening. I've seen worse."

"Eric and Ky?"

"Not sure," Hunter replied evenly, not willing to admit anything in front of Masters.

"Meredith Flynn?"

"She can take care of herself, Boss. She shot the first of Burdette's men." Of course, then she lost that handy dandy pistol of hers, but Hunter wasn't about to share that intel.

Alex didn't miss a beat. "Jed's been worried sick since you guys missed last night's report in. Who the hell are we up against, Hunt? Columbian guerillas? Indigent tribes?"

"Mercenaries and assholes," Hunter replied, startled it had been less than twenty-four hours since this debacle started. "Ask Jed if he's ever heard of a guy named Burdette. Between him and this jerk I'm holding prisoner..." He turned expectantly to Masters. "Name, rank, and serial number."

His prisoner shifted his weight from one foot to the other under his awkward load. ""Travis Masters, but I'm not a Marine anymore."

"I've got news for you," Hunter bit out, "you never were. What's Burdette's first name?"

"Albert."

"Who the hell's Teach?"

"Roger Teach. He's some joker who's buying Burdette's company." He looked to be telling the truth, but one way or the other, Hunter would soon know.

"Travis Masters. Albert Burdette. Roger Teach. Got it," Alex said. "What are these guys after?"

"Not sure, but this takeover has all the ear-markings of corporate espionage. When can you be here?"

"Jordan and Lee are on their way to you now."

"That all?"

"I'm in Caracas with Zack, David, and Adam. You need more?"

"Maybe," Hunter admitted. "Remember Vadodara?"

Alex should remember. Vadodara, population of more than two million, in Gujarat province, India, was the tightest squeeze Hunter had ever lived through to talk about. He and ex-Navy SEAL, Adam Torrey, were on one of those *easy* missions that went sideways before they'd known what hit them.

They'd found themselves outmaneuvered and facing an army of hundreds. Seemed the kid they'd been sent to extricate owed the wrong guys a gambling debt. Alex saved Hunter and Adam's bacon by calling in a few favors from a no-kidding United States Naval destroyer stationed off shore in the Sea of India.

He'd pulled them out in the nick of time. Well, maybe not exactly in the nick of time. Adam did go home with a bullet hole in the left cheek of his buttocks when he dived to cover the diplomat's son. He should've let the kid take the hit. Hunter would've. The little shit might have learned something. As it was, he'd never even said thank you for saving his sorry ass.

"Can do," Alex replied. "Mother's already tracked the GPS signal you called in on. Anything else?"

A pack of Marlboro Reds would be nice. "That ought to do it."

Another growl rumbled all the way from Alexandria, Virginia, and that was why Hunter loved working for this guy. They spoke the same language, even understood each other's grunts, growls, and expletives. Hunter had no doubt that Alex was planning ways to make the guy responsible for this nightmare, suffer. He was like that. He might chew his employees out like a mad dog with a bone, but God bless the fool who stepped on any TEAM member. Nothing made Alex madder. Or meaner.

"Expect to see Jordan and Lee within the next twenty-four hours. The rest of us won't be far behind."

"Copy that." Hunter ended the call and turned to Masters. "Stop."

Seth was barely holding on. His head sagged and the scalpel hung limp in his fingers.

"About time," Masters muttered.

By then, he was covered with sweat—not that Hunter gave a shit. He gestured his pistol toward the wide trunk of a nearby tree. "Set him down. Slow and easy."

Seth slipped to his butt and leaned tiredly against the jungle giant, fighting to hold his head up. He needed more than just rest. A stiff shot of whiskey wouldn't hurt. Maybe a transfusion.

Hunter tucked his pistol in his belt. The second Masters' hands were free, Hunter secured them behind his back with several loops of a handy vine. He tugged an extra tight knot. "Take a seat backside this tree. You okay, Seth?"

Seth waved one hand, his eyes closed. "Yeah. Just need... a minute to catch my... breath."

Masters settled cross-legged. "What now, tough guy? We gonna have a tea party?"

Hunter crouched between Masters' knees, his knife back in his hand. This particular knife had been made for the Two/Four. Comprised of infantry and support personnel, the *Magnificent Bastards* were second to none in combat action and declared it often, loudly and proudly.

"You know how this works. You answer quick and sure—I won't hurt you. You waste my time? I'll stick you where it counts."

"Them's a killer's rules," Masters muttered.

With a lightning jab, Hunter lanced his kneecap and twisted. "And so it begins."

Masters jerked his knee to the side. "Shit! Okay! Ask, damn it. What do you want to know?"

"Who do you work for?"

"Already told you. Albert Burdette." Masters jerked his head back toward his camp, a desperate glint in his eye. "He's second-in-command at Brinkman Exploration. Used to own it, but times have been bad."

"Who owns it now?"

"Some asshat named Teach."

"Roger Teach?" Hunter watched closely for deceit. "Who's he?"

"Some big shot out of California. Guess he wants to be the next Bill Gates."

Bill Gates sure as hell didn't get rich like that. "Why kill the MI team?"

Masters couldn't spit it out fast enough. "If McCormack's prototype fails, Burdette gets another chance at the DoD contract. His active camouflage system is better and cheaper. Least that's what he says."

"All this killing over a defense-industry contract?" Something about Masters' confession felt hollow.

"You bet." His head bobbed like that of a good boy sitting in the front pew at church on Sunday morning. "There's big money in DoD contracts and not just from the States, either. England, France, and Canada are all watching MI's

ActiveCamouflage development. Russia and China, too. It's the next level up in warfare, fighting an invisible enemy. Shit. Don't stab me again. I'm bleeding enough already."

Hunter shot him a guarded glare at that pathetic whine. Seth was the one bleeding. Masters just thought he was. "Are you telling me Burdette's in league with other countries, our enemies? That he's a spy? Who's he working for?"

"Shit, I don't know," Masters said quickly. "I just know active camouflage technology is hot buzz on the international scene. If he's smart, he's talking to Peking and Moscow. I would."

"Why torture Seth? You had him restrained and his mouth taped while you were cutting on him. What good did that do?"

Masters hesitated one second. The blade flicked so fast he could only yelp and jerk backwards, his shin bleeding now. "Shit. Damn it! I did it to draw you and the rest of your team in." He barely avoided another stab. "Damn it! Stop it! We knew you guys were out there watching us. Shit, you were picking us off one by one, so we let him scream a little at first. But we wanted you inside the net. Figured you military types would do something heroic to save your buddy's life if you thought he was dying."

Rage built to a dangerous level inside Hunter. That familiar red haze that blinded him to logic boiled to sputtering, roiling life in his head. As much as he wanted to stick that blade deep in Masters' throat and listen to him gurgle his last breath, he restrained from exacting vengeance. Rules were rules. Killing a man too soon wasn't how this game was played.

"That was your way of trapping me? Lure me in with a man who could no longer scream when you cut him?" *Jesus Christ. What if I hadn't gone looking for my guys?*

Masters stuck his chin out. "It worked, didn't it? Here you are."

He was also one of those *military types*, only the traitor had used his training against his brothers-in-arms. Bastards like him made it damned hard to remember to play by the rules.

"Where are the rest of my men?"

"How should I know? We only grabbed this guy the first night."

Hunter flipped his knife, handle over blade until he caught it again, the tip still pointed at Masters. Sweat dripped off the ex-Marine's chin. Apparently, bullying a defenseless opponent strapped to a table was okay, but facing an armed opponent who could fight back? Not so easy.

"Besides," Masters gulped. "What about all my guys? Where's Poncho?"

"You need any help back there yet?" Seth called weakly.

"You'll be the first to know if I do." Hunter answered casually over his shoulder. "How you doing?"

"Good." The declaration sounded weak.

Hunter needed to hurry this final act. "Who's Poncho? Your dog?"

"One of my men," Masters hissed. "You sure don't mind killing everyone you come up against."

"You're right. I don't." Hunter flipped the blade again. "Why's Burdette after Meredith Flynn? How does she fit in?"

Masters shrugged, meriting another razor-sharp dig, this one in his bicep. "Damn it! Stop—!" The blade bit again, turning both kneecaps into bloody pincushions. "All right! I honestly don't know why Burdette wants Flynn alive. Shit! I can't tell you what I don't know!"

"Maybe if I taped your mouth you'd remember better?" Hunter ground out.

Masters paled.

"Take your clothes off."

"Aw, come on—"

Hunter let his knife do the talking.

"Shit!" Masters rolled, jumped, and hopped his ass on the dirt. "How the hell do you expect me to do that with my hands tied behind my back and you poking at me all the time? I'm bleeding! Knock it off."

Hunter really wanted to let his blade do more persuading, but Seth was weakening and Hunter needed Masters alive. He bit his lip and restrained his knife. "I can peel those pants off of you if you'd rather. Want some help, Sally?"

Demeaning the guy's manhood worked. Masters stretched his bound hands forward. Sweating up a storm and still dressed, he finally maneuvered both boots between his wrists and through the restraints. Sucking in a breath, he dropped both clenched hands to his knees.

Hunter cocked an evil eye. "I don't have all day. I've got a friend to get home. Remember him? The guy *you* were sticking with a scalpel? Seth?" His voice grated lower with every darkly enunciated word.

"Shit, I'm hurrying." Masters attacked his bootlaces with nervous fingers. Pulling the footgear off, he tossed both boots aside before he unbuckled his belt and wormed his way out of his jeans. Kicking them off, the silver buttons on his shirt went next.

Hunter watched as one by one, those buttons revealed a tattooed American flag. The paradox between an honorable man and a scumbag was never more apparent. For two cents, Hunter would've carved that symbol of freedom and pride off Masters' tainted skin.

There was no way Masters could get out of his shirt, not with his hands bound. But that wasn't the real reason for the game now, was it? Nope. This next part was all about intimidation and hopelessness. Humiliation. The idiot you were torturing needed to believe you meant business. Clothes meant security. Nakedness stripped that frail coat of armor away. No man liked his junk exposed while forced to face a vengeful enemy with a knife.

Hunter scrolled his eyes up and down the nearly nude bastard in front of him. "Boxers."

Masters shirt hung at his elbows. He glared, but he was smart enough to drag his shorts down, one side at a time. They gathered at his ankles.

"Kick 'em high," Hunter ordered.

"Shit." Masters kicked his underwear into the brush, biting his lip like the new guy on the cellblock. He was a pitiful sight, bloody-kneed, hairy-legged, and that big, wide yellow stripe running up his back and ending at his brown nose.

"Sit," Hunter growled. "Indian style."

"Shit," seemed to be the only word in Masters' vocabulary. Down he went, cross-legged on the insect-laden jungle floor. Sweat poured off his brow in tiny rivulets, and Hunter was glad for the added humidity of Amazon country. The feeling of suffocation added to the torture. And the fun.

He took one quick glance at the man's privates and grunted.

"Go to hell," Masters shot back.

Hunter leaned forward, his blade less than inches from the personal gear Masters might think twice about losing. He shifted backward, maybe realizing things were about to get worse.

Excellent.

"Let's try that last question again," Hunter purred. "Don't lie to me. Why's Burdette after Meredith Flynn? How does she fit in?"

A shudder rattled Masters right down to his hairy ass. He looked heavenward and blew out a huge breath. "I don't know. Burdette's been pushing us to find her, but he hasn't said why."

Hunter's blade left three sharp stiletto stabs up Masters' inner thigh. "I said don't lie!"

"Ouch! Damn it, stop!" Masters all but cried. "I told you everything I know."

Hunter doubted that. He grabbed his quarry by the neck and jerked him into his face. "I know damned well Burdette's after Flynn. What does Roger Teach have to do with her?"

"Why would I lie to cover for Burdette or Teach? They don't mean nothing to me."

"They meant enough that you tortured a man for them!"

Masters didn't break eye contact. "That's what they pay me for. Why do you do what you do?"

The damned man had nerve, but time had run out. Seth couldn't last much longer, not in the shape he was in. Hunter didn't have enough time to complete a more thorough *assessment*, or argue the difference between him and Masters.

"What's the lime-green crap in the hypos?"

Masters didn't blink once. "It's a designer drug, a combination knock-out, brainwashing mixture. The original plan was to hit hard, take you all down, and chemically brainwash you guys into believing you were the ones who'd killed McCormack's men. That was the only way Burdette thought Brinkman EX could get back in the DoD game. MI would take the hit and go down in flames. You guys would go to prison swearing you'd killed the MI team. Burdette would get what he wanted. End of story."

"Only you didn't expect Meredith Flynn would shoot one of your guys, did you?" Hunter couldn't resist the dig. A damned smart woman had fouled Burdette's subterfuge from the get-go. He couldn't help the swell of pride for his new, very sexy teammate.

Chagrin hung heavy on Masters' brow. "We didn't know we'd be up against Stewart's team, much less Annie Oakley, until we got here."

Hunter allowed a very small smile. As good as she was, Annie Oakley had lost her gun right out of the gate like a greenhorn. He pushed off the ground and knelt at Masters' side, the knife at the man's throat, ready to do the deed.

Masters tipped his head against the tree, glaring. "Death is all I expect from the likes of you. You're a killer, same as me. Just do it!"

Hunter wanted to. Masters knew it. He rolled his eyes, daring another Marine to take him on, but that seemed to be what Masters wanted—for Hunter to stoop to his level. To sink to the point of no return. Hunter had honestly thought he'd passed that point long ago, the point where a man was beyond salvageable or worthy of redemption or love. Lost forever.

Along came Meredith Flynn. She'd breathed life into his dark and ugly soul. She'd challenged him, made him remember how much love he'd once been capable of giving. How much tenderness. What light through yonder window breaks indeed. Her accusing question hung heavy in his mind. *'Are they dead, too?'*

Only his heart had heard, *'Are you dead?'*

For the first time in forever, he'd asked himself. *Is this all I'm capable of? Hunting assassins? Taking life?*

Honorable or not, Hunter found himself wanting to be the kid she remembered from a long time ago. He wanted to be more than just a damned good Marine.

Masters' carotid pulsed beneath the blade, full of fight or flight. And fear. With one deft nick, the world would be better off. Another mad dog would be put down to terrorize the innocent no more. Even now, Masters squeezed his eyes tight, trembling against the finely honed steel and expecting no mercy.

Only...

What would Meredith think?

Hunter stilled his blade. It quivered. It wanted to do its job, and he wanted to let it, but her sweet chastisement gave him pause. Was he no better than this despicable man whose life he now held in his own bloodstained hands? Worse, was Masters right? Was he, Hunter, cut from the exact same cloth? Was his soul as dark and lifeless, as unworthy of her?

Think. Alex Stewart's favorite damned word, now Hunter's conscience. *Think.*

A trickle of sweat beaded at his brow, perched, like him, to fall. This was one of those pivot points when a singular decision could determine the rest of his life. Why the prickly conscience now? Hunter knew the answer. *Meredith.*

He lashed out. One long fang-mark nicked Masters' leg from his bloodied shinbone to his pin-cushion kneecap. Masters whole body winced. He'd just taken one for his home team. The game was over.

Hunter leaned forward and wiped his blade on the shirt hanging from his victim's elbows. Master's winced then, too, but Hunter just did that to scare the guy. He rolled the cramp out of the back of his neck and pushed to his feet, then sheathed his blade.

"Bastard," Masters hissed.

Hunter gave him one last message. "Damn straight, and I'm proud of it. Now, go to hell." He punched Masters a hard one. Wouldn't Merry be surprised?

Rounding the tree, Hunter still had to answer to Seth.

"You end him?"

"No," he answered truthfully.

"Why not?" The recrimination in Seth's voice caught Hunter short.

"Because that's your job, buddy. The day will come. He's all yours."

Seth glared, but relented, the hint of betrayal in his eyes fading. "You bet your ass."

"Besides, you're a hundred times more important. Let's get you home."

It took Hunter fifty yards of carrying Seth before he paused to get a better grip on his buddy. Backing into the cover of vines and shadow, he stopped to catch his breath.

Seth leaned his face against him, his arms around his neck, barely holding on.

"Man, what's happening? Why'd we stop?"

"Shhhhh," Hunter cautioned. Now wasn't the time to speak. A group of ten or eleven men thundered down the path to the burned out TEAM camp.

Seth slumped weakly into his arms. "Let me down," he groaned. "I'm done, man. Let me die."

"Never," Hunter growled. He did what he should've done all along. Securing his rifle, he set Seth's feet to the ground long enough to hoist him over his shoulder like a brother. Burdett's men had better get out of their way.

CHAPTER EIGHTEEN

If anyone intended to shoot me, they'd have done it already, wouldn't they? Meredith rationalized on her way back to the cave. She still had that sneaky sensation someone was watching her, but she had yet to spy anything or anyone out of place. The birds still chattered like teenagers in the high school halls. Insects buzzed while frogs croaked and hummed. All of those creatures would grow silent if a predator was near, right?

She counted on it.

The first portion of the crossing was easy. Calm water pooled at her left. Her confidence soared. The challenge began at half-point where the river ran faster. Her boots were too large. They made walking on dry land an effort, but balancing on wet rocks with the current tugging at your soles? At this rate, she'd be doing the splits in the middle of the river. Not a pretty sight.

Stepping gingerly onto the first water covered rock, her right foot slid forward. She pressed the fruit against her chest to redistribute her load. Just as quickly, her left boot slid into the river. Hurriedly, she pulled it up and rocked backward, striving to keep her balance. One more wrong step, one more water-filled boot, and Hunter would never let her live it down.

This wasn't rocket science. How hard could it be to bring home the bacon, so to speak? Meredith turned cautiously, facing downstream and edging sideways. Step by step. Breath by breath. Flatter rocks were just a few feet away, some of them dry. She'd be home safe. Biting her lip, she picked up her speed. Her load shifted. Sticking her butt out, she ended up tilting her upper body forward. It was a struggle to keep those men's boots from slipping when—

SPLASH!

Downstream she tumbled, face-first with her mouth opened wide. The fruit went with her. Sputtering, she bobbed to the churning surface, flailing for anything solid to latch onto. A tree branch would've been nice. Her waterlogged boots pulled her down like concrete until her feet slipped out of them. Under she went, her good deed forgotten.

A powerful undertow dragged her under the lip of the rock edge she'd tumbled over. It was a fight to keep her face above water. She swallowed a quick mouthful of air, but down she went again. Her lungs clamped shut. *Courtney!*

Flashes of churning shadow and light fueled her panic. Every breathless kick took more effort. As hard as she tried to break the surface, the turbulence sucked her farther down.

Suddenly everything got worse. The icy-cold clench of a slithering tentacle circled her waist. *Snake!*

She screamed underwater, sucking in a lungful. The snake prowled overhead, reaching for her. Its fangs slithered over her shoulders and nipped at her neck. Shoving away from it, she flailed, but it was no use. The reptile bit into her hand and dragged her upward. How cruel!

Deprived of oxygen, nothing made sense. It must need her out of the water before it could eat her. Not happening!

She dug her fingernails into its hard skin, searching for its neck. She refused to be swallowed alive!

But damn it was a powerful beast, built of writhing muscle, and gripping the bones in her hand harder. Tighter. It dragged her upward, toward daylight. Meredith screamed one last bloodcurdling underwater protest as the mighty serpent slapped her on shore like a fish.

Landing facedown, her sodden hair hung like seaweed over her eyes, choking as the river spewed out of her burning lungs in wrenching gasps. The snake slithered alongside her legs, but she was afraid to look at it. Any second now it would strike and she would die.

But how odd. The darned thing felt—warm.

Strong hands flipped her onto her back. Two massive legs straddled her, and two very big paws took possession of her waterlogged breasts. She slapped at the beast when it squeezed her chest, needing to see what monster had hold of her, a snake or a gorilla.

"Breathe, Merry, damn it! Stop fighting me and breathe!"

Bleary-eyed, she ceased struggling. *Hunter?*

Meredith launched herself away from the river and under his chin. She sucked in an enormous gulp of air, and just as quickly, spat it in his face with a mighty, "Snake!"

Frantically, she brushed her wet hair out of her eyes, needing to see where that snake had gone. It was still out there. Coiled and waiting to strike. She was sure of it.

Hunter encased her inside the steel bands of his arms, his chin on the top of her head.

Scared, she tucked her feet under her legs. That snake was big enough it could get Hunter too.

"What the hell were you doing in the river? I told you to stay put." He didn't sound as angry as she'd expected, probably because her head kept knocking into his chin, making it hard for him to really chew her out.

She pulled herself into a ball until she was completely between his legs, not willing to offer any part of her extremities for that serpent's next meal. "F-f-food."

"Why were you on the other side of the river?"

"S-s-snake." She tried again. 'F-f-fruit. M-m-monkeys."

He stilled, and she could hear the thunder in his chest. Between her chattering teeth and his pounding heart, all they needed was a pair of steel drums and a steel guitar for an island beat that would've rocked the world.

Wait a minute. How'd he know I was on the other side of the river? "D-d-did you...? W-were you...?" She looked up at him, trying to form one coherent sentence. "You saw me?"

His brows slanted. "Yeah. After I got back with Seth. I took him inside, but you were gone. You scared the hell out of me, but there you were, playing in the river."

"I wasn't p-p-playing. I was d-d-drowning." She blinked the water dripping from her hair out of her eyes and lifted her hand to show him the fang marks. "And I saw a really big s-s-snake. Look. It tried to eat me."

"That wasn't a snake, Merry." Hunter tucked one hand under her thigh, pulling her close. "That was me. I kept reaching for you, but you fought me off until I had no choice but to dig into your hand to pull you out. My God, you're a hard woman to rescue."

She shook her head. He had it wrong. She knew what she'd felt, and it was long and slimy and cold and—it had latched onto her wrist and hand. Just like he'd said. And it was kind of hairy. She looked closer at her fingers. Her knuckles were bloodied and scraped. Not with fang holes, but with scratch marks. Blinking another trickle of water out of her eyes, she stopped shaking. "It was you?"

"I'm sorry if I scared you," he murmured into the top of her head. "Snakes don't like fast water. They don't frequent the rapids when they're hunting."

"Oh," was all she could say. This jungle had reduced her to a pitiful excuse for a female in one day. Raking her sodden locks out of her eyes again, she turned away from him, but he only clamped tighter and ordered her to, "Stay."

She stayed, not because he'd commanded her, but because she lacked the strength to stand. The river had taken everything—her resolve to be a good teammate and very nearly her life. Meredith leaned into Hunter's hard, muscled chest. The steady beat of his heart eased her panic, but just that fast the tears came. "I c-c-can't do this anymore. I'm not a-a-a soldier. I'm not a killer. It's all too hard."

"There now, you're safe." His lips kissed the top of her wet head while she clung to his forearm.

"I want to go home," she sniffled.

"Whatever am I going to do with you?" His hand smoothed a comforting trail over her head before it cupped her shoulder. "One minute you're brave and courageous, but the next you're fragile and sweet. How can a guy like me keep up with a woman like you?"

She had no answer, so she sat there and shivered within the warm barricade of his knees, legs and arms. The devious river murmured behind her. It couldn't be trusted. The jungle either. Only Hunter Christian was safe.

CHAPTER NINETEEN

He couldn't let go of Meredith for the life of him. Not when he'd come so close to losing her. Damned woman. Every smart cell in his brain screamed at him to keep his distance and protect his heart, but he couldn't, not with her quivering and crying the way she was.

Soon the spell would be broken, and they'd have to seek cover, but for this one splinter of stolen time, he actually knew what he wanted. There was no confusion in his heart. Only Merry.

He'd dragged her to the sandy side of the river, and there they sat, the cave within reach. As frightened as she was, she evoked that familiar storm of protective emotions. This woman commanded the alpha warrior in him, and she didn't even know it.

Hunter hungered for her, but married women were off his menu. Hell, all women were. He hadn't cared for a particular one in years, and yet—he had. He'd just stopped looking for someone better. Why pretend to be a vegetarian when he'd already tasted the most succulent prime rib? Why settle for less?

And yet he had settled. Too much always stood in his way—her husband for one. But Welch wasn't there. Hunter Christian was.

They sat curled together in a single beam of warm sunlight breaking through the immense emerald canopy overhead. With the mountain at his back, he felt some measure of safety. The tender feel of her body in his arms calmed the rampage in his heart. Like the magic of the moment, it wouldn't last, but for now, Welch, Masters, Teach, and Brinkman EX ceased to exist.

Even if he never told Meredith, Hunter was glad he'd let Masters live. He'd done that one thing in her honor. She sagged into him, limp and relaxed and calm, but holding on tightly. That was all he'd wanted, just once—for her to need him as much as he needed her.

A piece of her lost fruit bobbed in a small eddy offshore. "What kind of fruit were you going to feed me this time?" he asked playfully.

"I don't know," she said softly, pointing to the opposite shoreline. "A flock of monkeys was over there in that big fruit tree. See the one with flowers? I figured if they could eat that fruit, so could we. Only I fell and... it's all gone."

"Makes sense," he agreed, "but I don't think monkeys flock."

She sniffed. "It looked like they flocked to me. They swooped down from the trees. I watched them a long time, and then they just kind of flew away."

Hunter grunted, still holding her, the one thing he seemed to be good at. Meredith sounded dazed, and it was no wonder. The river could've swept her away, and he wouldn't have known where she'd gone. As it was, he must have walked past where she'd been struggling in the foamy undertow. The black clothes he'd badgered her into wearing had worked against her. He hadn't even seen her there. The thought scared the hell out of him.

She fit inside the contour of his body, between his legs, and snuggled up to his heart. He didn't want to move, but they'd been out in the open too long. After the confrontation with Burdette's men, he couldn't take the chance. He waited until she breathed easier, not quite ready to end the magic, but keeping a close watch on the shoreline.

"All I could think of was him," she muttered tiredly.

That did it. Magic time vanished with those seven blasted words out of her mouth, and Hunter was done being stupid. Holding her didn't mean squat if all she could think of was her jerk husband. Hunter loosened his grip, untangling her from his arms. "Let's move."

"What's wrong?" Hurt trembled through her voice.

Did he have to spell it out? He shoved off the muddy ground and away. "Damn it, now I'm as wet as you are."

"Sorry," she whimpered, looking around as if she'd lost something and swaying like she might go down again. She might as well have been topless. He caught everything beneath her shirt, looking down at her like he had a choice. Those damn blue eyes filled with exhaustion, and right past them, the tempting swell of perfect breasts rose with every gasp. Nipples peaked to perfection from the chill baited him to touch and taste.

"What's wrong now?" he barked, his hand extended to keep her upright.

"Nothing." She scanned the river, eyeing that one piece of fruit bobbing near shore. "I just thought... I mean... I don't have anything for dinner, and I... I really thought..."

Fighting the tug at his heart, he cupped Meredith's elbow to steady her, fully aware they needed to get undercover. She might be dazed and confused, but she wasn't hurt like Seth. She'd live to go home to—*him.*

"You ready?" he growled.

She nodded, but her knees buckled, and the next thing he knew, she'd latched onto the waistband of his pants with one hand, clinging for support. Meredith looked like a drowned rat, her hair hanging down her back. The joyride over the rapids had knocked her around a bit. Dark bruises marked her arms and legs. Somewhere along the line, she'd bumped her forehead. A goose egg rose out of the purpling knot over her right brow.

"You don't understand," she whined. "He's all I've got, Hunter."

Argh! I don't want to hear this!

That was the problem. He did understand, and it was ripping his heart out. Like every other time he'd thought of Welch with Meredith, Hunter lost his grip and his patience. She had to be the only person on the planet who liked the jerk. He tugged her along. "Try and stay upright this time."

"'Kay," she said softly, shuffling behind him, still holding onto his waist.

His sniper sense was on high alert, the same as every other throbbing part of his body. There was no getting near Meredith without going up in flames. Molten lava coursed through his veins, most of it pooled low and wickedly hot.

She's married, you moron. Knock it off.

He scanned the opposite shore as they edged toward cover. The minute she stepped one bare foot onto the slippery rocks that lay between them and the cave, he knew he was in trouble. Meredith let go of him. She was afraid to fall, holding herself stiffly and awkwardly. This wasn't part of the natural dam across the river, just a rocky stream fed by the waterfall overhead. If she wasn't careful, it could push her back into the river.

"Loosen up," he encouraged, his hand outstretched for her to grab onto. "It's not deep. Keep moving."

"Uh-huh," she said, her eyes on her feet and the gentle current swirling around her. Her voice turned tight and whiny.

"Meredith." He snapped his fingers, urging her to take hold. "Grab on. I won't let you fall."

Her gaze lifted, stabbing him with the tenderest, helpless blue eyes. He froze in the act of grumbling. He knew what he'd said, but now he wondered what she'd heard.

I won't let you fall...

But he had, hadn't he? He'd left her behind in a fit of adolescent temper after he'd found out she was pregnant. Had that one rash decision of his brought them to this point in time where they both stood the chance of being murdered?

"Kay," she whispered, interlocking her icy-cold fingers with his. The simple action felt like so much more. Shaky and uncertain, each time she teetered too far forward or to the side, he stiffened his elbow to balance her. Her fear had turned this calm portion of the river into a marathon.

"You good?" he asked at the halfway point.

"Uh-huh. It's just that you'd never understand. I really miss him."

Hunter counted to ten.

"And I've been away so long."

Then twenty. *Great. She's gonna start crying again.*

"And everything's gone wrong since I got here," she all but wailed, working herself into a crying jag for sure.

He counted to thirty and rolled the pain in his neck away.

"You don't understand. You don't have kids. He needs his mom. I can't die. You have to help me make it home alive."

Hunter stopped cold. How hard had she banged that empty head of hers? "What the hell are you talking about?"

Another drawn-out whine, and damned if she wasn't bawling her eyes out. Hunter gave up counting. It wasn't working for him.

"C-C-Courtney," she finally spat out, wiping her nose with the back of her hand, tears running down her face. "I wanna go h-h-home!"

There was no way they were going anywhere at this rate. She couldn't see to walk. Hunter took two impatient steps back to her, and, in one fell swoop, he scooped her into his arms and against his chest. Her arm curled around his neck and her ear landed over his heart. She was drenched and breathing hard, but damn it. They were going to stand there until he knew what she was talking about. "Who the hell's Courtney?"

The saddest blues stabbed straight to his stubborn heart. Her fingers squeezed the back of his neck like he was her lifeline. "Courtney's my son, Hunter. He's all I've got in the world. I need to live. For him. Please don't drop me." A shudder heaved through her body. "D-d-don't let me die out here. I have to make it home alive."

She's got a kid? A son? Courtney? Why's he the only one she's got to live for? Where the hell's Welch?

Wham! Bright, flashing neon numbers finally lit up inside his hard USMC head. Red neon. The kind that said, 'Listen up.' Maybe he didn't have her figured out. Maybe he never had. Swallowing hard, he begged to hear it again. "You... you have a son? Courtney, is it?"

Her head bobbed under his chin. "Y-y-yes-s-s. He's three. Oh, I wish I'd never come on this stupid beta test. Everything's gone wrong, and..." She set to hiccupping and sobbing, and what could he do? He'd already turned to humble pie.

Hunter held her close. He'd been wrong all along, but not only wrong. No. He'd been a flaming ass, needling her at every misstep, never giving her a break. Worse, never listening. Never once asking for her side of the story. He'd jumped to a hasty conclusion, marched off to war like a noble asshole, joined the Corps, and...

Oh hell. That was why she'd married Welch. She had a kid with him, but Hunter didn't get the sense that Welch was still in the picture.

"Merry." His heart beat louder than the rushing water around them. "Why's your last name still Flynn?"

She tilted her face upward, her lips so close he could already taste them. "I tried to tell you before. Eddy didn't want Courtney—or me. I've been divorced for years. I took my maiden name back, and I... and I just want to go home!"

"But Courtney's three?" That was nearly the same amount of time he'd spent in the Corps. Hunter's stomach dropped to his boots. What if she'd been alone all this time instead of carousing with Welch like Hunter had thought? What if—*oh, God, I am so dumb*—what if all the men in her life deserted her when she'd needed them most?

"Yes, he's three." She tipped her head back and wailed, "Eddy Welch is the biggest jerk on the planet!"

Despite the saddest, most adorable woman in his arms, Hunter tipped his face to the azure sky above, angry with himself. Welch wasn't the biggest jerk on the whole planet.

He was.

CHAPTER TWENTY

"W-what now?" Seth asked, his teeth chattering nearly as much as Meredith's.

Finally under cover again, she'd remembered that Hunter said he'd located one of his men, but poor Seth. He'd been sorely treated. The man needed stitches on his arms and legs, and she was scared. Still shivering from her near miss with the river, she was cold and wet, but he was in worse shape. Blood seeped from some of the cuts on his arms and legs. Others were dried and crusted. Some looked fiery red and infected. She sniffed one last time and forgot her problems. Seth needed her.

"I need to remove Teague's bullet first," Hunter stated, as if he did that kind of surgery every day. "But I have to go back and get the supplies."

Oh, that. Meredith cringed. It was no wonder he'd distanced himself the moment they entered the cave, crouching between Seth and Teague. She'd caused Hunter nothing but grief and extra work.

He'd fashioned a dry bed for Seth, but Hunter could only get so far from her. The problem with the cave was the low ceiling, not to mention the limited space. "When I get back, we'll operate on Teague and treat Seth. Are you up to helping me?"

"You bet," Meredith answered, kneeling by Seth, determined to be strong. If Hunter wanted to play doctor, she was ready to assist. That thought raised another scenario in her mind, but she pushed the sexual innuendo away. Despite his current good behavior, anything intimate between her and this ex-soldier was so not going to happen. Facing death had a way of defining a woman's priorities. All she wanted was to get home to Courtney. Besides, Hunter seemed unwilling to look her in the eye. He'd made it clear for days. She needed to back off. "What do you want me to do while you're gone?"

He tossed her a bundle of the clothes from Teague's litter. "Cover Seth. It's chilly and damp in here. I'll get some firewood before I leave. These men need to be kept warm."

She bobbed her head. The bloody clothes didn't bother her anymore. When Hunter stepped outside, Meredith unbuckled the belt holding the bundle together and shook out the clothing. Carefully, she laid the largest shirt over Seth.

He shivered, but politely ducked his head. "Thank you, ma'am."

"Are you thirsty? I've got a couple bottled waters left."

"Yes, please." He looked frail, his fingers clamped onto the thin material under his chin and shivering like he was. Without asking, she unscrewed the cap on the bottle and pressed it to his mouth. Seth swallowed noisily, licking his lips when he was done. "I never knew water could taste so good."

"I wish I had something for you to eat, but I don't." She wanted to tell him how she'd nearly died in the river, but her troubles seemed insignificant.

"I'm back," Hunter said softly at the cave entrance, his voice barely audible over the crashing falls. He'd brought an armful of dry branches. The cave didn't seem so glum once he sparked a small fire near the wall opposite Seth and Teague.

He knelt alongside his friend while Meredith shivered alone. Her shirt still dripped. So did her hair, but she was just wet and a little bruised. Seth was badly hurt.

"How are you feeling?" Hunter asked, dragging the backs of his fingers across his buddy's cheek. "I'm not detecting a fever."

"I'm good," Seth answered, despite his many knife wounds. "You got an extra gun on you?"

"Let's get you into a better bed first."

Meredith scrambled to fashion a thicker mattress out of the spare clothing.

"Thanks," Seth murmured as Hunter eased him onto the dirty but dry padding.

Hunter reached into one of his cargo pants pockets and pulled out a gun and a handful of bullets. Wrapping Seth's shaky hands around the grip, he placed the rounds on the ground where Seth could easily reach them. "There. Now you're armed. Do me a favor, though. Don't kill anyone 'til I get back. You might wake Teague."

"Sure, Hunt," Seth said, his teeth chattering. "Th-thanks."

"No problem. I've built a handy arsenal with all these bastards I keep running into." Hunter scanned Teague's sleeping face to the other side of him before he pushed up from the ground. "And you," he said sternly, his eyes finally locked on Meredith. "What am I going to do with you? You're still soaking wet."

She wilted beneath his direct scrutiny. Why did she feel like she was twelve-years-old and disobedient? Her hand went automatically to her hair, twirling a wet lock between her index finger and thumb. Mean Girl had no clever comeback. She must've gotten washed downriver with that invisible snake.

"You need a dry shirt. Find something to wear." He motioned to the other bundles tucked in alongside Teague.

"I will," she agreed, an odd tone of obedience in her voice. He was right. She needed to change. She'd caused nothing but trouble, and right then, he was sounding all authoritarian and bossy, like he was in charge. Like yesterday when they'd camped. Like just before she'd kissed him.

"Can you keep these guys company while I go back for the supplies?"

Meredith touched her fingertips to her lips, her feet shifting and one ankle stroking the back of her leg. She looked from Teague to Seth because it was safer than looking at Hunter. "Sure."

"And stay out of the water," he added. "By the way, do you know Roger Teach?"

She glanced up at that question. "No. Should I?"

"Just checking. He's McCormack's competition, some corporate raider and the guy funding these assassins."

"Hmmm." Meredith paused to think. Jed McCormack always had stiff competition. "I don't know anyone named Roger. I'm sorry."

A hint of a smile tugged at Hunter's stern lips. "But you do remember our code, don't you?" he asked more gently, testing her once again.

She paused. So much had happened during the last twenty-four hours. She raked a hand over her forehead, pushing her wet hair out of her face. "Hotel Charlie is you.

That's what you'll say, I mean, and I'll answer with Mike Foxtrot. My initials."

He offered a genuine smile and Meredith wanted to stand there and bask in the sight. It felt like the sun had just broken through a very dark storm cloud. Hunter Christian, the handsome kid she used to know in college was back in the house. Look at him. The elusive dimple she loved shadowed his left cheek. *That* dimple. The one he used to offer willingly instead of rarely. He almost looked like himself again.

"Catch you in a few, Mike," he said almost coyly. "Stay out of the water."

"Bye Hotel Charlie," she whispered, wishing he'd stay.

The cave seemed chillier after he left, but Meredith had no time to feel sorry for herself.

"I've been worried about you," Seth murmured. "Sure glad you and Hunter survived. Looks like you've been busy."

She tucked a couple more shirts around Seth, hoping to stop his tremors. "It's more like Hunter's been busy. I'm afraid I've caused nothing but trouble this afternoon. How did you escape?"

"Good old Hunt showed up like he always does. The guy's got a nose for trouble. Masters was gonna kill me, but the next thing I knew, Hunt was standing there like John Wayne coming to my rescue, like everyone better git out of his way. The next thing I knew, that Masters jerk-off—ahh, I'm sorry ma'am. I meant that butt-hole..." Seth looked up at the ceiling, his eyes brimmed and shiny. "Sorry, ma'am. I can't speak kindly of the man who was cutting on me. I just can't."

One tear trickled down the side of his head into his ear, and Meredith wanted to cry right along with him. She crouched at his side. "It's okay, Seth. I've known a few buttheads in my life and a couple assholes, too. What did Hunter do next? Tell me about it. I want to hear everything."

Seth swallowed hard. "I ain't never been tortured before. The Army tells you what to do in case it happens, but..." He bit his lip, blinking the moisture out of his dark eyes.

"Seth," she whispered, smoothing her fingers over his brow. "You're not there anymore. You're here with Teague and me. You're armed, and I'm going to do everything I can to take care of you. Can you keep a secret?"

He blinked and wiped his face with the back of a shaky hand, finally meeting her eyes. "Sure."

"I lost my gun," she whispered, glancing over her shoulder as if Hunter might be listening. "I was in the shower at camp when I heard the first gunshots, but with Teague hurt and Hunter showing up and all the crazy racket, I set my pistol down. I guess I just forgot to pick it up again. Hunter's been mad at me ever since."

Seth frowned. "You lost your gun? Oh, man. That's bad."

She frowned in mock dismay. "Hey. You're supposed to encourage me. I'm not a soldier, remember? I'm an amateur at all this combat stuff. I got frazzled when we retreated, and it—" She shrugged, "—just happened."

A small smile tugged at his tired mouth even as he scrunched his nose. "But you lost your gun."

She rolled her eyes as dramatically as she could. "You're as bad as Hunter. I'm never telling you anything again."

He coughed a quiet, little snickering kind of a cough. "You see, ma'am, losing a weapon is a big deal in the military. A guy or gal in a combat zone would get an Article 15. That means they'd lose a few grades, at least half their pay for a couple months, and they'd get sixty days' restriction and extra-duty. That's only if the top brass decided they liked 'em enough to keep 'em. Or they might send 'em packing to teach 'em a lesson. Didn't you have a holster or anything for your weapon?"

She did a Vanna White maneuver, gesturing with her hands down over her soggy shirt and bare legs. "What you see is what you get, buddy. I was in the shower, remember? I was lucky to get out with my underwear. Hunter made me wear one of the guy's shirts and a pair of boots that he, umm, acquisitioned along the way, but..." She cringed. "I lost the boots in the river, and I can't bring myself to put on a pair of those dead guys' pants."

Seth smiled the most endearing smile, his eyes scrolling over her wet shirt. "Sweet."

She punched his bicep very gently. "I was right. You're as bad as Hunter."

"Hey. Still alive here," he reminded her. "Not dead yet."

"Well, maybe I'd better cover up then." She looked to the dry shirt she'd set aside for herself. "Do you promise not to look?"

"Scout's honor," Seth declared hoarsely.

She pivoted on her heel. "I doubt that."

He shrugged. "A guy's always gonna look. But if you're worried, step around above me where I can't see you. I don't think Teague can neither."

Teague was still out cold by the looks of him. Stalking back over to the pile of clothing, she selected the smallest pair of trousers she could find. A scrap of paper caught her eye. Tucked in between Teague's litter and the bundle of clothes she'd been going through, it was facedown. Lifting it off the damp floor, her heart jumped. The photo was her high school graduation picture. What on earth was it doing there?

Rubbing the dirt off of it, she read what she'd written that crazy day when she'd found out she and Hunter were both going to the same college. *Someday we're going to be famous! Love you, Hunter Christian! Your best girl, Merry!*

Ah, the overpowering need to end every thought and sentence with an exclamation point back then. The wide-eyed innocence of high school graduates who thought they knew it all. The gullibility of youth...

But why was her photo in this cave of all places? Hunter must've dropped it, but that begged the question—why? Was he cleaning out his wallet? Had he thrown it away? Was he looking at it again after all these years? The thought that he might have been doing just that, touched her. She secreted it in the pocket of the trousers she planned to wear.

Meredith made quick work of shrugging out of the waterlogged shirt and into another smellier, but drier one. Buttoned up into the trousers with her borrowed belt pulled tight and feeling a lot warmer, she sat cross-legged with Seth again. The dirty clothes might not fit or look good, but being covered went a long way toward feeling better. Darn it. Hunter had been right about that, too.

Seth latched onto her hand. "Where's everyone else?"

"I hate to tell you, but Lyle and Dan were murdered last night. We still don't know where Eric and Ky are," she said somberly, not wanting to tell him about the body dump. "Tell me how you got caught."

He gulped. "Me and Ky were headed back to camp. He had his flashlight and was maybe four steps ahead of me. All of a sudden, two guys jumped us. We never saw 'em coming.

Before we could get our guns up, we were out cold. Least, I was. I woke up strapped to one of them metal tables like you see in operating rooms. Then they started cutting on me..."

She squeezed his hand tighter. "Why? What did they want?"

"You. They kept asking me where you were hiding, and what you knew about the ACS, and where you lived back in the States. Honest, ma'am, I tried real hard not to tell 'em anything, but they kept asking and cutting, so I... I..." He sucked in a shuddering breath. "I'm sorry. I told 'em everything I knew."

"But Seth." Meredith placed her other hand on his forearm. "There's nothing to tell. It's not like I'm a spy or anyone important. I don't know anything that isn't already public knowledge."

He swallowed hard. "I told 'em you're as pretty as my old girlfriend, that you're the gal running the beta test, that you work for MI. That Jed McCormack must like you a lot if he sent you all the way down. That... that..."

"It's okay," she soothed. "My friends already know that. I'm nothing special."

He gulped. "Didn't matter what I said anyway. It's like they didn't believe me. Like they figured I was smarter than I am. Then they taped my mouth shut."

"Oh, my God, why?" Meredith shivered at that revelation.

"Guess they didn't want me to make any noise."

"Do you know what happened to Ky? Was he tortured, too?"

"I never did hear him. Course, I was making a lot of noise all by myself til they, you know."

Meredith changed the subject. She couldn't see Hunter leaving a man behind. If Ky had been in that camp with Seth, Hunter would've rescued him, too. "Listen. We're both safe now. When Hunter gets back, we'll get you cleaned up and bandaged. There are antibiotics in the medical kit—some painkillers, too. I'll fix something for you to eat. I noticed you have a tattoo."

"Ma'am?"

She nodded toward Seth's bicep. She'd seen the heart and the single word in the center of it. *Mom.* Two raw knife slashes defaced it, but the message was clear. Seth loved his mother.

"Oh, yeah. All the guys were getting 'em," he explained, "so I figured, why not? I know it's cliché, but I don't care. Mom had a nasty bout with cancer when I first joined the Army. I felt bad being so far away while she was going through chemo and radiation and all that crap, so I put her in my heart. As sappy as it sounds, this tat helped us both get through it. Mom knew she was always in my heart, and having her name on my arm seemed like she was with me no matter where I went."

"So she recovered?"

"Yes, ma'am. She did." Seth brightened despite the shivers. "Mom's got more energy now than ever before. You should see her go."

"What kind of cancer?"

"Melanoma. She loved working in her garden all summer long without a hat. Now she knows better. Sometimes we've got to learn the hard way, huh?"

Meredith nodded. Experience had certainly been the only teacher she'd listened to. "Hunter is covered with tats. What's the one on his back about?" She didn't mean to talk about him behind his back. Well, maybe she did. Just a little. This wasn't gossip. This was intelligence gathering among friends.

"You mean that big old boot print? Ahh..." Seth's eyes clouded. "That's a tough one. The next time he's got his shirt off, read what's written between the tread marks. You'll see."

The thought of Hunter's handsome bare back brought a needy ache to the pit of her stomach. She changed the subject again. "Where are you from, Seth?"

"Chicago. How about you?" His grip hadn't loosened, but he seemed calmer the more they talked.

"I'm one of those California girls," she admitted.

"Ah, that explains it then."

"Explains what?"

"Hunt. He's from California, too. You two knew each other before, didn't you?"

"Why would you think that?"

"The way he was staring at you after the paintball game. He had that look in his eye."

"He had a look?" she asked, secretly delighted. "What look?"

Seth shrugged. "Not sure how to explain it. Kinda like he was glad to see you only he didn't want you to know he was glad, only he couldn't take his eyes off of you, neither."

A wave of wiggling warmth swept up Meredith's insides. *Oh. That look.* "You're right. Hunter and I grew up in the same neighborhood outside of San Diego. We went to the same schools. Even went to college together for a little while."

"He cares for you, you know."

That took Meredith by surprise again. She looked away, wishing it were so. "I doubt it. If anything, I'm more of an inconvenience to him. We don't seem to do anything but fight when we're together." *And kiss. And push each other's buttons. And get all worked up only to be rejected.*

Seth squeezed her hand. "Nah, I can tell. He's one of the toughest guys I've ever met, but he gets a funny look when you're around. I seen it just before he left to get the supplies. Trust me. He cares."

She laughed it off. "Probably because he's counting the minutes until this operation is over, and I'm out of his life for good. You're seeing things." Meredith withdrew her hand from Seth's. "You need to rest while I check on Teague. He's been awfully quiet."

Seth pulled the skimpy shirt up to his chin. "Just give Hunt a chance, will you, ma'am? If he's as mixed up as I was when I came home, he doesn't know what he wants yet. And he's mad."

"Hunter's always mad," she agreed. "Explain that to me."

"It's just the way it is," Seth said quietly. "Not sure 'bout Hunt, but every time I killed someone, it kinda felt like I was losing a piece of my soul. Like the sun wasn't shining so bright anymore. Like I was never gonna be happy again, you know? Kinda like when I found out there wasn't a Santa Claus. It sucked."

That tender image of little-boy Seth helped. "You're one of the good guys. Get some rest." She lifted her backside off the ground, thankful for the diversion.

"So's Hunt," Seth answered. "Just cut him some slack. He's been in some awful tight spots."

Meredith wanted more details about those other tight spots, but saved questioning Seth for another day. Talking about Hunter had reopened the painful past. She should've never married Eddy. It was a mistake from the start to sacrifice her heart. That fatal error had sucked the joy out of her life. Eddy never wanted a son. He was a trophy hunter and she'd blown the trophy wife image the day she told him she was keeping her baby.

If she'd been smart, she would've told Hunter she was pregnant as soon as she knew. Yes, he would've been angry and yes, there would've been hurt feelings, but there was no doubt in her heart that he loved her. Hunter wasn't as mad as he was hurt. He would've eventually listened—then.

Hunter was not an indecisive man. He wielded confidence like a deadly weapon, but the look on his face when he'd asked how old Courtney was? That look was a cross somewhere between a goldfish gasping for air and the cat that ate the canary. *Priceless.*

She could've sworn she'd heard the gears in his brain spinning as he did the math, and hopefully, came up with the correct conclusion this time. The dumbass thought she'd loved Eddy? Heavens no! There'd only been that one night between them, and she preferred to forget it. The creep hadn't even touched her on their wedding night. He'd been too drunk. Every day after was just another exclamation point to her very foolish mistake.

Meredith's chin stuck out. It was time to clear the air and tell Hunter everything, because—she loved him. She always had, darn it.

Teague's eyes were opened when she shifted to his side. "You're awake," she said, her hand to his brow to check for a fever.

A bemused smile tugged at the corner of his mouth. "Where are we?"

"Safe for now. Hunter found a hollowed out space behind a waterfall. He's gone to get the supply crate. He'll be back soon."

"You two managed to bring a crate of supplies with you? MI or TEAM?"

"Yes, one of the MI crates and we've got a couple first-aids kits, too."

"Thank God." Teague arched his back. "Seth is right you know. I saw Hunter after the war games. He was definitely keeping an eye on you."

"Was that right before he walked out and went back to his camp?" These guys needed to knock it off. Ganging up on her didn't help keep her mind off Hunter.

The glimmer of a shadow at the waterfall caught her attention. Her first thought was it might have been caused by a cloud passing in front of the sun, or maybe Hunter. Her second thought was there was no way he could've made it back that fast. Dread's icy fingers clutched her throat. Something was out there. Man or monkey or—snake?

"He tends to go off by himself when he's had enough bullshit," Seth said. "Hunt's a loner. Always has been."

"Why's that?" she asked to keep the conversation going in case that glimmer was her imagination. Neither Teague nor Seth appeared to have seen anything out of the ordinary. Not wanting to be the hysterical damsel in distress again, she moved to Hunter's gear bag, still open at the foot of Teague's litter. Seth had a gun. She wanted one now too.

"Soldiering," Seth replied. "A guy who's been in combat tends to spend a lot more time by himself. Just the nature of men, I guess. We've all got things to think about. You ever served, Teague?"

There it was again, nothing more than the hint of a shadow. A ripple in the watery curtain. Casually, Meredith selected a revolver like the one Hunter had given Seth, then shifted it behind her back.

"Sure did," Teague muttered. "Air Force. Ended up in Pakistan."

She backed up, filled with a need to check the chamber on her piece, but not wanting the men to notice.

"Air Force, huh?" Seth said. "I figured you for a Navy man."

The air inside the small cave seemed more crowded. Fuller. Another ripple in the waterfall looked as if an invisible hand had parted the liquid curtain. Where was Hunter when she needed him?

"You wouldn't happen to have some water around here, would you?" Teague asked.

Her eyes were glued to the entrance instead of her patients, but no slinking reptilian form slithered toward her. None dropped from the ceiling either, but she couldn't shake the sensation that she and the guys were no longer alone.

Panic whispered, *'S-s-s-s-s-s-n-a-k-e.'* Mind-numbing shivers confirmed it. Paranoid or not, Meredith raised her weapon.

There it was again!

"Hey, what's going on?" Teague lifted up onto one elbow, grimacing. "Why the gun?"

She jumped at his question. "Because something is out there and it might be a—"

"Damn, you're good." Eric's mellow voice filled the hide-away as he materialized right before her eyes, panel by blinking ACS panel. *Darn him!*

"Eric! You scared me! I could've shot you!" By then her heart was pounding hard enough to beat the band, and her butt was stuck in the farthest corner of the cave.

"Hey, man," Seth muttered like it was no big deal. "Where you been?"

Eric was a sight for sore eyes, as dashing as ever. Meredith scrambled to him. "You're alive?"

He held his hands out for her, and that was all it took. She didn't hesitate before she was in his arms and hanging on tight.

"There, there," he murmured as he turned her around. "It's been a tough couple days, huh?"

Want to or not, tears brimmed her eyes. "I thought you were dead."

His hand caressed her wet hair before it came to rest on the back of her neck. "You sure know how to throw one helluva beta test, Mrs. Flynn."

CHAPTER TWENTY-ONE

Just damned great.

Hunter took one step inside the hide-away only to catch Meredith in the act again. She looked damned cozy in Eric's arms. Didn't it figure? He'd turned his back to secure the supplies, and she'd already moved on. Hunter bit his lip, angry enough to knock Eric on his ass even though he was damned glad to see the guy.

Hunter shot him a nod and a curt, "Where the hell have you been?"

"Hey, Hunt," Seth muttered. "Glad you made it—"

"Hunter!" Meredith dropped Eric like a hot potato and barreled into Hunter, surprising him. "I thought I saw another snake, only it was Eric, and…" She lifted that pretty face, and right there in front of God and all the guys, she planted the biggest, wettest kiss on his lips.

Who the hell was Eric anyway? Seth or Teague for that matter? They faded clear away. All Hunter heard after Meredith got in his face was a couple of guys muttering somewhere in the ozone. Sounded like they were on Mars.

Suffering from a sudden attack of sensory overload, he could barely handle the delightful taste of this woman's sweet mouth on his, her hands threading through his hair. Damn, she could kiss.

Warm caramel oozed into his veins, soothing all of his ragged edges, filling the cracks in his soul, healing him from the inside out. Fire roared over him, scorching his doubts and negativity away. Grabbing her into his arms, he took charge, lifting her off her feet, and this woman gave as good as she got. She growled for more, groaned for more, and his hands found her backside.

"Ahem." Big-mouthed Eric's caution only seemed to make Meredith pushier, but Hunter was happy to comply with her demands instead of Eric's hint. TEAM business could take a break.

At last, he eased away from her very determined mouth. "Merry. I mean, Ms. Flynn. Oh hell, Meredith."

Eric chuckled. "Do you two need a time-out?"

"Or a room?" Even injured Teague had to offer up his two cents worth.

When Seth murmured, "Sweet," Hunter angled past Eric, headed to his gear bag. He didn't need a damned audience. "Here," he growled, tossing Meredith the matching holster to that weapon in her hand. "Don't lose it this time."

She caught the holster, smiling.

Latching onto her wrist, he dragged her outside where she immediately got wet again. He hoped. As hard as he was, he wanted her wet and ready. They needed time alone and privacy for what he had in mind. *If only.*

He scanned the riverbanks while she secured her holster and weapon. She was no more than buckled up when he turned her roughly into his arms and kissed her again. But one kiss wasn't enough, and they were too exposed. He dragged her into the first available curtain of vines.

"What is it with you?" He had to ask. This wasn't the same woman he'd left a couple hours ago.

"You love me. I know you do," she said. "Go ahead. Deny it."

He gulped. *Damn. She's had too much time to think.*

"You thought I was still married. You thought I was cheating on Eddy the way you thought I cheated on you, didn't you? That's why you've been angry with me, isn't it?"

But you did cheat on me. His gaze hit the bottom of her chin. Now was not the time for true confessions. She'd had her chance, well, maybe not. He *had* left town after that slap in the face of finding out she was pregnant. What difference would rehashing the past make now? He didn't want to know how much she'd loved Welch.

She kept going, her chin lift a definite come-on. "Let me tell you something, Mr. Hunter Christian. I didn't cheat on you. Well, technically I did, but not like you think. I made a stupid mistake, and trust me, I've been paying for it ever since. I never should've married Eddy. Heck, I never should've given him the time of day. I know that now, but you need to understand why I did what I did."

She took a deep breath. "Remember the big beach party dance after SDSU won state? The one at Eddy's parents' beach place? All of us cheerleaders were still underage and drinking. I had too much. I admit it. I was excited, but everyone kept congratulating me and Eddy for being *brilliant*—" She curled air quotes beside her bobbing head, "—and you know how he was."

Meredith bit her lip, her thumbs under his chin now. "He was the star quarterback and I was star-struck and naïve and stupid and, oh God, I was an easy target, Hunter. I'm not saying it was just his fault, because it wasn't. The bottom line is I got pregnant that night, Hunter. I thought I should give him a chance because he was the father. I really thought he loved me. How could I tell you what I'd done?"

Damn, I need a smoke. Hunter took a full step back from her, needing distance. His head reeled at the much-romanticized dichotomy of a good girl with a bad boy. The last thing he wanted to hear about was her good times with a prick like Fast Eddy.

"Oh, no, you don't." She took a step forward, her fingers interlocked with the collar on his shirt. "You don't get to keep running. Not anymore, Hunter. That was why you joined the Marines, wasn't it? Because of me? Because of what I did to us?"

Well—yeah. He couldn't bring himself to admit what a fool he'd been back then—yes, for her. What a fool he still was. Knowing she'd divorced Welch soon after she'd married him didn't help. It only added further verification. Welch was her first time and they had a kid together. And a kid was a forever kind of a deal. Mother's didn't divorce them, and that made everything more—complicated. What if Courtney looked like his father?

Not that it really mattered. Hunter dragged a hand over his head. No innocent little kid should be held responsible for his old man's transgression.

"I cheated on you, Hunter, and I'm sorry." Tears brimmed her sad blue eyes. "It was stupid and wrong, but I can't change what happened. Courtney is Eddy's son."

Hunter swallowed past the hard knot in his throat. Felt like a steaming pile of camel shit.

She stuck her chin at him. "You've been mad at me since then, and I don't blame you. I tried to love Eddy, but I never did. I couldn't. There was only one man for me, only he left before I had a chance to explain what happened. So you've got two choices. You can tell me you love me or..." She bit her lip. "You can leave me again."

Hunter turned his back on her. He had to. Meredith made this course correction sound easy, but he'd had more than three years of what he'd truly believed was betrayal under his belt. Hell, her deceit was the foundation of the badass he was today. The anger and resentment from what he'd thought happened between Meredith and Welch had fueled his adrenaline before going into combat and firefights. He'd only been able to take those first kill shots because every insurgent he'd lined up in his crosshairs had morphed into Welch. How many times had he imagined killing the guy with his bare hands?

A shudder answered that unspoken question.

But now wasn't the time for relationship counseling or whatever Meredith thought she was doing. Hunter had wounded men to consider and a blown operation that had gone damned ugly. Armed assassins were hunting him and her. He needed to get Meredith back inside and let bygones be—

Damn. Her warm body melted against his back—the lowest blow, second only to her gentle fingers splayed across his chest. Her head pressed between his shoulder blades as if she needed to feel the words of his heart instead of his mouth. "I never stopped loving you, Hunter, and even if you walk away from me now, which is what I deserve, I still will."

He closed his eyes and counted to ten. A thousand could-bes rang every cautionary light in his dumb jarhead brain, but what *was* happening drowned them out. What was it his mother used to say? Sometimes people get what they deserve; sometimes they get what they need? Shit. Meredith had made mistakes, so the hell had he.

She chose that moment to loosen her grip. "Do you hate me so much that—?"

"No!" The truth sprang from his lips. Hunter clamped his hands over hers before she could release him completely. He had a better idea of what went down now. Did she cheat on him? Technically. Did he forgive her? Absolutely. Could she forgive him? "I never hated you."

Twisting around, he faced her. "I was just so gawddamned mad. You're right. I joined the Corps after I saw you ride away with him Christmas night. By then, I knew you were pregnant and getting married, and I went crazy. I couldn't believe you chose him over me." He closed his eyes and wished he were a smarter man. All of this could have gone differently if he'd only given her the chance to explain back then. "I can't say I wouldn't have been mad as hell, but I do wish I hadn't left without hearing your side of it. I was wrong to leave the way I did."

"I don't know if I would have told you anyway. I couldn't bear to break your heart, Hunter." A tear spilled out of her eye. "Not in person…"

It had to be the damnable tropical heat. Sudden moisture blurred his vision. Meredith was suddenly all starlight and twinkles and—*love.*

"It was never you over him, Hunter. He was Courtney's father. I honestly thought he deserved the chance to raise his son, but I was wrong. Eddy married me in January and he left me three months later. He wasn't even there when Courtney was born. If there were any way possible, I'd go back in time and do everything over again. I'd run to you and tell you what happened and that I was pregnant. I'd trust you. I'm sorry I hurt you."

"I should never have left. You needed me."

"You were hurt and I was getting married and—"

"I was stupid."

She offered a small smile. "It's nice to hear you say that, but this was all my fault. We were kids, Hunter, and kids make stupid mistakes. What do we do now?"

He lifted her hand to his lips. "I blamed you for everything."

"And I condemned you for leaving me when I was the one who cheated." She pressed her face into his chest, breathing hard and trembling. "I love you, Hunter. I always have. Don't let the mistakes we made yesterday destroy what we could be today. Stop running. Forgive me and let me love you."

He closed his eyes and let the past drop dead at his feet. "There's nothing to forgive. You're right. We both made mistakes, but you may not want me anymore. I've done things; my hands aren't lily white and I'm not sorry. I did what I had to do."

She pressed herself in closer, as if that was possible. "I'm not your judge. You're honorable and protective and… Please. Let me in again. Let's pick up where we left off."

A single golden ray of warmth spilled into the pitted craters of his heart. With Meredith in his arms, he could almost believe again. Maybe that ragged heart could heal.

Placing a small kiss into the top of her wet blonde head, he set himself in the center of the target again. Bull's-eye. One hundred points. Winner take all. With the next words out of his mouth, she'd have the power to kill him for sure. Whispering the words that had tortured him nightly for years, he did as she asked. He let her in. "I love you, Merry."

She raised her eyes. "I know."

The distasteful memory of her marriage nagged at Hunter. There was only one way to erase it. Make love with this woman. Claim her with his body, his scent, his soul. Join with her. The primeval instincts of a warrior raged with the barely existent civilized man within.

Hunter encased her sweet face in his big hands, a precious pearl caught between rugged workday tools, blistered and rough as sin. Her chin tilted a fraction upward, encouraging him to jump off the ledge.

Very slowly, he dipped his head to accept the offering. The rug that had been jerked out from under him all those years ago settled back beneath his feet. The sweetest taste filled his mouth; the sweetest perfume, his nose. The savage caveman within him roared to power, only to be tempered by the gentle man he used to be.

Hunter kissed her softly. Passionately. He gave his mouth license to trail wet kisses over her chin and tender nibbles down her neck.

She clung to him, returning fervent kisses to his forehead, her fingers splayed through his hair, hugging him to her. Maybe even forgiving him the way he'd forgiven her. When her body demanded more, he eased his mouth away from her far enough to look into her eyes again. Timid hope still shimmered there.

She had to understand once and for all. "I'm going to marry you the first minute we're out of here, but mark my words. You're already mine. Heart. Body. Soul." He lifted her off the ground, her ass once more clutched in his hands. "And everything in between. Got that, Meredith Flynn? I'm going to marry you."

The most glorious smile lit up her face. She kissed the end of his nose. "You're all I've ever wanted, Hunter. You're my heart and..." Another kiss branded his nose. "My soul and..." Moist lips and a hint of tongue blessed his mouth with, "And everything in between."

He pulled her into the most carefully suffocating embrace he could. This was why he'd gone to war. Meredith was everything good and pure and right with the world. She was worth fighting for, and now that he had her back, he wouldn't screw it up again.

CHAPTER TWENTY-TWO

"So you're the one who's been toting the supplies all this time?" Eric asked.

Meredith caught the playful undertone to his voice. "Yes. Why?"

He seemed amused. "Let me show you something."

Seth was cleaned up, doctored, and bandaged. Eric and Hunter had already performed minor surgery on Teague and removed the bullet in his chest. During that intense surgery and while Eric held Teague in a stronghold, Hunter sent Meredith to the entrance of the cave, supposedly to watch for intruders. She knew better. He hadn't wanted her to witness the pain poor Teague had to endure while his new, good buddies *helped* him.

Afterward, Hunter and Eric had disappeared outside and had shortly returned with two huge fish, already cleaned and skewered. They knew how to roast it, too. Having something more substantial than fruit to eat made a difference in her outlook. Teague's and Seth's, too. Both men fell asleep after they'd eaten.

Cracking the lid of the supply crate, Eric removed the bottled water, the MREs, the medical kit, and everything else. Reaching into the bottom of the container, he pulled up the three sealed plastic boxes Meredith hadn't had time to investigate yet.

"You, my dear, are Dorothy from *The Wizard of Oz*. You've had your hands on the ruby slippers the minute you grabbed hold of this handle. You could've been home by now, provided you used these to get inside Burdette's camp."

"I what?" Okay, now he made no sense at all.

"What are you talking about?" Hunter took one of the boxes and broke the seal. Out came an ACS suit, only the emblem on the chest of this one declared ACS_3. "I didn't know there was a third prototype. Hey, there's a rifle in here, too." He peered into the bottom of the supply crate. "Look. Tackle."

"Yeah, yeah, you and your fishing." Eric took over. "If you recall from our intelligence briefing, ACS_1 is designed to camouflage men and women in a multiplicity of combat environments. Once some of the bugs are worked out, ACS_2 will camouflage vehicles and heavy armament, short-range missiles, bunkers, stuff like that."

Hunter grumbled, "I'll believe that when I see it."

Meredith couldn't help but smile. Pessimism still hovered around him like a grim shadow of his former self. Oh, the plans she had for that grumpy man. Her whole body thrummed in anticipation of taking him on. Or under.

"Oh, yes," Eric replied. "It'll work, Hunt. Believe me. I've been working closely with Teague, and—"

"You're the mole," Hunter accused.

Eric blinked. "You knew?"

"Hell, yeah. How else could three geeks in camouflaged underwear take down Ky, Seth, and you as fast as they did?" Hunter grunted like that was a no-brainer. "No way could they have hit three trained covert operators unless someone told them how to look for us. I knew it wasn't Ky or Seth. It had to be you. You're a fat-assed snitch, Reynolds."

Eric grinned. "Exactly. I came here to train the MI team, not you guys. You're the pros, remember?"

"You bastard," Seth rasped from his makeshift mattress. "You got me killed."

"I got you shot with paint," Eric corrected matter-of-factly. "I was in collusion with the good guys, Seth, not Burdette. There is a difference. Teague and I were the only ones who knew the beta test included the ACS_3. Alex and Jed thought the fewer who knew, the more sound the results and the integrity—"

"I'm shooting them in the face right after I shoot you," Seth promised steadily, his eyes still closed. "Soon as I feel better, you're going down, Reynolds."

"Are you comfortable?" Meredith asked Seth.

"Yes, ma'am. Just planning me some payback." His fingers were interlocked on his chest, but all of them were wiggling. "Only I won't be using a paintball gun."

Eric shot Hunter an amused grin. "Now I'm really worried."

"You should be," Seth promised groggily. "I'm buying me a taser and an Uzi. Now shut the hell up. Some of us are trying to sleep."

"Anyway." Eric lowered his voice as he lifted an ACS_3 out of its box. He set the boots, rifle, and helmet aside. "These little babies are state-of-the-art third-generation. They don't just mimic environment like one and two do."

Meredith's ears perked up. Why did she not know this? "That must be what Teague meant. He said you knew something, Eric. I thought he was delirious. He was talking crazy, telling me there's two and three of something. I just didn't know what."

A shadow darkened the sparkle in Eric's eyes. "I'll bet he thought Burdette's men got hold of these suits when they overran our camps. That would've been bad. Burdette might have gotten everything he wanted."

"And more." Hunter held up one of the syringes he'd recovered from his close encounters with Burdette's men. "If Masters was telling the truth, Burdette planned to kill off Jed's team and brainwash us guys into believing we'd killed 'em. He's here to discredit MI's work in the ACS field once and for all."

"How'd you know?" Eric asked.

Hunter stilled. "I have my ways."

Meredith gulped. Translation: Masters was most likely dead. The dark side of Hunter seemed contrary to the gentle man who lay beneath the rough exterior of that hardened warrior. He was the ultimate bad boy—lover, poet, *killer.* He took her breath, and not always in a good way.

Eric didn't wait for further elaboration. "The ACS_3 takes environmental mimicry one step further than the first prototype. Whereas the first system mimics surroundings through holographic imagery, the third contains imbedded infrared crystals to cool or warm the soldier wearing it."

"Are you telling me they'll disguise a guy's heat signature?" Hunter's brows lifted.

"And negate the enemy's use of thermal imaging." Eric purred. "That's exactly what the ACS_3 is supposed to do— make a man invisible at every level."

"So a soldier in full-up combat gear would be completely undetectable? Not even night-vision goggles would pick him up?"

Eric nodded. "It's amazing science that will revolutionize the—"

"Wait a minute." Hunter lifted a palm to Eric's face. "Are you telling me the MI team would've been able to see us, that they would've killed me, Ky, and Seth, while we had no way to intercept or defend ourselves? You didn't think you needed to tell your own team something important like that, buddy? You traitor."

"I'm telling you, Hunt," Seth murmured sleepily. "The guy needs to die."

A frown creased Eric's brow. "Give me a break, Hunt. You're the one who shot everyone on the MI team in the first go 'round, remember? It was you who proved ActiveCamouflage isn't a failsafe, that it isn't the perfect answer."

"Yeah, well—"

"Well, nothing. You weren't using night-vision optics when you did it either, so knock off the traitor bullshit. I'm no snitch. What do you care if MI upped their game and made it harder for you to kill them? You'd still have been the last one standing, wouldn't you?"

"Yeah, well..." was all Hunter had to offer.

Meredith caught his covert glance in her direction. The man was all testosterone and ego, no doubt thinking of when he'd captured her. She could tell. He was more than a little proud of himself for undermining the MI beta test without using high-tech to do it. *The brat.*

"So how do we use these bad boys to go after Burdette?" Hunter changed the subject. "Stand outside their security fence and shoot 'em with more of your poison darts?"

Eric beamed. "You liked that, huh?"

"It sure surprised me that someone else was taking those guys out," Hunter admitted. "You saved the day."

"Wait a minute." Meredith held a hand up for silence. "Poison darts?"

Hunter pointed at Eric. "Me and Seth were on our way out of Burdette's camp. Eric gave them a damned good reason to let us go."

The TEAM's lead agent grinned like a little boy at Christmas, his brows lifted high and a sparkle in his eyes.

"And you wanted one for a pet," Hunter said sarcastically to Meredith.

"What?" she asked. "I don't get it."

"The poison he used comes from those pretty tree frogs you were yammering about this morning," Hunter explained.

"I wasn't yammering." She caught another covert glance and a smile. "I just thought those little guys were unique and colorful and—"

"Cute," Hunter cut in. "Admit it, Meredith. You thought they were cute."

She rolled one shoulder. "Maybe."

"Not all tree frogs are poisonous," Eric explained. "I wasn't sure I'd even found an actual poison-dart frog until the first man dropped. I was looking for a brown phantasmal. It's a tiny little bugger, but it secretes a chemical through its skin that's a hundred times more potent than morphine. The brown one I found must've been good enough. Whoever that guy was I shot, he never knew what hit him. Sure scared the creep with him though."

"Jonesy," Hunter said. "Not sure who you hit first, but he's the guy you took out while we were escaping. Sure made everyone think twice about stopping me and Seth."

"At least he died quickly—not what they intended for Seth," Eric murmured.

Hunter thumped Meredith's kneecap. "Jonesy is the guy you shot in the leg. I overheard him talking. He planned a nasty payback for you, so I'm damned glad Eric caught up with him first. But whatever you do, don't touch the frogs in this jungle." His brow spiked with his usual bossy attitude and his index finger in her face. "They're not cute. They're dangerous."

"I wasn't going to." She ducked her head into her shoulders, wanting to kiss him again. Or that finger.

"So what's the plan?" Hunter asked.

"You tell me." Eric's voice lost the excitement. "We can wait until morning or we can go after them tonight. Either way, we're outnumbered."

"How many do you think?"

"I've dropped five, no make that six. You?"

Hunter held up seven fingers. "Seven, if I count the two kills with the stakes."

"That was quick thinking, Hunt, but there's at least a dozen more guys in that camp, unless Burdette's brought in reinforcements," Eric said grimly. "I've been listening for chopper blades since you grabbed Seth, but I haven't heard anything. Have you?"

Hunter indicated negative. "I contacted Alex. He's got men in country and headed our way. Jordan and Lee. Zack, David, and Adam, too."

"And Alex?" Eric made it a question.

"What do you think?"

"I think we take Burdette's camp come morning."

Meredith interrupted. "That's still six-to-one odds, guys. You'll be outnumbered."

"Won't be the first time." Hunter winked at her before he turned to Eric. "Have you seen the fence?"

"There's another running to the north of us, just beyond Burdette's camp. What's up with them?"

"Damned if I know. Seems Burdette wants to run the table. Keep everyone out while he hunts us to extinction."

Eric shook his head. "It doesn't make sense. I get the green shit in the hypos, but the fence looks like it's meant for something bigger than a few guys."

"Wish I had a couple of Mother's Tattle Tales," Hunter mused, "or a Flyby. Then we'd know."

Again, Meredith had no idea what these guys were talking about.

"A Tattle Tale is a listening device—a bug. A Flyby is a tiny drone with satellite capability and video," Eric explained when he noticed her blank look. "We've also got a smaller drone that looks like a dragon fly. Sweetest little spy ever. Mother tagged it TEAMdragon. She's our world-class spy-gear provider. If we had one of those babies, we could scout the perimeter, map Burdette's fence line, and get inside his camp in nothing flat."

"Maybe inside one of his rigs." Hunter turned to Meredith. "You'll stay here at our rear flank. Keep Seth and

Teague company until the guys get here. Can you handle that?"

"But why don't we just wait for Alex and his guys?" That seemed like the best answer, and Meredith didn't want Hunter and Eric taking chances they didn't have to. She'd already lost two friends.

Hunter scowled. "It doesn't work that way. A man doesn't sit in his cave waiting to die. He strikes first."

"The best defense is the best offense?" she asked.

"And surprise is always the best defense," Eric added. "Burdette knows he's got us outnumbered. I don't get it though. He should have his men already hunting us."

"They are, but he's hired a bunch of losers. He only had one spec ops guy last I saw..." Hunter lifted his shoulders like a kid caught with his hand in the cookie jar.

"That gives you eight to my six, you bastard," Eric groused.

Meredith put her palms to the sides of her head. "I can't believe I'm hearing this. You're keeping score?"

"Maybe," Hunter mumbled, a mischievous glint in his eye.

"It's a guy thing," Seth said. "Like football stats. Passing. Rushing. Receiving—"

Hunter punched a fist into his palm. "Touchdowns."

Football she understood. "How will I recognize your guys once they get here?"

"They're ugly as dirt," Eric muttered playfully. "No, really. Jordan's never without his Ray-Bans and a ball cap. He'll probably lead. Lee will follow. They'll be wearing cammies with black polos. Course, you won't be able to see their shirts with all their gear. They're both tall drinks of water, built for speed and agility, not like your friend here."

Hunter stuck his chin out. "Lee's bigger than I am."

"Yeah, but he's light on his feet. You're just... big."

Meredith agreed. She'd seen the ropes of coiled muscle across Hunters shoulders and down his arms. His back. She didn't know who Lee was, but no man could hold a candle to Hunter.

He punched Eric's bicep hard enough that he sagged backward, but still smiled. "Damn, Hunter. Don't go breaking my arm. I might be your only ticket out of here."

"You might get me killed, too." Hunter punched him again. "Meredith, I'm going to catch another fish to tide you over 'til we get back. You want me to bring back a couple of those fruity things you caught? I hear they float real good."

The wickedest gleam leapt right from his eye straight into her heart. He'd actually teased. She lowered her lashes, planning for the second she had Hunter all to herself.

CHAPTER TWENTY-THREE

Team confidence turned high once Eric arrived. Teague drifted between a deep sleep and a drowsy slumber. Meredith had insisted Hunter and Eric situate both injured men, so they faced the cave entrance and could better defend themselves. The poison darts were off their offensive line-up though. Eric hadn't secured the tree frog, damn it. He'd let it get away, and along with it went a surefire way to neutralize Burdette's men.

"It's not like I had a safe place to store it," Eric grumbled. "Give me a break, Hunt. It wasn't a pet."

"Strategy, man," Hunter shot back at him, wishing he had a smoke. The craving gnawed at quiet times like this. "Winning a war is all about strategy and foresight."

"Hell if it is. The little bugger was poisonous. What'd you want me to do, stick him in my shirt pocket? If I'd ended up dead because I was playing with a frog—"

"I'd laugh my ass off," Seth murmured from the dark where he was supposed to be sound asleep.

"Shut it, McCray," Eric hissed. "Hunter doesn't need a wing man."

Hunter crouched near Teague's litter, lining up his arsenal of confiscated weapons. Not counting the stainless-steel revolvers, the tactical ARs and all the ammo, several walkie-talkies, one garrote, and miscellaneous flash bangs and grenades, he was feeling pretty secure.

He also had an impressive array of streamlined, folding, or fixed-blade knives. Too bad none were as good as the one he carried. Titanium-coated. Serrated blade. Perfect grip. And all that in a package that came in just a hair over eight ounces, and fit a man's pocket perfectly. Or his hand. Definitely his pride. Endowed with the USMC emblem for *The Magnificent Bastards*, there was no better blade in the world. And to think, he used to read literature. Sometimes, those days seemed like forever ago, and that guy with stars in his eyes? Another animal all together.

There was an exquisite, though primitive, art to combat and war, to strategy, and converting that strategy to mission success. Maybe combat didn't have the precise rhythm of the iambic pentameter of John Keats' prose, but it was poetry nonetheless. A fluid dance between enemies. A fierce sort of ballet between sniper and headshot.

From his first drill on the parade field, Hunter sensed the resounding steadiness and the cohesive beat in the marching boots of a USMC battalion. There was an innate beauty in flying cover for his brothers and sisters in the field, a camaraderie and an adrenaline rush the likes he'd never gotten from reading Chaucer or Tolkien.

"You want me to look at that hole in your chest?" Eric asked, nodding toward Hunter's collarbone.

He shot an evil brow at Meredith. "Who told?"

She shot an equally evil glare back at him. "Not me."

"Knock it off, Hunt, I'm trained to spot tough guys like you who don't think they need medical help when they really do." Eric winked slyly. "Want me to look at it, or not?"

"Not." Hunter let it go. He didn't need anything a smoke wouldn't cure.

"Where do you think Ky is?" Eric shifted the subject. "I haven't seen a sign of him since the first night, have you?"

Hunter nodded toward the entrance for them to take the conversation outside. "Be right back, Meredith. Stay put."

She looked up and smiled. Her hair caught the glow from the flashlight. It was one of those picture-perfect moments that took a man's breath away. There she was in the spotlight again, his reason for living. He had it bad.

Hunter grabbed an extra pair of boots and the compact fishing pole he'd found in the supply crate. Once outside, he answered Eric. "Meredith and I came across a body dump earlier today. I didn't want to say anything in front of Seth, but I saw four bodies for sure. There may be more. I hope not, but Lyle was there. We might find Ky if we poke around."

Eric grimaced. "Poke or puke?"

Hunter had no answer. All body dumps were disgusting.

"God, I hope he's not there." Eric blew out a long-suffering sigh. "That would kill Eden. They've been through enough."

Despite his gentle nature, Ky Winchester was one tough SOB who'd survived torture at the hands of some madman on the outskirts of Kabul, then found the woman he'd fallen for while on another crazy TEAM op. He'd married into the FBI family, a first for The TEAM. Until now, life had turned around for Ky and Eden. They'd just had a baby boy. Things were looking up.

"Let's hit the dump first thing in the morning," Hunter replied. At the beginning, they'd all thought this op would've been more fun than work. So much for that thinking.

"Knowing if Ky's there or not will give us the motivation to storm Burdette's camp and finish this crap shoot."

"Storm?"

Hunter nodded. "I'm not going in soft. We're going to hit 'em hard and leave 'em bloody. Or dead. It's all the same to me."

"I saw it going another way," Eric hedged, a devious lift to his brow. He and Hunter were at the edge of the river by then. The full moon overhead created a shimmering mirror of silvery water in the shallows. "You've still got all the hypos you confiscated, don't you?"

Hunter grinned. That was why he liked Eric Reynolds. Two-timing, sneaky snitch or not, the man knew his way around the human body, and maybe a little bit of the brain, too. "What are you thinking?"

"You know me. I like turnabout being fair play."

"Revenge," Hunter restated the euphemism.

"Not necessarily," Eric clarified. "Think of it as a fully loaded dose of karma. What goes around—"

"Comes around." Hunter grinned. "You're thinking of brainwashing them like they planned to do to us?"

Eric shrugged. "There's one way to find out. At least I can inspire them with the desire to not lie, which hopefully will get the truth out in the open, maybe even indict them. That ought to throw a wrench into what's behind this mess. Did you know some guy named Roger Teach owns Brinkman EX now?"

"So I heard." Something about the name still bugged Hunter.

Eric bumped him with his elbow. "You still got your sat phone?"

"It's in my gear bag. I took the batteries out of it after I thumped Masters, so Burdette couldn't track us. Alex is already checking into Burdette and Teach."

Eric sighed. "I hope he had time to pinpoint our location before you unplugged."

Hunter clapped his buddy on the back. "It's the boss we're talking about. Of course, he did. Are you going back inside?"

"Yeah. I've been on the run since this started. I'm beat. How about you?"

"I'll sleep when this is over. Tell her I'll be in shortly."

"Her?" Again with the devilish eyebrow lift.

"Knock it off, Reynolds. I told Meredith I'd catch another fish, that's all. We might be gone a while tomorrow."

Eric crossed his arms over his chest and grinned. "It's not like you to take a shine to one of the ladies we bodyguard, Hunt. What's up? Is this one special?"

"No," shot out of Hunter's mouth before he could think, but this was Eric, his buddy. "Yes," he admitted. "She's a friend from college." *Kind of.*

Eric had the quirkiest smile on his face. "I'll tell her you won't be long. Happy fishing. Don't fall in."

Falling in wasn't the problem. Tomorrow's mission was. If things went south and Hunter didn't make it back alive, Meredith would need plenty to eat until Alex and the guys showed. She would survive, damn it.

"Hey, I almost forgot." Hunter nodded at the waterfall. "Something of yours survived the fire. It's in my gear bag."

Eric spun on his heel, the moonlight washing his face. "What?"

"It's a small metal case. Go ahead and take it." Enough said. Hunter wasn't going to pry. If Eric wanted to share the story behind that little girl in the photo, it was up to him.

"Thanks Hunt," came out tight and emotionless. "I owe you one."

Hunter let his best buddy off the hook. Some things were hard to talk about. "I found Ky's glasses, too, but don't tell Seth his *National Geographic*s didn't make it."

Eric nodded, still facing the cave. "'Night, Hunt."

"G'night."

He waited until Eric disappeared behind the waterfall. Whoever that little girl in the picture was, Hunter had never seen Eric so uptight, so closed off. There was a sad story there. It might come out someday, but it might not. Hunter let it go.

Kicking out of his boots, he shed his shirt and pants, and doused himself with a mist of the industrial-strength bug spray he'd carried in his pants pocket. Donning the extra pair of boots, Hunter prepared to get that relaxing stroll, maybe a swim in the river.

He snagged a handful of berries from a bush along the riverbank and selected the calm pool for his midnight fishing hole. It had already proved its worth when he and Eric had successfully wrangled a couple slippery ten-pounders before. It would work again. Still waters ran deep, and he knew hands down that more big mouths lingered below the rippling surface, waiting for something to fall their way.

He tossed the berries in first, then cast his lure into the middle of the silvery moon's fractured reflection, tugging the line to make sure it wasn't dragging bottom. The pole was nothing fancy, just a hollow plastic grip that held extra hooks and lures, a telescoping rod, and a fifty-pound line. The concept was simple. *Bait 'em, hook 'em, and eat 'em.*

It wouldn't take long now. The line vibrated as something nibbled, tasted, and tested. Good enough. He reeled the line in, teasing his prey, and cast again along with another handful of berries, baiting the underwater life with nothing more than water disturbance.

An old Scottish verse ran through his mind. *The best laid schemes o' Mice an' Men Gang aft agley...* Robert Burns. "To a Mouse." Wasn't that the truth? Like this *vacation* operation. Like joining the Corps. *Like falling in love again...*

CHAPTER TWENTY-FOUR

Holy shit!

Meredith couldn't think of another way to describe the breathtaking scene laid out before her. She'd carefully crossed the river to speak with Hunter in private, not expecting the dazzling sight that met her eyes. This crazy, angry, wonderful man was fishing. In the river. Stark assed naked. *Who does that?*

His strong back was to her, every last muscle delineated by the silvery touch of moonlight on his skin. The tattoos on his biceps and back rippled. Meredith licked her lips, wanting to run her tongue over every last swirl of that ink. Just because.

Edging closer like a stalker, her pounding heart sapped the strength from her knees at the sight of the twin moons smiling at her. The man's backside was hard muscle. The hollows of his butt cheeks rippled with shadow when he pulled the line taut and high.

"There you are," he muttered, his deep voice washing over her. "Come to daddy."

Oh, I am so coming.

Her feet moved forward in automatic response, but her faltering steps were no match for the long-legged stride of the alpha male in the river. The sinews in his calves flexed the farther he ventured from shore. What fish could refuse his command? She couldn't, not with her brain atwitter like it was. Hooked. She was hooked. Heck, she'd be flopping on shore just for the sheer joy of being caught—and landed—by him.

Make that bedded.

Stout thighs, thick and marked with power, drew her eyes once more to the tight backside of an aesthetically endowed man. At least Hunter hadn't had that part of his anatomy inked. Adonis wished he looked so good in the buff.

The sheer size of Hunter's shoulders made her think of football and all those beefy workhorses at the fifty-yard line. Only they were encased in pads and protection. They had no necks. Hunter had an elegantly straight neck atop rippling shoulders, made more masculine with the inky definition of a tribal tattoo and that obscene boot print. Even the snake curling around his arm seemed somehow tame in comparison to that boot.

Hunter didn't need protection from anything in the river, but she might.

"Got you now." He twisted sideways as the silvery creature at the end of his line surfaced, thrashed, and sent a hearty splash heavenward. While Hunter reeled it in, Meredith crossed her legs and eased to the ground. *I can't take this. He's beautiful. Every last inch and crevice and... I can't take this.*

This perfect male specimen, her friend and past rival, had become her guilty pleasure. The hastily made bandage was missing from his chest, but he seemed none the worse for wear. The only way he could possibly top this strip show would be if he—

Oh. My. God.

Hunter turned around, holding the wiggling trophy in the moonlight, his other trophy aimed directly—at—her. "You thought you'd get away, didn't you? Forget it. Tonight you're mine."

Meredith flopped to her back, careful that her holster didn't stab her. *Yes. Yes. Yes. I'm all yours. Tonight. Forever.*

"Merry?"

Her body cringed all the way to her toes.

He stood over her with both hands on his hips, grinning like a very naughty boy. The fish flopped at his feet, and— what was that man thinking? The mischievous dimple was back in full force. It didn't seem to bother him that he was nude and damned proud of himself, but that amazing arousal between them wreaked havoc with her pulse, her heart, and her eyeballs. Especially her eyeballs.

"Hi," she squeaked, busted for looking, guilty as sin, and ready to do it again.

He extended a hand to pull her to her feet. The tattooed snake came with him, its red eyes dark and watchful. "What are you doing out here?"

"I. Don't. Know." She latched onto the tips of his fingers, below the knife in the snake's head. The brat had to know what his state of undress did to her. *What DO you say to a naked man?*

In one quick instant, Hunter lifted her high above him, his hands strong at her waist and Meredith was breathlessly, happily caught. "You... you didn't come," she breathed down at his handsome face. The man looked good with moonlight in his eyes, but—gah! Heat flooded her cheeks at her poor word choice. "I mean, you didn't come *in,* and I... I wanted to say goodnight." *Or something a little more brilliant.*

He groaned as he let her body slide down his chest and abdomen and thighs. The friction of his naked body against her ignited a trailing wildfire from her tingling breasts to her core when she landed with his knee between her legs.

"Goodnight, Merry," he said softly, his smirky lips close enough to taste.

As if there was any way she was leaving now.

Unbidden, her hands reached for her naked warrior. There was nothing soft or gentle about Hunter's body, only hard edges and angles, sheer strength that fueled her feminine softness with a scorching need to never let him go. She'd become a wet and willing sheath for the weapon he was.

"You should go back. Get under cover." His voice dipped temptingly deep. "It's not safe out here."

Meredith leaned toward him, her chin raised, and her fingers gentle on his chest. "But you're the one who's hurt, not me."

His eyes flickered to the branches overhead. "I have an idea. Let's go topside where we'll be out of sight."

Okay, that wasn't exactly how she saw her night going. Topside? As in up into the mammoth kapok tree whose trailing branches she'd been hiding under? He wanted to climb trees? Now? The man might be part Tarzan, but she wasn't Jane.

Before she knew it, he'd climbed onto the hefty branch hanging over the riverbank, completely comfortable with his nudity. Once seated a good ten feet above her, he locked onto the branch with both legs, tilted forward. She reached for him, and…

Swoop! She found herself sitting on the wide branch next to him. But this jungle was no place to play around. He was mighty dangerous too, but they should be inside the cave, not up in a tree like a couple of monkeys. Only this was Hunter. Crazy, risk-taking, murderously protective, and very naked Hunter.

He wrapped his arms around her with a sexy, "Come here, you."

Meredith barely had time to blink before his mouth crashed into hers with a ferocious hunger, his teeth nipping, his lips pulling, and his tongue lapping at her as if she were edible. The feel of his bulging pectorals beneath her fingers and the scant brush of chest hair made the sensual attraction stronger.

She wrapped one wrist around a wandering vine for balance and the other around his neck, tasting his moist mouth and lips, his tongue. Loving the sting of his whiskers on her skin. The smell of him. The warmth of him. Her appetite for him grew with every touch and nuzzle.

His very adept fingers popped the buttons on her borrowed shirt. "These have to go."

There was no chance of them falling. The branch they were on was smooth-barked and wide enough to stand up and walk across. Other branches stretched and vines dangled nearby, but talk about a crazy place to be necking or petting or whatever they were doing.

He cupped her jaw, his mouth making tender, passionate love with hers. The taste of him was rich and decadent in the history of all forbidden males. He was the ultimate bad boy. An untamed beast of a man in a god's body. She inhaled the sweet, smoky scent of clean, manly sweat, the essence of the male body she'd missed.

Before she knew it, she was on her feet and her holster dangled off a branch within reach. Her borrowed pants were wedged between two forked branches. Reduced to nothing but her bra and panties, she latched onto a leafy vine, drawing it across her nakedness. She had it wrong. Hunter wasn't Tarzan. He was Adam and this was paradise.

With a wave of his hand, he brushed the vine aside, a delightful glow of male adoration lighting his handsome face. His lips pursed into an O. His dark eyes glistened as they roved over her body. He must've liked what he saw; he licked his lips like he was ready to dive into a feast.

With one hand, he reached behind her and unsnapped the bra. The straps slid to her elbows. Arm by arm, he tugged it free as he took in her nakedness. Dipping low, he trailed a line of warm, wet kisses down her sensitive neck.

"Oh, Merry." Reverence whispered against her skin, his voice achingly deep.

Fire bloomed in her belly. She had no idea where her bra ended up. She could only gasp at the chills the suckling lips on her breast drew out of her. The fiery heat of his manly mouth turned her wanton. Closing her eyes, she let go of the branch and clung to Hunter. This was what she'd wanted all these wasted years. Who she needed. This man. This once in a lifetime match.

His tongue bathed her sensitive nipples with liquid fire, carefully attending to one with his mouth while he cupped the other, massaging and softly pinching her nipple. The whiskers around his mouth scraped when she arched into him, offering everything she had into his keeping if he'd never stop doing—that.

Moonlight filtering through the branches spilled over his broad shoulders. She saw it then—the trusting boy within the battle-hardened man. The only thing he had hold of was—her. Meredith reached up to latch onto the fibrous vine straggling overhead.

He groaned when she stretched, his mouth filled with her. Suddenly, there wasn't enough air in the jungle. A raging fire roared through Meredith, scorching her with need. Her nearly virginal body wept for wanting him. She stroked one foot against her other calf, her body clenched and aching. "Hunter," she begged.

"Not yet, Merry," he murmured as he dropped to his knees.

Tears filled her eyes as a sharp ache for this warrior unfurled in her heart with a good stiff snap like a flag in the wind. God, she loved Hunter. Meredith wrapped both hands on that vine, prepared for what might happen next. Drenched and needy, she wanted him seated deep inside. She let his name be enough because—it was. "Hunter."

He growled as, very slowly, he kissed his way to her hip, then bathed her navel in sizzling heat that drove her crazy. No man had ever taken this kind of time to pleasure her. His fingers were gentle, his mouth demanding but firm.

His fingers dropped to her hips and peeled her panties down. She stepped out of them and there he stopped, placing another fervent kiss just below her navel.

Meredith looked down to the top of his head, his short-cropped hair glistening in the ambient light from the moon. Barely able to breathe, she wrapped the vines around her hands. Quivering. Waiting. Hoping.

Hunter blew a slow heated breath at the juncture between her legs. "God, I wish I had a bed," he muttered. "I'd lay you down and eat you up."

A wellspring of moisture unleashed, and Meredith couldn't stand still. "Then do it," she begged.

Hunter lifted to his feet, and she could've killed him. The tease!

"Not here, Merry. One taste and I won't be able to stop. I'm saving dessert for later." A soft glow lit his eyes as he settled his palms to her now over-sensitive ribcage.

"But I want you," she breathed, her voice a growl.

He cocked his head. "Where? Tell me."

She captured his hips between her legs, casting her eyes down their as yet uncoupled bodies. "There. Right there."

A smoldering smile cracked his left cheek wide open. Ah, that sexy dimple!

"And I want you screaming when I'm done with you, Meredith, but this isn't the place and we've got neighbors." His voice turned into the rumbling growl of a hungry jungle cat. Hunter palmed her ass in his big warm hands. "Trust me?"

She nodded, the vine wound around her hands and her body throbbing. "Always."

"Then get a good hold, Merry." Slowly, he lowered her, impaling her inch by incredibly hot inch. She dropped her lashes and watched it happen. Her nostrils flared at the rich sultry scent of their sweaty bodies.

She arched backward, thrusting her belly forward. That brought him forward. Hunter nuzzled his nose between her breasts, spreading fire with his tongue even as his velvet shaft settled deep, claiming what she'd always known belonged to him. Her body. Her heart. Her soul.

She ground her hips into him, gasping with unadulterated pleasure that she finally had the right man where she wanted him. She clung to the vine as Hunter took her by storm. He backed her into the wide trunk of that tree, and, with determined strokes, he pistoned into her with force. She met each stroke with equally determined energy, granting more access, and forcing him to reach deeper. He complied, his body in sync with hers.

And she flew. Her body launched a bottle rocket of scorching light that ravaged every last nerve. The stars! A whimper escaped her throat as he clutched tightly, his fingertips digging into her hips as he found his release, too. This man was her Fourth of July fireworks. Her one true love.

Meredith gripped the vines tighter and pushed for more, milking every last inch of him, needing all he had to give. Aftershocks surged up her spine, forcing her body to clamp onto him, to hold him where he belonged.

Hunter groaned in the crook of her neck, his hands at the small of her back. Heavy breathing filled the air, their hearts pounding together in the jungle heat. She let one hand go of the vine to hold Hunter's sweaty head against her, wishing this moment wouldn't end.

His tongue lapped up the valley between her breasts. "Next time," he whispered breathlessly, "we'll do this right. I'll bed you in silk and rose petals. I'll cover you in kisses and chocolate. Whipped cream. Strawberries. Bubbles."

"And you?" she asked, the rough feel of her warrior between her legs the most comforting thing she'd felt there— or anywhere—in a long time.

"And me." Hunter lifted his head as he engulfed her inside his arms, still breathing hard. "You can let go of that vine now." He shifted his weight while he lavished her neck with moist kisses. "I love you. Can I ever tell you how much, Merry?"

Meredith dropped her arms around his neck. Leaning her forehead onto his chin, she sighed as the tattooed snake on his arm circled her. "You just did."

CHAPTER TWENTY-FIVE

"Shhhhh," Hunter whispered when he landed, but Merry couldn't seem to stop giggling. The notion that they'd just made love in the tree like a couple of monkeys seemed the perfect ending to what had, until now, been a ghastly day. Maybe she was out of her mind, or beyond the point of exhaustion, but the dangerous night had turned her silly. It could've also been because, for the first time in years, she felt truly loved.

Hunter didn't know, but her contentment made him wonder what she'd endured with a man like Welch for a husband. He knew damned well she'd been hit; he could tell by the way she flinched when he made a sudden move. Had any of their time together been good?

He caught her clothes first, the holster second, as she eased out of the tree branch and into his arms, still completely naked.

"Ouch," she hissed. "I've think I've got slivers in my butt."

He kept careful eyes on the jungle as he handed her clothes to her. His moment of joyful idiocy had long fled. He'd put her at risk in one out-of-control moment of passion and that wasn't smart. Hoping to not be a complete douchebag and ruin their first time, he spun her around and popped her ass. "No you don't. Put these on. Be quick."

"I will," she whispered, the silliest smile on her face. Hell. How could they go into the cave with her grinning like that? She had the perfect *I've-just-had-sex glow* in her eyes, and normally, he'd be damned proud he'd put it there. But Eric would surely notice. Hell, all the guys would notice a light like the one in her eyes. Meredith was happy, and that made him happy. He wanted to shout it to the world. Just. Not. Now.

He left her briefly and strode beneath the overhanging branches to retrieve his clothing on the riverbank. Within minutes, they were both presentable. His shirt still hung in the shadows because, truth be told, he didn't much like wearing some asshat's clothing any more than Meredith did. He snagged the three fish he'd caught on his way back. "I was going to roast these tonight. Now I'm not so sure I'll have time."

She leaned into him with her arm around his waist as they walked toward the hideaway together. "We could make an outdoor oven."

That took him by surprise. This woman had a few tricks up her sleeve. "You know how?"

"Sure. We'll need to dig a foot deep hole, maybe two feet wide. Flat stones make the best oven, but not river stones. They might blow up. And banana leaves. Oh, yes, and dry wood. Go get the matches. I'll find something to dig with."

He caught her wrist before she could escape. "Oh, no, you don't. The fish will keep just fine where they are until morning. Let's call it a night. We both need some decent shut-eye."

"Aw," she sounded like a little kid. "I don't want to go in. Just fifteen more minutes?"

He knew better, but caved like the sucker he was.

He chose a shadowy spot beneath the tree they'd been in. Backing against it, he lowered to the ground. Her plump backside fit nicely between his legs. They were no more than seated when she pointed to the riverbank where a dog-sized rodent sniffed at the stones. "Ewww, look. A rat."

"Might taste good," he whispered, his chin in the crook of her neck.

"Don't say that." A full on body shiver wiggled through her. "I'm not eating rat meat. Never."

With her small hand in his, he rubbed his thumb over her wedding ring. "Why the ring?"

"It keeps men away."

That helped. "All this time, I thought you were married. So why the divorce?"

Her shoulders lifted. "From the start, we wanted different things. I wanted Courtney. He wanted himself, I guess. The day I brought Courtney home from the hospital, he moved out. Said he needed space, only he never came back. By then I had a restraining order anyway."

"He hurt you?"

"He, umm, played rough." The tremor in her voice gave her away. "He could be mean. Most of the time it was over stupid stuff, like which movie to see. Everything had to be his way."

"Did he hit you?" Hunter had to know how bad things were.

Her lashes fell. "Yes, he…" She cleared her throat. "He did."

She seemed to have a hard time saying Welch's name. Fine by Hunter. He curled her into his arms, inside what would forever be her safe zone. "He'll never hurt you again, trust me." *Because I'll kill him the next time I see him.*

"Did he hurt your son?"

She shook her head. "He's never seen Courtney."

Un-fuckin'-believable, sprang to Hunter's lips, but he reduced it to, "Just as well. Courtney's too good for him." He spun the ring on her finger. "Is this his?"

"No. Mom gave it to me the day Courtney was born. She said it was a New Beginning ring to celebrate the birth of a brand new life for both of us."

"Where's *his* ring?"

Meredith grunted. "Where do you think? I threw it in the toilet and flushed it away."

Wasn't that the perfect comeback? A smile cracked his face at her vehemence. Hunter lowered his chin into the crook of her neck and let the comfort of holding this woman—*his woman*—seep into his soul. He was a lucky man. "I'm sorry for all the questions. I just needed to know. It's behind you now, Meredith. You're not alone."

"Us." She wiggled against his chest, her fingers on his thighs. "You mean it's behind us. I did learn some things while I was married to him, though. Like how strong I am. How resilient. The time I spent with him was a fire I had to walk through to get where I am today."

"The refiner's fire," he muttered, hating that she'd suffered, but thrilled she'd finally seen Welch for the lying POS he was. "Walking through crap does tend to change us. Did you ever finish college?"

"No. I'm taking night school on and off to get my engineering degree, but it's tough. I've got Courtney, and I can only take a class or two at a time. That's why I like working for Jed McCormack. He pays for any education his employees need, even if it isn't related to our jobs. How about you?"

"Yeah. Online classes. No big deal."

She twisted in his arms to look at him. "Good for you! What degree?"

"Business Management. I figured it'd help get me a job once I left the Corps."

"I'm so proud of you." She wrangled an arm around his neck and gave him a squeeze as if he'd accomplished something great.

"Yeah, well, it's not like I'm rich and famous like Welch."

Meredith shivered. "He has gotten wealthy awfully fast, hasn't he?"

"He certainly knows how to get around people. Sounds like we've all come a long ways from where we started."

"Isn't that the truth?" She snuggled her backside into him. "These last three years have been busy. Hey, I found something in the cave. My high school graduation picture, the one I gave you. Did you drop it?"

Ahh, damn. He scratched his scruffy cheek. "I left it with you when I went to find the guys, in case I didn't come back. In case—"

"Were you breaking up with me?"

"Yes. Maybe. Having you beside me after all these years but still married to him... I don't know." Hunter ran a hand over the top of his head. "It was ripping my guts out. I shouldn't have kissed you like I did last night, but I couldn't stand being so close to you and not being able to touch."

She hooked her fingers over his forearms, tracing the outline of his snake. "I like touching."

Those three words filled the empty hole in his heart with an ocean of warmth. How she did it, he didn't know. He was just damn thankful she was finally where she belonged.

"Tell me about your tattoos. They seem so... hostile. Why'd you cover so much of your body with ink?"

Where to begin? "It's a guy thing. You wouldn't understand."

"Try me."

Oh hell. "Which one do you want to know about?"

"The one on your back. It doesn't make sense. A boot print looks like someone stepped on you. Is that what you think life's done?"

In a word—yes. "That's not what it means. It's for my friends who died over there. Gary Jennings' name's at the toe of the boot because he died first. In Ramadi. The next tread down is Luke Casper. Coming home to nothing did him in. He committed suicide."

Meredith twisted around to kneel between his legs. "You carry them with you. Everywhere."

"It's the least I can do."

"I'm sorry."

"Why? You didn't do it."

Her fingers strayed to the eagle on his chest. A fine American eagle, and one he was damned proud of. She traced the words outlining the symbol of America. *Betrayer. Liar.* "Were these for... me?"

Hunter closed his eyes and told the truth. "At first, yes. I was mad at the world back then. I took it out on everyone, but later it meant the real betrayers, the ones who make a buck off wounded vets. The ones in Congress and Hollywood who stab us in the back."

She let out a deep sigh. "I'll never be able to tell you how sorry I am."

"It's over," he declared, turning her back to his chest again "It's done. It's what we do from this point on that matters."

"Is that really why you joined the Marines? Because of me and... him?"

Hunter nodded. "Like I said, I was mad at the world. I needed to get away so I did. End of story."

"Do you regret being a Marine?"

That was one thing he was sure of. "No. Never. It was the hardest thing I've ever done, but, hell yeah. I'd do it again." Hunter sank his nose in her hair. "So tell me about Courtney. What's he look like?"

"Me." Just hearing her son's name softened Meredith's body. She melted into Hunter, hugging his arms over her breasts. "Courtney is the smartest three-year-old in Mrs. See's preschool. He's blond and blue-eyed, and he needs a haircut, but I may never cut it. I love his shaggy, little boy look."

"But he never saw his own son?" Hunter avoided *that* name. "Not even when he was born?"

Meredith stiffened. And didn't the difference in her body language tell Hunter all he needed to know? Little Courtney didn't have a real father. Sperm Donor-Dad didn't count.

"It was just as well. Things between us were already strained. When I called to tell him I'd gone into labor—"

"You what?" Hunter couldn't stop the hiss. Wasn't that just like Meredith, to keep reaching out, trying to fix things and people that were broken? *Like me.*

She shrugged. "I know. It was stupid, but yes, I called him. Divorce is so final and, I kept hoping I could turn it around."

"But he abused you."

Meredith sunk into his arms as a sigh escaped her. "I honestly thought that one look at his son and he'd…" Another sigh. "I thought he'd grow up, Hunter. I thought he'd come to his senses and want to be a father."

He'd have to be a man first. "You'd still give him a second chance? You'd let him see Courtney after all this time, wouldn't you?"

Meredith ducked her head. "It's not like I have to worry about it. It's been three years and he hasn't met Courtney yet, but yes. He is Courtney's father. It could happen."

Hunter rolled his neck at the sharp stab of protectiveness he felt for a child he hadn't yet met. "Was anyone with you?" *Please don't tell me you delivered your baby alone.*

Her head bobbed. "Mom drove me to the hospital and Dad came up later. They're the ones who counted. They're watching Courtney now."

"Your parents left San Diego? They live near you?"

"They moved to Richmond last year after Jed hired me. I'm glad they did."

That was good to know, but regret slapped his hard head again. Hunter lifted her ring finger to his lips. "I'm sorry. I should've been there for you."

She twisted her neck to face him. "You had no way of knowing, Hunter. Let it go."

But he had no intention of forgiving himself, not until he'd made amends. Courtney needed someone to teach him the best rivers for fly-fishing and how to tie flies and cast and—all those important things boys should know. "When we get back, I'm taking you and Courtney fishing."

Meredith snuggled under his chin. "He'd love that."

As the night grew quiet, they talked more about Courtney and the Corps, their parents, and the friends they'd had in common. Finally, it was time for bed.

Scanning the jungle one last time before they broke cover, Hunter drew in a deep breath. The air was full of the delicious scent of his woman. It seemed all their past mistakes and missteps had distilled into this one perfect drop in time. They had a second chance at a bright future.

In case Meredith didn't know, he made it crystal clear. "You're sleeping with me tonight."

CHAPTER TWENTY-SIX

They woke up in each other's arms, her back to his front, and he wanted her. Meredith held perfectly still. Eric, Seth, and Teague were still asleep. So was Hunter, for that matter. Only certain parts of his anatomy were wide-awake and poking her backside.

Wow. What a difference a day makes. Parts of her were sore this morning, but they were all smiling. They'd had wild monkey sex their first time together. *How crazy was that?*

Hunter grunted, his breath warm at the nape of her neck. Meredith couldn't detect one molecule of submission in the man. Even the knife wound in his chest had held no sway over him. He'd brushed it off like it was nothing. The puzzle remained. How had the sweet man she'd once known gotten so tough? So hard?

Wrong word to think. He grunted in his sleep, poking her butt in the process. With a noisy groan, he rolled to his back and stretched both arms over his head. By then she really had to go. Quietly, she eased to her knees and then her feet.

"Where do you think you're going?" Ah, that sexy, grumbly morning voice was enough to make her stay—if she could've.

"Umm. Out?"

"Not without me, you're not."

She couldn't resist patting the eagle on his chest. "Then hurry it up, Monkey Boy. I can't wait all day."

Shaking his head, he exited the cave first, scanning the jungle for several long minutes before he waved her to join him. "Don't call me Monkey Boy," he growled, his hand instantly on her ass. "The guy's will never let me hear the end of it."

With one sharp swat on her ass, he led the way across the rocky dam to the jungle side of the river. The low sun in the east filtered through the wall of trees. The fish were staked where he'd left them, but protective vibes now shuddered off Hunter. "Make it quick, Merry. Don't go far."

"You got it," she agreed. His tension made her nervous. It took less than five minutes to take care of business.

By the time she rejoined Hunter, last night's catch dangled from the end of the sharp stick and he had a sturdy five-foot branch in his other. "Take this. It's for Seth. He'll want to get on his feet today."

"He shouldn't. He needs to rest."

"Trust me. He'll get up if he's ready or not. Let him."

Because he's just like you, she thought. *He'll think he has to protect me.*

Hunter tugged her ahead of him to lead the way. "Let's get moving and back under cover."

Meredith marched over the rocky path to their cave with Hunter at her back. Sure enough, Seth was on his feet when she cleared the waterfall. She offered no womanly I-know-better-than-you advice, just handed him the walking stick. "Here. Hunter found this for you."

"Hey, thanks." Seth took the branch and beamed as he fit it under his arm. "Just what I needed."

The camp sprang to life. While Hunter roasted the fish, Eric took the injured men outside. With flashlight in hand, Meredith reorganized what was left in the supply crate. She set out the last of the bottled water as well as the water filtration system and the empty plastic bladder that went with it. Like it or not, they'd be drinking filtered river water by the end of the day.

Before she knew it, breakfast was done. Eric had settled Teague and Seth back on their ragged mats. Teague was already asleep while Seth lay on his side, his walking stick close at hand. Hunter and Eric's gear bags were parked at the cave entrance, along with two ACS_3 suits. Both he and Eric had strapped on their holsters and weapons.

It was time to say goodbye.

"Don't worry about us," Eric offered with a wink. "We'll be back before you know it."

Hunter straightened from where he'd been checking his bag and came straight to her. "I have to do this," he said, his voice low and stern as he cupped her head in his hands. "You've got enough food to last the day and enough ammo to defend yourself, but don't be a hero. If you need to go out, keep to this side of the river. Be vigilant, Merry. Stay under cover."

"I'll take care of her, Hunt," Seth offered, his voice firm with conviction.

"And I won't let you down," she promised, her chin up but her heart pounding at the very real fear of sending her man into combat.

Hunter's eyes were dark in the dim light, but they stayed riveted to hers. "Understood, Seth, and thanks, but Merry—"

He pressed his lips to her forehead and whispered, "I've never had so much to lose. Please, be here when I get back."

She clung to his wrists, her throat nearly too full to speak. "I will. Just make sure you come back."

He held onto her for a long minute and she was afraid. Her tougher-than-nails man was trembling. Eric stood facing the waterfall. Seth was studiously picking something off his second-hand shirt, and Teague was peacefully asleep. With one last nod to her, Hunter gathered his gear and left with Eric. All she could do was nod and let him go. And worry.

She settled cross-legged to the spot where they'd slept. It had been less than forty-eight hours since he and his men had landed, and now he and Eric were off to perform the ultimate beta test.

"Take a nap," Seth encouraged, one arm across his forehead.

But she couldn't. Instead, she joined the ranks of women all over the world and she prayed with tears threatening. *Please keep him safe. Please bring him home. Please.*

At midmorning, Seth yawned and declared, "I'm going fishing."

"Are you sure you're up to it?" she asked.

"You bet." He climbed to his feet, wincing as he angled his walking stick for better balance. "It's just a matter of sitting still long enough to let the fish come to me. What about you, old man?" He tapped Teague's foot with his crutch. "You want to come outside and sit a spell?"

"Sure," Teague muttered. "In the shade."

Seth grunted. "This whole side of the river's in the shade, and if I remember right, there's plenty of vines on the granite face. What do you think?" he speared Meredith with that last question. "Is there enough cover to keep us out of sight?"

"Me?" she asked, surprised he wanted her opinion.

"Yes, ma'am. You've been across the river a few times. What are we up against?"

Meredith lifted to her feet and dusted her hands over her thighs. "The river flows east from here. This cave's in a natural stone corner, and yes. There are plenty of vines and brush to keep us secure. We've got two more waterfalls at our left. They're a lot higher because the granite wall slopes eastward. A dam of boulders and logs stretches across the river, but it can be slippery. Trust me on that."

Seth smiled. "Whitewater's a killer, huh?"

She bobbed her head, not wanting to dwell on her near death experience. "The river runs slower on the opposite shore. We'll have to cross over if you want to fish."

Teague grunted. "I can't walk that far. Guess fishing's out."

"The only way anyone can approach us is from the north?" Seth asked.

"Yes, unless they drop down the cliff above us." She hadn't been this nervous before, but with Hunter gone— anything seemed possible.

"I doubt they'd do that even if they knew where we were," Seth muttered. "They're mean, but they're not the brightest guys. We still need to be on the lookout for Lee and Jordan, though, so I'll take first watch."

"Sounds good," she admitted. "I'd rather keep to this side anyway. That way I can see anyone coming at me."

Seth winked. "Now you're thinking like a Ranger. Can you help me get set up?"

That she could do. While Seth secured his weapon in his holster, Meredith gathered up a couple extra pants for cushioning to sit on and followed. He was just as cautious as Hunter had been, scanning the riverbanks before he let her join him outside. The narrow trail to the sandy shore became drier the farther from the cave they walked, and the shade was dense.

Seth selected a shady spot between the granite wall and a curtain of flowering green. By the time she had Teague situated under cover, Meredith was sweaty and spent. Lifting a hand to shield her eyes from the sun, she scanned the opposite shore, looking for—*him.*

"Come sit between us." Teague patted the empty spot between him and Seth. "I might not be much help at fishing or cooking, but we need to stay together, no matter what."

"You're right." She did as requested, her mind set on the men gone to fight an enemy that outnumbered them.

Seth plucked his shirt away from his chest. "These black rags will help us blend into the shadows. No one will see us as long as we keep still."

"Ah-huh," she agreed. Hunter and Eric's only advantage lay in the miracle of the ACS_3, but now, Meredith doubted the technology she'd once been so proud of. Theory was all well and good in the research lab, and paintball war games were nothing but play. Reality was a thousand times different.

Compassion for the mothers of soldiering sons and daughters swelled within her. Sitting there with her heart in her throat, Meredith truly understood the torment of women left behind. It was her man in the line of fire today. Statistics and test results faded to gray. Leaning into the tree trunk, she whispered another prayer. *Please bring them back safely. All of them.*

Tired after her late-night escapade, her sleepy mind drifted to the man she loved. His hesitant smile. His strong hands. Hunter might think he was hard as stone, but Meredith knew better. She'd cracked that tough exterior. Inside he was all heart.

Teague hummed some old cowboy song. Seth sang along quietly, something about the streets of Laredo, and Meredith drifted off to sleep in the company of snipers...

Eric didn't ask about Meredith, and Hunter didn't offer. Men didn't talk about their loved ones and the sweet life they'd left behind, not with war in their hearts.

Instead, they moved silently westward to the body dump, the grim duty of finding some trace of Ky their first goal. The uneasiness of the day nagged at him. He should be the one protecting Meredith, not his buddies.

He kept going until the nauseating odor assailed his nose. Bodies in decomp smelled the same the world-over. The bile at the back of his throat and the disgust worsened the closer they got.

Hunter buried his nose and mouth in the crook of his arm, relying on his shirtsleeve to block the stench. His eyes watered, but his heart hurt. Ky was a good man. What was left of him might be in this foul mess, but it'd be damned hard to know for certain. Only a DNA test could identify him now.

Eric eased some guy's outstretched arm to the side when he stepped with care into the tangle of cadavers. "Come on, buddy. Speak to me if you're in here, Ky."

Hunter stifled his gag reflex and joined him, looking for anything that resembled the man he'd fought beside on covert ops, or teased in the office. There was a day when Ky had been the shy man out, but only because he hadn't acclimated to civilian life yet. Overeager one moment, he'd pull back the next and shut down, not talking for days. Alex called it shell shock. Harley called it PTSD, but it was all the same. Crap by any other name.

Then along came an FBI agent named Eden...

God, please don't let Ky be in here.

"I'm listening," Eric murmured to the corpses as he took another step, his boots gently nudging fingers, arms, and feet out of his way. "We've come to take you home, Ky. Are you in here? Talk to me."

Hunter kept looking, trying to see beyond the bloat, the milky-white stare or the empty eye sockets, the ravaged flesh. How Eric could talk to these mangled bodies with respect as if they could speak to him was a feat all unto itself. He must see something Hunter didn't. Hunter's stomach protested, but this was what real men did. They found their buddies and they took them home, no matter what.

Hunter wondered at the cosmic rule: *When it rains, it pours.* Why'd this have to happen to Ky? The kid deserved to live the rest of his life in peace with Eden and his son.

"I don't think he's here," Eric said as he straightened. "None of these bodies have the same build. Ky's athletic. These guys are all bouncer types. Big boned. Heavily muscled."

Silently Hunter agreed. Eric would know. A medic, he'd seen his share of mangled and dead bodies.

"We're done here." Eric's eyes weren't even watering.

"I'm not leaving this jungle without him," Hunter insisted even as he turned on the path to Burdette's camp.

"Understood. I feel the same way, so we'll keep looking for him. Are you ready to disappear?"

"Been ready for years," Hunter replied, except it didn't exactly feel truthful, not after yesterday's revelations. His life had changed in the blink of two sexy, baby blue eyes.

Eric led the way. They walked single file through the brush until he lowered his rifle and gear bag to the ground alongside a stand of twenty-foot tall bamboo, the plants gently knocking against each other. "Let's gear up before we get any closer."

Hunter complied, scoping the way ahead while he proceeded to garb himself in the high-tech world of invisibility. The suit was loose, made to overlay cammies, holsters, and the tonnage of gear a man in combat carried. It stretched, a good thing for a guy his size. ACS_3 was meant to fit over a soldier's uniform, leaving him wiggle room to conceal necessities like the holster at his ankle.

But it was heavy. Along with technology came an interior built-in battery system with a harness that hung down his back beneath the jacket. That could pose a problem. He had to know. "What's the shelf life on these batteries?"

Eric shrugged into his jacket, lowering one shoulder while he tugged the sleeve on. "Twenty-four hours. Enough to get in and out."

Good to know.

"How do you want to go in?" Hunter asked while he adjusted his helmet, a high-tech brain bucket with a built-in heads-up display. He'd no more than put it on when a map displayed in muted green inside his visor, while various other tactical information showed to the left and right. GPS coordinates, his, at the moment, he guessed. A transparent button labeled NVG, which left him wondering if the suit intuitively turned night vision on or if he'd have to activate it. This was a holy shit new world in combat readiness.

"Good morning, Agent Hunter Christian," a woman's soft voice said confidentially into his ear. "All systems are not online at this time. Shall I activate them for you?"

The damned thing talked to him. That was weird.

"Umm, sure," he answered, wondering how his helmet knew who was wearing it.

A set of crosshairs illuminated dead center of the display, overlaying the map. That meant this thing was integrated with his ACS$_3$ rifle? As Seth would say, 'sweet.'

"I'm sorry, Agent Christian. All systems are not available at this time," she reported. "If you wish a higher magnification on your scope, tell me, *'zoom.'* I will increase up to twenty-five-millimeter magnification until you tell me, *'stop.'* An illuminated tactical reticle is available, as are thermal imaging, target statistics, and laser lock. Will you require thermal masking for this operation?"

"Wait. I have a laser?"

"Yes, Agent Christian." The automated voice maintained a pleasant feminine tone he could get used to. "The rounds in your MI3 first-generation prototype automatic rifle are heat-seeking smart rounds specifically designed for modern warfare. Once you laser-mark your target, you can't miss."

"Damn. I have *got* to get me one of these."

"Shall I enter an online order in your behalf? The ACS₃ is available for five-point-seven-five million dollars per unit."

"Umm, no. Thanks." He mentally corrected his Christmas wish list, but wow. This ACS₃ was every Marine's dream. "So how do you know I'm Agent Christian?"

"My recognition software identified your fingerprints and bio-metric profile when you handled your helmet. Is there a problem?"

He shook his head. "No, hell no."

"Will you require thermal masking for this operation?" she asked again.

"Affirmative."

A shiver of cold air spilled down the back of his neck, engulfing his body as the high-tech, heat-signature-blocking technology sprang to life. *Holy shit.* A guy could get used to this space-age gear pretty damned quick. It'd make desert combat easier to endure.

By the time he was done with the ACS₃ helmet's indoctrination, Eric was garbed and waiting, his visor up and that same lop-sided grin on his mouth. "Jed makes a nice system, doesn't he?"

"Hell, yeah. Alex needs to upgrade our gear."

"Not going to happen. Not at the hefty price tag."

"So I heard. How do you plan on going in?"

"Same way you did yesterday. Through the front gate."

Hunter hadn't zipped up yet. He reached into his pants pocket and pulled up one of Burdette's hypos. "You think one dose will be enough?"

Eric pursed his lips. "It's hard to know how much we'll need for a mental suggestion to anchor. I don't want to kill anyone if I don't need to, so let's start out with half a hypo. If we need to up the dose, we will."

Hunter stifled his comeback. Burdette's guys deserved killing, and he had the perfect weapon to do it. "How do I plant a suggestion? What should I say? *Please play nice, asshole?*"

Eric rolled his eyes. "How about we tell them they can only speak the truth? That from now on, they won't seek out or hurt any MI or TEAM agents? That ought to mess them up plenty."

"I can do that. Here. You'll need these." Hunter handed over three hypos and one vial of the green shit before he zipped up "We ready?"

Eric pocketed his portion of their chemical warfare. "You need to know that one of the flaws of Active Camouflage is the technology itself. Without the MI laptop to control full integration, we won't be able to communicate with each other. If one of us goes down, we'll have no way to know, so be damned careful."

Hunter tapped the side of his helmet. "Then it's a good thing our helmets come with a digital clock. Meet me at the gate in one hour. By then, we'll have a better idea of what we still need to do."

"Hopefully, we'll be done by then."

"Don't jinx us before we get started."

"Move out," Eric whispered, a bit of a tease in his voice, "and whatever you do, don't shoot me in the ass like you did in Beirut."

"Stay out of my line of fire then." Hunter lowered his visor, immediately checking his six for Eric. Beirut was one of those nightmare ops. They'd been taking a blitz of enemy rounds when Eric had run straight into Hunter's line of fire to rescue a downed man. Hunter had creased his left butt cheek, but damn. Until then, he'd had no idea that USMC medics thought they walked on water. Eric was the hero that day. He'd hauled ass to save lives and work his special brand of miracles before he'd treated his own wound.

Eric lowered his visor and blinked out of sight, panel by panel. Hunter depressed the switch on his palm pad, triggering his suit to fade just as Eric's had. The ACS_3 invisibility system worked flawlessly.

"You're invisible," Eric reported. "Me?"

"Out of sight and out of mind." Hunter stepped to the side of their forward path. "You lead. I'll follow."

"Just make some noise once in a while, would you? You get scary quiet when you go ghost."

"That's the whole idea. This suit just makes it easier."

"Which reminds me. Tap the pad on the right side of your helmet to shut down the voice in your head."

"My computer woman?"

Eric grunted. "Yeah, her."

Hunter shut her down and followed his agent-in-charge. Eric made for a good ghost, too. He was sneaky and quiet. The only way Hunter knew his buddy was ahead of him was the occasional ripple in the jungle scenery.

After twenty minutes, they were at Burdette's camp. Eric halted in plain sight. The place appeared to be in lockdown. The lawn chairs were gone. No guys were sitting around, shooting the breeze. The tent Seth had been tortured in was gone. The fifty caliber, belt-fed, M2 machine gun resting dead center of the camp testified to the new rule of the day—paranoia. Sandbags circled the machine gun nest. One guard sat inside the circle, puffing on a cigarette that instantly jolted Hunter's need for nicotine. Odd. With all the crap going on, he hadn't thought about it until now.

Hunter took a wild guess and ended up being right when his gloved palm met with the resistance of Eric's shoulder. He just needed to let his senior agent know where he was. Eric jumped at the contact. *Message received.*

The security filament blanket covering the narrow compound shimmered on the updraft, but so did a perimeter of newly installed trip wires outside the fence. Hunter bumped Eric and nudged his boot to get him to look downward. A shoulder bump, the signal for A-OK, message received, came back at him.

That was the last he saw, but not really, of Eric. Invisibility didn't lessen the taste of adrenaline on Hunter's tongue or his need to get down on his belly and crawl to keep out of sight. He rolled the intense pinch radiating out from his neck to his shoulder. This new world of out-in-the-open *covert* work would take some getting used to.

It didn't take long for one of Burdette's men to shuffle through the gate. Hunter and Eric hotfooted it inside. As planned, Hunter rounded the first rig and headed out back to intercept as many of Burdette's men as he could.

Three bodies were already there. Burdette included. All had been executed. One shot to the center of their foreheads. Another in their throats. Small caliber. Plenty of black stippling. Damned close range.

Holy shit. Things had just gone from bad to worse, but Hunter had no way to notify Eric. He rounded the rear of the first rig and stepped up to the man lounging on a stack of wooden ammo crates behind the fifty-cal. Just as the tip of the hollow needle would've entered his opponent's neck, another guard climbed out of the first trailer. He'd no more than started toward Hunter when he swayed to one side, then toppled to his knees and fell over.

Gun Boy jumped to his feet. "Hey, McMillan. You okay?"

Knowing exactly where Eric was, or had been, steadied Hunter's nerves. He caught his unwary prey in a chokehold, hitting him with the hypo at the same time. Gun Boy relaxed forward, hugging his weapon like a little kid with a teddy bear.

"Stop telling lies and keep your fucking hands off Meredith Flynn," Hunter ordered in a muffled voice. Maybe not the perfect mental suggestion, but one he meant with every beat of his heart.

If that quick and easy takedown didn't make him feel like the friggin' sandman, nothing did. There he was, putting guys to sleep and whispering sugarplum dreams instead of killing them. Meredith would be proud.

He ducked back between the rigs and kept to his appointed rounds. Arguing came from his left at the rear of the second trailer. A louder debate came from inside. A roar. The sounds of a scuffle. Or a knockdown drag-out.

Hunter headed left. Three guards, make that three mutineers, stood behind the rig, discussing how or if they should take Masters down. One craned his neck around the far corner and freaked. "Shit, guys. We've got men down."

By the time he looked back, his fellow traitors were also down. Hunter moved fast and number three went to sleep, again with the stern admonition to tell the truth and leave MI and The TEAM agents alone. Especially Meredith.

Hunter traded the empty hypo for the full. He hadn't used Eric's recommended half-dose, though, more like half of that. Peering into the camp, he spied five more of Burdette's men sprawled on the ground. All asleep. But where was Eric?

Hunter tapped his helmet. "Can you target an ACS₃ suit in the vicinity?"

"Yes, Agent Christian," that calm automaton voice of hers answered. "Each helmet comes with a tracking chip."

The crosshairs dead center of Hunter's head's up display rotated to the left, zoomed out, and placed Eric at the passenger door of the same rig's semi, less than ten feet away. Helmet Lady advised, "Previous readings confirm target acquired is Agent Eric Reynolds. Shall I terminate?"

"Sh-shit no. Don't kill him!" he stuttered, instantly aware how powerful this suit could be in the wrong hands and how much he sounded like a fool. He'd have swiped his brow if he could have. Mental note to self: *Don't ever—ever—piss her off.*

"Understood," she responded emotionlessly, like the cold-blooded killer computer program she was. Another note to self: *This suit could cause additional friendly-fire accidents. Strict protocols were needed before ACS became regular GI. More testing. Lots more testing.*

"Wait a minute. Previous readings? Eric's been in one of these suits before?" *The snake!*

"Yes, Agent Reynolds has participated in several preliminary ACS₃ trials."

Several? Hunter tapped his index finger on the plunger in his hand. Maybe good old Eric needed a shot of this truth serum—in the same cheek Hunter had shot in Beirut. "Lock onto him without shooting him. I just need to know where he is."

"Affirmative."

Now that he knew Eric's exact location, the game changed. Hunter proceeded directly to 'Go.' Rounding the rig, he stopped at the side door in time to duck a shot. The trailer door opened and a bleeding body tumbled out.

"Does anyone else think he's in charge?" Masters roared from inside.

Hunter looked up at the angry man, now back in a black uniform. Masters looked a little worse for wear. Welts circled his wrists. The right side of his face testified he'd been dragged. Fine by Hunter. He hadn't expected the jungle life would've eaten Masters *entirely*. Tasted maybe. A man could only hope.

"Then get the hell out of here. All of you! Next man takes me on will get the same. Clark, bury this SOB."

Clark tried to move around Masters at the doorway only to be grabbed by the throat. "Don't think I won't," Masters hissed into his reddened face. "I know damned well you're behind this little mutiny. I've had enough of your whining. I tell you to do something? From now on you'd better be on it like stink on shit."

"N-no, sir," Clark mumbled. "I mean, yes, sir."

Hunter stepped back and made room for the party just in time. Masters shoved Clark down the steps and dropped to ground level not two feet from Hunter's position. His men followed, all nine of them. He stalked forward, glaring, his fists clenched. "I'm finding that bitch today if it's the last thing I do. Teach wants her dead or alive. Dead works just fine for me."

Hunter's ears pricked to attention. *Dead works for me, too. Only it will be you. Not Merry.*

Masters halted at the bizarre scene laid out in camp. He was down to eight men in his renegade army and losing ground fast. "What the hell's going on?" he roared.

His eyes widened when Eric moved in quickly and sent another unsuspecting mercenary to dreamland. Hunter added insult to injury, and Clark crumbled alongside the body he was supposed to bury.

"Gawddamnit!" Masters drew his pistol and backed against the trailer. What was left of his nervous men followed. "Who's out there?"

Like an invisible guy would be dumb enough to answer? Hunter rolled one shoulder. *Time to change tactics.*

"Agent Hunter," Helmet Lady's soft voice interrupted the standoff. "Enemy combatant approaching at your rear. ETA seven seconds and—"

Hunter flattened his back to the side of the trailer just in time. Masters was panicked enough to—BLAM!

Damn. He'd just shot his own man.

"Son-of-a-bitch!" Masters hissed, his weapon lowered a mite too late.

Hunter had seen this kind of panic before. Fear spread like wildfire and it made men do some crazy stuff. These guys were running scared.

He upped the ante and stabbed the closest man's bicep, then ducked behind the rig. Sure enough, when that man keeled over, several of Masters' men fired wildly.

Hunter crept back toward Masters and hunkered low. His heads-up display adjusted the crosshairs when Eric crouched to stick the leg of the man nearest him. As the guard dropped, Eric rolled beneath the trailer and out of range.

Hunter smiled. *Good thinking, Reynolds.* Since he was already at ground level, he did the same.

Masters and what was left of his quickly diminishing army sprayed their weapons in all-out panic, killing plenty of jungle greenery while Hunter and Eric delivered two more shots.

Down went those guards and Masters came unglued, veins bulging off his forehead and down the sides of his neck. "I know you're out there, Christian! Fight like a man! Show yourself!"

CHAPTER TWENTY-SEVEN

The steady *slap-slap* of rotor blades in the distance woke Meredith.

"Don't move," Seth whispered, his palm warm and gentle on her wrist. "We've got company."

Meredith finished another slow stretch. The sun was high, but they were safely concealed by ivy and shade. The helicopter sounded far away. "How long will it take for your boss to get here?"

Seth pointed directly across the river. "I meant them."

That got her attention. She eased upright. Sure enough, two men in dark green cammies stood on the opposite bank, looking upriver before they scanned the opposite shoreline and then downriver.

"Recognize anyone?" Teague looked pretty sleepy, too.

"Jordan Hannigan and Lee Hart," Seth murmured, his voice low and eyes on his buddies. "Keep still. Let's see how long it takes them to spot us."

"Hannigan and Hart, huh? Sounds like a vaudeville act." Teague's pistol rested comfortably on his stomach as the pair of snipers crossed the dam over the river. They paused at the third waterfall, but not once did they falter or seem off-balance. One stayed outside scanning the shoreline, his short stock weapon snug to his chest while the other ducked into the cave.

"Which is which?" Meredith straightened to see them better. The one tramped out of the cave. Both bent their heads together, obviously perplexed.

"Lee's the taller of the two," Seth answered. "Jordan's cap is backward."

Jordan lifted his shoulders at whatever Lee had just asked. Both were a slighter build than Hunter, but obviously ex-military judging by their alert, rigid posture. It didn't hurt that Jordan's baseball cap declared *TEAM* in bright gold, or that both were armed exactly like Hunter. Meredith's heart skipped a beat.

"Why the cat-and-mouse game?" Teague asked when Lee's gaze zeroed in on the shadows behind the vines. "Why not let 'em know we're here?"

"Just want to see how long it takes two jarheads to locate regular Army," Seth replied smoothly.

In seconds, Jordan and Lee joined them. "Alex said you cut yourself shaving again," Lee said when he spotted Seth. Nodding to Meredith, he tipped two fingers to his forehead. "Afternoon, ma'am. Are you ready to get back to civilization?"

A swell of relief filled her. "I am."

"Then let's get these guys ready to travel." Lee knelt alongside Seth and patted his shoulder, right where he'd been cut. "Where's it hurt?"

Seth grimaced. "Not there. Leave me alone."

"Here?" Jordan poked the very visible bandages Meredith had personally applied.

Seth shrugged away from his friend's teasing manhandling. "Get your grubby paws off me."

"Can't help if we can't touch," Lee teased. "Come on, man, seriously. Let's see how you're doing."

Seth stilled when Lee peeled back the bandage on his bicep. The teasing stopped. "Did you kill the SOB who did this?" Lee hissed.

"Not yet." Seth pulled the bandage back down and pressed the tape to secure it. "Where's Alex?"

Lee scanned the sky. "Looking for a place to land. He's in a private chopper. We would've been here sooner, but damn. These jungles are full of snakes. Where's Hunt?"

"He and Eric left early this morning for Burdette's camp," Seth said. "I was hoping they'd be back by now, but—"

Jordan lifted to his feet. "I'm on it," he told Lee.

Seth pointed north. "The camp's nearly two clicks that—"

"Don't worry. I know right where Burdette's camp is," Jordan assured as he tapped his forehead. "Mother's pulled more satellite images than you can imagine. Trust me. I'll find them."

"Stay in touch," Lee ordered Jordan.

"Always do." Without another word, Jordan crossed the dam and ducked into the jungle.

"Is there anything left to salvage from either camp?" Lee asked Meredith.

"I don't think so. We managed to get one supply crate, but I think Burdette's men destroyed everything else."

"Would you like to call home?" A gentle smile lit his eyes as he lifted the sat phone off his belt.

Meredith nodded and latched onto the phone. "Thank you."

Courtney answered her parent's phone on the third ring. "Hello?"

She couldn't hold back her tears. "Hi, sweetie. It's me."

The connection rattled as he shouted, "Gramma! It's Mama!" Then a bright, "I making brownies!"

"Are you helping Gramma?"

"Ah-huh!"

Meredith could almost see those sweet little blue eyes. Right now he'd be twisting the phone cord on her mother's old reliable wall unit until he was tangled in it.

"I miss you, Mama."

"I miss you too, and guess what?"

"What?"

"I'm coming home real soon. Maybe tomorrow."

"Oh, goodie!" Meredith listened as the receiver hit the floor on Courtney's end. He must have run to tell her mother the news.

Finally, her mother took over. "How are you, Meredith? How's your beta test going?"

"I'm good, Mom," Meredith hedged. "The test went fine. I'm just tired. It's been a long couple of days. I should be home in the next day or so." *I hope.*

"Well, don't worry about a thing. Court's doing fine, so take all the time you need. Your father and I are taking him to the zoo tomorrow and..." She paused. "You need to know that your ex has been calling."

Meredith's blood ran cold. "Did he say what he wanted?"

"Oh, yes. He talked my ear off the first time. He wanted to know where you were and what you were doing with your life."

"You didn't tell him, did you?"

"Heavens no. I never had any use for that boy. He did say something about getting back together though. Be prepared. That man wants something."

"Don't worry, Mom. He burned that bridge a long time ago. Hey, guess what? I met an old friend down here."

"In Brazil?" her mother exclaimed. "Who on earth could that be?"

"Hunter Christian." Just saying his name set that fire in Meredith's belly to glowing.

"Oh, for heaven's sake. What's he doing down there?"

"It turns out he was part of the beta test."

"That boy sure had a crush on you."

Meredith closed her eyes, remembering the latest crush of his hard male body against hers. "He still does, Mom. He's looking good." *Really good.*

"Does he live on the East Coast, too? That would be nice."

Meredith smiled. "I'm not sure where he lives, but Mom. He asked me to marry him."

Dead silence.

Meredith shook her phone. "Mom? Are you still there?"

"Meredith Olivia Flynn," her mother scolded. "Are you serious?"

"I thought you'd be happy."

"I am, but you've only been gone a few days and… Are you sure about marriage? It seems quite fast and—"

Meredith's breath caught. It was like watching a chameleon change colors. One minute the jungle was nothing but leafy green. The next, an armed and camouflaged warrior in face paint and shadows stood on the opposite shore. Ramrod straight. Shoulders back. Looking straight at her.

Alex Stewart had arrived.

"Meredith? Are you there?" her mother called.

"Yes, Mom. Listen. I have to go. I'll call when I know for sure when I'm coming home. Give Courtney a kiss and a hug for me."

With a curt chin lift, Alex acknowledged her even as his eyes tracked the river's tumultuous journey from east to west. His gaze flicked from the top of the falls and back to her, his face as hard as the granite wall behind her.

"You know I will. Take care of yourself. I love you, Meredith."

"I love you, Mom. Tell Dad hi for me." With that, she signed off as three other men uncloaked to Alex's left, all in the same tactical gear. She cocked her head in disbelief at the sight. None had relied on Jed's ActiveCamouflage technology, yet there they were. Invisible one moment. Poised for war the next.

Electricity crackled when Lee met Alex at the edge of the river. The three men with him seemed an extension of that energy as a lively discussion ensued. The kindly looking American-Chinese agent gave Meredith a gentle nod of respect. David Tao, one of the men behind the much-publicized takedown of the Black Dragon Syndicate in D.C.

The one who resembled Alex in physique and stature, smiled as he crouched near Seth. Adam Torrey. His plane crash in the Pacific had led to an unexpected coupe for McCormack Industry when Paul Reagan, one of Jed's fiercest adversaries, ended up being the killer behind the supposed *accident*. His only surviving heir, Shannon Reagan, dumped every last one of Reagan's proprietary secrets on Jed when she washed her hands of her father's betrayal. Another story for the books.

But the third warrior at Alex's side was Hunter all over again, only this man had a wide-open smile that seemed to say, *'Let's play!'* Zack Lennox. In the flesh. Every woman's idea of hot-and-heavy eye candy, plain and simple.

Dark scruff covered his chin and shaved head. Broad-chested, with a heavy backpack strapped to his shoulders, he trudged past Alex, dropped one knee to the ground and shrugged his over-sized pack off. Peeling it open, he pulled out several foil packages. "I brought lunch. Anyone hungry?"

That was Zack. A capable sniper with a penchant for gourmet food that he fixed himself. But Alex was all business. "Sit rep first."

"Assume Hunter and Eric are still engaged at Burdette's camp," Lee replied. "Jordan left to assist. We've recovered one of the ACS_3 units, still in the MI supply crate. Hunt and Eric have the other two. Seth and Teague are both stable and ready to travel."

Alex glanced at the men, both reclining in the shade. "Can they walk?"

"That depends," Lee replied. "How far away did you land?"

Alex nodded downriver. "Two klicks east. The pilot's waiting."

"They'll need help getting there." Lee cupped Meredith's elbow. "Boss, this is Meredith Flynn, Chief Engineer Teague's assistant."

"I know who she is." Alex's demeanor softened, which only made Meredith more nervous. She offered her hand, which he accepted in a gentle grip. "Hunter said you took the first shot, Ms. Flynn. Damned good job. Jed says you're levelheaded, one of his best. I'm glad to finally meet you."

This man was Jed's equal, a mover and shaker in his own right, but Meredith refused to be intimidated. Strengthening her grip, she hoped she gave Alex as good as she got. "It's good to finally meet you too, Mr. Stewart. I would've preferred your presence here as a measure of our success rather than our failure."

"Call me Alex, please. You haven't failed yet, Meredith," he replied warmly, releasing her hand. "I'm sorry you lost two men though. We'll assist with body recovering. Do you know where they are?"

Saliva pooled at the back of her throat just thinking about the tangled mess of corpses decomposing in the jungle. Somewhere. She glanced toward the jungle. "Umm, yes, they're—"

Again, Lee saved the day. "I'll handle it, Boss. We'll transport Seth and Teague first." He turned to Meredith. "Would you mind staying with them at the chopper until we're ready to fly?"

She balked. She'd meant to be there when Hunter returned, not two clicks east.

Lee continued. "Meet Senior Agent David Tao, our resident martial arts expert. Junior Agent Adam Torrey, and the guy with the food is Zack Lennox. David and Zack will accompany you to the chopper. You'll be in good hands."

How could she not do her part? Meredith stifled her worry and just like that, lunch was served and good old-fashioned camaraderie enveloped the beleaguered team like a comforting blanket. Alex turned into Seth and Teague's personal servant, making sure they were fed first. David and

Zack catered to Meredith. David pulled out a collapsible three-legged stool from his pack while Zack spread a red-and-white checkered cloth, picnic style.

Lee's sat phone rang when Jordan reported in. He hadn't made contact yet, but he had passed though both the MI and TEAM camps. He'd encountered no resistance and was advancing on Burdette's camp.

Alex and his men continued exchanging information, but the angst of their initial encounter diminished. The scene resembled a picnic until Lee's phone rang again. When he signaled Alex, Alex lifted to his feet and disappeared into the jungle without a word.

CHAPTER TWENTY-EIGHT

"Fine. I give. I give!" Tough-guy Masters raised his hands in surrender.

Hunter relieved the startled man of his weapon while Eric lifted his visor and reverted to visibility.

"I should've known it was you, Reynolds," Masters griped. He knew he'd been beaten, but he had no idea where to shoot without killing more of his men. Most of them already lay useless around him. A couple snored. "Shit, you guys are as dumb as Burdette."

Hunter de-cloaked, his rifle—not his hypo—trained on the last standing enemy combatant. "What are you talking about? Why'd you kill him?"

Masters gestured at the silent rigs. "Why not? The dumb bastard thought he could get his company back. Thought if he destroyed McCormack, he could corner the defense market. Thought if he brought Flynn back alive—" Hunter hated the way Masters twisted that word, "—he'd be rich. Well, I've got news for you. He ain't getting nothing back. The dumb bastard also thought I worked for him."

"Enough with the games!" Hunter roared. "Spit it out or I swear I'll kill you right now."

Masters leered, nodding toward the number one rig. "But that's where you're wrong. It *is* a game. This board's been set up for months and the pieces are moving. You think because you won here today that anybody cares? The kid's already dead. So's that sweet little thing you've been banging. Shit, she's no brighter than Burdette. Mrs. Tight Ass Flynn is yesterday's trash. She just doesn't know it yet."

"What kid?" Enlightenment dawned on Hunter. *This was about Courtney?* He charged, knocking Masters down to the ground. "I'm gonna ask you one more time. What's Meredith got to do with Burdette?"

Masters laughed in his face. "Nothing."

"Then who's trying to kill her?"

"Teach. Who'd you think?"

"Who the hell is Teach? Why's he want her dead?"

"Roger Teach, you moron!" Masters spat. "The guy who now owns Brinkman EX. The guy who's gonna own Alex Stewart's ass before this op is through. The guy who's gonna own you!"

"Hunter!" Eric's voice finally got through to him, but all he could see was the baleful gray eyes glaring up at him. "Back off," Eric tried again. "Come on. Let's get him back to camp. We can work on him there."

Hunter complied only because Eric made sense. Jerking Masters to his feet, he growled into his ear, "Meredith's not going to die. You are. Get moving."

"What about the rest of these guys?" Eric asked. "We can't just leave them here, not like this."

"Bet me?" Hunter twisted Masters' arms behind his back. "Alex will be here soon. They'll be safe until then. Besides, nothing can get inside this compound. Take a look inside both rigs before we leave, though. You know. For Ky."

Eric took all of five minutes to accomplish Hunter's order. "Not here. They're both torn apart and there's plenty of blood spatter in that one." He nodded toward the first rig. "Who else is dead besides Burdette?"

"Two more guards," Hunter stated. "They're out back, shot execution style. Grab a key fob out of one of these guys' pockets to open the gate. We've got what we came for. Let's go."

After Eric located a fob and opened the gate, Hunter pushed Masters forward, glad hell week was nearly behind him. But Masters' answers had offered no peace. Hunter still didn't know why Roger Teach had targeted Meredith or her son. He might just have to use some of that green shit in his last hypo on Masters.

Then there was Ky. Time was short and his missing friend compounded Hunter's anxiety. When Alex arrived, the operation would be over. Alex would evacuate his team and what was left of Teague's to safety. Where would that leave Ky? Deserting a fellow soldier wasn't in Hunter's playbook.

Just then Jordan broke cover on the trail ahead of him. "Hey guys."

"The boss is here?" Hunter asked.

"Should be right behind me," Jordan responded, peering at Masters. "I heard shooting. Everything okay?"

Hunter nodded. "It is now. This guy's still got some explaining to do, but we left everyone else back there." He released Masters arms. "You two make sure this bastard gets back to camp?"

"Sure thing." Jordan pulled a pair of cuffs off his belt and secured the last enemy standing.

"Where are you off to?" Eric asked.

"I'm making one more sweep for Ky," Hunter explained. "He's got to be here somewhere."

"This is a big damned jungle," Eric stated the obvious, his weapon now in the center of Masters' back.

"Yes, but we're fenced in, remember? He's got to be close by. Now that I'm wearing all this technology, I'm scouting the perimeter before we leave. I might have to fly out of here today, but I won't leave the country until I know what happened to him."

"Alex contacted Brazilian authorities," Jordan said. "They'll be here soon. Why don't you wait for them?"

"Call it a gut feeling." Hunter turned toward the burned out camp that had briefly housed his team. "You heard Masters, Eric. Alex needs to put a security detail on Meredith. Her son, too. He needs to take down that damned electric fence and find out who the hell Roger Teach is."

"Will do," Eric answered. "Let me get Masters to Alex, and I'll come back and help. You're right. Ky's got to be here."

While Eric headed one way, Hunter went the other. He veered southwest, his heart aching for his lost friend. He tugged back into his ActiveCamouflageSystem helmet, enough to reactivate his visor. Ky had disappeared the first night. If he'd been wounded, there had to be some trace of him between both camps. Maybe a blood trail.

"Trace Ky Winchester's biometrics," he ordered the ACS_3, hoping that information was somehow stored in its computer chips.

"Working."

Hunter left his helmet unstrapped, but kept his head on a swivel as he moved swiftly through the brush and vines. Ky wasn't hiding, but something catastrophic had happened to him. Seth hadn't seen him in Burdette's tent, yet he'd been with Seth during the initial attack. Just one last look, that was all Hunter wanted. One last sweep through the area. Just in case.

"Agent Winchester is not in this grid."

Hunter slapped an open palm to his thigh. Didn't that figure? "How large is this grid?"

"One square mile."

"Then search the next one."

"Working."

Ky's disappearance made no sense. It was as if he'd vanished into thin air. Frustration mounted. On Hunter's way out of camp, an odd moan similar to the wintry wind whistling through windows and doors caught his ear. He cocked his head to zero in on where that noise came from, but the jungle stilled. Great. Now he was hearing things.

"I'm not leaving you, brother," he explained. "I'm coming back, and when I do, I'm bringing reinforcements."

As if in answer, another barely audible whistle. Hunter turned toward the sound, sure he'd heard it this time. He put the helmet back on and re-engaged ACS_3. "Identify that noise."

"Working."

While she worked, Hunter marched toward the sound that came from, oddly, the same place Seth had said he and Ky were intercepted. Brushing through the thick undergrowth, the whistling grew louder.

"Do you hear that?" he asked the lady in his helmet. Stepping off the trail, he followed his gut. Not ten yards into the brush, he spotted a curling wisp of—fog? It looked more like someone had left a cigarette butt smoking instead of grinding it out. *What the hell?*

Too late he remembered another geological feature carved out by the mighty Amazon. But by then, he was tumbling face forward into Pitch. Dark. Nothing.

CHAPTER TWENTY-NINE

Meredith couldn't move her gaze from the jungle. Surrounded by men who could easily take on whatever it threw at them, her unease still grew. It had been slow going to the chopper. Adam and David carried Seth while Lee and Zack transported Teague, but they'd made the trek without incident. Seth and Teague were now ready for transport, both resting in litters outside the Army drab chopper. Lee maintained constant vigil at her side.

"Ma'am?" He tried again. "The boss wants us aboard when he gets back."

"Not yet," she pleaded. "Please? Hunter's coming; I need to know he's okay."

Lee bowed his head and stepped away, another polite gentleman like the others. The careful way these guys handled Seth and Teague had caught her eye. Their initial rough treatment had been replaced by an almost protective guardianship over their wounded brother.

The sun had dropped in the west when Eric and Jordan finally appeared with their prisoner. At first glance, he looked like the same kind of man as they were, but the glint in his eye took Meredith back a step. His sneer of contempt left her cold and afraid.

Lee stepped in front of her as if to break eye contact. "Is this him?"

"Travis Masters," Eric introduced the prisoner. "Ex-Marine if his tattoo's not a lie. Murderer. Scumbag. You know the type. He's the one who tortured Seth and killed Burdette."

"Go to hell," Masters muttered, jerking his elbow out of Eric's grip.

Meredith took another step back. She turned toward Seth, now raised on his elbows and scowling across the distance.

It happened in the blink of an eye. Eric leaned behind Masters, his hands on Masters arms. "What the hell have you—?"

Masters whirled on Eric, cuffs dangling off his wrist. He plunged a dagger into Eric's abdomen, not once but three times.

"No! No! No!" Meredith shrieked as she ran to help. This couldn't be happening!

BLAM! A single shot ripped past her, the thunder of it stealing her breath. Meredith froze, afraid to move. Time stopped for the one long eternal second as she met Masters' grim stare.

"I'll be damned..." Masters blinked wide eyes across the clearing. Past Meredith. To Seth. To the gun in Seth's hand.

"You'll be *God damned,* you bastard!" Seth roared at him. "Go to hell!"

A red fountain gurgled out of Masters' windpipe as he toppled to the dirt, and

chaos took over. Lee and Zack were on Eric in seconds. They ripped his shirt open, both frantically working to staunch the blood. Meredith ran for a medical kit, but Zack had already spread emergency supplies alongside Eric. Where they came from, she hadn't a clue. He and Lee worked furiously as they filled all three wounds with some kind of aerosol foam that slowed the blood loss.

God, this can't be happening.

Eric hadn't made a sound since he'd fallen. Pressure bandages came next, both Lee and Zack working in sync as if they'd performed this exact sort of first-aid before. Lee's eyes were grim, but not once did he hesitate. "He's losing too much blood. We need to get him to a hospital now."

Zack answered with a grunt, one hand compressing Eric's wound while he ripped the thick roll of tape clamped under his chin with his teeth. Meredith took the roll and tore strip after strip while he secured the slippery bandaging. Seth was on his feet, handing Lee supplies despite his own injuries.

Lee tucked his sat phone between his ear and shoulder. "There's no time, Boss. David and Adam will wait for you and I'll send the chopper right back. Stay put." He ended the call and hooked the phone to his belt, gesturing to the waiting helicopter. "Ms. Flynn, please. You're coming with me."

Zack and Adam loaded Eric aboard along with Seth and Teague before they took their seats. Meredith sat on the bench beside Eric and Zack, praying for the man dying at her fingertips and all the men she'd left behind.

In minutes, the chopper lifted vertically. It hovered over the immense sea of emerald green rippling below. Her heart reached through that canopy, wishing for that elusive more with Hunter she never seemed to get.

Meredith wiped a single tear. And she left.

The terror ride wouldn't end.

Dropping what felt like several hundred feet landed Hunter into a roaring torrent of churning ice-cold water. The subterranean rock tumbler seemed hell-bent on polishing off any part of him of that protruded, like his fingers, his elbows, and his nose. He'd already lost the ACS$_3$ helmet. With no way to see, he thrashed for any handhold to stop himself from the relentless pounding, but he found no purchase. Only water. Thunder. And the most helpless sensation of being ragdolled by the serial killer benignly called Mother Nature.

He tumbled end-over-end while everyone he'd ever held dear flashed through his battered brain. His mother and father. His friends. Meredith. Like Ky, they'd never know what had happened to him. He'd unwittingly become one of those question marks that would forever haunt them for the rest of their lives.

Son-of-a-bitch!

Cursing the universe, he rolled, make that floundered against the current's merciless grip. He'd only succeeded in cracking his head. Knowing he was close enough to hit a solid edge should've offered hope, but it didn't. Just as quickly as he'd made contact with what might have been his salvation, he'd lost it. Hunter had no choice. The underground river swept him away and away he went.

At last the watery spin cycle ceased. The current slowed. Smooth edges whispered past his fingertips. Stone ground against his chin. Then his chest. His knees touched bottom. The toes of his boots dragged. His battered hands reached for something—anything—with enough substance to support his weight.

Finally! A rock ledge. His fingernails clawed for a solid grip, but the water tugged him away. Kicking for his life, he fought the river until, inch by inch, he dragged his cheek and chin onto a cold, smooth surface. With his boots dangling in the water, he dropped facedown to what felt like concrete but smelled like dirt. It was good enough for what followed the moment he was stationary. Grit-filled water spewed from his throat and nose until he could vomit no more.

Sucking in a searing, labored breath, he coughed and sneezed and sputtered to clear the water out of his burning lungs. His drunken tilt-a-whirl ride to hell was over, but the sensation of falling wasn't. There was no light in this place to get his bearings. No glimmer. Only a cold black darkness that left him eerily disoriented and dizzier than hell. He couldn't tell down from up. Hunter clung to the cold rock like a drunk to his sidewalk, while he willed the urge to hurl away.

Everything hurt. For the time being, he seemed to be on stable ground that didn't move. Well, maybe. Hunter honestly couldn't see enough to tell for certain where he was. The solid mass beneath his aching ribs declared he'd stopped moving, but try telling that to his stomach and head. They hadn't stopped rolling from the rock polisher he'd crept out of.

With no strength left to care what happened next, Hunter closed his stinging eyes. How would he get back to Merry now? The din of wherever-he-was deafened, and his head hurt with a magnitude of ten on the migraine scale that ended at five.

Soaked to the core and scraped raw, he toed his boots nearly off, but then worried they might fall in the river. Hunter eased to his butt. There wasn't one molecule of his body that wasn't bludgeoned and bruised. Bending one aching knee at a time, he pulled his feet out of the water and removed both boots. He knotted his socks and tucked them inside his boots next. A warrior always kept his footgear dry.

He rolled to his side, shivering as he tied the laces together and hung the boots over his neck to make sure he didn't lose them. Wet leather had never smelled so good. Exhaustion from that simple survival instinct claimed him, and Hunter went willingly into oblivion. *Rest now. Worry later.*

He slept until the noisy river woke him again. By then, his tenderized muscles had gone stiff. Breathing hurt and he was certain his eyes were filled with slivers that raked the inside of his eyelids. Wiping a hand over his face confirmed that it was better to endure the pain instead of clearing it away. His eyeballs watered profusely at the contact, but nothing brought relief.

Fear whispered there was light in this deep, dark cavern; he just couldn't see it.

Holy shit.

Lying there in the dark with his clothes drenched, his body beat to hell, and exhausted to his bones, the irony of his predicament struck him. He'd finally found the one person on the planet he'd ever loved, only to lose her with one lousy misstep? What an unlucky bastard he was.

Hunter hugged his boots while he completed a quick mental self-assessment of what hurt the worst, his back, head, or—hell, everything else. There was no contest. Every muscle screamed at the brutal gauntlet he'd survived. Even his ears were tender, as if the river had sanded his skin. Make that peeled. *What now?*

Like he had choices. His eyes, if they weren't damaged, were useless without light. The babbling brook on steroids alongside of him drowned out any rescuer calling to him. If there was a way out of this cavern, it'd be a fucking miracle.

He shivered as his cold, hard reality sunk in. He'd lost every last bit of the ActiveCamouflageSystem. He had no pistol. No holster. No knife. Hell, he barely had fingerprints or fingernails left. This was bad. Really bad.

Falling through the Earth's crust like he had explained one thing though.

He now knew what happened to Ky.

CHAPTER THIRTY

Meredith didn't know which city she was in, and she didn't care. Life came to a standstill while the best physician on staff at the local hospital performed emergency surgery on Eric Reynolds. Seth and Teague were already in a recovery ward after undergoing their own medical assessments. Lee and Zack sat in the tidy waiting room with her. But she'd never felt more alone. She paced the checkered black-and-white flooring, counting how many tiles in each rotation.

Poor Eric. The look in his bright dark eyes had gone from shock to bleak nothingness so quickly. And Masters? He'd bled out in less than a minute, maybe just as surprised by the turn of events as Eric had been.

Meredith turned on her heel to make another lap. She didn't know what happened to Masters after Seth shot him. She didn't care that no one ran to his aid. For the first time in her life, she was glad a wicked man had died and died hard. She only wished she'd been the one to put Masters down before he'd knifed Eric.

Now I sound just like Hunter.

But Eric was the sort of man a girl instantly felt a connection with. He was kind and thoughtful, handsome and dashing and...

Is the sort of man. *Is kind! Is thoughtful!*

She closed her eyes to keep the tears at bay, ashamed she'd used the past tense to describe him. He wasn't dead yet. He couldn't be.

Is! Is! Is!

"How is he?" Alex barked the second his boots hit the emergency room floor. But when Meredith turned to face him, his eyes flickered away from her to Zack. "Well?"

Her heart pitched to the linoleum. *If you're here, where's Hunter?*

"We're still waiting, Boss. Eric's been in surgery for hours. Seth and Teague are doing well. Do you want to talk with them?"

"I want answers," Alex shot back at him. "How the hell did this happen?"

Lee growled as he bowed his head. "Then Seth can't help you. From what we can tell, Masters slipped his cuffs. He grabbed a knife from somewhere, might have had it up his sleeve. Hell, I don't know."

"Where's Hunter?" Meredith asked, her throat tight and her heart pounding.

Hard blue eyes skewered her through. Her breath caught. Alex commanded his men like General George S. Patton with a steady touch of Jesus Christ thrown into the mix. Patton because he knew how to lead. Reputation had it that Alex's men would literally follow him into Hell. Jesus Christ because, for all his steel and take-no-quarter attitude, Alex was also known to work a gentle miracle now and then. He pulled his ragtag team of soldiers and misfits up by their bootstraps, and his men and women loved him for it.

"Where is he? Tell me?" She hated the pleading cry in her voice. "Alex?"

"I don't know yet, Meredith," he answered quietly. "That's why I'm late getting here. David, Jordan, and I have been all over the jungle searching for him. Hunt's vanished into thin air, just like Ky."

Meredith jumped to her feet. "What do you mean vanished?"

"He's not responding to the sat phone he had. We can't find any trace of him or Ky, and believe me, we've been all over that fenced-in couple of acres looking for him."

Lee cupped her elbow, holding her in place even as he declared, "We need to go back."

"Don't you think I know that?" Alex snapped. "We're all going back. David, Jordan and Adam are still there."

"But..." Meredith's voice caught in her throat. "But... where could he be? He should've come back with Eric. Why didn't he?"

Lee's arm snaked around her shoulder. "He'll be okay, ma'am. Hunt's tough. You know that. He's a scrapper. A survivor. By the time we get back there—"

"No!" She burst with fatigue and stress. "He's not that way at all! He's a poet. He writes songs for me, and he's... he's kind and gentle and—"

"Hunt?" Lee's brows lifted like McDonald's golden arches. "Are we talking about the same guy?"

Tears filled her eyes at the gentle tease. Lee might've thought he was comforting her, but these guys only knew the hard side of the man. Meredith clapped her jaw shut and stowed her heart. Turning her back on them, her fears got the best of her. She lifted a clenched fist to her teeth. First Lyle and Dan. Maybe Ky. Maybe Eric. Now Hunter.

The jungle had taken too much!

Lee's hand on her shoulder brought her around. His green eyes filled with kindness for which she had no resistance. "I'm sorry, ma'am. I didn't mean to upset you. We will find him. *I'll* find him."

That was the last straw. A muffled sob hiccupped out of her as her heart caved in and the floor came up. Down she went to her knees—hard. Lee went with her, but Alex and Zack quickly joined them, all crouched at her side, penitent and striving to shelter her from more grief.

"Lean her back," Alex ordered. "Give her room to breathe."

"She's exhausted," Zack muttered. "Poor gal. This operation's been a nightmare."

And it was Lee again, his palm firmly pillowing the back of her head.

She grabbed onto his hand. "I can't lose him," she cried, her heart stuck in her throat.

"You won't," Lee promised. "Look at me, Meredith. Open your eyes and look at me."

She gulped and did as he asked.

"Hunt's searching for Ky, I know he is," Lee told her firmly. "Think about that for a minute. Hunt never could leave a man behind. Do you think we're any different?"

She honestly didn't know what to think, so she said what came to her mind. "But there are snakes in the jungle. And monkeys. A panther. I saw it. And bugs. Spiders."

Lee nodded once. "They'd better stay the hell out of his way then."

That actually—helped. Meredith took a deep breath. She needed to stay strong. Hunter would be back. Lee and Alex would find him.

She knew it to her soul.

Moving—make that crawling—hurt like hell. The wicked river had sandpapered his face to the point it felt like a massive third-degree burn. The continual stream of salt water dripping out of his hair stung his eyeballs and tenderized cheeks. His shirt and pants were reduced to strips of ragged cloth that didn't do much to keep him warm. He was wet, but he still had his boots.

The cold was good for something. It got him off the ground and kept him moving. Walking slowly warmed him. A little. Until his feet bumped into something and he stumbled to his knees.

"Holy shit," he cursed out loud—not like he could hear it. The roaring water behind him suppressed all noise. But the thing at his feet was definitely a body. A rigid body.

Hunter lowered to his knees and investigated as little as possible to determine if the corpse might be his friend. Gingerly feeling his way down the length of the stone-cold person, he stopped at the feet. Tennis shoes. Size elevens maybe. It wasn't Ky. He wore steel-toed work boots, sometimes loggers.

Dragging the guy back the way he'd come, Hunter rolled the body into the river, not willing to share his only refuge with a corpse. Then, because he refused to sit on the wet ground and feel sorry for himself, he recommenced the slow shuffle, listening carefully to avoid the edge. A damp wall finally came within reach. Pitted and hard. Sheer stone.

"This sucks!" he bellowed, finally able to hear himself. "I find the one woman I care about and this is what happens? Shit!"

Edging alongside the wall brought no change of terrain or surface. He kept going because he couldn't stay where he'd fallen, could he? There might be a way out of there. He had to try, didn't he?

The ledge seemed to widen. The noise of the river lessened, or maybe he was becoming deaf. At any rate, Hunter continued the journey he'd set his bare feet to. Shuffle along. Grope. Curse. Start again. He was just getting a good temper tantrum up when his fingers touched cloth. And skin. Bare warm skin.

"Shit!" he hissed. *Not another body.*

Only this one was upright. It felt warmer. Drier. It moved. Startled, he jerked away.

Two rough hands grabbed the back of his neck. "Hunt! God, it's you! It's really you!"

A very dim light flickered across his face. Only then did Hunter realize the river had done its worst. He was pretty much blind.

But he wasn't deaf. Ky hugged him, crying like a blubbering baby. "Oh, man! I thought I was lost for good!"

Hunter stiff-armed him. Didn't Ky get it? He wasn't found. They were both lost.

CHAPTER THIRTY-ONE

They searched the fenced-in area for three days until Alex insisted Meredith go home to Courtney. By then she knew some director out of Japan had ordered the fence built prior to filming the latest, greatest monster movie. The electric fence was a realistic prop the director shut down while the search for Hunter and Ky continued.

"No, ma'am. I'm not going anywhere," Alex reassured Meredith at the hastily constructed helicopter pad.

Geologists, spelunkers, and other search-and-rescue teams had been brought in to canvass the hidden caverns of the mighty Amazon River. Teams of men with dogs had located the tiny crevice Alex suspected Hunter had fallen through. Alex expended fortunes exploring underground caves and caverns, but still, no sign of Hunter or Ky.

With a heavy heart, Meredith relented. Courtney needed her. "Call me the minute you find him."

Alex had turned into her most faithful servant. "You know I will."

She cast her gaze up to the surrounding trees that even now reached tendrils of greenery into what had become another TEAM camp. Zack and Lee had become fixtures, leading group after group into the jungle. They'd set up camp and tents where satellite images mapped a ten-mile radius of the place where Hunter was last seen. Then a twenty-mile radius.

To make her melancholy deeper, Eric Reynolds had survived—on life support, which was a good thing, but still. He hadn't come to since he'd fallen, and his chance of a full recovery worsened every day he remained in the coma. Airlifted to the States, he now rested in the best hospital Washington D.C. had to offer.

"I hate to leave," she whispered more to herself than Alex. "Hunter's here. I know he is."

Alex didn't speak, just stood silently at her side until she'd made her decision and said goodbye to the man she might never see again. The rotors tore tears from her eyes when the helicopter lifted off, taking her to a waiting plane. One layover set her down in Miami, and then she was home.

Brazil seemed so far away.

Ky became guardian angel and provider, something Hunter had never needed and didn't know how to accept. Alpha males hated weakness with a passion.

Little annoying things morphed into monsters. Bigger things into rage. Had Eric remembered to warn Alex that Meredith and her son were in danger? Who was that Teach guy anyway? What could the CEO of Brinkman EX possibly have against a working mother with a kid? Was he after her because she worked for Jed? But mostly—

How the hell do I get out of here?

"I'm going exploring again. Do you want to come this time?"

Ky had asked the same damned question the last three days. Hunter had yet to oblige. The weak battery in Ky's penlight had given up the ghost—not like it mattered. There was nothing to see in a world gone bat-shit dark.

And that was another thing.

As regular as clockwork, hordes of bats swarmed down from the ceiling on their way somewhere else. Hunter figured they came and went at twelve-hour intervals. All that flying-silent-with-sonar crap was bullshit. He could hear 'em dropping en masse from somewhere high overhead. In seconds, their parchment-thin, leathery wings brushed over his hair and all but collided with him on their way out. Their squeaks, screeches, and whistles sounded like flying chipmunks drunk on a combination of crystal meth and Everclear. The damned things couldn't seem to fly straight.

But mostly they annoyed him because they could get out while he couldn't. They had a life. A goal. Freedom to come and go. He had next to nothing.

"I made it maybe thirty more feet yesterday," Ky hinted in his non-assuming way. "Straight up."

"Was it a path out of here yet?"

"Not sure, but I did find another ledge. It looks, I mean, it felt promising."

Hunter grunted. Big whoop. A ledge. Was that supposed to be a breakthrough? They didn't even have a decent set of clothes between the two of them. Neither had anything left of their shirts but rags. Their pants and boots seemed to have withstood the river's battery. As for their skin? Plenty scraped, cut, and shredded. He'd been in a few barroom brawls in his life. This one had them beat.

"I've been thinking." Ky was the kind of guy who accepted whatever Hunter dished out without once striking back or arguing. He would've made the perfect lifer. He just kept on keeping on, no matter what.

When he didn't share what he'd been thinking, Hunter gave in and asked, "What?"

"Well, I'm no expert, but it seems to me this river used to be a lot deeper. Something gouged that ledge out. It might have taken millions of years, but that ledge up there has to be the result of natural erosion. That's all it could be. It sure wasn't man-made."

Hunter rolled his eyes, not caring much about the geological formation of his prison. He'd lost his drive. It had been a good four days since he'd last eaten. The water tasted like wet sand, and he was blind. He couldn't for the life of him figure what kept Ky going. Yet Ky was damned near as regular as the bats. The guy spent more time exploring the walls of this cavern than he did the solid ground.

"It makes sense, Hunt, if you think about it. Look at lakeshores the world over. When the water level decreases, it leaves a ledge. A shoreline. Judging the size of this cavern, this river's been rolling for eons."

"Can you see?" Hunter asked quietly, his fists clenched tight.

"You still can't?" Ky moved in closer, his fingers brushing Hunter's bare forearm.

Gritting his teeth, Hunter faced away. If he could see, he wouldn't be asking now, would he? The fall had done him in, but everything was blurry and dark. He didn't know if it was him or if there really was no light in this place.

Hard hits to a man's skull damaged delicate things like retinas. The only thing he'd seen semi-clearly in days was the very dim light from Ky's flashlight, but now even that was gone. And he was worried. Blind men didn't make good soldiers. They didn't even make good men.

"The ceiling in here is covered with some kind of crystal. It glows. Or maybe it's fireflies, some kind of bug or larvae. It almost twinkles, like it's moving," Ky explained what Hunter already knew. They'd had this audio tour of the cavern—how many times before? A dozen? More?

It started again. Way high ceiling. Stalactites hanging down, some so large they'd created walls and columns. Stalagmites aiming upward to join with the stone dripping from above. Churning river aft. The cavern wall starboard unless you faced the opposite direction. Something glittering overhead. Blah, blah, blah.

Hearing about it again didn't mean squat. Hunter needed to see it for a change. He cut Ky off. "Stow the tour."

"Your blindness is probably temporary," Ky encouraged.

But compassion irked Hunter. "You better get climbing. The bats will be back soon."

"You know, that's another thing. Where are they coming from? And where do they go when they leave?"

Hunter turned his face up to the glowing ceiling he couldn't see and began counting to ten. Ky tended toward kindness. Hunter tended toward rage. The two didn't have much in common.

"Come with me," Ky offered again. "You can't stay here forever, and I'm not leaving without you."

"Who said anything about leaving?"

Ky sighed. "You're making this harder than it has to be, Hunt. Instead of us both pressing forward, which makes sense, I have to keep coming back to this spot in the river because you won't move. How do you expect to get rescued if you won't try?"

"I can't see," Hunter reminded him. "How do you expect me to climb sheer stone?"

"It's not sheer. There are plenty of foot and handholds. I'll help you. You'll see."

"No. I won't," Hunter hissed, tapping an index finger to his temple. "Blind as a bat. Handicapped asshole coming through, remember?"

He didn't need to fall again, either. Hunter wouldn't admit it to Ky, but he'd gotten as twitchy as an FNG, as in the fucking new guy in his squad. The river he could hear. He knew where it was, and what it would do to him. But this planet had already proved it hid some ungodly drop-offs. He couldn't afford to make another mistake like that last one and drop into Dante's final level of Hell. Uh-uh.

When Ky took off to play Daniel Boone, Hunter didn't do much more than hunker down and wait for him to return. Besides, Ky was gone for hours at a time, and what good had it done? He'd found a ledge. Big fucking deal.

"Hunt." Ky wouldn't let up. "We need to stay together. I'm worried I might not find my way back one of these times. You could be stuck in here forever."

"Wait a minute," Hunter growled. "Are you telling me I'm holding you up? You'd be better off without me?"

"No, but I don't intend to sit down here and wait to die, either."

The river faded to background noise compared to the roar inside Hunter's head. Had this pipsqueak just called him out? It felt like it, but the worst part? Ky was right and Hunter knew it. He swallowed hard, fighting to get his tough-guy persona back. Fear of falling into that maelstrom of a river had stopped Hunter cold, but blindness was a deeper kind of fear. It made him as helpless as a baby, and it rattled him to his core. It shamed him. Tough guy Hunter, scared? Hell, yeah.

"There's a pair of conjoined stalagmites at my six," Ky continued patiently. "I always start there, swing right, and head west, at least it feels like west to me. Anyway, it's to your right. I figure the underground river's got to flow the same direction as it did upstairs. The Amazon was running west to east, wasn't it?"

"It was," Hunter grumbled.

"So heading west ought to take us uphill."

"What's uphill?"

"Hell, I don't know," Ky admitted. "I just don't want to go down. Up seems like we'll run into a tunnel or chimney or… or something, maybe a way out. There are only two ways we're leaving alive. Either we climb up the first hole in the ceiling that we run into, or we go back into the river and swim for our lives and hope it eventually dumps us into the Amazon."

"Go back into the river? Hell, it's a death trap. It could go on for miles. We won't have to worry about being dumped into the Amazon because we'll be dead." Everything out of Hunter's mouth sounded mean and impatient. Condescending. He couldn't make it stop.

"But what if we find a break in the topography that leads to a way out?"

Hunter clenched his fist, wanting to hit something besides stone.

"Do you feel better now?"

"No!"

"Me either. The point is we're still breathing, Hunt. There's still hope. Lee *is* coming."

Hunter twisted around to stare at the location of Ky's voice. *Are you kidding me? Lee is coming?* What nonsense. Was Ky insane? No one was coming. Couldn't he get that through his thick skull? They were lost in the last place anyone would think to look—under-fucking-ground!

"You and I have been in worse spots," Ky murmured, his voice firm. "Lots worse, Hunt. You know you have."

Hunter turned away. Ky was fixing to go down Memory Lane again, only it wasn't one of those nostalgic trips you took pictures of.

"I wanted to give up and die once. As god-awful as it was in Nizari's torture chamber, I still learned one thing."

Hunter stilled. Ky and Lee Hart were the only two men he knew who'd personally survived torture, and both by the same twisted Taliban bastard in Afghanistan. Nizari. The Taliban banker. Hunter had seen the scars—at least the ones on their arms. Neither covered them up anymore. He had to admit, he was in awe of men who had survived what they had.

"The night Lee found me was a lot darker than this." Ky's voice took on that far-away quality. "Nizari had a new kid on his team. He needed practice. The jackass worked me over good. I thought that was who'd opened my cell door that last time, that he'd come back to dish out more of the same crap. I was so fucking scared I thought I could smell the blow torch in his hand."

Ky drew in a shuddering breath that ended in a groan. "Hell, I was blind then too, so I know how hard this is. That's when I sensed Eden, but honest to God, I thought I'd lost my mind when she came to me like she did. The point is, Hunt, the guy in my cell that last time wasn't there to stick me or burn me. It was Lee. He showed up and he saved me."

The poor guy's breath came in short huffs as he relived his time in Taliban Hell. "And you know what Lee did, right there in the middle of that stinking five-by-five toilet they kept me in? He took me down off that gawddamned hook, Hunt, and he hugged me like I was his little brother, and he talked to me, and he promised he'd come back for me. He promised, Hunt. He gave me a knife so I could defend myself while he was gone. God, I didn't want him to leave. I didn't know it then, but Nizari had Tess, too."

Tess, as in the woman Lee married. Hunter could barely swallow. This part of the nightmare he didn't know.

"Lee gave me something before he left, Hunt. He gave me hope. That's the lesson I learned that night. To hang on. To never quit. Listen, buddy, I don't know what's going to happen to us. I just know. I can feel it in my gut. Somehow. Someway. Lee is coming back for us. He did it before, and he'll do it again. If you're still with me, well..." Ky sniffed, and that was the lowest blow. This trip down Memory Lane had hurt him to share.

Hunter blew out a long, deep sigh. Ky had just offered what every soldier, jarhead, and sailor did for his fallen brethren—a hand up. Damned if it wasn't time to man up, blind or not. Hunter seriously doubted Lee was coming, but point well taken. Ky's heartfelt persuasion made sense. They did need to keep together. There was safety in numbers.

But tough guys didn't ask for help. Hunter hadn't in years, not unless he was already pulling a full load and barking orders at others to do the same. "We might at least find out where these bats are getting in," he replied begrudgingly.

"It'd be nice," Ky agreed, his voice steadier.

The damned ball was back in Hunter's court. It really was time to grow a pair. Face' his fear. Take the risk. Maybe fall again. Maybe die. What the hell? Wasn't that what Marines did? Keep on going until they dropped? "When are we leaving?" he asked.

"Right after breakfast." Which meant right then, since there was no breakfast unless a guy wanted to suck on dirt.

Hunter's stomach pinched in response. The slim possibility of eating again was another good incentive. He squared his shoulders and pushed up from the stone floor one last time. "Are you ready then?"

"You bet."

"Lead on." Hunter groped through the inky darkness, instantly meeting Ky's bare shoulder. The guy was already facing away as if he'd known all along he could get Hunter to follow. *The shit.*

Ky clapped a hand over Hunter's. "I'll get you to the wall. There are plenty of handholds once you get there. It's easy-going at first. Once you get a few feet up, keep the starboard stalagmite at your six for counterbalance. That way you won't fall. Keep talking so I know where you are, okay?"

"Copy that," Hunter said, shuffling slowly only to lose touch with Ky right off the bat. He lurched forward, out-of-control panic hurrying him despite the fact that Ky couldn't have gotten more than a foot away.

Ky halted until Hunter made contact again. "You good?"

Hunter allowed another grumble, but swallowed some of his pride. It went down over the lump in his throat. Felt like his heart. "This is going to be a damned slow walk."

"What's the line about the journey of a thousand miles begins—"

"With one long drop into Hell," Hunter bit out.

"Yeah, well, that first step was a killer," Ky admitted, "but the only way out is up."

"Walk a mile in my shoes," Hunter volleyed right back with another worthless adage.

And so it began, the climb away from the river that had tried to kill him.

Ky's advice was sound. The wall was a conglomeration of wannabe mounds of wet stone pushing upward to meet the dripping stalactites directly above them. Mother Nature didn't seem to have a good handle on the whole patience concept. Now that his socks and boots were dry, getting a foothold had become easier.

"You have a girlfriend?" Ky asked, his voice bouncing an echo from somewhere overhead as the sound of the river below grew quieter.

"Yes. How's Eden?" Hunter declined to offer further personal details. The thought of never seeing Merry again hurt too much.

"The last time I saw her and Kyler, she was good." Ky's voice dropped a decibel. "She had a funny look in her eye the morning I left. The baby's been sick. She hates overseas tours."

"All women do," Hunter offered. He hadn't left a girlfriend behind on any of his tours, much less a wife and son. Compassion for what his partner was going through flared to life. Ky'd been stuck in this cavern longer than Hunter. It had to be killing him to think of Eden and his boy.

"She's psychic, you know," Ky said. "Eden didn't say anything, but I knew she was worried this time. I told her it was no big deal, that I'd be back before she knew it. That this op was easy."

Hunter grunted. He'd thought the same thing.

"She couldn't seem to let go when we said goodbye, and she cried." Ky's tone dropped another pitch, and all Hunter could think of was the stars in Meredith's eyes after she'd climbed out of that tree. She'd glowed as if she'd been lit up inside, like her heart was shining out of those baby blues. He hadn't wanted to let her go, either.

"We're going home," he offered, determined that two could play this encouragement game. He was willing to give hope a shot. For Ky's sake. For Eden. For Meredith.

Ky grunted. "We're here. Lift your arms over your head and feel this."

Hunter complied. A ceiling of cold, wet stone met his fingertips, then his palm. "This the end of the road?"

"Not exactly. It's only a foot wide at this point and it runs for as far as I can see, which isn't far." Ky latched onto Hunter's extended hand. "Now feel here. Get a good hold."

Hunter reached to his right, fingering the edge of the ceiling. "What's this?"

"The lip of the ledge we're going to be walking on."

"Shit," Hunter hissed. "It's narrow. You've been on it?"

"It's narrow right here, but yeah, I've been up there."

Hunter swallowed hard. How the hell was he going to get onto that ledge? He'd have to dangle over free air to do it. What kind of crap had Ky gotten him into?

Ky's palm clapped Hunter's shoulder. "You oughta see the look on your face right now."

No wonder! "It's over my head. And it's narrow." He bit his lip rather than say: *I can't*. But damn. This would be a leap of faith into pitch black nothing.

"It's narrow because it's just a lip, Hunt. Don't worry. We're not climbing onto it just yet. It's a guide for now. A handrail over your head. About thirty feet ahead, you'll notice the path we're on inclines. In another forty or fifty feet, the way forward joins with this ledge and turns into a stair-like terrace. The steps are uneven as hell, but we won't be climbing a wall anymore and we'll keep moving up."

Hunter gulped. He'd always been one of those 'buck up' guys in the Corps. After failing every physical challenge when he'd first enlisted, he'd made it a point to never show weakness. He'd pushed himself until he was not only tougher than most, but toughest of all, top dog and damned proud of it. Humility was something he'd left in the past with poetry, prose, and Meredith. Having to admit he wasn't as good as Ky at rock climbing wasn't his forte.

"You still okay?"

"Why wouldn't I be?" But then he had to admit, "Now that I know I won't have to play Spiderman and hang upside-down over the river."

"Me too," Ky agreed. "The first time I saw this ledge, I thought it was a dead end. I thought what a cruel joke to get this close and not be able to get out of here, but then I kept going. Glad I did. You lead for a while."

Hunter balked. *Lead? Me? A blind guy?*

Ky nudged his right. "Take it slow. The path is narrow, but the way is clear."

"You quoting scripture now?" Hunter groused.

"Not so much." Ky leaned into him, forcing Hunter to move. Of all things, he was learning to trust his right-hand man the hard way. Shuffling to his right brought his foot to what felt like a ninety-degree angle. Lifting that stubborn foot, Hunter climbed his first step. Then another.

Okay, so Ky was right again. The graduated steps made progress easy, but damn. They were only about eight inches wide with a drop off at his right if that updraft meant what Hunter thought it meant. He used the rock edge overhead as a guide until it narrowed and joined the path he walked. By then, he was out of breath and possibly standing at the edge of a cavern. Cautiously, he lowered to his butt and—*Oh, hell no.* His feet dangled over nothing but air. Not wanting to look like a sissy, Hunter leaned back and planted his elbows firmly on the rock behind him, his palms splayed flat. Just in case.

Ky settled alongside, breathing hard. "What'd I tell you?"

"What's out there? What am I not seeing?" Hunter asked quietly.

"You're missing a majestic view, my friend. Those glowing things on the ceiling look like stars, and I can't hear the river anymore, can you? That alone is a relief. It's still dark, but the ceiling's a deep bluish, purplish hue. If we weren't trapped belowground—and if you were Eden, I might call this place heavenly."

"But we are getting higher."

"Oh, yes."

For the first time in days, Hunter almost felt—hopeful.

CHAPTER THIRTY-TWO

Meredith took off work the first day back from Brazil. Her mother had flown back to California, and Courtney needed his mom. But truth be told, she felt sick at heart. After she dropped her mother at the airport, she crossed the Potomac to the hospital in D.C. If she couldn't be with Hunter, she needed to at least offer what comfort she could to his friend.

The physical therapist had just finished a session with Eric when Meredith and Courtney arrived at his room.

"How's he doing?" she asked in a whisper, as if Eric were merely sleeping. He looked pale, his tanned complexion pasty white. "I thought he was on life support?"

"Who? Eric Reynolds?" The therapist smirked. A beefy guy of around two-hundred-fifty pounds himself, he shot Meredith a comical look. "No way. They might have thought that in South America, but the minute we got him admitted, his doctor pulled the plug. He's been breathing fine on his own. Mr. Reynolds is no wimp. He's still in a coma, but all he needs to do is wake up. Are you his girlfriend? Fiancée?"

"Just a friend," she explained as she looked around his room. One flower arrangement after another lined Eric's countertop. Greeting cards lay unopened at his nightstand.

When the therapist left her alone, Meredith didn't know what to say. Eric breathed as if he were sound asleep. An IV line snaked beneath his covers. Several other lines ran between him and the monitor.

"Is he takin' a nap?" Courtney asked solemnly, his trusty teddy bear tucked under his arm. Bear, once golden and clean, had been Courtney's first Christmas present. He might look a little ragged, and the once bright green, checkered ribbon around his neck resembled a faded rag more than a ribbon, but that was one beloved teddy bear.

"No, honey. Eric got hurt when Mama was in South America. Remember the world map I showed you and where Brazil was? This man was down there with me."

Courtney pursed his lips at the oximeter on Eric's index finger. "Did he get cut?"

"No, honey. He had an accident while we were working and he's... sick." There was no need to frighten her son with particulars.

"Shhhhh. He's sweepin'," Courtney whispered to Bear.

"Yes, he's very sick and when we're sick, we need extra rest, don't we? Remember when you had a tummy ache and spent the whole day in my bed?"

"Uh-huh, and you gave me a red Popsicle." Her little boy's face brightened. "I don't wanna go to Benzawaya."

"No, you don't." Meredith tousled Courtney's hair at his attempt to pronounce a terrifically big word. "You want another Popsicle, don't you?"

"Uh-huh," Courtney mumbled, his interest in Eric already spent. "Me and Bear wanna go."

"Just a minute, honey." Meredith stepped closer to Eric. What a lady-killer. No man should be blessed with the thick dark hair and thicker eyelashes that Eric had. Elegant dark brows edged his forehead. His skin was clear and unscarred, and his nose was straight. Someone had shaved his face and combed his hair, a neat part on the left.

Right then, he resembled a sleeping Prince Charming, only the fairytale was all wrong. There was no Sleeping Beauty or Cinderella wringing her hands and waiting for him to wake up. Why wasn't some gorgeous gal curled at his side and sick with fear that she might lose him?

If Hunter had been the man in that bed, Meredith would've camped out and moved in. She'd be lying alongside of him, whispering prayers and promises to make him want to live. But Hunter wasn't there, was he? God, where was he! The not knowing clenched her stomach all over again. Alex promised he'd call the minute Hunter was found but it had been days. Days! Her fear for him was eating her alive.

Life is so unfair!

Trembling, she swallowed past the knot in her dry throat and lifted Eric's limp fingers in her hand. He was Hunter's friend. He needed to know what was going on in her world.

"I don't know if you can hear me or not, Eric, but I thought you should know. Hunter disappeared that last day. He and Ky are still in South America. I have to go back."

Eric gave no indication he'd heard, but she'd expected none. Her heart hurt for him. Tears brimmed. "Alex and your friends are still there. They promised they'll stay until they find him and Ky." She gave his hand one last squeeze. "You'd better be on your feet by the time Hunter gets back. He'll want to know what happened to you and I… I don't want to be the one to tell him."

Eric's fingers didn't even twitch.

Meredith blinked back her tears. They'd make Courtney feel bad, and she couldn't do that. She leaned into Eric's ear.

"Thank you for being Hunter's friend. For being mine, too. You're a good guy. Don't sleep too long, okay?"

A girlfriend would've kissed him, but Meredith had none of those conflicted feelings. She ran the back of a gentle finger along his cheek instead, wishing for a reaction. He looked so alone in his quiet hospital room. Almost forgotten. "I'll come back to sit with you every day until I leave to search for Hunter. I promise."

Courtney tugged at her hand. "Come on, Mama. I wanna go."

"Sleep tight," she whispered as she patted Eric's arm before she stepped away.

The walk to the elevator was her undoing. There she was, leaving him alone. The helplessness of her situation overwhelmed. She couldn't find Hunter. She couldn't help Eric. Her eyes brimmed, and damn it. She wiped a quick hand over her face. Why didn't he have a good woman in his life?

The drive home to her townhouse, took longer than expected because Meredith stopped for a bag of Popsicles. Pulling into her numbered stall, she spied a familiar face peering at her from the open window of a racy, red sports car parked nearby.

Immaculately trimmed black hair slicked back on his head. Tailored navy blue suit. Crisp white linen shirt, open at the front enough to reveal dark curly chest hairs. Expensive Italian leather loafers. Eddy Welch hadn't changed at all.

"What's he doing here?" she grumbled to herself.

"Who, Mama?" Courtney asked from his booster seat behind her.

"Never mind honey." She pushed the stick shift into park and grabbed her purse and the Popsicles off the passenger seat.

By then Eddy was opening her door for her, all cavalier and gentlemanly like he'd never been before. "Meredith. Good to see you," he said politely while he ducked low, peering past her into the back seat. "Hey, Courtney. Remember me?"

She caught Courtney in the rearview when he turned shy and lowered his face into Bear's fluffy fur. Meredith refused Eddy's hand. "Why would he remember you? It's not like he's seen you before."

"You're right. I was just hoping you'd showed him some pictures or… something."

She cut him no slack. "Why are you here? What do you want? I still have a restraining order, remember?"

Opening the rear door of her very affordable compact vehicle, she leaned in to unfasten Courtney's seatbelts. Knowing her ex was no doubt making the most of her position and getting an eyeful of her ass, she pulled Courtney into her arms as quickly as she could. She shifted her son to her opposite hip where he didn't have to see the stranger in his life.

Meredith tossed her head to get her hair out of her eyes and turned to face the only man on the planet she could honestly say she hated.

Eddy lifted a bandaged hand to her view. "I know about your restraining order, but I... I had an accident recently. It got me to thinking, and, well, I thought I'd risk it coming here."

He was playing the sympathy card? Really? *What an idiot.* That boat sailed the first time he'd slapped her.

"I'm busy." Clutching the Popsicles in one hand and Courtney in the other, she kneed her car door shut. "It's naptime. We don't have time to talk."

"Okay," Eddy said quickly, his palms forward. "No problem, Sweetheart."

"Don't call me that," she warned him. "Those days are gone. You lost the right to whisper sweet nothings a long time ago."

"How well I know." His gaze hit the pavement, and Meredith couldn't get away from him fast enough. Reconciliation with Eddy was a foregone impossibility.

Been there. Done that. Got the stupid T-shirt and ripped it to shreds!

"I talked with your mother," he offered weakly. "I just called her to say hi. It was no big deal."

"She told me." Meredith's annoyance at having to deal with him again grew stronger with every step she took. With her car keys stuck between her fisted fingers clutching the bag of Popsicles, she prepared for trouble. If he made one wrong move...

"She told me you were happy. That you had a good job. That kind of stuff."

He didn't follow her, so why was he here? What'd he want? Meredith had to know. She came to a full stop and faced him. Leaning his hip to the driver's door with his ankles crossed, he was as handsome as ever. Only now she knew better.

"What are you doing here? What do you really want?"

Eddy folded his arms over his chest, his suit jacket wrinkling as it stretched over wide shoulders. He'd been working out. Who cared? "Nothing. Honest, babe—ahh, I mean, Meredith. I just wanted to see him." He nodded his chin at Courtney. "I've had a lot of time to think these last couple weeks. I finally get why you hate me so much."

He looked sad. Honestly contrite. For a full second, her heart softened, but Meredith knew better. Eddy was up to something. He wanted her to ask what happened to his *poor* hand, and that would open the door to more conversation, wouldn't it? There was a time she'd believed everything he'd said, but her trust in him had ended badly. Why should she believe him now?

"So tell me." She poured on the sarcasm, still keeping Courtney protected on the opposite side of her body. "If you're so smart all of a sudden, why do I hate you?"

"Because you should." He shrugged both shoulders with what seemed like honesty. "I was a jerk. I treated you badly. I'd just like the chance to make it up to you, that's all."

"No," she said unequivocally. "It's too late and I'm not interested. There's nothing you can do or say that will change what you did. You need to go."

"Okay. I get it. Really, I do. You're right. But he's still my son."

Meredith's hackles lifted. Was that a threat? "No, he's not. You said you didn't want anything to do with him or me, remember?"

"I was under duress."

"No, you weren't. You were under Georgette. Or Twila. Or whoever your bimbo of the week was then," Meredith bit out, surprised she sounded as bitter as she did. But how dumb did he think she was?

When Courtney whined and leaned his head into her neck for comfort, the discussion was over. She had more important things to do than argue with her ex. "You know what? I don't care. We're not your problem, so leave us alone. Goodbye."

"I'm making him my heir, if that helps." Eddy's eyes brimmed.

Meredith had to look twice. Were those tears? Was he crying? Was there nothing this joker wouldn't try? Her lips thinned. *Nope. Not buying this act either.*

"I've made more than my share of mistakes. I'd like to do one thing right in my life, Meredith. I make good money. It'll all go to him if something were to happen to me."

"Fine. Whatever. Do what you want. Put him in your will." She stood firm in her decision. If Eddy truly were sincere, she had no qualms about him bequeathing the universe to Courtney, but that was all. There would be no joint custody. No fatherly visits solely intended to get into her pants. A man who'd thrown his only child away didn't deserve a second chance.

"Thank you," he said meekly, and again Meredith had to look twice. Who the heck was this guy? She almost didn't recognize the snake she'd married, divorced, and tried like heck to forget for more than three years now.

"Goodbye, Meredith." He pivoted and walked away.

She watched him go, offering not one word of sympathy or regret. The man had his nerve to come begging to be part of Courtney's life again. Okay, so he hadn't exactly asked for that, the jerk. Come to think of it, all he'd wanted was to give Courtney what Meredith would never be able to, even if she worked overtime for the rest of her natural life. He wanted Courtney to have—everything. Could she really allow that kind of wealth to happen to her son? The effects would be mind and soul altering. Was this just another barnstorming tactic to run over her? To borrow Hunter's word: *Shit.*

"He your friend, Mama?" Courtney asked, his head still against her chest, his nose buried in Bear's fluffy ear.

"No, baby." Meredith placed a kiss on the top of his head. "You met my friend in the hospital, remember?"

"Oh, yeah." Courtney covered his eyes with chubby baby fingers, peeking up at her. "I forgot."

"Do you remember his name?"

"Spot!" Courtney declared with a mischievous chuckle.

She giggled with him as she unlocked her ground-floor entry door. "Not Spot, silly boy."

"Bear!" Courtney was into his funny-boy routine, the encounter with his biological sperm donor forgotten.

"His name was Eric Reynolds, and he's one of the good guys."

Glancing over her shoulder at the sound of a loud engine, she glimpsed the sleek red sports car pulling out of overflow parking. So that was what Eddy drove these days. No doubt it was over-the-top expensive. Probably foreign-made. Like she cared. The engine revved. It was so like Eddy to draw attention to himself.

She turned her back on him again. Closing her door, she secured the deadbolt with a definite click. She set Courtney to the floor, and off he ran with Bear. There was no way Eddy could worm his way back into her life, but what had he meant, *if something were to happen to me*? And what had he done to his hand? It was odd he hadn't offered details.

"Mama! Popsicle!" Courtney squealed. "Me and Bear hungwy!"

Instantly grounded, Meredith peeled a treat for her son. One for Bear, too. She might never make the Fortune 500 club, but so what? Wealth didn't make her happy. Courtney did.

Besides her father and son, the only other man she loved was two thousand miles away by land, but only a heartbeat away by soul.

Alex would find him. He had to.

CHAPTER THIRTY-THREE

After days without food, the time had come to call a halt to the constant march to nowhere. Hunter sat with a thud, his legs and boots dangling over the ledge of what very well could be one helluva drop-off.

"Don't sit so close to the edge." Ky's hand on Hunter's bicep pushed his back to the wall behind him. "It's a long way down."

Hunter let him push all he wanted. Ky wasn't any stronger than he was. They'd walked and climbed and climbed and walked, but nothing had changed. Absolutely—damned—nothing. But at least they'd tried. It was small consolation and a tough way to end up, but the facts were speaking pretty loud and clear. Hydration wasn't the problem. They could suck water off the walls. But food? An unsolvable problem that gnawed relentlessly at both of them.

Until Hunter got tangled up in that floating spider web.

"Shit," he cussed, swatting the mass of sticky strings away from his head. The damned thing came out of nowhere, probably floating on the perpetual draft inside the cavern.

Ky reached around him. "Let me see that."

"Get this crap off me." Hunter fought the webbing, his fingers knotted around the toughest damned filaments he'd ever come across. And it was muddy. Probably full of spiders the size of housecats, judging by the insanely thick strands.

Didn't it figure? Starving to death and they'd run into a man-eating spider?

"Hunt. Stop moving. Let me grab onto it and—"

"It's roots," Hunter declared.

"That's what I thought." Ky pulled a long tendril away from Hunter. "Damn. It's hanging down from the ceiling."

"I'm just glad it's not spiders."

"I thought you were going over the edge for a minute there," Ky teased. "Then I'd have to drop down to river level again and haul your sorry ass all the way back up."

"Can we eat those roots?" Hunter asked, the gnawing pain in his gut the only thing on his mind.

"Hell, I don't know. Should we try?"

"Why not? Plants point up. Roots point down." It made better sense before he said it out loud.

"It's covered with white pearls. Not sure if they're berries though. They feel more like... oh, my hell. Mushrooms."

"Have you ever eaten wild mushrooms?" Hunter gulped, salivating at the mere thought of something edible.

"Nah-uh. You?"

"Sorry, I didn't run with the pot smoking, mushroom-munching crowd." I was one of the good kids back then. *Like Meredith.* That familiar pain sliced another cut in his already damaged heart. What he wouldn't give for one more kiss. One more taste.

His fingers had already plucked several of the knobby tidbits off the root. Looking down into the hand he couldn't see, common sense stopped him from popping one into his mouth. A psychedelic trip to La-La Land was one thing, but poison? Was he hungry enough to risk never seeing Meredith again?

"One of us could try a tiny piece. The other could watch and see what happens." Ky's excitement radiated in his voice. God, they were so hungry.

The choice sounded logical. Hunter gave it a fifty-fifty chance. Eat and live or—die. He swallowed hard, his gut gurgling to life at the prospect of having something in it. "I might not be able to hold you back if you decide you can fly."

"Who said I wanted to be the white rat?" Ky chuckled. "Go on, Hunt. You're the risk taker."

Hunter had the feeling he should drop them over the edge and shove the root away, but he didn't. Temptation taunted the hell out of the weakness in his trembling limbs. Food. This was food at its simplest form. It was a sign he and Ky were meant to live—wasn't it? "It might be worth a shot."

Just that fast, Ky flip-flopped. He slapped Nature's gift out of Hunter's hand. "No, Hunter, don't do it. Everything in that jungle upstairs was trying to kill us, remember? What makes you think it's any different down here? I was just messing with you."

"Yeah, only..." Every mushroom hadn't fallen. Hunter rolled the last tender edible between his index finger and thumb. He held it up to his nose and sniffed it. The thing sure smelled like a mushroom. He blew the dirt off and set just the tip of his tongue to it. Tasted like—dirt. He licked his lips, hungrier than he'd ever been in his life and desperate enough to do something stupid. *Fifty-fifty, remember?*

He rationalized. "Think about it. Ky. We could've stayed at ground level, but look where we are now because we took a calculated risk."

"Rock climbing's a little safer than eating mushrooms that might be poisonous."

"Is it?" Hunter turned toward Ky's voice. "You gave me a choice down there: Move or lay down and die. Now we have another choice: Eat and maybe live, or starve and surely die. I'm not seeing much difference between then and now."

"No, Hunt," Ky declared adamantly. "I'd never let you risk your life like that for me. It's not worth the chance. We keep moving. We don't eat until we know for sure what we're eating won't kill us." He brushed the last mushroom away.

"You made me drop it," Hunter grumbled, watching it disappear into the darkness below. It glowed. A tiny little star dropping slowly out of sight. *Hmmm, falling star. Hmmm.*

"I can see!"

Ky clutched his wrist. "Really? Hunt, really? You can see?"

An odd thing called a smile cracked the dry skin on Hunter's cheeks. "Yeah, man. No kidding. Maybe those were magic mushrooms after all." He scrubbed a hand over his face, rubbing his bleary eyes. Gradually, the cavern came into shadowy but sharper view. The ledge he was on, too. Instinctively, he backed away from the edge and into the wall behind him. "Shit, we're high."

Ky fist bumped his bicep. "What'd I tell you? Keep holding on and something good's bound to happen."

"Yeah, well…" Hunter swallowed hard. One misstep would've sent him to his death. He focused on Ky's grinning face. Nope. Not going to think about the height or falling or…

Damn. He squinted, but couldn't detect an opposing wall. If there was one.

Ky thumped his arm. "Look up."

Hunter followed Ky's blurry pointing finger to the ceiling, which was a lot closer than he'd suspected. More clumps of roots dangled downward, some dotted with phosphorescent fungi, but beyond those roots? What looked like an earthen, as in a no kidding, dirt ceiling.

"You're right, Hunt. Plants point up; roots point down."

Hunter scrambled to his feet but kept a palm flat to the wall to steady his equilibrium. Now was not the time for taking chances. "Trees are on the other ends of those roots."

Ky's smile about split his face. "What are you gonna do when you get out of here?"

"Kiss the first person I see," Hunter declared emphatically, but then he really looked at his friend. The man's once bright amber eyes were sunken and his cheeks were hollow. His hair was messy, and a thick, short beard covered his chin and throat. Hunter reached out a hand and squeezed his buddy's thin bicep. My God. His body was cannibalizing itself.

"Are you… are you really okay?" Ky surely didn't look it. Skeletal maybe.

"I am now. Come on. Let's keep moving."

Hunter let the lie pass knowing he probably looked as bad. Re-energized, they pressed forward. The ledge had widened to a path they could walk side by side. Having his sight back made an incredible difference in Hunter's morale. Thinking of Meredith didn't hurt either. He turned back into a leader, every step more certain.

Any minute now, they'd find a way out of here.

After hours, his enthusiasm lagged. Real spider webs hung between massive clumps of dark chandelier roots. Real spiders too. Only these eight-legged creatures didn't glow.

They were just big. And fast. They dropped out of nowhere. Or maybe they jumped. He batted another palm-sized creature off his head. "These attack spiders are getting old."

"They're a good sign though," Ky said. "Spiders catch flies and other bugs. We've got to be getting closer to the surface. If there are enough bugs to keep the spiders alive, they can keep us alive too."

Hunter kept his mouth shut. Close only worked with horseshoes and hand grenades. It wouldn't mean anything if they couldn't catch a break and find a way out of this cavern.

"You ever eat a spider?"

"No, and I'm not going to start. Tell me more about Eden and Kyler," Hunter said, hoping for distraction amongst the increasing webs. Some looked like tunnels; some looked like nets stretched from the wall to who knew where. That monstrous spider in the *Lord of the Rings* trilogy came to mind. Look what happened to Frodo? Wrapped in a silk cocoon, saved for a late midnight snack. Goosebumps wriggled up Hunter's bare arms.

A soft sigh hissed out of Ky. "What's there to tell? Eden and Kyler are everything. We named him after Lee Hart, you know. His full name's Kyler Lee. You ever see *Wonder Woman*?"

Hunter smiled. Yes. He'd seen *Wonder Woman*, and her name was Meredith.

Ky rattled on, and Hunter let him talk. Down below, there hadn't been a single web. What else might live closer to the surface? Rats? Mice? Snakes? Another smile cracked his lips at the memory of Meredith's blood-curdling shriek when he'd killed that first snake. That woman had a good set of lungs. And she was fast. She'd almost made him believe in time travel, the way she'd been standing beside him one second, then throwing a hysterical fit behind him the next. Hell, she'd almost made him believe in a lot of things. And that one night in the tree? That hot sex they had? The love he'd seen in her eyes?

He stumbled, his mind topside when a flurry of bats engulfed him and Ky. This flock didn't just bump. This was a full-on assault, as if the bats were funneled through a narrow opening and all trying to get in at once. Either that or they were scared and didn't care what they hit.

Hunter gave up fighting them off. He turned his back to the horde and covered his face and head with his arms and hands, ducking to avoid contact with the rabies-carrying little beasts. "Shit," he hissed as one bat body after another pummeled his back, shoulders and neck.

"I never liked Batman," Ky grumbled, his voice nearly lost amongst the high-pitched whistles and squeaks.

At last, the onslaught diminished. Hunter scraped the creepy feel of the flying creatures off his arms and the back of his neck. "That's it. Those bats are getting in somehow, and I'm going to find out where."

Ky brushed his hands over his bare arms and chuckled.

"What's so damned funny?"

Another chuckle. "It's about time. You sound like yourself again."

Hunter growled. "Move it, Winchester. Let's get the hell out of here."

As promised, Meredith, Courtney, and Bear paid Eric another visit. His condition hadn't improved, so she kept the visit short. The best part was running into Seth on their way out. By the time they were on their way to ground level, she knew Hunter hadn't been located yet, but Alex had called in more men and machinery.

"The boss is one determined guy," Seth declared. "When he says he's gonna find Hunter, you can take that to the bank."

"I hope so. It's been over a week."

"Is this your son?" Seth nonchalantly handed Courtney a big silver coin.

"Yes, this is Courtney," she answered. "Can you tell Mr. McCray thank you?"

"Ah-huh. Thanks," Courtney mumbled, his eyes aglow. "Look, Mama. I got a dollar."

"It's one of my challenge coins from the Army," Seth explained as he crouched to her son's level and tapped Bear's black plastic nose. "I see you brought a buddy with you. Good thinking. What's his name?"

"Bear." An attack of shyness wiggled through Courtney's little body. It wasn't often he let an adult get this close without hiding behind her.

"I bet you're the kind of guy who takes good care of his mama too, aren't you?"

Another "Uh-huh," and a wiggle.

Seth looked up at Meredith. "How about you? Are you hanging in there, Mom?"

The gentle question caught her by surprise. For the first time she noticed his eyes were the same color as Hunter's, a deep, dark coffee brown with caramel sprinkles. Delicious eyes. Tender eyes. A quiet confidence radiated from him.

"I'm good," she replied, wishing she were more than that. "How about you? You went through more than I did."

"Shucks, no need to worry about me. I'm headed back down south in the morning," he admitted as he rose to his feet.

"To search for Hunter?"

"Yes, ma'am. To see if we can find both Hunter and Ky."

"I need to come with you," she said, her heart torn between her son and the man she loved.

"No, you don't." Seth nodded at the little boy standing between them. "Your first job is here. You take good care of my buddy and Bear. Let me find Hunter and Ky."

Courtney's face lit up. "I is your buddy?"

"You bet. You and Bear are both my buddies." Seth tousled the boy's hair, but his gaze drifted to her. "Don't worry. We've got a few months of good weather left. We'll find them."

She cringed. Would it take that long?

"Anyway, I've got to pack. I will be in touch." Seth offered a half-salute to Courtney. "You take good care of your mama, okay soldier?"

Courtney offered a left-handed salute right back, his other hand still hanging on tight to Bear and his prize for being that good soldier. "I will," he promised. "Bye, buddy."

Meredith could've cried. Seth, a complete stranger, had just made her son feel like a man, something his own father had never attempted. Not even once. Eddy was such a loser.

She lifted Courtney to her hip and made it all the way to her car before she noticed the flaming red vehicle parked across the busy street. Eddy Welch waved, a big grin on his face like she should be happy to see him.

"Darn it," she cussed as she unlocked her car and strapped Courtney in.

"Aw, Mama, you sweared," Courtney scolded quietly, Seth's coin still clutched tightly in his right hand. "And Bear heard it, too."

"I know," she apologized. "Mama's sorry. I shouldn't say words like that, should I?" If he only knew what she was thinking.

"Nope." His eyes lit up, but he'd lost interest. "Look it. A motor scooter!"

Meredith gritted her teeth, blew out an impatient sigh, and turned to face Eddy as the biker roared by, in the hospital zone no less. By then he'd climbed out of his pricey sports car but ducked back inside to pull out the latest fad that every little boy on the planet wanted. How he'd gotten the bright red trike with monster black plastic wheels in the front of his snazzy little car was another thing altogether. The toy must've been riding shotgun.

She gritted her teeth. The big shitty grin on his face didn't help her parental position one bit, especially when he focused on Courtney and exclaimed, "I bought this for you!"

Of course, her three-year-old promptly forgot everything she'd taught him about stranger danger. "Mama! Look! It's for me!" he squealed.

Meredith crossed her arms, blocking Eddy's view of the child he thought he could buy. "How dare you? What do you think you're doing, showing up with that instead of talking about it with me first?"

He turned his typical megawatt smile on her. It used to work. Not today. "Just giving my boy a birthday present."

"It's not his birthday."

Eddy shrugged. "I know. Geez, do you think I forgot my own kid's birthday?"

"Only for the last three years." Her foot started tapping. "What's this really about?"

"Repentance, Meredith," he admitted. "It's a late birthday present. I've come to ask for your forgiveness. That's all."

Her foot tapped harder. Darn, he was good, but he was lying through his teeth.

He set the trike on the street as traffic rolled by. "I don't expect you to understand. You've been the good parent, and I get it. I've been the absentee father. If you want me to leave again, I will. But before I go, you need to know that I meant what I said. Look at this." He drew a sheaf of folded papers out of his inner suit pocket. "I had my lawyer draw it up last night. Got him out of bed to do it, but he can stand the overtime. I pay him enough."

Meredith accepted the documents. The first page took her breath. Right there in black and white. Eddy Welch was worth eighty-three-point-one-billion dollars. She swallowed hard. There were a lot of zeroes after that eighty-three-point-one. This man was more powerful than she'd suspected. She'd had no idea.

The document went on to itemize his assets, a multiplicity of banking institutions and various investments, but her eyes kept pulling back to—eighty-three-point-one-billion dollars. *And all this time, Courtney and me have been living in a low rent neighborhood and eating macaroni and cheese.*

Not that she hated her tidy apartment. She didn't. It was small, but clean. She liked her neighbors. They were decent hard working people. She'd made good money at McCormack Industries, and with her next raise, she'd be able to afford something nicer if she wanted to move. But wow. This was some serious cashola.

Her heart pounded at the top line of the document: *I bequeath to my only living heir, Courtney Flynn, the whole of my estate in the event of my untimely death.*

She leaned her hip against the car, her head spinning, but her heart not yet believing. At least he'd gotten Courtney's legal name right, but this was a scam. It had to be. Eddy wanted something. That was how he worked—dazzle his friends with bullshit and rob them blind when they turned their backs. If Courtney could've heard what naughty words she was thinking right then, he'd remind her again about swearing.

"Do you have any idea how hard I've struggled to make ends meet?" *You pompous ass.* "Your son and I have been living on hand-me-downs and tuna casserole. Why didn't you go back to court to increase your child support if you care so much? Why now?"

His lashes dropped. "I'm sorry, Meredith. I'm only doing what a father should do for his son, what I should've done all along. I can't change the past, but I can make sure that Courtney has everything he needs from now on. Give me a chance to make things right. That's all I'm asking. Read the second page."

Swallowing hard, she flipped to page two, her hand shaking. What? Courtney would begin receiving a monthly stipend payable to her as custodial parent, beginning in seven days. No limits. No qualifications. No strong-arming.

"No," she managed to spit out of her dry throat. "This is too much. We don't need—"

"It has nothing to do with need, Meredith. It has to do with what's right. I get it now. You've proved yourself a thousand times over. You, a single mother, are the better parent. You've made more than a decent life for your child while I've done nothing but send a monthly check. Let me make amends." He looked down the street as he raked a slender hand through his dark hair. "It's obvious you don't need me in your life. I get it. If you'd prefer, I can save everything in a trust until he's of age. It's your call. I bow to your command."

She didn't know what to say. He'd let her struggle for years with the minimum child support, and yes, she could've taken him to court for more, but she hadn't. Of course, if she'd known then what she knew now…

Eddy was richer than most of America, maybe the world. But bottom line, she'd never wanted his money. To hit him up for more child support had always seemed an admission that she couldn't make it without the almighty Eddy Welch in her life. Not so. She could, and by God, she had.

"No," she said again, handing the portfolio back. "Give it to charity. Heck, give it to someone else. We've done fine without you. I don't want it and Courtney doesn't need it."

"Okay." Eddy slid the document into his jacket and picked up the trike by its handlebars. "But will you explain to him when he's older how you turned him into a pauper?"

Courtney whined from inside the car, kicking the back of her seat in excitement. "Mama! Kin I keep it? Me and Bear wanna see it!"

"Come on," Eddy muttered, his voice low and confidential. "This is a big decision. It deserves more consideration. Why don't you sleep on it? Let me take you to lunch. At least let me give him his present."

She gulped. A plastic trike was one thing, but the world—something else entirely.

"Just lunch. Just the trike. That's all."

He nodded, his gaze on Courtney again. Eddy almost looked—honest.

CHAPTER THIRTY-FOUR

"What the hell is that?" Hunter squinted, the mass of roots and spider webs stretching upward and beyond him brighter than the others. It didn't just glisten with glow-in-the-dark fungi anymore. This bunch was bigger. Animal-sized bigger. *Maybe lizard. Dinosaur? Dragon?*

That was what weeks without food and not enough water did to a guy.

The farther up they'd climbed, the less condensation on the walls. The air turned more humid with every faltering step, yet neither man's body could produce a drop of sweat. Literally running on empty, they wouldn't last much longer.

He scrubbed the hallucination away and looked down at his feet to catch his balance. Dizziness plagued him. His dry eyes stung. His lips were peeling and chapped, and damn, he was thirsty.

Ky grunted behind him. They were both on their last legs. Had been for… hell, Hunter didn't know anymore. Time was a non-player in this never-ending journey to nowhere. He'd lost track of it the day he fell.

The lighted web in the ceiling began another lackadaisical twirl.

"It's gotta be a spider nest," Hunter muttered, but his gut told him differently. He looked again, his neck extended forward, like that helped him see better. *Not so much.*

Ky dropped to his butt with a weary groan. "I'm dizzy, man. I need to hold still for a minute. Everything's spinning."

"No," Hunter said, even as he sat with Ky. "We've got to stop... resting. One of these times... we won't be strong enough... to get back up." But sitting sounded like a good idea. He wished he'd thought of it.

Ky chuffed another nothing non-answer. He'd been doing that more often. Walking slower. Stumbling. Needing help getting to his feet.

At first, finding those tree roots and spider webs was a morale booster, but that was days ago. Neither of them dared chance eating the roots and risking a slow painful death. This latest mass was just more of the same and just as worthless. Millions of trees grew topside and they all had roots, so why had he thought escape from this underworld realm of stone and starvation was imminent? It wasn't. They'd gotten excited for nothing.

"I'm so damned tired," Ky wheezed, his normally optimistic voice dull and flat.

"Yeah. Me too." Hunter leaned his back to the wall. Now was the time to grab a few ZZZs.

The total lack of food had become irrelevant in the slow race to the surface. His stomach didn't hurt anymore. Hunter recognized it for what it was—the body's way of coping. The urge to curl up and sleep compelled him to face the truth. There was no way out. He'd never see Meredith again. Never kiss her lush warm lips. Never breathe in the flowery scent of her pretty blonde hair. Only the dried up skeletons of him and Ky would be found—if anything.

Hunter growled at the bitch called Karma. Those spider thingees were one of her dirty tricks. False hope was what they were. Damn her to hell...

Rambling—another sign that he was losing his mind. He flicked the dusty dirt off his fingers. There was one last thing he had to do before he died. With great determination, Hunter gritted his teeth against the burning ache in his joints. Everything creaked, even his jaw. Like an old, old man, he rolled to his hands and knees and searched the flat ledge for something to scratch out a few words with.

His body would be found someday. When it was, he wanted Meredith to know.

Hunched over, his butt in the air and his nose to the ground, he found a suitable rock, suitable because it was the first one his fingers touched. It would do. Slowly, he scratched two stick figures into the stone floor, a lady and a guy. A crooked heart between them.

That made him chuckle. A crooked heart. Ha. Wasn't that the truth?

In the center of the heart, he etched, "Mike Foxtrot."

Over the stick figures' heads, he carved a five-pointed star with a long tail. Of all things, a single tear dripped out of his grit-filled eye to land square in the middle of the lady stick figure's round head. That was all the artwork he had strength for. No more words. No signature. Just that. Meredith would know what it meant.

He stretched his dying body beside the message. His forehead hit the dirt as he whispered to the only woman who mattered in his miserable life, "I love you, Merry."

"Whatcha... doing?" Ky asked weakly from where he'd collapsed, his arms spread crucifixion-style.

Hunter licked his dry lips and whispered, "Wishing... on a star. That's all. Just..."

Wishing with all my heart.

Eddy showed up at her place in gray dress slacks and a pale-blue button-up shirt instead of jeans and a polo or T-shirt. He obviously hadn't planned on the local hamburger joint for lunch. It shouldn't have surprised her. They never were on the same wavelength.

For now Eddy sat between her and Courtney. He'd satisfied her three-year-old's appetite with a cheeseburger (hold the catsup and pickle), fries, apple juice, and a toy made in China. Thankfully, Courtney was ecstatically unaware of the adult power play in process. He sat sharing his fires and fry sauce with Bear and chattering to his best bud as if the perpetually smiling stuffed animal was listening.

Meredith had ordered a sweet tea, not anything pricey enough to be beholden to the man who thought he could buy her affection the way he'd bought her son's. Each time Eddy stretched his arm along the back of the booth, she moved away from him until she was up against the edge of the seat. She kept her cell phone at her fingertips. Lee might call with good news on Hunter and Ky. God knew, she needed some.

"I was thinking more of fine dining," Eddy admitted, his eyes out the window on his expensive wheels.

"Maybe another time." *Like never.* Meredith tapped her phone, wishing it would ring. She had both Seth and Lee's numbers, but hadn't called either man yet. She trusted them. They'd call as soon as something broke.

Eddy's eyes brightened. "Really? You'd go out with me again?"

She stalled, biting her tongue for thinking she had to be nice in front of her son.

"To tell you the truth, the place I had in mind is on the Chesapeake, near Annapolis. You'd love it. We could spend the day on the beach. I'd love to take Courtney sailing, and—"

"I'm not interested, remember?"

"But sweetheart." Any closer and he'd be on her lap. "It'd give me a chance to get to know him better."

But sweetheart nothing. This was just a means to get to her through Courtney. "If you want to get to know him, why aren't you sitting by him?"

Eddy's nose wrinkled. "Because..."

"Mama, I hafta go potty," Courtney announced proudly, his cute little chin lifted because he'd remembered in time. Well, almost.

"I think he already did," Eddy whispered as he stood to let her out of her seat. "I didn't want to embarrass him. Sorry. I'm not good with little boys yet, but I'd love to learn."

She rolled her eyes, suddenly back in time and not sure what to believe. Eddy said the right words, but she wished not one ounce of Welch blood flowed through that darling little boy's veins. Her way forward would be clear then.

Eddy intercepted her just as she reached for Courtney. "It's time I figured this fatherhood thing out. Would it be okay if I took you to the bathroom, Son?"

That word. *Son.* Eddy had said it smoothly, as if he'd never missed a single birthday or Christmas morning, first step. But the biggest smile crackled across Courtney's face. Why wouldn't it? Eddy had bought everything the little guy had hinted he'd wanted at the counter. And what could she say? Technically and biologically, Courtney *was* Eddy's son. Darn it.

"Yeah!" Courtney exclaimed, his eyes bright as if he suddenly had a new best friend. "I goin' potty. I a big boy now."

"I see that," Meredith answered, her motherly instincts on high alert. What could she say? Courtney seemed genuinely happy to be spending time with his father, the deadbeat. Only Eddy wasn't legally a deadbeat, either. He'd never missed a child support payment. All he'd missed was—everything else.

"But you're injured," she offered lamely.

Eddy scowled, shaking his gauze wrapped hand like it was nothing. "I'm tough. What do you say? Do we have your permission?"

She handed him the emergency change of little boy clothes she always carried in her trendy, mother-sized backpack. "I'll be waiting."

He smiled, and off the father-and-son team went, hand in hand, like real fathers did with their sons every single day. So why did that make the hair on the back of her neck stand up? Instead of waiting, which drove her crazy the minute Courtney was out of her sight, Meredith went for a refill. The counter was close to the restrooms. She could hear if anything—

No. Nothing will happen. Eddy's not evil. A jerk, yes, but he'd never hurt Courtney.

Still, Meredith breathed a sigh of relief when they exited the restroom, her little guy jabbering away and still hanging onto his father's hand. When Eddy handed her the plastic bag that held the wet clothing, one brow lifted. "You didn't have to wait outside the door."

"I hope you washed your hands, Courtney," she said with a gulp. She'd been caught loitering like a suspicious woman, but so what? One happy meal does not a father make.

"And I used soap," he said proudly, his two very clean little hands waving at her for proof. "Daddy helped me reach."

She choked on her sweet tea. *Daddy?* "Wh-who helped you?"

"Him." He pointed to Eddy. "My Daddy."

Eddy scooped Courtney off the floor, and wrangled him onto his shoulder. "I can't very well have him calling me Mr. Welch, can I?"

A few other choice names came to mind, but no. Courtney did have to call his father *something*. Meredith just wished it wasn't *that*. Things were moving too fast. She bit her tongue while *her* son, the little guy she'd nursed through midnight earaches, scary bouts of colic, and other childhood illnesses—all by herself—squealed with delight on his ride back to the table.

This time, Eddy made sure to sit beside Courtney. *What a surprise.* Then he made it a game to see who could eat his cheeseburger the fastest. Meredith tried not to stare, but she couldn't help noticing that, like him or not, he seemed to be making an honest effort. Courtney and he looked good together. Almost happy. Almost believable.

Then why did her gut pinch with apprehension? Oh wait. Could it be the multiple times he'd bullied her? The time he'd slapped her? Had he really changed or was this just another scam? She tucked her palm under her chin and stared out the window, wishing it was Hunter sitting across the table.

"So tomorrow then?" Eddy's question snapped her out of her reverie.

"Excuse me. What?" she asked, not understanding.

"Tomorrow," he said, very deliberately. "I'll pick you kids up at nine. We can be at my cabin by noon. Courtney can't wait to go boating."

"I going fishing, Mama," Courtney blurted out, his blue eyes wide and sparkling as he bounced in his chair.

Figures. First the trike. Now there's a cabin and a boat.

"When did we decide we were going to your cabin?" she asked haughtily.

"You said you'd consider dinner another day. I just assumed..."

So that was it. He'd set this in motion when he'd taken Courtney to the restroom. He'd baited his child with boating and fishing and all those guy things she hadn't offered *her* son. And, oh yeah, he'd also made sure Courtney knew he was his father. Darn him. Eddy would sabotage her at every turn by buying his son's love, like that was hard to do with a three-year-old.

She steeled her resolve. "Sorry. I have work."

His chin dropped. "You're right. I'm coming on too strong, aren't I? Another time then."

"But Mama," Courtney whined. "He my Daddy and I wanna pway with him."

"No, Son. Your mother's right. I've been gone awhile…" *Like most of your son's life.* "…and I understand. You finish those fries and I'll take you home."

"But I wanna go with you, Daddy."

And there it was, her chubby cheeked angel had just resorted to the oldest trick in the Shirley Temple playbook— pitting one parent against the other. It hadn't yet been twenty-four-hours, and the line was drawn in the sand. The three-year-old was hooked.

She cocked a cold shoulder of disdain at Eddy, while she lifted to her seat and told *her* son in no uncertain terms, "We're leaving. Grab Bear. Now."

"But, Mama—"

"Listen to your mother, Courtney." Eddy tucked Bear under his arm, then grabbed hold of Courtney and flipped him over his head and upside down so he landed, straddling Eddy's shoulders. Giggling. "Do it again!"

Just like that the argument was over. God, she wanted to hate him, but legally, Eddy was Courtney's father. Did she owe Eddy a second chance with her? No way.

Did he have a right to see his son? Certainly. Fathers had rights. Especially wealthy fathers. It wasn't an unreasonable request, and any court in the country would agree with him. She'd never agree to joint custody, but what harm was there in letting him get to know his only child? Supervised visits only. At first. If he proved to be a fit father—maybe more.

Meredith held her breath at this sudden change in her life. "What are you doing? You drop in out of the blue and disrupt my life and…." She waved a hand at the crumbled lunch debris on the table. "What do you really want? If all this is a scheme to get custody—"

He slipped a hand inside his suit jacket. "Here. Maybe this will put your mind to rest."

She glared at him even as she unfolded the single sheet of what felt like fine linen paper. The seal of the State of Virginia in the upper left hand corner looked official, but it was the title of the document that took her breath. *Voluntary Relinquishment of Parental Rights.*

He'd done it. He'd signed on the line. The document was witnessed and notarized, and she honestly didn't know what to think. "Why would you do this?"

"Because I may not be good enough for you, Meredith, but I do know how your mind works. You don't trust me, and I don't blame you. I've given you no reason to. You think I've come back into your life just to take Courtney. Let that piece of paper be my solemn word that you and you alone will retain all rights and custody of this fine little man you're raising. I'm not here to steal him. I just want to get to know him better. I want to be, in some small way, a part of his life. Call it guilt or penance, but I need to make sure he's provided for the rest of his life. Is that too much to ask?"

"Umm, wow. I don't know what to say." She swallowed hard, her mind racing as she handed the document back.

He waved it away. "It's yours. Keep it."

Meredith tucked the paper alongside Courtney's animal crackers in her backpack before she was composed enough to face Eddy again. By then Bear was stuffed in front of Courtney. Her son's smiling eyes beamed. Could she refuse him this chance to know his real father? She bit her lip already knowing her answer.

"One day, Eddy." She hated the tremor in her voice. Why did it suddenly feel like she was toeing the edge of a very deep precipice? In the dark? On a windy day? "I'll give you this one day with your son, but I'm not kidding. We need to be home by eight tomorrow evening. I have work the next morning," she lied.

"No problem." Eddy smiled that cocky half-smile she'd thought handsome a long, long time ago. "Eight p.m. it is. Bring a warm jacket for you and Courtney. Autumn on the Chesapeake can be breezy."

"No sailing." Meredith pushed her motherly authority. "You know I don't like being out on the water."

"Since when?" Eddy gave her a tentative smile.

Since I'll have to be out there with you.

"Come on. Loosen up. Live a little."

"No sailing, Eddy," she said more firmly. "I mean it." This was no happy family. There was no sense making this one-day event what it wasn't.

"Okay, okay." He shrugged. "Bring a coat anyway. We can always go for a long walk. Maybe we'll find some shells. Have you ever been beachcombing, Courtney?"

Meredith took a long sip of her tea while her son jabbered. Eddy seemed to have changed. Didn't he?

The damned spidery light got brighter. And annoying. Hunter growled. He must've dozed off. He watched distractedly as the light split into separate beams and descended from the ceiling. Nothing made sense anymore. Loud voices echoed continually inside his head. The world spun, or maybe he was doing the spinning. It all felt the same when a man was dreaming. Or hallucinating. Or dying…

The spider reached down and snagged Ky first by its very long pincers. Hunter would've fought it off, but he couldn't make his pinkie move, and besides. That spider was big. And hairy. The arachnid came for him next, only other spiders had joined in by then. They argued as they wrapped him tight, and the oddest thought showed up. *Does it hurt when a spider sucks you dry?*

Guess I'll find out.

Up he went into the spider's lair. Nest. Web. *Whatever.*

He just didn't expect it to be so bright when he got there. Some guy had his hands all over his face, peeling his eyelids open and pouring a ton of stark-white burning sunlight into his head.

"Sh-shit. B-back off," he croaked, his mouth too damned dry to get the words out. Turning his head to the side, the cold lips of a canteen collided with his mouth. Spiders and water? Sunlight? The world had turned upside-down and everything hurt. His eyes. His body. Even his boots. *Holy hell.*

"Hunt," someone kept calling to him out of a long dark tunnel. "Hunt. Come on man, wake up. Open your mouth. Take a good long drink."

He batted the nonsensical eight-legged beast away, not going to be any monster's desiccated human-dinner roll. The brightness dimmed and the fog in his head lifted.

"There you are." That same guy cuffed his cheeks until Hunter wanted to scream. "Hunt. Take a drink. Come on, man. Don't go dying on me now."

Then leave me the hell alone.

"Easy now." The man poured water through his cracked lips until it finally made sense. He'd been rescued. Him and Ky. Again with the water, and Hunter's brain re-engaged. He latched onto that bottle and swallowed. Water! More! Then he chugged. Then the guy kneeling over him turned into Lee Hart, and Hunter choked the water all back up.

He didn't mean to but damn. Lee had rescued them just like Ky'd said he would. How had he known? Who cared? The big tough guy leaning over him looked beautiful. Hunter grabbed Lee's face the same second tears stung his dried-up eyeballs. "Lee!"

"Yeah, Hunt. It's me. Jesus Christ, we've all been looking for you lucky bastards."

"But it's really you." Hunter didn't think twice. He pulled Lee into his face and planted a kiss on his surprised friend's mouth.

Lee jerked to the side, spitting and wiping his lips. "You do that again, Hunt, and I'm dropping your sorry ass back down that hole we just dragged it out of."

Hunter squeezed his eyes shut. So. Damned. Happy. What a small word. He was beyond happy. He was thrilled. Ecstatic. Oh hell, he was—alive.

"Ky?" he asked, hoping with all his heart Lee gave him the right answer.

Lee cupped Hunter's head to the left. "See for yourself."

"Hey, man," Ky groaned hoarsely, staring at Hunt. He was flat on his back with good old Zack Lennox kneeling over him with another canteen. "You ain't gonna... kiss me next... are you?"

Zack chuckled. "Don't think I've seen that one before, Hunt."

Hunter choked up, but disguised it by puckering his lips and blowing Ky a kiss instead. "We made it, buddy. Just like you said. Gawddamnit, we made it."

"I told you he'd show up." Ky sounded so damned bad, his lips cracked and peeling, his voice so ragged it hurt listening to him. How he'd gotten sunburned made no sense until Lee started smearing some kind of gel over Hunter's forehead and cheeks.

"You two look like a blowtorch worked you over. Or one of those sandstorms in Iraq."

"River," Hunter croaked. "Sand. Rocks. River." It made sense before he said it.

"There's a river running underground?" Zack asked. "You fell in it?"

Hunt could only nod. "Long ways... down."

Lee's big palm landed square in the center of Hunter's chest. "Take it easy. The chopper's on its way to pick us up. Alex is going to kick your ass. You two guys cost him a fortune."

"Alex... here?" Hunter asked.

"Hell, yeah," Zack said. "How'd you guys survive this long?"

You call this surviving? "How long?" Hunter had to know.

"Two weeks," Lee replied.

Hunter closed his eyes. Meredith. God, he missed her.

"I need you to calm down," Lee said sternly.

"I am... calm," Hunter insisted, the pounding in his heart a little on the loud side, but nothing he hadn't heard before.

Lee shook his head grimly. "No, you're not. You guys are both in rough shape, but your heart's beating like crazy.

Relax, Hunt. Come on, guy. Think of something peaceful for a change, okay? You're going to make it. Promise."

Hunter closed his eyes and willed the tender feeling of Meredith's lovely body into his arms. Even he could hear his heart pounding a thousand hoof-beats a minute on its race to some imaginary finish line. He needed to calm himself before...

Jesus Christ. Not this again.

Lee muttered something Hunter couldn't understand, right before Lee bellowed, "Son-of-a-bitch. I'm losing him!"

The darkness of the cave slithered out of the jagged cleft, and Hunter fell a thousand miles into—nothing.

CHAPTER THIRTY-FIVE

"Mama! Look at me!"

Meredith looked up from her beach chair to her son's squeal for attention. The day was sunny and warm. Comfortable in jeans and a periwinkle blue sweater top, she'd opted to let Eddy have what he'd declared he'd wanted most: time with Courtney. Unfortunately, that meant father and son now stood at the bow of Eddy's grand sailboat, serenely anchored off the private dock of what Eddy called his *cabin*.

With historic Thomas Shoal Point Light Station just down the bay, the location couldn't have been more perfect—or exclusive. Interestingly, Eddy had no neighbors. He owned this entire stretch of beachfront property.

Courtney had worn his favorite *Elmo* T-shirt. Jeans kept his legs warm and kid-sized boots protected his feet. Eddy cut a dashing figure in navy blue slacks, a white Henley with nautical red and blue stripes across his chest. She'd had no idea he'd taken up sailing, but it fit him. He seemed a natural.

The only reason she'd allowed Eddy this private time with Courtney was the happy smile splitting her son's face. She couldn't deny it. He deserved a relationship with his father, and as long as Eddy doted on him, Meredith could endure a few supervised visits.

But if Eddy's house was a *cabin*, she was the pope.

She'd had the tour. With floor to ceiling paned-glass windows at the front, and an open deck at every level, his three-story, very elegant home faced the South River, one of the Chesapeake's many tributaries. Built of dark gray granite rock and golden cedar, the home was stunningly offset by a charcoal slate roof. Set back in the pines, the house had a cozy feel, although the dramatic security lighting when they'd first arrived had made it impossible to miss.

Talk about pricey. Luxurious bedroom suites comprised the entire second level; a gaming center complete with billiards, an enormous home theatre, and a soundproof reading room/library occupied the third. But it was the widow's walk at the highest peak of the roof that gave her pause.

Romantic folklore held it as the watch point where many a lovesick woman stalked while waiting for her seafaring man to return. It seemed an odd feature for a man Meredith knew for a fact didn't have a romantic bone in his body. Yet, it was perfectly functional, its access acquired by a charming spiral staircase from the third level. An expensive old-fashioned, brass telescope stood in one corner, an outdoor rocking chair in the other.

Despite Eddy's rambling about high seas danger and swashbucklers during the tour, Meredith didn't linger at the widow's walk. She wasn't there for romance.

The only thing his *cabin* lacked was cell-phone coverage. Not enough towers, Eddy had said. Hmm. How about that? Not even a billionaire could buy everything.

But being out of range made her edgy. It had been two weeks since she'd come home, and she was on the verge of calling Seth or Lee. Hunter hadn't been found and Eric hadn't woken. Something had to give.

Drawing her knees beneath her, she waved back to her son. Courtney seemed totally smitten by his father's attention. Eddy did have a way with people. But that sailboat was another thing altogether. It looked more like a fifty-feet long yacht. To think she could've had all this once upon a time. Yeah, right.

Meredith waved one last time and made herself comfortable. She'd brought a good book to read, but she couldn't concentrate. Hunter kept showing up in the middle of every page. She only had to close her eyes, and she could see every last detail of him. That sexy wink. The way he shrugged when he didn't want to answer a direct question. The taste of his lips. Strangely, this day at the beach reminded her more of him than Eddy.

"Bye, Mama!"

Her head jerked up at that delighted announcement. Courtney stood at the bow of the boat, barely able to see over the side, but waving like the little trooper he was.

Meredith jumped to her feet. "Where are you going?" she called, her hands cupped to her mouth. Eddy didn't give any indication he'd heard as the boat headed out to sea.

"I goin' with Daddy!" Courtney waved happily as if his mother wasn't panicking.

Oh, no you're not! She ran to the dock. "Eddy! What are you doing?"

Not once did he look her way, but sweet Courtney kept waving. A bright yellow lifejacket covered *Elmo*, but worry still battled with logic. Eddy had promised no boating, yet there he went, turning that elegant craft toward the big beautiful bay that emptied into the unforgiving gray Atlantic.

She couldn't breathe. *He's got my son. He's taking Courtney.*

Her heart skipped across the waves to her reason to live. Eddy had deliberately gone against her wishes. He'd deliberately baited her son with the adventure of a ride in that fancy boat. She craned her neck to keep sight of that barely visible hint of bright yellow.

He'd better take care of my baby. He'd better make it a short ride. He'd better never do this to me again!

When the sailboat paralleled the shore, its prow pointed north, she lost sight of Courtney. Up came a billowing sail, then another much larger sail behind the first. When they caught the wind, the boat soared away, and Meredith's heart sank. Sheer panic took over. *Oh, God, what have I done?*

She ran into the house and pounded up the stairs to the widow's walk, needing to know everything taking place on that boat. Still talking herself out of a full-blown panic attack, she pivoted that telescope to the sea and adjusted the focus.

At last, the boat came into view, Courtney's little body too. Eddy had him locked in his arms, pointing at something high overhead. The little guy twisted to look at his father's face. She could clearly see his bright smile, and okay, that helped. Her heart stopped beating so hard. She could breathe. Why she'd gotten nearly hysterical over a little boat ride amazed her, but Eddy hadn't always been this thoughtful, and he'd thrown away his chance to be this—fatherly.

As she steadied the telescope, Eddy and Courtney turned at the same time. Eddy pointed directly at her. They waved like a normal father and son would do. Both grinning. Both happy.

Meredith swallowed her panic. She had no reason to suspect this new version of Eddy of anything other than wanting to be part of his son's life. He'd already declared Courtney his only legal heir. He wanted to give his boy everything.

It just seemed too good to be true.

When the sailboat sidled along the dock, Eddy lowered the sails. Her heartbeat resumed an almost normal rhythm. She angled the telescope for one last look at her handsome little boy on what would be his first and last sailboat ride. There he stood with the biggest grin splitting his cute face.

"I should've taken a picture," she scolded out loud. "He'd like that. It was an important event in his life." She would have if she hadn't panicked. But that was what happened to women who survived abuse. They always suspected the worst.

Calmer now, she spied her son at the bow, the sunshine on his face. It took so little to make him happy. But what was that black thing flying up high on the mast? Meredith peered through the telescope for a closer look. At last a gust of wind ripped the wrinkles out of the pennant, revealing a white skull and crossbones.

A pirate flag?

"You're not going anywhere."

Hunter peeled one eye open. He would've told Lee in no uncertain terms what he could do with that order—if he hadn't just discovered he had an oxygen mask taped over his mouth. If he hadn't been flat on his back in a hospital—in Brazil—where everyone around him was speaking Portuguese.

Lee sat perched beside him on a stool, his arms folded over his chest. It annoyed Hunter to be helpless, but he was too weak to care, much less do anything about it. Grunting, he let Lee think he'd won this round.

"You're lucky we got to you when we did. I didn't know you had a stent."

Hunter held up two fingers.

"No kidding. Two stents?" Lee pursed his lips. "Well, now you've got three, you dumbass. Why is that not in your personnel file? You had no business taking this assignment."

Hunter shrugged. A lot of things weren't in his personnel file, like the reason behind his disability discharge. He'd learned to love the Corps, but it seemed the Corps didn't love the heart condition he hadn't known he'd inherited from his father's side of the family. After his first aortic aneurysm, which came out of nowhere one day at Bagram, he'd persuaded his CO it was a fluke. Chances were it'd never happen again.

Hunter got the green light to go back to active duty. He was young. Otherwise healthy. He certainly had the right killer attitude. But five months later, he failed his physical. Another aneurysm. Another stent. That one tanked his career. The Corps would've kept him—at a desk job. Stateside. Hunter bailed.

"Meredith," he mumbled, fogging up the mask. *Just tell me where she is and if she's safe.*

"That's why you left the Corps, isn't it? Your heart condition?"

There seemed no end to the questioning, but now was not the time. Hunter tried again, but only succeeded in mumbling, "'Mehmip."

Lee leaned in a little too close, his brows furrowed like a son-of-a-bitch. Lee could look damned mean when he wanted to. "And still you smoke?" he hissed. "How dumb are you, Hunt? Are you trying to kill yourself?"

Hunter looked past Lee to the drapes that ruffled whenever someone on the other side hurried by. That was the real question of the day, wasn't it? Had he deliberately put himself in harm's way three years ago because he'd lost Meredith?

Yes and no. The dumb kid he was then had no way of knowing he'd end up in the Two/Four, one of the toughest regiments in the Corps. Yet it had served his purpose. Turning into a battle-hardened Marine had certainly changed his outlook on life and his moral compass. Hell, it changed everything that had made him the pathetic man he'd believed Meredith had tossed aside for Fast Eddy Welch.

Hunter had thrown his heart and soul into that noble mindset: The few. The proud. The Marines. He'd taken every tough assignment that came his way, and he was a fast learner because he wasn't afraid to die. At least that was what he'd thought… then.

Or was it the other way around? Had that abrupt about face in his life been a coward's way out? Would a smarter Hunter have humbled himself and sought Meredith out to learn what really happened? Would he have given her a second chance? Was he afraid to live? Was that why he'd run?

Pressing back into his pillow, he dragged one weak hand up to his face and jerked the oxygen mask off. Self-enlightenment could wait. "Not now, Lee. Where the hell's... Meredith?"

Lee's green eyes narrowed as he stuck a pointed finger in Hunter's face. "This discussion's not over. You and me are getting to the bottom of this bullshit death wish of yours. Count on it." Folding his arms over his chest again, he tipped back onto the stool. "As for Meredith, Alex sent her home. I'm not sure if he told her that we'd found you yet, not after the scare you gave us. He might want you to break the bad news yourself."

"She's in... danger," Hunter wheezed. "Roger Teach. Brinkman EX. Tell Alex. Hurry."

"Take it easy, he knows. He's got Mother and Ember looking into Teach and Burdette's holdings."

That helped.

"You would've been okay if you'd treated that knife wound, you know. It was infected. You had a first-aid kit. Jesus, Hunt, why didn't you?"

Meredith would get a kick out of this conversation. Hunter could almost see her chewing his butt like she did when he'd told her he'd taken a swim in the river.

He pushed the thought of her away. "Where's... Ky?"

Lee rolled his eyes. "Damn you're a hard-headed ass. Ky's on his way back to the States with everyone else."

"Everyone?"

Lee nodded. "Everyone except Alex. You know how he is. He won't leave until you're ready to travel."

"When?"

"Tomorrow, if your oxygen sat level improves, which is why you were on the respirator until this morning."

That explained the sore throat. "Why?"

"Because you had a damned heart attack in the middle of the jungle," Lee muttered. "Holy hell, Hunt. We've spent weeks tearing that fenced-in plot of land apart trying to find you and Ky, but the minute we do, you scare the shit out of us by going into cardiac arrest. I've never seen a man flash into hyper-medic-mode as fast as Zack did. Are your ribs sore?"

Hunter nodded. Hell, yeah. All of him felt pretty damned sore.

"Good! They ought to be broken. Zack pounded on you hard enough. Guess he lost a guy in the middle of chest compressions a few years back. He wasn't about to let you die."

Hunter made a mental note. *Zack. Lee. Damned good friends.*

"How'd you… find us?" His throat burned with every word.

"Blame that on the boss. He brought in a team of experts who map tombs like the ones over in Egypt and that crystal cave in Mexico. Those guys are good."

It was easier to let Lee talk. It wasn't often he had this much to say.

"They used geo-electric mapping to scan the underground terrain. You should've seen them. I've never worked with men so excited about what they were doing. They're the ones who found the chute you or Ky dropped into. Sucking quicksand nearly bought Jordan the farm, but finding that one shaft was the break we needed. They're the ones who went underground after you and Ky."

"What's geo—" Hunter waved his hand, "—whatever?"

"Geo-electric mapping." Lee shrugged both big shoulders. Calmer now, he looked laid back in his customary western shirt and jeans. "It takes three-dimensional images of whatever's underground. Oil and gas companies use it. Explorers. Environmentalists."

This rescue still felt more like a blessed miracle than practical science. "But there had to be hundreds of trails and ledges down there…"

Lee nodded, but his eyes shifted to the monitor. "There was. Like I said, those guys were good. We almost lost Eric though. This has been one hell of an *easy* operation."

God, not Eric. All the good news turned to gray. "What happened?"

Lee rolled both those broad shoulders at whatever he was reading on Hunter's monitor. Worry creased the corners of his eyes. "Take it easy, Hunt. Your blood pressure's spiking."

"Then tell me!"

After a slow, deliberate breath, Lee spilled. "Masters knifed him, then Seth shot Masters and we had to exfil out of there. Eric's in a hospital back in the States. He's in a coma, but he's holding his own."

Why did Hunter get the feeling Lee was holding back? "Did Seth kill Masters?" *He better have!*

Lee nodded. "Oh, yeah. One shot to the throat."

"Good." Hunter forced himself to calm. "I should've done that, but I needed answers and I… I…" *I wanted to be more than a cold-blooded killer. For Merry.*

The intensity in Lee's eyes softened. He always did see through Hunter. "You like Meredith, huh?"

"Yes," Hunter admitted, his pulse steady. "How was she when you last saw her?"

Lee rolled his eyes. "I'm not sure she's mentally sound. That woman thinks you're a lover not a fighter."

Great. What had Meredith said?

"Ky told me." Hunter changed the direction of this conversation, "'bout you and Tess and Nizari."

Lee arched a brow. "Is that right?"

"I had no idea."

"That was another bad night," Lee hissed softly. "I honestly didn't think we'd get out of there alive."

"Tess is amazing."

A thoughtful smile tweaked one corner of Lee's mouth. "She is. There's never a dull moment in my life."

"Guess we don't always know each other's stories, do we?"

"All I know is what I see, Hunt, and Meredith thinks the world of you. Damned if I know why, but she does."

Hunter wondered the same. "I've known her for years."

"What'd you do? Let the woman of your dreams get away?"

"Something like that." Hunter cleared his throat. "I'm... sorry. I've been—"

Lee waved him off. "Later. You can explain why you're a dumbass when we're home." He pulled a cell phone out of his front shirt pocket and tapped the screen. "Here. I've got her number. It's five o'clock on the East Coast. Call her." His green eyes were smiling when he shoved his wide shoulders around the drapes and gave Hunter some privacy.

Hunter pressed the phone to his ear. Meredith would be thrilled. Mentally calculating travel time and distance, she could be in his arms inside twenty hours or so—if the hospital discharged him as quickly as he hoped they would.

When the phone kept ringing, he ran his fingers over his head, wishing he were with her. Single mothers had it tough. She was probably on her way home from work right now. With Courtney. What did the little tyke look like? Hunter wanted to know everything. About Meredith's apartment. What kind of car she drove. Her favorite food. Everything.

She used to dunk Oreos in milk when she was a kid. Did she still? Had she taught Courtney to do that? Did they sit together giggling until their cookies disintegrated into soggy mush? That was when Hunter first knew he loved her, sitting at her mother's kitchen table. Meredith had the most adorable turned-up nose when it had soggy chocolate crumbles on the end of it.

But the phone kept ringing. He disconnected the call and let his hand drop to his lap.

Maybe next time.

CHAPTER THIRTY-SIX

Summoning all the patience she could muster, Meredith met Eddy and Courtney at the dock, her arms crossed over her chest and her toes tapping. "I thought we agreed no sailboat ride?"

Eddy cocked his head. "We did?"

"You're doing what you've always done, Eddy. You're not listening to me." Her hands dropped to her hips. "When I set boundaries, you sidestep them as if you never heard me."

His brows slanted. "If I remember correctly, you said *you* don't like being out on the water. You didn't say anything about not taking Court for a quick jaunt."

Darn. He had her there.

Eddy lifted Courtney off the sailboat and set him on his feet. "There you go, Tiger. Be careful. Don't fall. You're still a landlubber, Mate. You haven't got your sea legs yet."

Meredith crouched to catch him, but instead of running to her for a hug, Courtney took off for the porch with a squeal. "Aye, aye, Cap'n. I gonna win!"

"Not if I get there first!" Eddy called after him.

Meredith ran a hand through her wind tossed locks as she straightened. Had she heard right? Eddy was not only Daddy now, but Captain too?

Abruptly, she was in his arms. Before she could growl a warning, he'd covered her mouth with his. Mumbling for him to stop, she pushed him away, but he held on tight. When pushing didn't work, she dug her nails into his chest until he broke the kiss. "I said no."

"Ouch." He pulled back, rubbing his chest. "Nipple pinching, huh? That's new."

Typical. He twisted whatever she did or said. That would be the day she did anything remotely intimate with him. "Don't kiss me again. The only reason I'm here is for Courtney. You and me are over. Understood?"

"I win!" her happy boy crowed from the porch, his wind-reddened face wide with glee. Courtney did look as if he'd had the time of his life.

Eddy waved at him. "That young man of yours is intelligent, Meredith. We had fun out there on the water. I wish you'd come with us to smell the open sea and feel the bite in the wind and—" He sucked in a deep breath and thumped a hand to his chest. "God, I had no idea how much it meant to share this old boat with my son. This place. Look around. It'll all be his someday."

An unexpected dose of guilt for not trusting Eddy caught in her throat.

"But you are right. That kiss was out of line and I apologize. I guess I was overcome by the moment." He said all the right words.

She almost wanted to forgive him. "Behave yourself. We have a little boy to think of and he doesn't need to see displays like that. It'll confuse him."

Totally disregarding her warning, he grabbed her hand, but Meredith bit back her protest. She hated encouraging the illusion that they were together, but Courtney was frowning. He looked concerned, the last thing she wanted.

Shrugging out of his grip, she hurried to her son. "Did you see me waving at you?"

"Ah-huh. I did." He wrapped his arms around her neck. "Did you see me flying?"

"You mean sailing, son," Eddy corrected.

"And I want a boat!"

"And you shall have one." Eddy reached around them to open the front door.

"You don't need a boat," Meredith scolded, lifting Courtney into her arms. She nuzzled his neck to distract him. "You already have a new trike. Don't you want—?"

"Yes, I do, Mama," he argued, crossing his arms over his chest, his lips pinched into a pout and his brows furrowed. "I want a big boat. A really big one. Just like Daddy's."

Eddy lifted a salacious brow. "Well, I do have a big one."

And that was the last straw. No three-year-old needed to deal with sexual innuendo.

"We're done here," she declared, her Irish up. She set Courtney on his feet. "Get your jacket and Bear. It's time to go home."

"Oh, come on," Eddy groused. "Can't an ex-husband tease his ex-wife?"

"No. You can't. And you're not to jerk Courtney around either. He's your son, not some conquest to step over on your way to me. Stop manipulating him."

Courtney let out a bleat. "Daddy says I kin have one, Mama. He says I kin have anything I want."

"Sweetheart, we'll talk about that boat when we get home, okay?"

His bottom lip stuck out. "No. I staying."

Meredith took a deep breath and stopped arguing with a three-year-old. "Okay then. You stay here. It's too bad you don't have any pajamas or your blanket, though."

He blinked. "I kin stay?"

"Sure. I'm not going to fight with you, honey. If you want to stay here—"

He ran into her arms. "No, Mama. I going home with you."

She slanted a small smile of satisfaction in Eddy's direction as she picked her son up again. He might own the world, but she knew what made her little boy tick.

Eddy shook his head as he opened his front door, his eyes on the floor, and there it was again—the tender look that made her want to believe him. "You're right," he said, his voice subdued. "I've behaved badly. Like I said, I'm not good with kids, but don't leave, Meredith. Give me another chance. I can be better. I know I can."

Gritting her teeth, she set Courtney down. "Maybe another time. I think we've had enough visiting for one day. Go get Bear, Courtney. We're leaving."

He hunched over and whined, "But I don't wanna go."

"I know, but we need to. Get Bear or he stays here."

That did it. Courtney took off to find his best friend.

"I am sorry," Eddy insisted. "Listen. I can't help it if you're irresistible. Don't punish my son for what I did."

"You're not sorry." She faced him, whispering so Courtney wouldn't hear. "I don't care what I said, you knew I didn't want him out on the water. You fill his head with ideas a three-year-old doesn't have a clue about. A boat, Eddy? Really? You told him he needs a boat, and where does that high-and-mighty notion leave me? Suddenly, you're the hero, and I'm the witch who gets to tell him no—is that what you're teaching him? You show up with the world at your fingertips while all I've got to offer him is tuna casserole?"

With his palms splayed open, Eddy stuttered, "I... I didn't mean it like that. Honest. I—"

"What did you think you were doing, then?" she hissed. "He's three! He believes everything you tell him. Don't toy with that little boy's heart like you did mine, because right now, he thinks you're his hero. I don't."

"Bear's lost, Mama," Courtney mumbled behind her.

"I'm... I'm sorry," Eddy said. "Honest, Meredith. I was only trying to make up for being an ass."

"Then stop being one." She whirled away from Eddy and crouched down to Courtney's level, changing her tone and countenance. "Where's Bear?"

A tear tracked out of her little boy's eye. Manfully, he glanced at Eddy as he wiped it away. His lip quivered. "He lost, Mama."

"Oh, now stop fussing." She pulled him to her. "We'll find him. Did he go sailing with you?"

"Uh-uh," Courtney said sadly as he shook his head. "I not want Bear to get wet."

"Good thinking, Son." Eddy crouched beside them, contrition deep in his eyes. "I'll bet that rascal took off on his own adventure while we were sailing. Shall I help you find him?"

Meredith closed her eyes. How could he do this, twist her inside out until she didn't know what to believe?

Eddy pulled Courtney out of her hands and settled him high on his shoulder. "Come on, Court, let's find Bear. Then let's take your mother for a ride and to dinner, so she'll forgive us for frightening her, shall we?"

"Home," Meredith reminded him tersely, her toes tapping.

"Yes!" Courtney said excitedly. "And buy me a boat!"

"Probably not," Eddy dodged a direct answer. "Big boats are for big boys like me. Trikes are for little guys like you. How about if we settle for a nice dinner tonight? That'll make your mother happy."

"Home, Eddy." God, he was infuriating.

Up they went to the top level. But the higher they went, the more Meredith's instincts prickled. Eddy had Courtney all to himself again. She could barely hear their father/son banter until they stood at the third level banister when Eddy stopped to look down. *Over the edge. With Courtney tilted forward.* "Hey, pretty lady. Am I forgiven?"

"Not if you drop my son," she bit out. "You're scaring him, Eddy. Hold onto him."

Eddy glanced over his shoulder. "Courtney Welch isn't afraid of anything, are you?"

The little boy who wanted to please his father shook his head and breathed his first lie. "No, I not 'fraid."

Finally! Eddy reached one arm over his head and clamped onto the boy. "You're shaking. You okay back there?" Courtney's head bobbed even as Eddy tugged him into the safety of his arms. "It's all right, he muttered. "I'd never let you fall, big guy."

"C-Courtney Flynn," Meredith corrected weakly, so damned thankful her son was no longer in danger of tumbling over that banister.

Eddy tossed her another wink, nodding. "You're right. I should've known better."

You think! Meredith nearly collapsed with relief when they stepped away from that damned banister. Why did Eddy play these games? Or was he? She couldn't decide. One minute he seemed sincere, but the next he acted oblivious to his son's safety. Didn't he understand how little boys thought and worried? That had to be it. Fatherhood was an unknown frontier for this high roller, and he had a lot of catching up to do.

In seconds, naughty Bear was back on ground level with everyone else. Meredith scooped her son into her arms, still shaken at what could have happened. Didn't it figure? Eddy wrapped his arms around the family he'd deserted, his chin in the crook of her neck. "You're shaking. I'm sorry I scared you again," he murmured. "I can't seem to get anything right."

She swallowed hard and endured the embrace. It was obvious he had no clue what to do with children. "It's okay," she whispered. "You'll learn, just… don't ever take chances, okay? He's small and he doesn't know better and it's our job to protect him." *And I'd die before I let anything happen to him.*

Eddy nodded against her hair but kept his hands where they belonged and not on her ass. "I suppose you want to leave now," he said sadly.

Meredith wasn't that cruel. Eddy seemed earnestly trying to get this fatherhood thing figured out. She couldn't blame him for making mistakes when she'd blundered through enough of her own as a new mother. Kids didn't come with instructions. She'd had time to grow into motherhood. Eddy might need the same consideration.

She swallowed her overly protective edge and decided to end the day on a positive note. "How about a long ride and dinner on our way home?"

He eased back, looking down at her. "I truly am sorry."

"Let's just go." She needed to put this day behind her. "Where are you taking us?"

"McGinley's," Eddy replied as he retrieved her jacket from the front room.

Of course. The trendiest nightclub restaurant on the bay. Why choose some place reasonable where a child might actually fit in?

"Wait. I need my backpack." She'd stashed it beside her jacket on the leather recliner. "I'll get it."

Eddy shook his head. "You women and your purses. What's in it? A gun?"

What an odd question. Her lashes hit the floor as she tugged the backpack over one arm. Did he already know she'd brought her conceal carry at the last moment—just because? "A change of clothes for Courtney, remember? He needs his jacket, too."

"Already taken care of." Eddy grunted as he corralled Courtney's arms into the correct sleeves. "Come on then. You want to be home by eight, and home, you shall be."

Hunter couldn't get out of Brazil fast enough. He'd tried to call Meredith before he boarded the flight home, all without avail. Sitting in comfortable first class didn't alleviate the growing sense that something was wrong. Neither did the long, direct flight into Dulles International Airport, northern Virginia. He doffed his seat belt as soon he could and paced the jetliner.

Lee fell asleep before lift-off. Alex took the window seat and perused one of several newspapers he'd picked up in the airport. "You're wearing a hole in the carpet."

Hunter growled to himself and sat. "Guess you're right."

"Mother's still checking into Roger Teach." Alex thumbed another page, then shook the folds out of his paper.

"And?"

"Whoever he is, he's a slippery one. It's as if he didn't exist before he took over Brinkman EX seven months ago."

"How is that possible? Everyone leaves a paper trail. Bank accounts. Birth certificates."

"You'd think so." Alex seemed absorbed in whatever article he'd come across.

"Are you telling me he might be CIA? Mob? A foreign spy?"

"I'm telling you he's in for a surprise if he thinks he's smarter than Mother."

Hunter replayed Masters' threat. *I'm finding that damned bitch today if it's the last thing I do. Teach wants her, dead or alive. Dead works for me.*

"He wants Meredith dead, Boss. Her son too."

"So you said," Alex murmured, "which is why I sent Maverick and Taylor over to her place this morning. Don't worry. They'll take care of her until you land."

Maverick Carson and Taylor Armstrong were two of the best agents on The TEAM. Hunter trusted them. Meredith would be safe.

Lightning flashed off in the distance. Rain pelted the windows. Hunter stared past Alex out the window, hating the confinement of an all-night flight from Caracas. He needed to be on the ground. Now.

CHAPTER THIRTY-SEVEN

Eddy could be charming when he set his mind to it.

"My usual," he ordered the maître d' when they'd arrived at McGinley's. A waiter escorted them through the crowded restaurant into a private dining room at the back of the restaurant. Overlooking the Chesapeake, the elegant room came complete with soft lighting, a lavish fresh flower centerpiece, and a staff of two waiters. Another stood waiting off to the side with a carafe of ice water.

Safe in her arms, Courtney dodged the strange gentlemen dressed in crisply ironed white shirts and pressed black slacks. His best buddy, Bear, stayed tucked under his chin for protection from all things adult.

The table had already been set with Irish crystal and silverware, but the booster seat in one of the chairs caught her eye. Eddy must have phoned ahead. That was unusually thoughtful. Maybe there was hope for him after all.

"Come to me," he commanded Courtney, his arms outstretched to take the boy from Meredith. Courtney hesitated for less than a second. Okay, that was another surprise—her son transferring eagerly into his father's arms when he'd been shy the day before. Meredith gulped. Between all the gifts and Eddy's fatherly attention, she was losing ground fast.

Eddy turned his attention to her, a twinkle in his gray eyes as he held a chair for her. "May I seat you?"

"Yes. Thank you." She took her place next to Courtney. "This is very nice. I can only imagine how much this is costing you."

His brow lifted in a devilish arch. "Actually, they let me eat here for free whenever I choose. I own McGinley's."

Wow. She so didn't realize what it meant to be wined and dined by a billionaire. Oh, wait, yes, she did. Jed McCormack was a billionaire, only one would never know it to look at him. He was so—normal.

Eddy settled at the other side of Courtney. "I'll just bet you're a macaroni and cheese connoisseur."

Courtney pursed his lips. "I not a con-a-sour. They're scary and they eat people."

Meredith couldn't contain a giggle. "Not a dinosaur, Courtney. A connoisseur. That's someone who likes to eat good food."

"Like mac-n-cheese," Eddy added.

"Oh, yeah! I like mac-n-cheese." Courtney's eyes brightened as he clapped. "And I like pisghetti and hotdogs and hangebergers and noodles..." He took a big breath, "and oh, yeah. Popsicles!"

Meredith interlocked her fingers under her chin, her elbows on the table. Her son did like to eat.

"And pizza and ice cream." His brows slanted. "Only not 'matoes. They're icky."

Eddy caught her smiling. "There's the girl I used to know," he said, lifting his water goblet in a toast. "You look radiant tonight, Miss Flynn. What would you like to eat?"

She reached past Courtney to clink glasses with Eddy. "I'm a mac-n-cheese gal myself." He might as well get used to it.

"I bring you to the top restaurant on the East Coast and you want simple fare?" He shook his head, tsking. "Knox? You heard the lady. How's the mac-n-cheese here?"

Knox, the blond waiter with his hair neatly parted on the left, stepped forward. "We only serve the best," he said with a nod to Courtney. "Would you prefer chocolate milk or apple juice with your entrée, young Mr. Welch?"

"His name is Courtney Flynn," Meredith corrected before this misunderstanding went any further. "And he'll have..." She cocked a brow at her son, who by now was hanging on every word.

"Root beer!" he declared hopefully.

Eddy ran his pinched thumb and finger over his lips, and all eyes were on Meredith. The scene around the table felt like a happy family. It was just possible Eddy would make a decent father after all. "Then root beer it is. You do have root beer, don't you?"

"Yes, ma'am. Nothing but the best for Master Flynn."

The meal couldn't have gone better. The service was excellent. The unobstructed view of the Chesapeake at night defied description and the mac-n-cheese was by far, the best Meredith had ever tasted. Courtney finished every last morsel. The root beer disappeared as quickly.

"I done," he announced, resting his fork on the edge of his plate as she'd taught him. "I tired, Mama."

"Me too," she admitted. The day had gone far better than she'd expected.

"Would you care for an after-dinner drink, ma'am?" Knox offered, an elegant white napkin laid his forearm. "A liqueur? A brandy? Perhaps coffee?"

"An Irish coffee would be nice," she said.

"Yes, ma'am." His gaze shifted to Eddy. "Your usual, sir?"

Eddy nodded, his eyes glowing and focused on her. "I think I see a pattern," he said, his voice full of silk. "It's taken me these last three years of living alone to realize that you're content all by yourself, Meredith. You're strong and competent. You work hard and you take excellent care of your son. What's more, you're happy. You don't need anything from me, do you?"

That came out of the blue. Her cheeks blushed with warmth. "I'd appreciate your friendship for Courtney's sake."

"You'll always have that, Meredith Flynn." He enunciated her last name carefully. "But you don't need a man in your life to direct you or provide for you, do you? You do quite well on your own, even though you have very little to your name."

"I have everything I want or need." She turned to the sleepy boy between them. After that delicious meal, Courtney was on carbohydrate overload, his eyelids heavy and his cheeks flushed.

"Yes. I believe you're right." Eddy sighed. "You do have everything you need."

Not once during the meal had he stretched his arm across Courtney's back to snare her fingers or brush her shoulder. It was a relief not being hit on for a change. "What's come over you?"

"Nothing." His gray eyes were hooded, making them sexily dark. Eddy always knew how to use that smoldering look he had going for him. "I've just been watching you today, as I'm sure you've noticed. I owe you an apology. I know I was hard on you the short time we were married and, God…"

He shoved his fingers through his hair and looked away as if he was embarrassed. "To say I behaved badly makes me sound like a decent person when I wasn't." The muscles in his neck constricted as he swallowed. "I hurt you and worse, I deserted you and Courtney when you needed me the most. I'm sorry. I'm truly sorry."

She blinked, not sure what to believe.

"I'm not asking you to forgive me." He kept his eyes on his plate. "In so many ways, you're stronger than me. I respect that about you. I need you to know that I'm afraid I'm smitten all over again with you, only it's too late, isn't it? I've made the one mistake that can't be fixed with money. I've lost your trust. It only follows that I've also lost you forever, haven't I?"

Meredith lowered her gaze to the crystal cup of Irish coffee Knox had just placed in front of her. "Water, ma'am?" he asked politely.

"No, Knox. Thank you. This looks perfect." She waved him away, flustered at the tenderness emanating from the man she'd tried for so long to hate. It took her a moment before she could look her ex in the eye again. "You hit me, Eddy. You hurt me. I can forgive you, but I can't forget that. None of it."

His head bobbed. "Understood, but because of my former abuse, I'll forever remain your most humble servant. To my death," he said quietly, his tone somber and more than a little sad. "I stand in awe of you, Meredith. I've met royalty and celebrities the world over. I've dined with wheelers and dealers. Hell, I've hosted the Vice President on my sailboat, but you, the mother of my son, are the most brilliant woman I've ever known. Truly. You've just eaten a beggar's meal, yet you sit there with a contented smile that makes you shine." He reached behind Courtney for her hand and lifted it to his lips. "Courtney is a very lucky little boy, and I'm a fool."

Embarrassed by all the flattery, she eased her hand from his, willing to accept his kindness, nothing more. Eddy always did have dreamy eyes. The last thing she needed was to get sucked back into them.

"And that lucky little boy is now sound asleep," she said.

Eddy cocked his head, his eyes full of tenderness at the child between them with his chin sagging on his chest. The Irish coffee was forgotten. Eddy pushed back his chair and scooped Courtney into his arms, covering him with his jacket. "I think I promised to have you home by eight. We'd better leave now."

They left McGinley's through a private rear exit. The valet must have known they were ready to go. He stood next to the open sports car door, ready to assist wrangling Courtney into the very limited back seating area.

"Next time, remind me to drive one of my SUVs," Eddy muttered as he all but climbed into the back seat to strap Courtney in. "This will never do in the future."

There it was again, a future plan he hadn't yet vetted through her. Oh, well. She shrugged her annoyance away. Maybe it was the pleasant way the day had gone, but she'd finally seen something in Eddy's eyes that made a friendly relationship with him seem possible. She rested her hand on his back as he secured her son with loving care.

Immediately, he stiffened. "Don't. Please don't."

Startled, she pulled her hand back.

Pushing the driver's seat into position, he turned to her. "You have no idea how much your touch means to me, Meredith. My soul craves to have you back in my life, but you've made it perfectly clear I've lost that privilege. Don't tempt me more than I'm able to bear."

She gulped. Wow. He looked—beaten. "Thank you for a very good day," she murmured.

He nodded, escorting her to her side of the car. "I'm afraid I haven't kept my promise. It's nearly eight now."

"It's no problem if we're a little late getting back. Thank you, again. This has been wonderful."

Resolutely, he shut her door and climbed into the driver's side. "Do you have Bear?"

Meredith looked over her shoulder at her sleeping son. Bear wasn't in sight. Eddy scrambled out of the vehicle. "I'll be right back."

In no time at all he returned with the prized plush. "Shall we leave then? Or would you allow me the simple pleasure of the first sleepover with your son? Your son, I repeat, not you. I shall be the perfect gentleman. You have my word."

It might have been the mac-n-cheese. It certainly wasn't the Irish coffee. But the slightest hint of concern didn't even flit through her mind. Eddy seemed sincere, nothing like the brash, over-confident bully he'd once been. Could it be true? Had he changed? Did he deserve one last chance to make things right with Courtney?

Meredith looked at that sleeping boy who, despite his blond hair and blue eyes, still resembled his father. She took a deep breath and decided to give her ex another chance. "Just this once."

"But what about your job?"

Oh, that. "I'll have to call first thing in the morning."

He handed over his cell phone. "Then call now and leave a message. Tell them where you are and who you're with so they don't worry. There's no coverage at my place, remember?"

Meredith lifted his phone out of his hand, upset for telling a lie in the first place. Oh, the tangled web she'd tried all her life to avoid. She dialed her office and left a quick voice mail message explaining that she wouldn't be in the next day. That'd be a surprise to Paulette, Teague's secretary, since she already knew none of the MI team was scheduled.

Handing the phone back, Meredith caught that same tender look in Eddy's eye. "There, all done."

"You think you're clever, don't you?" he asked, one brow raised.

What on earth was he talking about?

"I'm beginning to understand how devious you are."

What could she say? Silence filled the car.

"You love that little boy in the back seat more than anything, don't you?"

"Of course," she whispered. "Courtney's my life."

Eddy pressed the ignition button and the sports car rumbled to life. "I wish you were talking about me," he said wistfully.

Meredith had to look away. This was a different side to the guy she'd once fallen in love with. But he was right. That day was done, and it hadn't been love to begin with. It was a young girl's infatuation with the most popular jock on campus. Nothing more. The privilege of being her husband and the man she adored now belonged to Hunter Christian. "Just drive."

The sun had barely risen when Hunter's flight touched down at Dulles. He dialed Meredith as quickly as he could. Still no answer.

Alex had his phone clamped between his shoulder and ear. "They what?"

Hunter's hackles lifted at the anger in his boss's voice.

"When? She's been off the grid since yesterday?"

"Who?" Hunter damned well needed to know.

Alex shot him a dark look. "Maverick and Taylor went over to Meredith's yesterday, but she wasn't there."

"They lost her?"

"They never had her," Alex bit out.

Lee lowered his cell phone. "I just talked to Mother."

"And?" Hunter and Alex barked in unison.

"She's not getting a GPS signal from Meredith's phone, so either the battery's dead or she's out of range."

"Bullshit," Hunter roared, his gear bag slung over his shoulder as he headed for the exit.

"Wait up." Lee called to him. "Where are you going?"

"To find her."

CHAPTER THIRTY-EIGHT

She allowed herself one long, languorous stretch on waking. From her head to her toes, Meredith felt rested. As promised, Eddy hadn't bothered her, but she felt uncomfortable sleeping in one of his T-shirts. This would never do.

Easing away from Courtney, still sound asleep beside her, she scurried into the in suite bathroom. She took a quick shower and used several guest items on the counter to brush her teeth and hair. Changing back into her jeans and sweater, she ventured forth.

By then, Courtney was gone. Bear too. Feeling proud for giving Eddy a second chance with his son, she fluffed her hair before she made her way downstairs. Divorced people could be friends. Other couples did it all the time.

Better yet, she intended to call Seth. If he and his guys hadn't located Hunter or Ky yet, she was headed back to Brazil.

The delicious aroma of coffee drew her into the kitchen. After helping herself to a steaming cup of caffeine, she leaned over the granite kitchen sink to peer out the window. There stood father and son at the bench on the front deck.

Eddy was patiently explaining the black cloth in his hand. Courtney looked intent, his forehead wrinkled as if he was thinking extra hard. Meredith's heart warmed. They looked good together.

But what was that in Eddy's hand? Oh. That pennant from his sailboat. That silly pirate flag. What was it called? The Jolly Roger?

Startling revelations sprang to life. Something about Jed's competition. Someone named Roger Teach. Hunter called him a corporate raider, and a corporate raider was a—pirate.

Oh God, no.

Where the hell is she?

Hunter's fist crashed the steering wheel of his SUV. He was on his way to Meredith's townhouse in Falls Church, Virginia. The day before, Maverick and Taylor had illegally entered her place, and they'd found no evidence of foul play, but something wasn't right. She wasn't answering her phone.

The cell phone in his hand rang, startling him. Mother.

"Are you getting any GPS signal from her yet?" he asked without the customary hello.

"No, but Ember backtracked her cell phone. We've got the last signal narrowed down to a hundred-mile radius near—"

"That's not helping!" He punched the wheel again, the cell phone tucked in his neck.

"Shut up and listen," Mother barked back at him. A petite woman with premature white hair, she ruled the office with an iron fist of genius technological skills and a touch of gossip. "Let me finish talking before you bite my head off. We've also been digging into this Roger Teach guy who took over Brinkman EX."

Hunter stilled. The name still bugged the hell out of him.

"We might not be able to tell you where he came from, but we can tell you what he's been up to the last few months. Besides hostile takeovers of three floundering corporations, Brinkman EX included, he's been buying Chesapeake watershed property along the South River, east of Annapolis. Ember's contacted several real estate offices in that area, and guess what? All the agents know him. The second any parcel becomes available, they have instructions to contact him first. He grabs it up, no questions asked, and no price is too high."

Hunter's fingertips worried the steering wheel. "So?"

"So Ms. Flynn's last call came from the southernmost area Teach owns."

Hunter stilled. "Who is he, Mother?"

"I think you already know him. I'm sending a bitmap to your phone. You tell me."

Hunter swiped his cell phone to incoming mail, tapping the image from Mother. It downloaded quickly. "Shit. It's Eddy Welch. Track his cell phone."

"Already done, *Junior Agent*," Mother shot back, like she meant to put him in his place. He was, after all, the new kid on The TEAM. She'd been there like, forever. "He's got a home near Redemption Bay. I'll send you the coordinates. Begin there and tell me what you find, and Hunt?"

"Yes?" He had his foot to the pedal as he executed a drifting U-turn and pointed the SUV north by northeast.

"This guy has the money and means to do anything. Be careful. He can make you disappear."

"He can try."

Meredith couldn't breathe. Her mind skittered over signs she'd missed. Details she'd seen, but ignored or rationalized away. Every. Little. Thing.

Dominoes slammed, each a lightning strike to her heart. Roger Teach. The name itself was a twisted combination of Blackbeard's real name, Edward Teach, and the pirate flag, the Jolly Roger. And standing on the deck at this moment, with his hands on her son, was—Roger Teach. The man who'd sent men to kill her in Brazil. The one behind Lyle and Dan's deaths and Seth's torture.

It all made sense. Crystal-clear, scary sense. The unlikely reunion with her ex just when she'd returned—alive—from South America. The hard press to convince her that he just wanted more time with his son. *How could I have fallen for his lies again?*

Eddy Welch was—*Roger Teach.*

She turned on her heel, taking in the grand home around her. Everything was an elaborate ruse, and…

Oh, my God. I've fallen for it. Hook. Line. And—anchor. Not only that, she'd brought Courtney along with her like a lamb to the—she could barely think it—slaughter.

Reeling, she stumbled backward, searching for the edge of the kitchen island behind her before she fell. *It can't be. He wouldn't kill Courtney and me, would he? He couldn't. Not after…*

Oh, yes. Even after all he'd said and done to convince her otherwise, Eddy Welch was perfectly capable of murder. She knew it to her soul. He'd blended just enough truth with his lies to make her believe he'd truly changed.

Inconsistencies screamed at her. How had Bear gotten all the way up to the third level yesterday when Courtney had left him on the couch in the front room? And Eddy's injured hand. Where was the bandage he'd made so sure she noticed the first day? How had he hurt his hand? Or had he? Why did he relinquish his parental rights—or did he? Were any of those legal documents real? How easily could a man like him reverse every last one of them? She cringed. *I should've had a lawyer look at them.*

A sinister shiver whispered over her neck. Was that why he'd wanted her dead, to get custody of Courtney? Was that his end game? It seemed an extreme measure for someone who could obviously buy off any judge in the country. That was another reason she'd never asked for more child support. He could've taken Courtney away from her without batting an eye. Powerful people always got their way.

Meredith didn't have time to connect all the dots. Killing her might make his life easier, but she doubted that was all he wanted.

Where's my gun?

Taking the stairs two at a time, she ran for the backpack still safely tucked beside the nightstand where she'd left it. Courtney had slept with her. At home she'd have made sure the gun was stored out of his reach, but last night she'd felt better with the backpack nearby, only now...

Her bag was too light. Shit! She'd done it again. She'd left her weapon behind, and now Eddy had her pistol. And her son.

Oh, God! What am I going to do!

Gulping her panic away, she settled down to think. Now was the time to summon Mean Girl. There'd be no helpless feminine screaming or running around like an idiot without a brain. If nothing else, Eddy had to believe he had the upper hand. That she believed him. That she was just that stupid to fall for him again.

She hadn't brought just a weapon and a change of clothes for Courtney in her backpack. Hurriedly, she opened the small plastic first-aid kit and removed the elastic tape. Very quickly, she made her way back downstairs to the kitchen with her backpack and selected three of the smallest knives from the knife rack. One went into her backpack. She taped another to her ankle under the hem of her jeans. The last one went inside her shoe. He'd never suspect.

Meredith cleaned the broken cup from the floor and wiped up the coffee, fighting her stupidity as much as her failure as a mother to protect her child.

"Come on, Daddy." Courtney's sweet little voice sounded outside. "Let's get Mama."

She peeked out the window and banished the guilt she felt for falling into Eddy's trap again. It could wait. Father and son were already coming in the front door.

Compose yourself, Mean Girl snapped. *Meet him in the eye. Don't let him know that you know. Don't let him know you're scared. Buck the hell up. Get moving.*

Mean Girl sounded a lot like Hunter.

"Mama," Courtney called. "I home. Where are you?"

"I'm in here," Meredith answered back, still gripping the counter for support. But that would make her look weak, and weak would give her away. Jittering out of control, she turned her back on the kitchen door and reached into the cupboard for another mug. Stalling for time, she shot what she hoped was a cheerful smile over her shoulder when Eddy and Courtney entered.

"Would you like a cup?" she offered in her best fake, I'm-not-scared-to-death voice.

Eddy lifted the cup in his hand. "Already on my second. Go ahead. It's about time you joined us, sleepyhead."

"Mama, look what Daddy gived me." Courtney barreled into her legs, and at last she could breathe.

"What now?" She set her coffee to the counter and crouched to his level, using her long hair as a curtain to take a good hard look at her son. He looked as happy as ever. Still safe. She cupped his sunny face. *What have I gotten you into?*

His eyes sparkled. "I got money and Daddy says it's gold." There in his grubby little hands lay a battered gold piece, a very old coin with worn away edges.

"What's this?" she asked Eddy.

"Ah, it's nothing." He shrugged. "Just a sixteenth-century Spanish escudo. It's part of my collection of doubloons. I'd like to show the collection to you someday."

"Kin I keep it?" Courtney asked.

What could she say? She gulped, her throat dry and tight. Why was Eddy doing this to her son, plying him with wealth he had no concept of? Every muscle screamed to grab Courtney and run.

"You gave a priceless treasure to a child?" she asked, intent on keeping up the façade.

Eddy cocked his head, studying her. "It's not like I robbed the Smithsonian of some artifact. That coin only goes for one K."

"A thousand dollars?"

"Yeah, why not? Are you okay?" His brows slanted. "You look... off. I thought you'd be rested when you woke up this morning. What's going on? Are you mad?"

A complete idiot is more like it. She played it cool. "I'm just ready to go home, that's all. This place is too much, and now this gift—"

"Give me a break, Meredith. You let your boyfriend give him a piece-of-crap, but you won't let me give my own son something worthwhile?"

"Seth isn't my boyfriend. He's just one of the guys I worked with in South America. And the coin—you know what? I don't need to explain anything to you."

Eddy's eyes darkened. "No, I guess you don't. So what now? You want to go home as soon as possible, right?"

"Yes." She held her breath. *It couldn't be that easy, could it?*

He scowled, closed his eyes, and shook his head. "Great. I'll bring the car around."

"Go get Bear," she told Courtney.

Her poor little boy still stood at her feet with that gold piece in his palm. "No," he said firmly. "I wanna stay here with my daddy."

The labor-intensive work of her son's first three years of life came undone after just one day with his father. Defiance. Greed. Temper. It didn't get any better than this.

She knelt to explain. "We're going home, Courtney. Do you want to leave Bear here until we come back? That would be okay with me if—"

"By the way," Eddy interrupted with a lazy drawl that was so not like him. "Courtney needed clean underwear this morning. You were still asleep, so I helped myself to the extra clothes. Do you always carry a gun in your backpack?"

And there it was. Out in the open. How could she hide her shock? "I do carry, yes," she admitted without batting an eye. "Where is it?"

"In a safe place."

The old game commenced. Power play. He took until she broke. Not this time.

"I want it back." She pushed the limit.

"No." He rolled one shoulder, his eyes gone black. His upper lip twisted into a sneer. The real Eddy Welch stepped forward. "Get in the car," he spat. "Both of you. Now."

Meredith stood her ground, easing Courtney behind her. "We're not going anywhere with you."

Lightning struck. Eddy backhanded her, his knuckles harsh on her cheekbone. She dropped to her hands and knees on the floor, seeing stars.

"Mama!" Courtney shrieked, his little body instantly tucked into her side.

Inky black waves swarmed her vision. Courtney became her only touchstone. She pulled him under her, trying to catch her breath and balance, afraid to let him go.

"I gave you everything!" Eddy boomed from somewhere overhead.

Blood dripped off her lip to the floor, narrowly missing Courtney's frightened face. She still had those knives. She wouldn't go down easy.

CHAPTER THIRTY-NINE

Meredith climbed slowly to her feet with Courtney clinging to her leg, hiding behind her. The knife that had been taped to her ankle was now firm in her hand, and she was ready. Deadly calm stilled the pounding in her heart. She didn't want to do this in front of her son, but she would defend him to the death.

"You never did know when to back off!" Eddy bellowed, his index finger pointing to the floor at his feet. "Courtney, get over here, you little bastard! Now!"

She kept her son firmly behind her while she back-stepped toward the kitchen exit. "He's not a bastard, and he's not—"

"Who the hell are you kidding? Yourself? He's Christian's boy, not mine!"

"Hunter? How could you think that? I never—we never—"

Eddy lunged, his hand at her throat as he pushed her back against the counter.

"Run!" she screamed, but Eddy snagged Courtney's shirt collar before he could get away.

"Eddy! Courtney isn't Hunter's child. We never had sex. I swear. I—"

"You think I give a shit who fucked you first?" Eddy hissed, his nose in her face while Courtney struggled. "You never were much for brains. Tits and ass, maybe, but things that mattered? Never."

The knife in her hand slashed his cheek on its way to his neck. His eyes flared, then—*blam!* He smashed her into the sink, pushing her off her feet. The knife flew. Courtney screamed and kicked.

"You scheming bitch!" Eddy stuck an elbow in her back, fastening her to the counter while he rubbed his bloody cheek over his bicep. "You cut me."

"Please, don't hurt him. I'm the one you want."

"Yes, you are." He let her drop as he angled Courtney under his arm. "What else do you have up your sleeve?"

"Nothing," she lied.

"We'll see about that." He marched out the back door and into his four-car garage.

"No. Don't," she cried, running after him. "Wait! Eddy! I promise. I'll do anything."

"Mama!" Courtney cried, his little body turned sideways. "Help me! Help!"

Eddy activated the trunk release to the sedan parked beside his sports car.

"Not that! No! Don't!"

He rolled Courtney into the trunk and slammed the lid. Huffing, he leaned his butt to the trunk and crossed his arms over his chest, seemingly oblivious to the terror-filled cries behind him. "Strip," he hissed.

"Mama! I scared! Mama!" Courtney's screams reduced her to begging.

"Stop it! I'll do whatever you want. Just don't hurt him. Let him go."

"Then do what I said. Strip."

She complied quickly. Kicking out of her slip-ons, her sweater and jeans hit the concrete next.

Eddy's eyes tracked down her body to her feet and up again. He'd always played rough and hard. Right now, she'd let him do whatever he wanted to do—to her. Meredith stopped the strip show when she got down to her bra and underwear. The only weapon left to her was now buried under her jeans. "Now let him go."

"Turn," he commanded.

She made one shaky revolution.

He smacked his lips. "I've got to hand it to you, sweetheart. You're still one hot babe."

Her little boy's cries shredded her heart. She raked a quick hand through her hair. "Please, Eddy. He's choking. Can't you hear that? He's just a little boy and he's scared. I'll do whatever you want me to do, just, please, let him go."

"It isn't Courtney you need to worry about." With one quick step forward, he slapped her head sideways only to whip her around to face him again. With her eyes watering, she jerked her knee up. At the same time, she lowered her head, intending to take out that arrogant nose of his. Maybe break it.

But Eddy was prepared. Dodging, he twisted her arm behind her back and hoisted her face down onto the trunk lid. For one brief second, Meredith was thankful Courtney couldn't see what might happen next. Eddy pushed her cheek into the cold, hard metal. He wanted her to scream, but she wouldn't. Courtney was terrified enough.

"You should've died in South America," he hissed, his body pressed against her backside. "Don't think I won't take what I want, 'cause I will." He kneed her legs apart, his erection still in his pants, but scaring the hell out of her. "I've got news for you, Meredith Bitching Flynn. I lost the taste for poor white trash three years ago."

With one final hair-wrenching shove, he backed away and she slid off the trunk. The second her feet touched down, she turned to face her worst nightmare. "Let him out, Eddy. Let us go. I won't tell. I promise. Just—"

He stood with his legs spread, his arms crossed over his chest. "Tell what?"

"That you're R-R-Roger Teach."

He held a palm to her face. "Shut up. Get dressed. If your ass isn't in the front seat when I get back, it will be the kid's turn on the trunk lid, and I promise, it won't be pretty. I'll enjoy it, but you won't."

She gulped. He wouldn't!

The truth hit her in the face. He would. Eddy wasn't just a pirate. He was a predator.

"Now!" he barked, and she ran for her clothes. He went back inside his cabin, but was barely gone when he returned with a fifth of something in his hand. No glasses. Just the booze, a handful of zip-ties, and a roll of black tape.

"You're not sitting," he growled, a glint of pure evil in his eye.

Meredith hurried to slip into her shoes.

"Leave them. You won't need 'em where you're going."

She hurried to the passenger seat. "It's going to be okay," she called frantically to Courtney, trying to infuse courage she didn't feel. "Be a brave boy for Mama. Can you do that, baby?"

When he didn't reply, her heart sank.

Eddy pushed the bottle at her. "Hold this. With both hands."

She complied, shaking from head to toe while he secured her wrists and ankles with zip-ties, then taped the bottle inside her clenched hands. And Meredith knew. There was no way out of this alive.

Eddy tilted his head toward the trunk, where Courtney's cries had grown weaker. "You and me are going for a little drive. When we come back, you're going to be all I ever wanted in a woman, aren't you, Meredith?"

"It's dark in the trunk," she reasoned. "He's scared. Please don't do this."

"You're going to be all I ever wanted, right?" The whip in his voice stung.

"Y-y-yes. Just let him out. Let him sit up here with me."

Eddy cocked his head to the side, blackness swallowing his eyes. "That's not how the game's played." Reaching for the bottle in her grip, he unscrewed the lid. "Drink up, Meredith. The party's just beginning."

She balked. Big mistake.

Yanking her wrists upward, he mashed the bottle against her lips, spilling its contents over her chin and into her mouth. She spat the fiery drink out, but he lifted the bottle again. "We can do this the easy way, or I can get your kid out of the trunk, and we can do it the hard way. Now drink, or..."

She swallowed, not sure what liquor spilled fire into her empty stomach. Coughing, she choked, but he just kept pouring.

Finally satisfied, Eddy stopped the torture and ran a hand over the back of her head, petting her. "I knew you'd listen to reason." He started the car, hit the garage door opener, and backed onto the brick driveway that led to the isolated road.

Meredith wiped her mouth into her bicep. "Where... are we going?"

"You'll see." Shifting the car into drive, he headed away from the shore and connected with the nearest highway. Once he set the cruise control, he cupped her chin and turned her to face him. "I really shouldn't have hit you. I can't have you looking beat up on your first day back to work, can I?"

She blinked, trying to understand. "I'm going to work? Like this?"

"You are now. None of this would be happening to you if you'd just laid down in Brazil. Hell, Meredith. All you had to do was die, but no. You had to learn how to defend yourself. What'd you think I was going to do? Hurt you?"

She couldn't answer.

He pulled onto another highway, chuckling. "Looks like none of that self-defense bullshit did you much good. Get it through your head, sweetheart. I'm bigger and smarter than you. Always have been. You're just a dumb blonde who's been in my way for years."

"Wh-why?" She needed to know what he intended before she lost consciousness. As it was, the alcohol was working fast.

"Time for another drink."

Feigning compliance, she lifted her arms, but only pressed the rim of the bottle to her lips.

Eddy snapped his fingers under her nose. "Do you want me to get the kid out of the—?"

Tears filled her eyes. She gulped the nasty liquid, her heart breaking for her poor little boy. "At least tell m-me wha-zzz goin' on. Why are you doin' this?"

He grunted. "All this time I thought you were slowing me down and making me look bad, but now I'm actually glad Masters and Burdette didn't catch you. It took this little family get-together for me to realize you're more valuable alive than dead. That kid back there is my ticket."

"Ticket to w-what?" She peered sideways at him. The inside of the car whirled in one crazy circle around her. Planting both bare feet flat to the carpet didn't help. Eddy looked like he was leaning sideways. Or maybe it was her.

"To you. Jed McCormack likes you, doesn't he? You can get close to him, right?"

"Yes-s-s." Her nose itched. Her cheeks flushed with heat. She ran her nose over her bicep to keep it from dripping.

Eddy squeezed his long fingers between her legs. "And that's what I need you to do. Get close to old man McCormack. Give the rich, old ass a kiss on the cheek. Let him grab your ass while you give him a present from me. Can you be a good girl and do that?"

"Why sh-should I?"

"Because that's the only way you'll get the brat back. Drink up. You'll need to be good and drunk for this next part."

Forced to take another scorching swallow, she let the tears fall. Whatever Eddy had in mind, she'd never be drunk enough.

He used to cruise at eighty. Today, Hunter didn't care what speed limits he broke as he raced toward Redemption Bay. Miles of interstate flew by while acid chewed at his gut. Meredith and Courtney needed him, but damn it! He wasn't where they were.

Finally, he left the freeway behind and zeroed in Welch's last known location. Autumn colors blazed everywhere, but they meant nothing to Hunter. It took twenty long minutes of winding back roads before he sighted the unmarked turnoff to the beach. It ended at one helluva mansion tucked into the trees. A ritzy sailboat shifted placidly against the dock.

He parked in the shadows to the south of the place. The pistols under his arms stayed where they were, for now. When three loud raps at the front door elicited no response, Hunter tilted back on his heels to peer into the picture window at his left. He could detect no signs of trouble. Pulling the pistol from under his left arm, he tested the doorknob. When it turned, he rolled one shoulder before he entered Welch's home.

The stark silence of the place unnerved him. Weapon up, he walked through the entry to the staircase at his right. No sounds came from above. It was still possible someone was up there, but if they were, they were quiet. He opted to search the ground level first.

Quietly, he passed a lavish dining room on his right, a large bathroom at his left, and a pair of closed doors that, upon opening, revealed an expansive bedroom to his right. A light beckoned him into the largest kitchen he'd ever seen, but Hunter's heart stopped at the doorway. Obvious signs of a struggle. Smears of blood on the floor and countertop. Several unopened fifths of high-priced Scotch near the sink.

An opened toolbox on the floor near the rear door. Scattered tools.

Fear drove him past the kitchen island to the slice of light at the far door. He stopped at a two-step landing into the garage, hoping to God, Meredith was still there. He'd found four stalls. One limited edition Bugatti Veyron. A bright red Shelby Mustang. A black Hummer. One empty stall. But not one damned clue as to where Meredith was.

Hunter dragged his cell phone out of his jeans pocket, not like that helped. He had no bars. Packing enough adrenaline-laced frustration to give him a heart attack, he backtracked through the home, searching for a landline to contact Alex. There wasn't one. No wonder Meredith hadn't answered his calls.

Back in his car, Hunter left Welch's mansion in the dust. He pushed the SUV, squealing its tires around corners as he approached the interstate. More acid pinched his gut. It was damned odd that Eddy Welch didn't have any kind of phone coverage at such a plush estate. He was rich enough.

Hunter's cell phone rang. Tucking it to his shoulder, he snapped, "Talk to me."

"Where have you been?" Mother snapped back at him. "I've been trying to reach you for nearly an hour!"

There wasn't time for lengthy explanations. "I was at Welch's. Meredith's not there. Where should I be?"

"You mean to tell me Welch doesn't have cell service?"

"I don't have time for this, Mother. Tell me where he is." *Where Meredith is.*

With a huff, she settled down. "Hook onto I-95 the first chance you get. Go north toward Baltimore. That's the direction Welch is headed right now."

Hunter floored the gas pedal, daring Maryland's finest to pull him over. The interstate on ramp was just ahead. "Don't lose track of him."

"Not happening," she promised. "I'll be in touch as soon as I know more. Of all the nerve, no phone service…"

Hunter disconnected in the middle of her rant. He could barely catch a decent breath knowing Meredith's ex was behind everything that had happened in Brazil. He cursed traffic and road construction, but mostly, he cursed himself for jumping to the wrong conclusion years ago.

He was cruising through Baltimore when Mother rang again. "He just turned onto Maryland 543, south. It looks like he's going to Aberdeen Proving Ground. Listen to this. Ember's been digging through every property and business Welch owns. Two and a half years ago, he took over Barclay Enterprises, a private company that detoxifies federal landfills and contaminated wells. The Army contracted them to detox and manage prolonged containment of all the wells on Aberdeen. You're closing in on him. He's only got a half-hour lead."

Hunter hung up. Aberdeen was a sprawling facility of more than one hundred square miles. It might as well have been the moon.

CHAPTER FORTY

Meredith peered through heavy eyelids at the blur of gray light outside her window. It was raining. Maybe.

Eddy kept talking about weather and sailing. He'd covered her with a blanket, only she wasn't cold. If anything she was burning from the flame in her gut. The alcohol had done its best to render her unconscious, but she'd fought blacking out.

"Courtney," she breathed. "Where's... Courtney?"

No answer came back to her. Only a sickening buzz in her head and stomach. Her door opened, nearly dropping her to the ground. Some guy pushed her upright. *Oh. Eddy.* She chuckled to herself, sure she was losing her mind. *Eddy always did pop up in the most unlikely places.*

He knelt at her side and patted her cheek like she was an imbecile. "Come on now. Wake up. You can do this. There you go."

Eddy had three heads and four faces. They kept bobbing back and forth until she closed her eyes to make it stop. Pink elephants couldn't have convinced her any better. She was way over the legal limit.

But not yet. She had to save Courtney.

Eddy pulled her bare feet to the side and onto the gravel shoulder, but when she tilted forward to get to her feet, he pushed her back. "You don't need to get out. You just need to see."

She blinked the fuzziness away, trying to focus. "W-what you sayin'?"

"I said sit. Stay. Watch. Enjoy the show if you can. It'll be fun, you'll see." He flicked her chin with a snap of his index finger. "Hell, you might even learn something today."

"'Kay," she mumbled. Sounded easy enough.

Something thumped from way back in the car. A little boy screamed, "Mama!"

Meredith snapped out of the dead zone she'd slipped into. *Courtney!*

He screamed again, his voice ragged with terror.

"Courtney! I'm here. I'm coming!" Lurching out the door, she landed face-first on the gravel, bound hand and foot. Sharp edges cut her cheek and chin as the world turned into a tilt-a-whirl, but she didn't care. She had to move. To run!

"Give him to... to… me," she ordered. "Don't h-h-urt him!"

Eddy didn't answer, just shouldered Courtney and marched into the short grass, growing smaller and smaller until he stopped a hundred miles away. She watched through tears, fighting delirium. Crouching to one knee, he lifted a very large gray dish, then dropped it to its side. Maybe a satellite dish? She couldn't tell. Nothing made sense.

The gravel under her nose smelled sweet and damp with rain and tears.

"Courtney!" she called to her baby.

"Mama!" he got one last ear-piercing scream off, but then—he was gone.

She couldn't see Eddy for a moment, but then he popped up out of the ground like a rabbit. A very ugly, mean rabbit. With four ears.

"It looks like Welch has parked."

"Where?"

Mother sent the coordinates inside Aberdeen. "The guards at the gate won't give you any trouble. Alex already greased the skids, but listen. Aberdeen has multiple contaminated areas. Be careful. Welch's car is at one of them."

"Copy that," Hunter said.

Aberdeen Proving Ground. Not good. The Army facility, infamously known for producing tons of mustard gas and other toxic gases during World War I, was now home to extensive tracts of contaminated land, water, and buildings, not to mention significant amounts of buried ordnance. The Environmental Protection Agency listed APG as the most serious uncontrolled hazardous waste site in the country. What was Welch up to?

At the gate, two armed soldiers stopped Hunter, but after he explained who he was, they waved him through. Barely mid-morning, the day was sunny and pleasantly warm, a nice shift from the intense heat of the jungle. A light shower spattered his windows while worry radiated down his leg and into the accelerator. Hunter stepped on the gas. It didn't matter. By the time Hunter made it to the designated coordinates, he'd missed rescuing Meredith again.

"Fuck!" Welch's car was gone.

Scrambling to his feet, Hunter glared at the vacant fields stretched out on both sides of this gravel road. He walked a quick circle around his SUV, then expanded it by twenty feet. Then forty. At sixty, he cupped his hands to his mouth and bellowed, "Meredith! Can you hear me?"

Nothing but the breeze whispering through the grass came back to him. Pissed, he widened his search. Welch hadn't come all this way for nothing.

Out of nowhere, a whimper had just sounded. Hunter stilled like a mannequin. Within minutes, another soft cry drifted to him from the east.

He cocked his head to hear better. The breeze also carried the salty odor of the nearby Chesapeake to his nose. A jet engine sounded high overhead. The partly clouding sky let loose another smattering of raindrops, but Hunter tuned everything out, striving to hear that one particular sound again, that child-like whimper of distress.

"Talk to me," he whispered to it—or her. "Say it again, Merry. I'm here. Help me find you."

Another wisp of a cry, and Hunter's thigh muscles bunched as he exploded off the balls of his feet and ran. He saw it in the distance then, some kind of a concrete cap setting askance at the lip of a metal ring the size of a rusted Hula-Hoop sticking out of the ground. The yellow sign above the ring declared: *Danger. Ground Water Radiation Site. No Entry.*

Hunter pulled up short of the well and peered over the edge. He hadn't found Meredith, but there in the bottom of the twenty-foot deep, concrete-lined hole, was a very young boy. Curled in a fetal position with his knees tight to his chest, he cried.

Hunter's heart melted. "Courtney?"

The child lifted to his knees, but there was no way he was Meredith's son. This little guy had sad almond-shaped eyes. "My name is Bradley," he said, his face shiny wet and barely visible down there in the dark. "Are you with... him?"

"Am I with who?" Hunter asked, his mind back at the twenty-foot tow strap in the rear of his SUV. It might be long enough to reach this frightened boy. There was still time to find Meredith.

"With M-Master?"

"I don't know who Master is," Hunter explained gently, "but I'm getting you out of this hole. I'll be right back." He stopped his big mouth from automatically saying, *'wait here.'*

Hunter knew what to look for now. On his run back to the SUV, he noted five more yellow danger signs in the immediate vicinity. He called Mother, his temper up. "Get Aberdeen's installation commander on the line."

"Why?" she asked softly.

"Because Welch's a flaming bastard!" Hunter snapped, but damn! People who hurt children were the lowest of the low.

If Welch was Master, and Hunter knew damned well he was...

If he'd put that little boy in the ground like a piece of meat...

If he'd committed the despicable act Hunter suspected...

Son-of-a-bitch! Hunter kicked the grassy stubble underfoot, as angry as he'd ever been.

"Mother," he ground out, fighting for control as he scanned the grassy field. "There's a kid in a contaminated well out here. I can see five more wells from where I'm standing, all of 'em uncapped, but there might be more. If Welch's done this, if he's stashed kids in each of these wells... Shit!"

This kind of brutality brought back every emotion Hunter had suppressed through all the deployments, firefights, and battles in far off countries. It was no wonder his heart now needed three stents to keep him alive. It was the only tender part left of him, and this kind of depravity—*this!*—was killing it.

"I need all base MPs and ambulances and, hell. I need everyone out here, Mother. This is so bad."

"They're on their way, Hunt, but is Meredith there?"

"I don't know." He glanced over his shoulder, hoping she was but thinking of that desperate boy asking if he was with Master. Had Eddy brought other men with him when he'd visited that poor little guy? Exactly how long had he been in that well? "I need the whole damned Army, and I need 'em now."

"They're on their way," she promised before the phone went dead in his hand.

He jerked open the tailgate of his SUV and was back at the first well within minutes, the sturdy tow strap over his shoulder. But he didn't dare move the child. He couldn't save him. Not yet. As much as he wanted to help poor Bradley, evidence of this horrendous crime scene needed to be preserved or Welch would never get what he deserved—at least not in a court of law.

Hunter peered over the edge at the awful pit where a child waited. "Bradley," he said as evenly as he could manage. "When was Master here last?"

"Today," the boy said, his neck craned upward and his bare feet shifting back and forth. "But he didn't want to play. Can I go home? Please, mister. Can you take me home? Please... please don't leave me down here."

The hysteria billowing up from the well from that little guy stopped Hunter cold. Play? Was that what this poor kid had been forced to believe abduction and assault was called? Was that what Welch had told him?

The poor kid stood on concrete that glistened, which meant there was water in the hole. Dressed only in what looked like a simple white T-shirt and swimming shorts, he clutched his arms. And he was thin. He had to be on the verge of hypothermia. Maybe starvation. Hunter didn't want to imagine what else. "Bradley, I'm not leaving you, buddy, but I need you to be brave for me while I check the other wells. There might be more kids here. I'll hurry. Can you do that for me?"

"There... there are more wells? More kids? Like me?"

The boy was crying, and damn. Hunter brushed his bicep over his face. "Yes, and I need to help them, too. Be brave, Bradley, just a little longer, because I'm not leaving without you. The police are coming. Will you trust me?"

"Y-yes," the terrified little guy replied. "I can be brave, but please don't... don't forget to come back. Okay?"

"I promise. I'll be right back." Hunter blinked as he stepped away. *What kind of monster could do this?*

He flew from one hole to the next. In each, a frightened, skinny young boy looked up at him with the bleakest, saddest eyes. Finally, well number five yielded his first clue as to Meredith: a small pair of clean little boy jeans off to the side. They looked the right size for a three-year-old. Maybe Courtney and Meredith were down in this well.

Hope unfurled in his chest until Hunter peered over the edge. Only a little blond-haired boy stood at the bottom looking up. He had to be Courtney.

"Hey, little guy." Hunter spoke softly so he didn't scare him. "Are you ready to get out of there and go home?"

All of the other boys had been quiet, but his little guy stamped his feet and shrieked, "I want my mama! He's hurtin' her!"

"It's okay. I'm here to take you home. Are you Courtney Flynn?"

"I not telling you nuthin'! I want Mama!"

By then, the MP's mobile-command unit was on scene, along with scores of soldiers ready to assist. Dog handlers and their K-9s commenced canvassing the area while rescuers were lowered into the wells.

Hunter waved a pair of first responders over to him. "Here! I'm going after this one!" In no time, he was geared up and anxious. It'd been a while since he'd rappelled. Backing over the lip of the well, he began his descent. "Courtney, I'm coming down. Make room for me okay?"

The frightened boy drew back against the opposite wall. Wearing only cotton briefs and socks, his hands clenched open and closed at his sides as Hunter made a quick descent.

When he touched down into the five-inch deep puddle, Hunter coiled the rope and took better stock of the boy's condition. Courtney's upper lip was swollen and bloody. An obvious handprint blazed high on his left cheek, and his chest heaved. "Stay 'way!" he shrilled, stamping his stocking feet in the water. "Stay 'way! Don't touch me!"

Hunter crouched where he landed and extended a gloved hand. "It's cold down here. Come on. Let's go."

In his scant playbook on childcare, that should've been enough to entice the kid to come forward, but Courtney hunkered into the opposite wall, his left shoulder jutting between them. The poor little guy shivered, too scared to move.

Hunter backed up as far as he could, but kept one hand extended. "I know who you are, son. You're Courtney Flynn. I'm Hunter Christian, your mother's friend, and I'm here to take you home. Let's go."

The child whined, his lower lip quivering but his feet firmly planted. "But I want Mama."

"And your mama wants you," Hunter said softly, his heart breaking for the little guy.

Courtney's nose was red and running as his slender throat worked a tremendous swallow. "You know Mister Seff?"

"You mean Seth?" Hunter asked, not sure where that came from "Yes, I know Seth. He's a good friend and I work with him. He's your mama's friend too."

"He gived me money." More tears streamed down the little guy's cheeks and that brave chin quivered. "But I lost it."

Hunter choked back the need to gather him into his arms. "It's okay. Seth's a real good guy. He'll understand, Courtney. Heck, he's probably got more where that money came from. Should we go find him, too?"

"And I lost Bear," Courtney squeaked, but why the little guy wouldn't take his hand concerned Hunter.

He dropped to one knee, wanting to be whatever this scared little boy needed in order to trust an adult male again. Cold water rippled across the six-foot gap between them, lapping up the poor boy's ankles and chilling Hunter's leg. So be it. The guys holding the strap and hoist topside would understand. "Who's Bear? Do we need to find him, too?"

Courtney's head bobbed. "Uh-huh. Pweeze."

"It sounds like you and me got some work to do, tough guy." Hunter opened his palm and curled his fingers.

"I ain't tough," Courtney whispered, his head shaking. "I just widdle."

Hunter coughed, fighting tears, damn it. "No, Courtney. You might be little, but you're the toughest man I've met in a long time, and I'm going to need your help to find your mother and Bear."

Just that fast, Courtney barreled into him. Clinging to his neck, he climbed up into Hunter's lap, his wet feet in Hunter's lap and his nose in the hollow of Hunter's throat. "He hurted me, and he hurted Mama, and he's scary."

The feel of that little body wrenched with sobs shredded every heartstring Hunter had left. He dared place a hand to the boy's back, cradling his head with the other. Courtney was so cold.

"Mama's lost," the tyke breathed a shuddering breath.

"Does she have Bear?"

Courtney hiccupped. "Nah-uh. My mean daddy took him."

Hunter wrapped his big arms around the tiny little guy, content to just sit there until Courtney was warm. "That mean guy's not your daddy," he explained gently. "Daddies don't hurt their children. They take extra special care of them and their mamas."

The saddest blue eyes scrolled up to meet his gaze. "And Bear?"

Hunter's breath caught. No doubt about it. This was Meredith's son. He had her same blue eyes. "Absolutely. Hang on. Let's get out of here."

Hunter signaled the guys topside. Not once did Courtney whine on the way up. He didn't let go either, and that was fine.

Finally, Hunter sat with Courtney in his arms on the hood of one of the ambulances, waiting on their turn with the medics. They hadn't found Meredith yet and that was troubling. Welch was more dangerous than Hunter had suspected. She wasn't safe.

The urge to offload Courtney and go charging after her was strong, but Hunter couldn't do it. As kind as all these guys were, the kid didn't need another stranger in his life. Not on what had to be the worst day of his life.

He was calmer now, but he wasn't talking. For the most part, he appeared uninjured but for his fat lip, reddened cheek, and obvious bruises around his neck left by a man's hand. That bastard Welch might not have molested him, but the kid had definitely been manhandled.

Someone brought a blanket. Hunter made sure to keep Courtney snuggled and his head hooded. He didn't need to see the guys in olive drab fatigues walking around and holding other frightened little boys, rocking them, and crying with them. One started singing *Frosty the Snowman*, and it was all Hunter could do to hum along. Poor old *Frosty* never sounded so sad.

His phone rang. Alex this time. As brusque as ever. "How's Meredith's son?"

Hunter brushed a hand over Courtney's head, content to let the boy snuggle. "He's a little roughed up, but he's tough like his mother. He'll be fine."

Alex's voice dropped a pitch. "Was he… assaulted?"

God, I hope not. "Not sure, Boss. We're waiting on the medics right now, but I don't think so. Welch wasn't here long enough." Hunter didn't dare go into specifics. "So what's the word?" The PG rated version of: *Where the fuck is she?*

"Maverick and Taylor observed Welch pulling into his place forty minutes ago. Meredith's with him."

"Where?"

"Woodland/Normanstone Terrace." An upper-class neighborhood north of Georgetown.

"Then what are they waiting for?" *Go get that son-of-a-bitch!*

Alex growled. "Because the gawddamned FBI's involved now. They gave me a cease and desist order until they get their agents in play. They want Welch for more than crimes against children."

"Shit, that's enough for me, Boss."

"Understood, but—"

"Aww, you sweared." Courtney peered up at Hunter, his lips pursed just like his mother's "Mama says decent people wike us don't hafta swear."

A smile cracked Hunter's heated face. "She does, huh?"

"Kin we pwease go find her and Bear now?"

"Kids." Alex chuckled. "When will you be done there?"

"Not until we get the all clear from the medics," Hunter answered Alex and Courtney at the same time.

"Bring him into the office when you can. Mother and Ember are waiting, and you know how they can be. He'll get plenty of mothering."

Wasn't that the truth? "Will do."

CHAPTER FORTY-ONE

Darkness. Her stomach pitched another fit. Meredith didn't know how she'd gotten from Eddy's vehicle into this bathroom. The tiled floor felt cool beneath her cheek, but it kept moving. Her head pounded and her tongue tasted like the floor. She would know. She'd sampled it.

A light burst into the room, blinding her, and suddenly, Eddy knelt at her side, his fingers soft and gentle on her cheek—like he cared. "Doing better?"

She turned away, never needing to see, smell, or hear him again. The liar. His feigned concern nauseated her more than the alcohol poisoning her system. Only the hole in her heart hurt worse. Nothing made sense, but she knew what she'd seen. Eddy had taken Courtney off into the grass somewhere, but he'd returned alone. Her son was lost to her. It was night and wherever he was he was scared and alone and...

God! How could she ever get him back?

"You can't lie here all night feeling sorry for yourself. Get off the floor. Let's get you into the shower."

Growling at her inability to function properly, Meredith pushed Eddy's hand away. She didn't need his help.

It didn't stop him. He scooped her off the floor as if she was nothing but air. The butterflies in her stomach turned cartwheels at the sudden movement, but he seemed ready for that. She found herself facedown and hugging the porcelain commode, sick at heart for all her missing son must be going through, and disgusted with her body's continual betrayal.

When she finished hacking up her intestines, he dragged her by her armpits to the shower and turned on the shower. Cold. Why expect anything different?

Meredith sank to her hands and knees over the drain, still retching. She'd always refrained from swearing, had taught Courtney there were better words to use, and more effective ways to express one's anger. Intelligent people didn't need to stoop to vulgarity. Not tonight.

She borrowed Hunter's choicest expletive. *Eddy is fucking going to die.*

Just. Not. Now.

When the water streaming over her back turned colder, an involuntary whimper escaped, but only one. She stifled another and swore she'd live long enough to see her son again.

Eddy turned the water off and tossed a towel over her. "Dry off. I need you coherent and gorgeous. We have plans to make."

She stayed where she'd landed, still facing the shower drain, still on her hands and knees. *Trust me. I've already got one.*

"Do I need to dress you, too?" he snapped.

"No," she rasped, fighting for control. *Don't touch me.* "I'm getting up." Slowly, she made it to her feet and faced the tiled wall. At least, it didn't move.

"You've got five minutes. Get dressed."

"I'm sick. I need to sleep." *So I can plan exactly how to torture you.*

"Yeah, well..." He slapped her wet backside with one hard smack. "Not tonight you don't. You need to understand the rules first. Then you can sleep if we've got time."

Meredith jumped at the rude contact, grimacing more from disgust than pain. "I'm coming," she murmured more to the wall than to him. "Stop hitting me."

"Then do what you're told." He snapped his fingers. "Step on it."

When the bathroom door closed behind him, she let the tears fall. The hole where her heart used to be hurt with a pain so deep, it took her breath. What was Courtney doing out there alone in the dark? This had to be killing him. She ran her fingers through her wet hair, tangling it into a knot.

Only anger kept her moving—only the thinnest shred of hope that Courtney was still alive. He had to be. A mother would feel a break in the maternal link with her child. She'd know if her son had been murdered, wouldn't she? The gruesome possibility pierced her soul. Despair dropped her to her knees. *Courtney!*

A sharp rap at the door startled her. "I don't have all night!" he bellowed.

"I'm... I'm coming!" she said to shut him up.

Standing there and utterly alone, Meredith lifted her gaze to her reflection in the mirror. It had been years since she'd seen that other woman staring back at her, that wretched one who used to cower and make excuses for the predator she'd married. Dark, wet blonde hair straggled over her shoulders and down her back, still dripping. No longer bright and bouncy blonde, the light had gone from every strand. Just like her soul.

Sunken, lifeless eyes glowered, unsmiling. No inner sparkle. No dreams. Meredith lost the thread of control she'd been clinging to. She slapped a hand to that pathetic reflection and…

Out of the blue, Mean Girl stepped forward with all of her beautiful attitude. Finally! *Stop feeling sorry for yourself and do something, Meredith. You won't get him back if you give up. Plan now. Kill the bastard next. Find Courtney and cry later. You can do this.*

Meredith nodded at her reflection as it—she—morphed into Mean Girl. The day she'd taken that last slap from Eddy over three years ago was the day her alter ego had first shown up. Without her incredible strength and conviction, the sweet woman Meredith used to be would still be Eddy's favorite whipping girl. Never. Again.

She steeled her spine. "I'm not giving up," she told herself with whispered determination.

Peeling out of her wet clothes, she dried herself and dressed in the silky baby-doll get-up Eddy had left on the vanity. No robe. Just that red piece of slutty degradation.

She dried her hair. Trembling from booze and anger, she clenched her fingers to make them stop shaking while Mean Girl chanted, *You can do it. Plan now. Kill the bastard. Find Courtney. Cry later.*

Meredith took hold of the crystal glass on the counter, filled it to the brim, and swallowed every last drop. She did it a second time. A third. Wiping the water on her chin with the back of her hand, she faced her future. This wasn't the end of her or Courtney. Not by a long shot. He was out there. He was!

The alcohol in her system wouldn't rule her much longer, and she would find him!

Her chin lifted. Her fingers curled to fists. Okay then. She'd do what it took to get Courtney back, but the second he was safe and sound, Eddy would die.

With her head down, she crept from the security of the bathroom. The light from his expansive living room beckoned her. Meredith made her way, one palm to the wall to steady her. "I'm here," she announced at the doorway.

Glittering gray eyes roved over her in one quick assessing glance. Eddy patted the cushion next to him. "Come here. I have a proposition, and you look like you need a cup of coffee."

No. I need a gun, and this time, Hunter, I won't lose it.

"I want Mama!" Courtney nearly fell off the examination table when he lurched for Hunter. "I want Bear!"

Hunter soothed one hand over the boy's shoulder to steady him. "It's okay, I'm right here. We'll go find Bear and Mama as soon as this is over, remember?"

The little boy hiccupped, and damn. Hunter turned into peanut butter and jelly. The MPs had insisted Courtney be given a physical examination before they'd let him leave Aberdeen. Hunter complied, even though it meant another agent on The TEAM would probably contact Welch first.

It couldn't be helped. Meredith's son needed someone he trusted in his corner, and for now, it was Hunter. But everything went from bad to worse when Hunter admitted he wasn't Courtney's legal guardian. The best he could offer up was Meredith's parents' names, and that they lived in Richmond.

He got the surprise of his life when the Army's contracted physician, Dr. Jeffs, called the Flynns for permission to examine their grandson. Meredith's mother vouched for Hunter sight unseen—after all these years. This whole day had been nothing but humbling.

For now, Courtney was dressed in bright blue flannel pajamas covered with cartoon cars and trucks. Fuzzy red socks kept his feet warm. A preliminary physical had been done, but the more Dr. Jeffs examined him, the more frightened he became until Hunter couldn't take any more. He lifted Courtney off the table and wrapped his arms around the kid to steady. "Don't be scared," Hunter whispered while the doctor sneakily placed a stethoscope to his back. "You're brave. Just like your mama."

Dr. Jeffs gave a listen, one brow raised as he met the challenge in Hunter's eye. "I don't want to do an invasive exam if I don't have to. Take a seat while I ask him a few questions."

Hunter settled into the nearest chair with his little boy buddy planted on his lap and hiding his face between Hunter's arms.

"Courtney, I'm Dr. Jeffs, but you can call me Randy," he said quietly. "What do you like best, chocolate or peppermint?"

Courtney twisted around, going for invisible, his face still buried in Hunter's shirt.

"Most kids like chocolate, but I've got candy canes and suckers, too. You can take them home with you if you'll answer a couple questions. Would you like that?" Dr. Jeffs asked.

Hunter kept rocking and Randy kept trying. He didn't touch the boy, just maintained a respectable distance, his arms folded over his chest while he took in every detail. "Did your mean daddy hurt you today?"

Stupid question. Courtney's head bobbed, but his face stayed tucked where he didn't have to look at the doctor.

"Your mama's afraid of snakes," Hunter whispered. "Did you know that?"

When the boy lifted a trembling chin and peered up at him, Hunter blinked. He'd seen the same sad expressions in Afghanistan and Iraq, on children without parents or hope. Splaying a palm over Courtney's back, he promised, "No one's ever going to hurt you again. I'll make sure of that."

Courtney glanced sideways as if he didn't want Randy to hear. "But I scared."

Hunter gave the boy what he needed. "I don't blame you. That was a deep hole you were in, but you're here with me now. Talk to Dr. Jeffs so nothing like that happens to anyone else."

Randy leaned forward, cupping his palms to his knees. "Can you do that for me, Courtney? Can you help me stop that mean guy from hurting other kids?"

The little guy swallowed hard. Still not acknowledging the doctor's presence, he cupped one hand to his mouth and whispered to Hunter. "He hit Mama, and he hurt her, and he made her cry, and he put me in a dark place, and it was noisy, and..." A big shudder shook his little body. "And he ripped my pants off, and he made me cry, too."

Randy pressed for more. "What'd he do then? Did he… touch you?"

Tears brimmed and the questioning needed to end. "He's had enough?" Hunter bit out.

"You're right, he has," Randy said softly, "but I think he's brave enough to tell me the rest of the story. Do you know what inappropriate means, Courtney?"

The boy peeked around the barricade of Hunter's big arms and nodded. "Ah-huh. It means nobody should never touch my private parts."

A gentle smile brightened Randy's face. "Good for you. Your mama taught you that, didn't she?"

His head bobbed. "She yost."

"But Hunter's going to find her, and you trust him, don't you?"

Another nod. "Ah-huh. He my friend."

Way to turn a jarhead to mush.

Randy continued the gentle interrogation. "What did your mean daddy do after he ripped your pants?"

Courtney rubbed his face against Hunter's bicep. "He screamed at me, and he said it was my fault cuz I go'd potty."

"And then what?"

Another heart-rending whine, but Courtney soldiered on. "And then he grabbed my neck, and he put me in a hole, and he left me all alone, and I was scared."

Hunter swallowed hard.

"Did he throw you in that hole or did he drop you?"

"Uh-huh. He had a wadder." Courtney seemed to have trouble with L-words when he was upset.

"Just one more question. Did your mean daddy give you anything today? Any candy? A drink? Anything?"

Hunter slanted an eye at Randy. Was he thinking Welch drugged the kid?

That lip again. "He gave me a gold dowwar, but I yost it, and I yost Bear and…" A big tear dripped out of Courtney's eye. "I yost Mama!"

Stop torturing him. Hunter barricaded the boy in his arms. "Courtney's a good boy. None of this is his fault."

Randy's eyes narrowed. "You're absolutely right. We're done here. I've heard enough. No more questions, Courtney. You did real good. Would you like a new friend bear to hang onto?"

The little guy gulped, his fingers in his mouth. "He yost, too?"

"He might be," Randy coaxed.

"Okay," Courtney murmured, his heart rate calmer. "I yike bears. Mama does too."

Hunter scrubbed a hand over his face. He had to. A different kind of pain in his chest kept twisting and pinching. This had to be how Meredith felt in the middle of the river that day when she was missing her little boy.

Randy's nurse must've been waiting nearby. She peeked around the curtain, her lips curved with a genuine smile. "Does someone in here like fuzzy bears?"

Courtney nodded. "Ah-huh, I do."

"Well, there's a hungry bear sitting at my desk right now. His name's Black Jack and he likes peppermint and chocolate," she teased. "Which do you like?"

"Choc-wat," Courtney said around his fingers. "Mama yikes choc-wat, too."

"Would you sit with Ellie while I finish talking with Mr. Christian, Courtney?" Randy asked.

The little guy looked up at Hunter. "He hurted you, too?"

Hunter could only whisper, "No, tough guy. He's scared of me." *Welch had damned well better be.*

Courtney mashed his face into Hunter's chest, his arms opened wide in a little boy hug. "I not ascared of you, Hunner. Not no more."

Hunter bowed his cheek to the top of the boy's head. "Go with Nurse Ellie. And don't eat all the chocolate." He didn't know how much more he could take.

Nurse Ellie extended a hand. "Come on, kiddo. Let's go rescue Black Jack."

"Don't leave without me, 'kay?" Courtney whispered as he slid to the floor.

Hunter winked. "Go meet your new friend, kid. I'll be waiting."

That seemed to help. Nurse Ellie distracted him as they walked down the hall, but with every step, Courtney glanced back at Hunter. He didn't look away until the notorious, chocolate-eating, Black Jack, was pressed into his arms. Cutest damned sight ever, that poor little kid hugging a bear like he'd found a long lost friend.

Hunter dragged a hand over his bleary eyes and got back to business. "You think Welch drugged him?"

Randy shook his head. "Child predators often do. It keeps their victim quiet, but I'm not seeing any signs he was. His blood work came back normal. I just needed to hear it from him. To be frank, there's no indication this boy has been sexually assaulted, but he still needs counseling after what he's gone through today. Will you make sure he gets it?"

"You bet," Hunter promised. "Meredith will do what needs to be done, and I'll help her."

"You weren't really planning to take him with you when you locate her, were you?"

"No, but he's a smart kid. He needed to know what was happening next. I have a couple lady friends back at my office who are dying to meet him. He'll be in good hands until I can call his grandparents."

"Ellie will make that call for you." Randy leaned back in his seat and blew out a sigh. "You never know. With the right handling, Courtney might brush today off like it never happened. Kids are resilient, but you and his mother will need to watch closely for signs of withdrawal or guilt. The world used to be a safe place. It's not anymore. He learned a hard lesson today at the hands of someone he trusted. He may experience out-of-control moments of anger or shame. He may have nightmares or regress to bedwetting."

"Got it," Hunter said. "He may have some PTSD."

"Exactly." Randy's eyes lit up. "I take it you've had some experience with post-traumatic stress?"

Hunter started to shake his head, but what the hell. If Courtney could man up, so could he. "I guess," he admitted. There was no sense lying.

Randy cocked his head. "Are you angry all the time? Hyper-vigilant? Do you have night sweats? Nightmares? Have you gotten professional help?"

Hunter swallowed his pride. Hell, he'd been angry for years. "I will now."

"Good." Randy held out a hand. "Have a good night, but understand—this child trusts you, and right now, he's fragile. He needs someone in his corner who'll fight the monsters under his bed. Another thing, find that dirtbag father of his and end the son-of-a-bitch."

The doctor's vehemence took Hunter by surprise. He shook Randy's hand with a sincere promise. "Don't worry. I intend to."

Exiting the cubicle, his gaze landed on Courtney sitting with Nurse Ellis and still squeezing the daylight out of that black plush bear. "Hey, buddy. You ready to go?"

Courtney dropped Black Jack and ran headlong into Hunter's arms. He crouched to catch him, but damn. The second the kid hit his chest, Courtney wrenched his heart all over again. "You safe, Hunner," he breathed. "I gotcha."

Didn't that beat all? It had been a long time since Hunter had been safe, or safe to be around, for that matter, but here was this little guy. Reaching out. Thinking of someone else instead of dwelling on his own nightmare. Yeah. This was definitely Meredith's son.

And someday, he'd be Courtney Christian.

CHAPTER FORTY-TWO

Being forced to stand-down and wait, having to rely on someone else's rules of engagement, made for the worst times in war for Hunter. Yet, there he and Lee were, hunkered down in a TEAM SUV, parked outside Welch's mansion in Woodland/Normanstone Terrace—waiting. Hunter sat in the driver's seat while Lee took shotgun. He would've been inside with guns blazing if he'd had his way, but no. The Feds were in charge, and everyone knew they moved at the speed of bureaucratic bullshit.

With Courtney safe with his grandparents, Hunter was free to engage—once he got permission from the almighty Bureau. That didn't stop him from setting up The TEAM game board with a little help from his friends.

Maverick and Taylor were now in the courtyard at MI, watching for Meredith and the dayshift to arrive. Zack and Seth were hanging out on the street outside McCormack Industries, handling the unexpected unknowns that never failed to screw up an operation. Murphy's Law never took a day off, and Hunter wanted them close at hand if needed. Mother was back at the office, backtracking the creator of that designer drug in the hypos he'd found.

Ember and her husband, Junior Agent Rory Dennison, were double-teaming Welch's vast empire of ill-gotten assets, digging into his financials and the history between him and his conquests. Rory had a theory that Welch wasn't just lucky in the corporate world, that he'd specifically targeted—or blackmailed—certain CEOs. For what, Rory didn't yet know, but he suspected it had something to do with what Hunter had found at APG.

Hunter let the Dennisons run with it. It'd be good to know how Welch had gotten wealthy as quickly as he had. The jock Hunter had known in college just wasn't that smart.

To put it mildly, Welch's mansion was outrageously extravagant. Red clay tiles topped the three-story Mediterranean-style residence. Hunter best guessed it at twenty thousand square-feet. Three stories. Stucco exterior. Arched windows. Manicured lawns. A multi-toned gray brick driveway curved around a concrete pool in the front yard, itself barricaded behind black iron fencing and overflowing with lily pads and water hyacinths.

When they'd been on duty, Maverick and Taylor had detected Meredith's soft voice soon inside the residence, but they hadn't gotten much more than muffled conversations since. It was almost as if Welch had intentionally soundproofed certain rooms in his home. *Interesting…*

The few snatches Hunter had detected of Meredith's voice hadn't sounded panicked. Distressed, yes, but she didn't seem to be in danger. So far, Welch had been civil with her—the only reason he still breathed. That and the very real fact that Hunter could get inside that house in seconds and end Welch if need be. God knew he wanted to.

His mind drifted back over the day. The final count out of Aberdeen was nine little boys, all under the age of ten. They hadn't been starved, but all had been sadly used and all claimed Welch kidnapped them. For now, their parents had been notified. Aberdeen's commanding officer held off releasing any information to the press, pending the alleged FBI *imminent takedown* of Welch. God, they were slow to move.

Alex was somewhere working contingency scenarios with Jed McCormack, Welch's primary target. He'd used Courtney to get to Meredith, and Meredith to get to Jed. That was the only thing that made sense. The question was how Welch intended to strike back. And when.

The bastard didn't know it, the FBI either, but they both had until sunrise to make their move. After that, Hunter was going in—with or without the Bureau's permission.

Suddenly, Meredith's voice came through his earpiece loud and crisp. "A… a bomb?"

Hunter stilled while Lee adjusted the highly sensitive microphone to better amplify the conversation. Hunter couldn't make out Welch's reply. Only paper shuffling, a snap and a click and a—slap?

"And I said…" Meredith's terse reply trailed off, but damn. Welch's garage door lifted just as a sliver of sunlight broke to the east. An immaculate silver Maserati GranTurismo eased out of the driveway and onto the street.

"Game time," Lee alerted The TEAM, relaying license plate number, make and model of car, and the direction Welch was heading.

A quick "Copy that," came back from Alex, then Zack and Maverick, then Mother. Hunter squinted through two sets of darkened windows, his and Welch's, hoping to catch a glimpse of Meredith.

"Do not break cover," Alex reminded his guys.

"Copy that," Hunter replied as he shifted the SUV into drive. *Not until I have to, Boss.*

As suspected, Welch hooked into I-66 and crossed the Potomac, then swung right onto Lee Highway, headed directly for Rosslyn, Virginia, the home of McCormack Industries.

"Coming straight to you," Lee informed The TEAM just as Hunter took a quick detour that put him ahead of Welch by seconds. He and Lee rolled to a stop at the intersection in time to watch the Maserati pass by.

"You're playing this awfully close," Lee muttered.

"I know," Hunter grunted. *Not as close as I'd like.*

Feeling lucky, he pulled a U-turn and parked a block ahead of the Maserati on the same side of the street. The passenger door swung open and there she was. Meredith. Still breathtaking, dressed to the nines in a slim red dress, one of those designs that hugged her hips and accentuated her full breasts. Hunter couldn't tear his eyes off the goddess in his rearview. If he had his way, he'd be out there with her. Protecting her. The FBI had better get their act together—soon!

"Here she comes," he told his guys.

But the woman was tense, her shoulders taut. Her spine ramrod straight. Her chin set and her face forward. The high-priced Halliburton carbon fiber attaché case in her right hand caught Hunter's attention. He'd used the same type of briefcase once in Indonesia when he'd exchanged a ransom for a kidnapped five-year-old girl.

"The queen is wired and carrying explosives," Lee apprised The TEAM. "You guys know what to do."

"I'm going in," Hunter decided, his hand already on the door handle. Either Welch had the detonator or he'd planted a timer inside the case. Or both.

"Stay," Alex hissed. "Cut her some slack, Hunt. Meredith's no dummy."

"Then everyone needs to stand down. Do not approach. I repeat, don't approach Meredith. Welch will blow that case in her hand if you do!" *I gawddamned know he will.*

Meredith came to a dead halt in the center of the MI courtyard. She seemed frozen, staring straight ahead at nothing. *She's afraid.* "You can do this, Baby. I know you can," he breathed, his heart pounding like a mother in his chest.

Damned if Jed didn't step out of nowhere, smiling in that easy way he had as he fell in step beside her. Hunter about lost it. "What's he doing here?"

"He owns the place," Lee replied.

"I know that," Hunter snapped as a chill shuddered up his spine. "Where the hell's the FBI?"

"Still in transit." Alex whispered so softly that a visual instantly sprang to Hunter's mind. His boss. Flat on his belly. His scope up against his eye socket. The crosshairs dead center of Welch's forehead. That picture of his lethal boss actually—helped. Alex had his six.

Hunter kept one eye on the Maserati behind him, the other on McCormack Industries ahead. Everything was up to Meredith now.

All Hunter could do was wait.

McCormack Industries

Established 1990

Rosslyn, Virginia

The gold lettering etched into the magnificent red sandstone, itself standing on end in a bed of red gravel, declared Jed McCormack's success for the world to see. Fingers of water trickled in grooves from the top of the monolith. In weathered copper, an artist's rendering of Jed graced the red brick walkway, almost as if the man himself welcomed visitors and business associates alike into his world. Darkened by time, the statue's smiling eyes seemed fixed on Meredith. She couldn't take another step.

Jed McCormack. Ever watchful. Extra kind. Almost fatherly.

Meredith Flynn. The liar come home to disappoint. The traitor. The destroyer.

Forced to endure a night of meticulous planning without much sleep, she'd come to MI wired to the gills with caffeine. Sporting a unique pair of wrap-around Oakley sunglasses, everything in her line of sight and every spoken word was now transmitted back to Eddy, hiding down the block in his sports car like the snake he was.

Choice had ceased to be an option. Motherly instinct controlled her every thought and desire, her every action and reaction. Today was about getting Courtney back, and, if she lived long enough—killing Eddy.

Paralyzed with fear, she stood stock still, her mind on fire with the treachery of her mission. Could she go through with Eddy's scheme? Could she cause untold death and misery, unimaginable destruction and suffering to others—just to save her child?

In a word—*yes*. Courtney would die a slow death at Eddy's hand if she didn't.

"Remember who depends on you, Mom," Eddy's sarcastic voice threatened through the earpiece secreted deep inside her ear. "Do this, and you'll get your kid tonight. Double-deal me, and you'll never see him again. I'll just send pictures. Maybe body parts."

Grinding her teeth so hard that her jaw hurt, Meredith took a deliberate step toward the classy entry to MI. She walked up to the doors. The reflection in that plate-glass almost looked like her. The simple red A-line dress with black piping fit her style. So did the practical black pumps. Even the sunglasses. From head to toe, that stern-faced woman staring back at her looked like the top-notch technical assistant to MI's hotshot engineer, Teague Horton. The spy within was hidden well.

"Hold up, young lady." Jed sprinted from behind, his hand outstretched. "Let me get that door for you." Tall, white-haired and regal, he never seemed out of breath or common courtesy. He ushered her inside as if he simply worked there instead of owned the place.

"Speak," Eddy prompted. "Open your mouth. Flirt. Kiss his ass. Do your thing."

She coughed, bile climbing up her throat at her deceit. "What are you doing here this early?"

"I might be asking you the same thing. Why aren't you home with your son?" Silvery brows narrowed over gray-blue eyes full of energy and life. Jed was a man above others, yet humble enough that he knew his workers on sight, and he called them by name.

"I, umm, needed to get my head back in the game," she lied just as she'd rehearsed.

"Are you sure? I'm not a slave driver." He stepped aside to let her enter first. "There's still time to leave. I wouldn't blame you. Go on. I'll cover for you."

"Don't you dare," Eddy hissed.

"I... I'm fine. Really." The subterfuge came easier. Meeting Jed was an added bonus to this awful day. With him at her side, she wouldn't have to submit to the customary screening all MI employees endured upon entry. With a world of proprietary information locked behind every door, security was the order of the day. Like it or not, the world had changed, and she was there to change it again.

Unexpectedly, the gentlemanly CEO reached down and relieved her of Eddy's deadly briefcase. She nearly shrieked. "You d-don't need to do that. Please. I can carry it."

He ignored her as together they circumvented the security system "A mother should be home with her son. Didn't that little guy miss you while you were gone?"

Her heart pinched at the cavalier way Jed had taken over, but what could she say? Unwittingly, her target had become her accomplice. And she'd let him. Like the coward she was.

"He's fine," she murmured, her resolve shaken. *What a lie. I don't even know where he is! I need help, Jed.* "If Xander doesn't need me, I'll go home. I just wanted to make an appearance."

Jed cupped her elbow and steered her toward the elevator, the briefcase still snug in his other hand. "Well, good, see that you keep it short. I need to talk with Xander myself. Might as well walk you to your office. Heaven knows mine can wait. Once I show up there, Donna will just expect me to work."

"Excellent," Eddy hissed. "You're good at this, sweetheart. You've got him eating right out of your hand."

She lowered her lashes, ashamed to her soul and hyperventilating at the high cost of betrayal. Jed was as good a man as any she'd ever known. No one matched his consideration for the military or his employees. *God, how can I do this to him? To my friends?*

This entire wing was devoted to research and development. It was geared toward helping the men and women who fought for freedom, at home and abroad. Guilt for her wicked intentions chilled her core. How could she ever explain this day to Courtney? Would he understand how desperate she was, or would he blame himself?

Darkness filled the elevator as it smoothly plummeted three levels belowground to the Research, Development, Testing and Evaluation Lab. Only Eddy had called it the kill box, and the darkness was in her soul.

When the elevator door hissed open, she reached again for the deadly briefcase.

"Oh, no, you don't." Jed shook his head, holding Eddy's brand of Armageddon at arm's length. "My mother raised a southern gentleman, Miss Flynn. You wouldn't want me to disappoint her, would you?"

She gulped at that revelation. "Your mom's still alive?" *How can I kill another mother's son? That's what I'm doing. I'm murdering sons and daughters, and—I can't.*

"Not exactly. She's up in heaven with my old man. Now, what's so important you had to leave your son? Courtney, isn't it?" he asked, his brow lifted in mischief.

"Jesus Christ, don't let him open it," Eddy snapped. "The bomb has to be inside the lab when it goes off, you dumb bitch! Get the briefcase back and stick it under your desk like I told you!"

I'm trying! Her throat clenched as tightly as her empty fingers. "Just reports and comments I made during the beta test. Please. Let me take it while you speak to Xander."

"It's no trouble." Jed seemed intent on escorting her to her desk, the briefcase still in his care. At the secure entry to the lab, he pressed his thumb to the fingerprint reader. Once the electromagnetic lock beeped its approval, he leaned into MI's next line of defense, the iris scanner. There was no audible signal that time. The latest technology in security simply authenticated the pattern in Jed's iris, and, just like that, she and the bomb were—in.

Meredith stopped as the thirteen-inch thick door hissed shut behind her. She and Jed were now standing inside the steel-reinforced walls of the world's finest research lab. Blast resistant glass doors lined the wall at her left, each one the entry to one of MI's top-secret research labs. The ActiveCamouflage suits. The stealth drone prototype. The next generation geostationary satellite system.

"Hey, Meredith!" Xander waved at her from across the bay. "Good to see you back."

Her hand lifted in a half-hearted response. This was the last time she'd see this place. These men. The walls would contain the blast, turning everything and everyone within this section of MI to ash. There'd be no fire because there'd be no ventilation. No oxygen. There'd be nothing left of—anyone.

"How's your headache?"

In a daze, Meredith blinked at Jed, not sure when he'd turned around to look at her, or how many times he'd asked that question. "My h-h-headache?"

He took a step toward her. "What's wrong? You're still wearing your dark glasses. I figured you had a migraine."

If you only knew. "Oh, umm, yes. A migraine." She was falling apart little by little. "I've already taken extra-strength pain reliever. Hope it works soon."

Jed reached for her, his fingertips barely skimming her jaw. He frowned. "You're trembling, Meredith. Are you sure you should be here today?"

God, what a question. "I, ah—"

"Let him keep the damned briefcase! Get your ass out of there," Eddy hissed. "If he's staying to talk with the engineer, your work's done. Move it."

It gave her no comfort to know that Eddy wanted her to live while everyone else would die. Swallowing hard, she bumped her butt against Xander's cluttered desk. Feeling behind her, she found a pen. A piece of paper. And courage. "You know what? You're right. I think I will go home."

"Now, you're talking." Jed gave her a thumbs-up. "I'll put this thing under your desk. Whatever's in it will keep for another day. You go home to Courtney where you belong. Get some rest."

Jed strolled to her desk and tucked the Halliburton beneath it. Meredith gulped. If this next part didn't work, her kindly friend and benefactor would die along with everyone in this part of the complex.

"Move your ass," Eddy ground out.

She jumped at the rise in volume inside her ear, but pushed the limit. Meredith took three steps toward Jed, her hands extended. "Can I just tell you what an honor it was to be selected to go to Brazil? Even though it didn't turn out like we'd planned, all versions of the ACS performed better than expected."

"What the hell are you doing?" Eddy shrieked.

Tenderness glowed in Jed's eyes. "I'm glad you came home, Meredith. I don't know what I would've done if I'd lost you. Dan's and Lyle's funerals will be early next week. I'm speaking at both, so I hope you'll be able to attend them."

Trembling, she transferred the now crumpled paper into Jed's palm with her sweaty handshake. "I wouldn't miss them. That was such an awful loss."

"That it was." Jed didn't bat an eye as he accepted her— gift.

"I'll blow you to kingdom come if you don't get your ass out of there," Eddy snarled. "Cut the bullshit and run."

"Have a good day, Mr. McCormack," she said, trembling at the risk she was taking. "I might just take the rest of the week off if you're sure you don't mind." *Because I may be in jail after I find my son and kill his father.*

Jed eased his hand from hers. "See that you do, now skedaddle."

Fighting to maintain her composure, Meredith turned woodenly to leave. She'd done all she could. Eddy's message to the world was right where he wanted it to be.

So was hers.

CHAPTER FORTY-THREE

"How about that, you do listen," Eddy grumbled. "I might have another job for you."

"No," Meredith answered quickly, keeping her head down as she punched the button to ground level. She didn't need to see any co-workers or friends. "You promised—"

"I know what I promised, but you've got the brains and the looks for this business. Who'd suspect a sweetheart like you? Once MI is dead, there's still General Dynamics. Hell, they're headquartered down the road from your place in Falls Church. It'll be a snap getting you in. All you've got to do is show 'em your credentials and wiggle your ass. You'll land a job in no time."

"No, Eddy," she ground out. "You can't make me—"

He laughed in her ear. "Want to bet? I'm the one holding the detonator. Just think. Northrup Grumman. Lockheed Martin. Maybe Boeing. With you in my corner, we could rule the world."

When the elevator opened, Meredith stepped inside. Her heart sank. Eddy Welch was insane. In less than thirty steps, she'd be at the front entry, but she'd never be free. Even if Jed deciphered her hastily scribbled message—even if he somehow neutralized the bomb, he couldn't get to Eddy in time.

Her courage wilted. There was no way out of this nightmare, not for her. Eddy would use and abuse Courtney to make her do his dirty work. In the end, she and Courtney would die.

She'd barely stepped out of the elevator when Xander bellowed, "Meredith!"

She jumped, her nerves strung so damned tight.

His face was flushed. He must've run up the stairs. "I thought I'd missed you. Here." He forced a blue MI award box at her. "Jed wanted you to have this before you left today. He said you could use it."

She shook her head and waved him off. Today wasn't a day for gratitude after what she'd done.

"Keep walking, Flynn," Eddy threatened, "or the kid dies."

You think I don't know that!

"Take it," Xander insisted, shoving the box at her until she had no choice. "Mr. McCormack was going to give it to you in some big ceremony later, but he thought you could use the cash today."

Meredith pressed the box to her chest. It felt heavier than the usual Mi awards. Did she dare hope? Had Jed awarded her with a—pistol? Was he omniscient or was he just that good that he'd known how desperate she was? Hope blossomed in her chest. As casually as she could, Meredith balanced that MI award box against her thigh. "Tell Jed thanks."

"You betcha." Xander chin nodded at the exit. "Go on now. He's waiting for you."

She glanced over her shoulder, half expecting to see Hunter. Could she be so lucky?

Maybe…

"You got five minutes to get your ass in this bucket seat," Eddy hissed. "I don't know what that crap was about, but I want to see what's in that box."

"I'm coming." She set a quick pace to Eddy's car. He wanted it. He was going to get it.

"Coming your way, Hunt," Maverick advised from MI's courtyard.

"Copy that. I see her." Hunter lowered his head, his gaze still fixed on that classy lady headed straight toward his vehicle. Meredith couldn't see him through the tinted windshield, but he had no trouble seeing her.

The Oakleys were still in place, but the Halliburton was gone. She seemed to have left her timid self behind. She carried herself proud, a small navy blue box in her hand at her thigh. Her chin was up and her stride seemed—determined. She had that look on her face, the same look she'd had when she'd yelled at him to stop swearing. She didn't see him though. Didn't glance his way. Just walked on by.

Throwing his arm between the two front seats of his SUV, he twisted his torso to maintain the visual. Lee had hunched down in his seat. "Your woman's got balls."

Yeah, I know. They're mine.

Meredith paused for a second at the passenger door Welch had just shoved open. She glanced to her left, then to her right, fumbling with the box before she ducked inside.

"FBI's in position," Alex murmured.

"Finally," Lee muttered.

Thank God! "Can we move on Welch then?" Hunter snapped.

"As soon as we—"

BOOM!

"Shots fired!" Lee bellowed.

Hunter scrambled out of the SUV. What the hell just happened? What'd Welch do to her? *So help me, I'll kill him!*

"You ain't got what it takes to make—"

"I said take your clothes off!" With another roar, the pistol in her shaky hand invited more sunlight in through the pricey roof of Eddy's ego-trip car. "You hurt my son. *MY* son! And you put him somewhere without telling me where. Believe me, I do *got what it takes*. Take your fucking clothes off!"

And now I sound just like Hunter.

Eddy stripped down to his boxers, balling his pants, shirt, shoes, and tie to the floor. The bully's hands actually shook more than hers. "Listen. If it's money you want—"

"I don't want your money!" This man didn't get it. "Toss your clothes out the window. All of them. Do it!"

Out they went, and there sat Eddy, his hands gripping his hairy knees and a glimmer of sweat on his brow. The man was nervous. Now Meredith understood why Hunter stripped the bodies of the men he'd killed. There was a certain power in humiliating this pompous ass. She pressed the barrel of the pistol that had been hidden in her award box to Eddy's temple. "Where is he, *Roger Teach*? Where'd you put Courtney? Tell me!"

He offered a twitching half smile, his fingertips drumming his kneecaps. "Pretty clever, huh, using a nom de plume when I'm plundering fat cats who—"

"Shut up!" Did he honestly think she cared? The police had to be on their way. She'd made enough noise. When they showed, her chance of getting her son back would be gone. "Where's Courtney?"

Eddy kept skirting the answer she needed. "You want revenge 'cause I roughed up your little girly boy? You want—"

"Enough!" She gritted her teeth and squeezed the trigger and—

The driver-side door jerked open. Just that fast, a man stuck his pistol in Eddy's neck. "Put your hands on top of your fat head, Welch, or should I call you, Master?"

Hunter? Oh my God! Hunter! But he was too early. "No!" Meredith cried. "Not yet!"

He ducked inside and peered past Eddy. "Hey, Merry. I'd let you have more time with your ex, but Alex has this crazy idea you might shoot him."

"Courtney?" she asked, her finger still on the trigger. And tempted. "Where is he? Do you know? Is he okay?"

"Don't worry, I found him yesterday at Aberdeen Proving Ground. He's safe and sound with your parents right now. They're spoiling him rotten." Hunter pocketed the detonator, bumping Eddy's nose with his elbow when he reached for it.

Meredith nearly laughed. Hunter did that on purpose.

Eddy growled, batting him away. "Watch it, Christian."

Wrong move. Hunter stuck his elbow in Eddy's throat and, while Eddy sputtered, nonchalantly asked Meredith,

"You wouldn't know what happened to Bear, would you? Courtney's been worried sick."

Eddy grunted, but Hunter looked... So. Damned. Good. Meredith could barely see past the tears in her eyes. Hunter talked as if he knew Courtney.

She nudged Eddy's head with her pistol. "I was just about to find out. Where's Bear?"

The jerk only shrugged. "Hell, I don't know."

Determined to get a better answer and maybe inflict of little justice, Meredith leaned forward, but the door opened and Lee leaned in. He reached around her, as if he disarmed angry women every day. "You're sure making a ruckus. Mind if I take that *major award* off your hands?"

She nearly chuckled at the *Christmas Story* reference, but this was no leg lamp she was holding. She had to be certain. "There's a bomb. Third level down. In the MI lab under—"

"Under your desk. Understood. Already taken care of," Lee replied. "Jed called in a bomb threat, but Zack and Seth couldn't wait. They disarmed it already. Look down the street."

She could barely believe what she saw. Crowds of MI employees in the street. Arlington County PD cruisers. Several FBI vans. *Thank God!*

"It's really disarmed?" She needed to hear it again.

"Of course. All us guys can diffuse explosives. Come on now," Lee persisted. "Jed wants his pistol back."

"But Eddy needs to pay," she whispered out of the corner of her mouth. And I want him to!

"He'll pay. Believe me, he'll pay." The glint in Hunter's deep brown eyes settled her once and for all. "Give Lee the gun. Courtney's sick with missing you, Mama. Let's go home."

That tender endearment was her undoing. So was that fatherly thing Hunter didn't realize he did so well. Her need for revenge stilled. Lee easily lifted the gun from her fingers. Eddy never looked so glum. "You're a bitch, Flynn. Always were. Always—"

The. Last. Straw!

Meredith launched across the console of that posh little car, her fists balled tight and she punched Eddy's big mouth. Hunter played along, opening Eddy's door as Meredith shoved his nearly naked ass to the curb. Down he went with a grunt, Meredith giving him hell all the way. Eddy didn't offer as much resistance as she'd expected—not after her knee landed in his crotch.

"You fight like a girl," he whined.

"I am a girl! "She balled her fist and landed a hefty smack to his lying mouth.

Somewhere in the distance, Lee asked, "You think we ought to pull her off?"

"Not yet," Hunter answered. "My girl's got this."

Wasn't that the perfect thing for her man to say?

Smelling victory, Meredith mashed the heel of her hand into Eddy's already bleeding nose. He rolled to his side to get away, but Mean Girl wasn't done with him yet. With one pointed knee in his kidneys, she cranked two of his fingers until he squealed. "You... you win. You'll never see me again."

"Time to stop playing," Hunter urged. "The FBI's here. He's their property now. Let me have him."

"FBI?" She looked up to several stern-looking federal agents. *Where'd they come from?*

"Yes. Captain Hook's been on their watch list for money laundering and insider trading, not to mention murder and his predilection for little boys. Looks like he'll be walking the plank."

"I don't think that's what they call it in prison," Lee muttered, "although it does have something to do with a plank."

Meredith didn't understand what Lee meant. Regaining what little charm she had left, she pushed up from the sidewalk and straightened her red dress, tugging it down over her thighs. Combing her fingers into her tangled hair, she dragged it out of her eyes and with a puff, she blew it off her face. By then, she looked halfway presentable. Her nylons were still shredded and so were her knees, but Courtney was safe. That was what mattered.

She tossed her head, her battle won.

Hunter winked. "Nice dress."

"She's a slut," Eddy hissed, and enough already!

Meredith whirled on her ex. With a mighty growl, she kicked him in the face with the very practical black pumps he'd forced her to wear. "Just! Shut! Up!" she yelled, punctuating every word with her heels. "Stay away from Courtney and me!"

Eddy squirmed, shielding his bleeding face with his arm. "She's killing me!"

Hunter was smart enough not to tell Meredith what she could and couldn't do. Instead, he crouched beside Eddy. "Then stop making her mad, Welch. She's lethal. Remember that."

Meredith stilled. Was this the same guy who'd given her hell for losing her gun?

Eddy glanced up at her through puffy eyelids. "Her? She ain't nothing."

Hunter secured his arms behind his back and hoisted him to his feet. "You're never going to learn, are you? Don't you know about the power of a woman? 'Cause I sure do."

Meredith's heart melted at Hunter's feet. The most charming mega-watt smile brightened his face. He barely had time to hand Eddy off to Lee before she plowed into him.

"I love you, Hunter Christian," she growled, her hands on the sides of his head, holding him in place.

"Not like I love you," he muttered hotly. "Marry me."

"Where? When?"

"Justice of the Peace around the corner. As soon as my best man can get here. You know the guy. Courtney Flynn."

Could he have said anything sweeter? "Done."

Lee Hart coughed politely somewhere behind them. "Ah, guys. The boss just pulled up."

Untangling herself from Hunter's arms, Meredith snaked her hand around his waist. *Ahh, this man's body.* She tucked her fingers into his belt while she settled under his arm. Next to his heart. Her war was finally over.

Looking down at her, he asked, "May I have the earpiece and wire you're wearing?"

"Sure. The sunglasses are in the car." Somewhere. "You can have the earpiece, but the wire's under my dress, and I can't—"

His eyes lit up. "I can."

Once again, it was just Hunter and her, two kids in love and lust like they should've been all along. He turned his back, shielding her from Lee and the rest of the world. "It's time to go home."

EPILOGUE

Never in a million years could Hunter have predicted that he'd end up with a wife and son after a deadly South American operation, nor that he'd be cured of his nicotine craving. But he was. The only thing he craved now was the woman sleeping in his arms, her blonde hair cascading off the pillow around her, her nose twitching against his chest like she couldn't breathe enough of him. The innocent gesture made him smile. Meredith's appetite for sex was ferocious, and he was happy to oblige.

As much as they'd played over the last weeks, neither seemed able to get enough of the other. It was as if they had to make up for their years apart, and the foolish decisions they'd made. With her ex safely behind bars, and Courtney thrilled that *Hunner* got to live with him and his mom, life couldn't get any better.

Except for one thing. Hunter was hungry for more make-up sex. It was well after midnight when he smoothed his fingers over the satiny skin of her shoulder and down her arm. Even in her sleep Meredith responded, pushing her bare breasts against his bicep. Heat flamed where only seconds before a steady ember had simmered. Her sleepy body arched into his and no words were needed.

They moved by memory over each other now. Easing a palm down her spine, he cupped one cheek of her plump bottom and rolled to his back with her. They were made for each other. They fit together. The delicious heat of her core worked magic on him. Arching his hips, he pushed into her slick warmth, reveling in the luxury of making love anytime and anywhere he wanted.

"Hmmm," she murmured, still mostly asleep, her head heavy under his chin and her breasts mashed against his chest.

If there was something better to live for, Hunter didn't know it. He clutched the swell of her hips and drove his love for her home with one deep thrust. She arched back, her hands on his pecs, her fingernails holding him secure. Captured in her silky curtain of hair, he set a gentle rhythm. Only after she cried his name to the ceiling, did he let himself fly with her.

A smile of male satisfaction curled his lips. It pleased him no end to please her. To shelter her. To provide for her and Courtney. Still locked together and breathing hard, he whispered, "I love you, Wife."

"You're up early," she murmured.

"I'm up all the time," he teased, thrusting deeper. They lay in silence until their bedroom door cracked open and the light from the hallway glanced over them.

Meredith stiffened. "Not again. That little boy's got radar or something. He's always catching us."

Hunter didn't mind what had become a nightly interruption. Quickly covering her with the blankets, he eased her to her side of the bed. If Courtney needed reassurance, Hunter meant to give it to him. "What's up, buddy?"

As usual, Courtney shuffled to Hunter's side of the bed. Dressed in his bright red, *Elmo* footie pajamas, he had Bear snuggled in one arm, while Black Jack dangled from the other. "I had a bad dweam, Hunner. Kin I sweep wiff you?"

"Sure thing." Hunter scooped his son off the floor and, after he made sure those *Elmo* PJs were dry, he settled Courtney between the sheet and blanket at his left. Their nightly ritual also included both Hunter and Meredith sneaking out of bed once Courtney fell asleep, to slip into their pajamas. But for now, with him and his bears snuggled between them, they were the epitome of a happy family.

The little guy had reverted to sucking his thumb and bedwetting, but neither Meredith nor Hunter let Courtney be embarrassed by what he had no control over. They did laundry together, even gave Bear and Black Jack a bath with Courtney when they needed one. Bubbles and all.

The Christian family went to the gun range where Courtney was learning the basics of hunter safety. How to properly hold a loaded weapon. How to aim. Why you never played with guns. Good and reasonable things like that.

They ate hotdogs and fries at a local Mom and Pop's Café afterward, and they always took Bear, and Black Jack, with them. Life at the newly purchased Christian homestead on the four-acre plot in Falls Church, was settling down. Hunter made certain of that.

He hadn't brought a dog home yet, but he planned to. Hunter had a good friend who raised the best German Shepherd pups in the country. Courtney would love another furry friend at his beck and call.

Unless Courtney brought it up, no one talked about the bastard who'd abducted him. For certain, no one called him *father or daddy.* Welch was simply Welch or—*that bad man.*

Son-of-a-bitch and *bastard* were reserved for Meredith and Hunter when they were alone.

Come to find out, those legal documents Welch had initiated, his will and his relinquishment of parental rights, were legal. Courtney was his heir, but no longer his son. That made adopting him easier. Hunter had already filed the paperwork.

As far as the promised billions Courtney was supposed to inherit? Hunter didn't give a good gawddamn if his kid ever saw a penny of that filthy cash. Welch would probably rewrite his will in prison anyway. Let him.

Since Aberdeen, Courtney had decided *Hunner* was the best. Anywhere Hunter went, Courtney was sure to follow, like the sweet little lamb he was. They'd grown as close as a father and son could be, but that was no surprise.

Hunter knew the day he'd found Courtney they'd be best buddies. Sitting there in the cold water like they had, a bond of brotherhood bound Hunter to Courtney more permanently than blood. It was the unspoken promise of men who fought side by side, who covered each other's asses, and who never left the other behind. Even though one of those men was only three and a half.

Meredith braced her head in her palm and peered over her drowsy son to Hunter. "Tell me again," she said softly. "How did you win Courtney's heart so quickly?"

Hunter stretched his neck to place a kiss on his wife's forehead. She loved this story. "I married his mother. You might know her. Meredith Christian. Sexy blonde fighting machine. Fierce Amazon-warrior type."

Meredith's brows lifted. "You mean the woman who lost her gun?"

He winked at her. "That's my girl."

"You guys are squishing me," Courtney grumbled sleepily as he wiggled between them. "Be quiet. Bear's sweepin'."

Even in the dark, Hunter saw the sparkle in Meredith's eyes. Was she crying? She did that a lot these days. She'd come out of that debacle with her ex a changed woman, still afraid of snakes and maybe a little meaner. Definitely a lot stronger. But ridden with a good mother's guilt. Hence, the tears.

She over-compensated, over-protected, and could get downright nasty if anyone laid a hand on Courtney. Hunter wasn't worried about that either. It might take her a while, but she'd adjust. She'd learn.

Like his pretty wife, Hunter learned his toughest lessons the hard way. He couldn't help wondering if those stents in his heart weren't due, in part, to his mistaking Meredith's running off with Welch for love. Knowing that had never been the case made a definite difference. Hunter's heart wasn't so ragged these days. He smiled more often and he teased. He'd remembered how to play. You might even say he was a happy SOB. *Ahem, make that a happy man.* He was still working on that not cussing clause in his marriage vows.

Eric Reynolds finally came out of his coma. In an unexpected turn of events, Zack Lennox had found Eric's boxful of secrets taped to his chest the day Masters stabbed him. Hunter was in the office when Zack laid it on Eric's desk. The look on Reynolds' face was telling. He'd opened his mouth like he wanted to talk, but nothing came out. No thank you. No explanation either. He'd just nodded once, then stuffed the box in his desk drawer and went back to work.

The day would come he'd have to face his demons, whatever they were. Hunter only hoped Eric's story ended as well as his.

As far as how Welch knew about the beta test, Hunter had found it damned—*darned*—peculiar that both Lyle Salaz and Dan Randolph were executed so quickly. It was almost as if they'd been targeted for execution. After voicing that opinion to Mr. McCormack, Jed had his security people dig into both men's research in the MI lab. They uncovered irrefutable evidence of collusion between Welch, Salaz, and Randolph. They'd been on Welch's payroll for months before the beta test, reporting on the top-secret ActiveCamouflage research.

Hunter wasn't surprised. He'd never liked the jerk who'd referred to heroic military members as *assets.* As for Dan, Hunter could honestly say he'd never met the coward. Apparently, Randolph never had the guts to look the people he'd betrayed in the eye.

Another interesting side note: From the first time he'd heard the name fall off poor Bradley's lips, Hunter found it peculiar Welch insisted the boys he had abducted called him Master. The name grated on Hunter, so similar to Travis *Masters.* It wasn't until the day after the bomb scare at McCormack Industries, that Ember and Rory stumbled across the connection. Eddy Welch and Travis Masters were cousins on Welch's mother's side of the family. But worse, Masters had been dishonorably discharged from the Corps and done time—for child molestation of a ten-year-old boy. It seemed Welch's ugliest character flaw ran in the family.

The Dennisons also uncovered why Welch had selected the corporations he'd targeted. It seemed the CEOs heading those businesses belonged to the same East Coast ring of pedophiles that Welch did. He was no financial genius. He just knew how to leverage a few illicitly obtained photographs against his *friends*. Hunter had to give Welch a shred of credit. The man certainly had the market on ego and pride locked up tighter than a pirate's treasure chest.

"You saved my son," Meredith whispered in the dark. "You didn't have to, but you did, and you saved me, too. I love you, Hunter. So does Courtney."

He reached over their sleeping child to wipe away the tear trekking down her cheek with the pad of his thumb. His fingers lingered in her hair, winding a golden curl between them. Because of Merry and Courtney, Hunter had stars in his eyes. He'd taken to reading poetry and stories again, though admittedly, most of those stories had to do with a little yellow bear named Pooh who lived in A. A. Milne's *Hundred-Acre Wood*.

"It's no big deal, Merry. I just love him. That's what fathers do."

She blew out a tremulous sigh. "All this time, he thought Courtney was yours. He thought I tricked him into marrying him. He called him that…" Another soft sigh. "… that ugly B word."

Welch thought Courtney was a bastard? What a flaming ass.

"Thank you again for saving us, Hunter," she murmured. "You've changed everything."

Meredith had it wrong. If anyone was saved, it was him. Tough Marine. Trained hunter/killer. Hunter Christian.

Yet that was precisely what happened. A scared little guy had dared reach out and trust a guy as lost as he was. In doing so, Courtney rescued Hunter as much as Hunter rescued him.

Any *silly old Bear* could see that.

THE END

Sneak Preview of Eric

Book 15

In the Company of Snipers

"Ladies and gentlemen, this is your captain speaking. Please return to your seats and fasten your seatbelts. We're in for a bumpy ride."

Again?

There was no need to return. Junior Agent Eric Reynolds never unbuckled once he'd lowered his butt into first-class seating and strapped in. Didn't matter which airline he flew. Didn't matter the destination. Only when all wheels touched down on planet Earth again would he think of unfastening that buckle. Screw physics. The science behind jet propulsion couldn't compete with the force of attraction behind Newton's law of gravity.

Didn't matter what eye-catching logo had been splashed across the tail or under the belly of this jumbo bird. It still fit Eric's definition of a damned rock, and rocks fell out of the sky, damn it.

There was no point talking statistics to him about how safe air travel was in comparison to automobile, train, or boat travel. He didn't want to hear all that logic on a good day when he had both feet flat on the ground. Facts didn't mean squat when a guy was dropping twenty thousand feet a minute out of a clear blue sky with nothing to say about it but *splat* and *goodbye. Adios. Sayonara.* Add rain, thunder, and lightning to the mix, and a paranoid man with a fear of flying didn't stand a chance. Bring on a double dose of Dramamine. *Or a Jack and Coke.*

The flight to Amsterdam from JFK had been one jolting bump after another. Up and down. Side to side, and, every so often, the jet shifted in all four directions at the same time until his stomach screamed.

He steeled what was left of his ragged nerves, digging his fingers into the armrests just in time. The aerodynamically-designed bird bucked, and anyone not strapped in hit the ceiling. They deserved what they got. What were they thinking walking around?

Black clouds taunted at every window. Lightning flashed, too close for comfort. The atmosphere beyond the thin skin of this jumbo jet sounded like a warzone. *Regularly scheduled, my ass.* Fifteen hours to Amsterdam was not part of Eric's regular schedule, not by a long shot. But there he was because, once again, his compassion had gotten the best of him.

Operation Find Finn started at the crack of dawn the day before with a curt bellow from his boss, Alex Stewart. "Sit room. Now."

All hands on deck complied. Ex-Army. Ex-Marine. Ex-whatever. Alex hired mostly ex-Marines, a given considering his prior career in the Corps. Eric guessed that was to be expected, not that he minded, since he was ex-USMC himself, a medic and a damned good shot. He'd never done the scout sniper thing, but there he was, working for one of the best in a company of snipers. Once a rifleman always a rifleman.

They filed into the Situation room where Mother, aka Sasha Kennedy, The TEAM's genius Girl Friday, was already seated and unusually somber. A chill prickled up Eric's spine then. His gut clenched like it used to at the call of man down when he'd been active-duty.

Something wicked had come down to The TEAM. He felt it zero down on him. It didn't help that most other agents were out of the office, already assigned and in the field. Zack Lennox in Cuba. Seth McCray somewhere in South America. Hunter Christian and Lee Hart on a black ops mission to only Alex knew where. Even Senior Agent Harley Mortimer was out of the country, no doubt in Afghanistan monitoring the spike in opium production for the United Nations.

Who didn't see that coming after decades of war and failed promises from the international community?

Others were assigned to local operations and security details. That left two senior agents, Mark Houston and David Tao, and two junior agents, Eric Reynolds and Jordan Hannigan.

Mother and her assistant, Ember Dennison, didn't count. Techies didn't do field work.

Eric had no more than parked his butt when the big screen overhead flashed to life. The camera angle panned out, revealing the bastard running the show. Dressed in the black robes of the current terrorist plague sweeping the planet, his face was masked as he gripped his victim's long, blond hair into a cruel topknot. The scimitar in his right hand cast blinding laser flashes at the camera lens.

But worse was the physical state of the poor kid on his knees. He couldn't have been more than twenty-five. Dark, black lines crisscrossed his entire torso. Possibly burns.

Maybe bloody welts. The victim had lost control of his bodily functions. Couldn't catch a decent breath.

Probable internal bleeding or punctured lung.

Wide, fear-filled swollen eyes, the barely visible whites red with blood. Strangled whimpers. Grunts. The camera lens cut close to a view of the guy's broken and bloody nose, his lips swollen and cut. His left front tooth was broken and jagged. His hands were bound in front of him, bloody stumps where three fingers had been clipped off. Both index fingers. One pinkie.

Eric's trained medical mind automatically worked damage control on the graphic scene. Definite extremity trauma. Internal bleeding. God knew what else. This was a race against time. Hemorrhaging required sustained massive transfusions and tourniquets. Shock, hypothermia, and the victim's unknown medical history could work against Eric no matter what he did. Pain control was a given. Damned rapid evac.

If Eric could've gotten to him in time. But he couldn't, and it was happening again. Someone's child was dying, and he couldn't do a thing to stop it.

"I am Abdul-Mutaal! You have forty-eight hours to deliver Finn Powers," the bastard towering over the victim demanded. "No more."

Abdul-Mutaal. The terrorist-de-jour thought to be hiding in Syria.

"F-Finn," the young man ground out, the shuddering panic in his voice unmistakable. "I'm... I'm sorry."

Eric couldn't bear to watch, but he did. With one swift stroke of that scimitar, the wicked deed was done. The camera lens caught the arterial spray as a young man a world away died. The bastard in charge pushed the poor kid's body aside while he shook the decapitated head at the camera with one last vigorous, "Forty-eight hours!"

The video blacked out. Thank God.

Eric dug his fingernails into the heels of his palms, willing his soul back to center, and his heart to stop jackhammering. He'd seen crap like this before. It wasn't the first beheading on live TV, and it wouldn't be the last. Frustration filled his gut. Until that last act of barbaric cruelty, Eric knew he could've saved that young man. At least, he could've relieved his suffering.

Working for the owner of the elite covert surveillance company of ex-military snipers, The TEAM, often brought the harsh realities of the world into the Situation Room. But that? Cold-blooded murder was what it was. Damned brutal.

Whatever contract Alex had just signed, whatever promise he'd made to save the world, Eric wanted in. Abdul-Mutaal needed one of those close-up-and-personal come-to-Jesus meetings the Corps offered free of charge. With a .338 Lapua Magnum. 16.2 grams.

Now, damn it.

"The young man whose death you just witnessed was Phoenix Berglund, an American citizen and a student at the University of Amsterdam. We believe his murderer is Abdul-Mutaal," Alex said, his palms also flat to the conference table. "Berglund's body was found in the research lab where he worked, but he was tortured elsewhere."

"Abdul-Mutaal's damned nervy to carry out a beheading in an Amsterdam University," Jordan muttered.

"He's an asshole is what he is. Who sent the video?" Mark pushed back from the conference room table, his thick

arms across his chest. He was a hard one to rattle, but even he'd turned a whiter shade of pale.

"Mutaal made the video, but one of Berglund's friends stole it." Mother's voice was tight, her tone edgy. It wasn't often The TEAM's genius techie came unraveled, but she was close, her manicured nails tapping a relentless clatter on the tabletop. "Phoenix and his friends were involved in some kind of a research project at the university, something to do with solar energy. They called it dynamic energy displacement."

"Your hacker friend got a name?" Eric knew Mother walked the thin line between providing superior technical support and outright breaking the law. That she wasn't behind bars proved her unique expertise. Hackers. The current version of Bonnie and Clyde, at least until the CIA and the folks at Langley turned them into federal agents or inmates at Leavenworth.

She glanced around the table, making eye contact with everyone present. Him last.

Eric's sixth sense sprang to life. She didn't want to name her hacker friend. Why not?

"Finn Powers," Alex divulged what she couldn't or wouldn't. "He's one of three young men Mother works with on her other job as a freelance game developer. All Americans. All living abroad and studying on a research grant in Amsterdam."

Powers? Really? That got Eric's undivided attention. Powers was his ex-wife's maiden name. A proud name—until Shea Powers Reynolds ran away. Ditched him. Filed for divorce. What a bizarre coincidence.

The name alone was more than enough to make him wonder, like he had every day for the last two years. Where had Shea gone? Why hadn't she contacted him since she'd left? Not that it mattered. He'd take her back in an instant if she'd let him. If he knew where she was.

He was just that stupid in love.

Alex drummed his fingers on the table, pulling Eric's attention back to the Sit Room. "Mother received the video an hour ago. Finn witnessed Berglund's murder and stole the SD card out of Abdul-Mutaal's camera. That one act of courage preempted this bastard's plan to release it to Al Jazeera for prime-time viewing. It was fast thinking to get one up on a psychopath like Abdul-Mutaal. He's got to be pissed."

"How can we be sure he's lost his advantage?" Eric wanted to know. Terrorists enjoyed broadcasting their acts of bloodlust and perverted cruelty. Beheadings on live television guaranteed a grim kind of respect, notoriety, and an influx of stupid, idealistic recruits.

Alex eyed Eric a full minute before he spoke. "Ember's monitoring all newsfeeds out of the Mideast in case he made a copy, but our source, Finn Powers, was pretty sure he didn't."

"There hasn't been a word of this murder on any news network yet," Ember assured Eric. "Our State Department hasn't caught wind of it, either. I called one of my friends to be sure."

Not like that meant anything. The State Department didn't often offer up intelligence until they had to. The CIA, either. Both federal agencies might know what went down in Amsterdam, but the world wouldn't until top-secret records were declassified decades in the future. Hell, this could be one of their undercover operations gone horribly wrong for all anyone knew.

Mother expelled a breath slowly in one long sigh through her pursed lips.

"What are you not telling us?" Eric asked her directly. "What's really going on? Why kill Berglund to get at Finn?"

She clenched her chin in her fist, breathing hard before she blurted it out. "Finn told me that he and his friends were in trouble. They were onto something big. Maybe illegal."

"What'd they hack into?" Eric growled, hating that someone from The TEAM might have to put his life in danger to save people who took stupid chances.

"Nothing. This isn't about hacking as far as I know, but Hugh Carlson paid them a visit at the university. He made all three of them impressive job offers if they'd work for him. When they refused, he threatened to steal their invention from them."

"Hugh Carlson? The narcissist billionaire from France? Why? What's so great about this—" Eric waved his hand at the blank screen. "—Dynamic energy displacement thing?"

Mother gulped. The woman should never go into black ops, not the way LIAR lit up in her eyes like it did.

"For hell's sake, tell him," Alex growled. "If you want Eric to save your boyfriend, tell him everything he needs to know."

With another deep breath, Mother spilled. "You won't believe it, but they've built the perfect force field." She swallowed hard. "I know this sounds like science fiction, but it's not. Dynamic energy displacement is a naturally occurring repulsion. Think of DED like a giant magnet with *north and south poles. Two magnets attract each other when their opposing poles align. It's basic science."*

Great. Another acronym. DED. How appropriate.

"And they repulse each other when you force north to north or south to south. Got that." Eric nodded. "The laws of natural attraction and repulsion, but how does that equate to a force field?"

"Because these three guys created a unique amplifier that boosts that natural attraction or repulsion. They've found a way to compress that energy, turning it into a—"

"Jesus Christ. A weapon," Eric finished for her. "Carlson wants the weaponized version of whatever they created, doesn't he?"

She nodded, her clattering nails enough to drive a man crazy. "Yes. It could be used as a weapon. In fact—"

"It could effectively be used as a long-range laser, nearly as powerful as a controlled solar flare—if what Finn told Mother is correct," Alex interrupted, two fingertips to his left temple. The man dealt with horrendous migraines, something Eric could help with if he'd let him.

"Carlson is dangerous. You've all heard his tag line: One Nation. One Network. One World. *He believes the man-made constraints of nation, country, and state have fallen to the wayside. They're obsolete. Like castles and national borders." Alex paused, his brows furrowed and the cords in his neck rigid. He made marble look relaxed. "In his mind, cyber-technology is the go-to strategy for world domination of market resources. His world domination. Think about it. If not for Carlson's CC, none of us would have cell service today, would we?"*

"*Right.*" *Eric got that much. The CC, or Carlson's Chip, as Carlson himself had named it, had done away with local cell providers in every country in a brilliant coup that monopolized the industry and took even know-it-all Wall Street by surprise. Hence the slogan:* One Nation. One Network. One World. *He also held a twisted and inflated opinion of himself and his abilities. The bastard was a genius, but he'd outright told the United Nations that he intended to take over the world. Get out of his way.*

Alex growled, "We won't know the extent of his madness until we get Finn Powers and Gordie Mikkelson out of Amsterdam and into U.S. custody. The Secretary of Defense is willing to send his Seal Team operatives in, but Finn asked for you, Eric. By name. You're lead on this op. Jordan will accompany. So tell me, how the hell do you know this guy?"

Eric shrugged, as baffled as everyone else. The only connection to Finn was that last name. Powers. "Never met him in my life, Boss. Where is this Finn person now, and how do you know all this?"

Mother glanced over her shoulder at Ember. "Show him."

Ember tapped her keyboard, bringing a final video to life on the overhead screen. Had to have been taken via Finn's cell phone, and a cheap one at best. At least the bumbling oaf knew to set his phone down to take a steady video clip.

An obese young man with Coke-bottle glasses peered into the screen. Unibrow. Crooked teeth. Big, wide nose. The guy was no looker. Typical geek type. Squinty-eyed. Unkempt. Probably talked techno-speak like Mother and Ember. Too bad he wasn't as good looking as they were.

Eric cringed when Finn stuck his face too close into the screen. Nose hairs. A boil or something that needed to be lanced on the end of his chin. This guy needed some serious time in the barber's chair. One of those reality-show makeovers wouldn't hurt. No way in hell was that guy related to Eric's ex-wife.

Finn's quavering and very effeminate voice pitched across the room. "Sasha. You know that boss of yours? The one you're always bragging about? I need him like uber fast. Time's short." He looked over his shoulder as if checking to see if he'd been followed. "Tell him to check his dedicated savings account, the one he uses to pay his personal taxes once a year. I transferred enough funds to get the job done. If that's not enough to get me out of the country, I can get more. Help me, Sasha. They're coming. Tell your boss to send his best. Send Eric!"

Eric's throat could not have gone any drier. He nearly rolled his eyes at the geeky term uber fast.

Your best? Me? How the hell do you know me, 'cause I sure as hell don't know you?

"Three million dollars was deposited in my bank account at midnight overnight," Alex said. "Ember tracked the transaction through a dozen Internet cafes and IP addresses scattered across the globe. Finn, or Mikkelson, or whoever sent it, is a damned good hacker, but the question is, where'd the money come from to begin with? I doubt three college kids had that much loose change laying around."

Eric lifted a palm for Alex to slow the information download. "Correct me if I'm wrong, but we've got two things going on here. Carlson wants the force field, and Abdul-Mutaal wants Finn. I get why Carlson wants Finn.

He's a rich bastard who wants the world, but what's Abdul-Mutaal's stake?"

"Presumably the same thing." Alex lowered his voice. "All we know now is that Finn needs protection, and we'll give it to him. According to the timestamp on the video, Berglund died at sixteen hundred hours yesterday, and that puts us inside a very tight forty-eight hour window. An international flight will eat up most of what time's left. Eric. Jordan. Gear up. You're going to Amsterdam."

The jumbo jetliner dipped, jolting Eric back to the present thunderstorm outside his window and another bout of queasy nausea. He glanced at his companion agent, Jordan Hannigan, Army Ranger in his past life, directly across the aisle. He'd stretched his long legs under the seat ahead of him and was sound asleep. Had been since the flight left D.C.

Damn him.

For what it was worth, Eric tightened his seat belt yet again. *Three more hours to the land of windmills and Hell.*

Thank you for reading Hunter!

Be sure to check out the rest of the guys and gals of Irish Winters' series: *In the Company of Snipers*

Other Irish Winters' books:

King of Hearts, Deuces Wild Series, *#1*

Joker Joker, Deuces Wild Series, *#2*

Smoke, Hearts and Ashes Series, *#1*

Ash, Hearts and Ashes Series, *#2*

Coming soon!

Seth, In the Company of Snipers, *#17*

One-Eyed Jack, Deuces Wild Series, *#3*

YOU are the key to this book's success!

Please tell other readers why you liked Hunter and Meredith's story by leaving an honest review at the retail site where you purchased it. Recommend it to your friends. Lend it. Most of all, enjoy it!

The best way to keep up with my new releases, giveaways, and actionable intel is to sign up for my spam-free newsletter at IrishWinters.com.

About the Author

Irish Winters is an award winning, Amazon best-selling author who, when she isn't writing, dabbles in poetry, grandchildren, and rarely (as in extremely rarely) the kitchen. More prone to be outdoors than in, she grew up the quintessential tomboy on a dairy farm in rural Wisconsin, spent her teenage years in the Pacific Northwest, but calls the Wasatch Mountains of Northern Utah home. For now.

She believes in making every day count for something, and follows the wise admonition of her mother to, "Look out the window and see something!"

Connect with Irish!
On Facebook: https://www.facebook.com/author.irishwinters
On Twitter: https://twitter.com/irishwinters1
Or at www. IrishWinters.com

9 781734 809732